Thrilling reviews for RHYANNON BYRD's Primal Instinct series from HQN Books

EDGE OF HUNGER

"Byrd successfully combines a haunting love story
with complex world-building."
—*Publishers Weekly*

EDGE OF DANGER

"Ms. Byrd had me first intrigued and then
spellbound from the first page to the last."
—*Joyfully Reviewed*

EDGE OF DESIRE

"[Byrd] serves up plenty of action and passion
that won't be denied.... Great stuff!"
—*RT Book Reviews*

TOUCH OF SEDUCTION

"This is a seriously sensual story with taut action
and a plot that doesn't let up."
—*RT Book Reviews*

TOUCH OF SURRENDER

"This is an ideal blend of suspense, romance,
action and intrigue, all set within
an amazing paranormal world."
—*RT Book Reviews*

RHYANNON BYRD

RUSH OF
DARKNESS

HQN™

Recycling programs
for this product may
not exist in your area.

ISBN-13: 978-0-373-77558-3

RUSH OF DARKNESS

Copyright © 2011 by Tabitha Bird

www.HQNBooks.com

Printed in U.S.A.

Dear Reader,

I can't believe that *Rush of Darkness,* the seventh book in my Primal Instinct series, is finally here. This definitely wasn't an easy book to write. Raine and Seth come from tragic backgrounds, and though they should be enemies, they realize that some emotions simply can't be denied. I love their passion, their chemistry—and the way this ruthless human soldier falls so completely head-over-heels for his little vampire. Seth might be a big, bad alpha male, but he isn't afraid to say what he wants and go after it. And when he goes after Raine, she discovers exactly what it means to be utterly possessed...and thoroughly loved.

Wishing you all much love and happiness!

Rhy

This book is dedicated with much love
and affection to the fantabulous Joy Harris,
who always makes me blush and laugh...
and who I never get to see nearly as much as I'd like to!
Thanks for everything, Joy!!

Acknowledgments:

As always, there are so many people
who deserve my deepest thanks:
My wonderful readers, whose support
and enthusiasm keep me going.
Endless thanks to each and every one of you!
My amazing editor, Ann Leslie Tuttle.
My incredible agent, Deidre Knight.
The awesome team at HQN
who are beyond compare.
The lovely Madison Hayes,
who puts so much time and effort into my books
that I'll never be able to thank her enough.
And last but not least, my family,
who mean the absolute world to me!

RUSH OF
DARKNESS

Only love can banish the darkness...

CHAPTER ONE

Paris, France

WHOEVER SAID THAT revenge was a dish best served cold obviously never had a taste for it, because all Raine Spenser could feel was heat—fever warm and searing through her veins—and it felt good. Better, in fact, than anything had felt in a long time, as if her life had finally been given purpose after so many draining months of weakness. Who cared if she was acting on visceral emotion rather than coolheaded logic? Her thirst for vengeance was an infusion of power ripping through her system, setting her on fire, and she liked it. A lot.

The May rain came down in a lazy, endless pour, drenching the city of Paris to its bones, the howling wind driving the cold drops against her face, and yet, she burned, aching with the need to catch her prey and make him pay for his sins. And for a woman like Raine, she was more than capable of dealing out a devil's load of violence.

Unique among the ancient clans—nonhuman races whose existence had been kept secret from the majority of humans for thousands of years—Raine was a woman from two worlds: that of the Deschanel vampires and the

Alacea psychics. Her parents had given Raine a childhood that was full of love, laughter and acceptance, and though they'd always done their best to protect her, she refused to make them a part of this.

This had to be *her* fight, and whatever happened, she would see it through to the end.

The young woman who had been raised in her parents' caring home, gone to university, then traveled the world as an environmentalist seemed another person now. One Raine hardly knew or understood. After being kidnapped at the beginning of the year and held prisoner for nearly a month, the hope that had once burned within her had been transformed into something distorted and dark. But then, these were grim times for all the ancient clans and the crossbreed knew she wasn't alone.

A war unlike anything that had come before was upon the world, though most of the humans continued on with their carefree existence, blithely unaware, believing the nightmares closing in on them were nothing more than mere figments of their imagination. But the nightmares were all too real, and if they weren't stopped, life for the humans and the clans alike was never going to be the same again.

Monsters once imprisoned had found escape, and now the men and women who had helped save Raine's life just months before were caught in the middle of a battle of epic proportions against a vile race known as the Casus. Immortal creatures that had been imprisoned for their gruesome crimes against humanity and the other clans more than a thousand years ago, the Casus had finally found a means of escape from the metaphysical prison called Meridian that held them. And although they could only escape one or two at a time, their numbers were steadily growing. But the most frightening part was that they were working to bring about "the flood," when all of their brethren would escape Meridian in a mass exodus, wreaking their vengeance upon the world.

And that's where the Watchmen came in.

An organization of shape-shifters whose job it was to watch over those clans who had survived the centuries, the Watchmen were the ones meant to ensure tranquility and peace. Though they lived in every corner of the world, it was a small unit of shifters from Colorado who had first begun the fight against the Casus. They were now established at a new compound in England called Harrow House, which was where Raine had been staying since last February, after they'd freed her from the madman who'd been determined to use her psychic powers to aid the Casus in their quest for freedom.

But while their fight was a righteous one, Raine wasn't working with the Watchmen or their allies. She had her own agenda—one she planned to carry out with deadly purpose, no matter the consequences.

Tonight, she was a predator. And she was on the hunt.

Peering around the corner of a thick, weathered building made of ancient granite, Raine could see her prey lurking in the distant shadows, his tall form hidden at the far end of a narrow alley. He was one of the escaped Casus shades, living within the body of a human host, the man's spirit destroyed so that the monster might wear his skin. Despite the rain, she was close enough to scent him, his sweaty stench overriding the wet stone-and-wood smells of the city, and she could sense his sadistic craving for pain and flesh. For that reason alone, she would have been justified in killing him, preventing him from taking another human life. But she had other reasons, as well. The Casus who lurked at the far end of that alley had committed unforgivable sins against Raine's family, and she wanted his destruction so badly she could taste it.

She might have been raised to abhor violence, but she wasn't worried about carrying out this creature's murder. Not when her motivation was so strong. After all, her mental powers had made it possible to see inside his mind. To see his past. To see visions of the cruel suffering he'd inflicted on others, before his imprisonment, as well as the carnage he'd carried out since his escape. He was pure, incarnate evil, and she wanted his death even more than she wanted her next breath. Even more than she wanted to survive.

Still, there were times when she was frightened by the ways in which she'd changed, wishing she could just go back home and forget the past months had ever happened. But her life had been irrevocably altered during the weeks of her captivity, to the point that she could *not* shake this seething need for revenge that had found life within her. And now that she'd given in to it, the darkness continued to spread through her a little more each day, her hatred bringing her a renewed surge of purpose and power. Instead of wasting away into nothing, her body had begun to heal itself, until she'd been ready to leave the safety of Harrow House the week before and head out on her own.

And now this bastard is mine, she thought, masking her scent as she slinked deeper into the shadows of the alleyway and released the razor-sharp talons on her fingertips. Her fangs dropped hard and fast as she gave herself over to that slick burn of rage firing through her and became one with the night.

She was a shadow. A wraith. And before this monster saw the dawn, she would be the one who delivered him into hell. She'd taken one of the prized Dark Markers from the Watchmen before she'd left their compound for just that purpose, knowing the ancient cross was the only weapon that would truly be able to destroy the Casus's soul.

Crouching down low, Raine gave free rein to her Deschanel senses, soaking in the sensory perceptions like a lung drawing oxygen from the air. The heavy beat of the monster's pulse filled her head as she started to go in for the kill, when a group of tourists suddenly came laughing down the street, ignorant of the danger they courted as they stumbled past the entrance to the alley. Her prey looked after them, contemplating their deaths, then shook his head and prowled toward the nightclub across the street, where he intended to choose his next victim. Though the ones ruling over the Casus had originally banned the monsters from human feedings, the Watchmen believed the restrictions had recently been lifted, considering the number of kills they suspected were taking place in cities all over the world.

The Casus had begun feeding for strength, which meant they were readying themselves for the next phase of the war.

Raine waited until the male had gone through the front doors of the club before retracting her talons and fangs and following him inside. Though she tried to get a clearer read on him, his thoughts came to her in disjointed fragments, but then, that was the best she could manage these days. Even though she was physically growing stronger, her mental abilities remained frustratingly shaky, still a far cry from what they'd been before she was kidnapped from the South American jungle where she'd been working and forced into those brutal, abusive weeks of captivity. Her body had mended from the ordeal, but her powers had not.

While most of the men in the club were dressed in black leather or denim, the women seemed to have chosen as little clothing as possible. Covered in faded jeans and a tight gray sweater, with her long blond hair buried beneath a black cap, Raine was clearly out of place, so she kept to the edges of the crowd as much as possible. Loud, pulsing music that seemed more computerized than instrumental battered against her sensitive eardrums, the acrid stench of sweat, alcohol and cigarette smoke assailing her highly developed sense of smell. As the chaos of the club closed in on her, scraping against her nerves, she struggled to follow the Casus's scent, but it was impossible.

Fearing she'd lost him, she came to a stop, searching the crowd with narrowed eyes, and it was then that she caught it. Not a mental warning, like something she might pick up with her Alacea powers. No, this was too physical, like a chill moving over the surface of her body, alerting the predator within her to nearby danger.

Someone was watching her, his searing gaze pressing against her skin, and she shuddered as if there'd been actual contact, her face burning as her pulse sped up in response. It wasn't that she couldn't stand to be touched, like many women who had suffered what she'd been through. But she still shunned any physical contact with others, wary of the memories that might claw their way back into her consciousness.

Wondering if the Casus she was following had been working with another, though she'd seen nothing to support that possibility in his thoughts, Raine shoved her way to the far side of the room. She pressed her back against the safety of a wall as she searched for the source of this newest threat, her intuition warning her that something was coming, drawing steadily closer. As a group of girls who looked far too young to be clubbing swayed by in a flurry of drunken giggles, she started to move along with them, using them as cover, until a warm, unforgettable scent washed over her. Reeling with shock, she stopped at the edge of the crowd, a low groan on her lips.

It can't *be him,* she thought, breathless, her pulse stuttering as that mouthwatering scent filled her head. *It would have been impossible for him to find me....*

But, somehow, the impossible had happened, because she knew *exactly* who stood behind her, his scent imprinted on her brain like a tattoo inked into tender skin.

Turning around, Raine came face-to-face with Seth McConnell, the tall, human male who continued to haunt her dreams whenever she dared to sleep. She stood frozen in place, the Casus she'd been hunting forgotten as she helplessly lost herself in the human's rough, masculine details. She wouldn't have thought it possible, but he was even more stunning than she remembered, the sharp tension around those dark green eyes and hard mouth lending a rugged edge to his sensual beauty that looked incredibly good on him. The stark cut of muscle beneath all that dark, golden skin was even more defined than before, as if he'd been pushing his body unbearably hard since she'd last seen him, nearly a month ago, and it suited him. Better than she cared to admit.

Yeah, he was built, and undeniably gorgeous—but he made her feel things she had no business feeling. Not for a man who had done the things that he'd done. Which meant he was off-limits as a friend, and most definitely as a lover.

Still, she couldn't deny that McConnell was seriously easy on the eyes, if a woman liked her men a little hard-looking, with a scintillating air of danger. And though it chafed to admit it, she was obviously one of those women. She loved the way his ripped body looked wrapped up in a black shirt and jeans, his feet covered in heavy black boots. Loved the way his cheekbones cut beneath his skin, his chin strong and square, with an arrogant jaw. She'd been told by his Watchmen friends that he'd worn his short, sun-bleached hair a good bit longer until the beginning of the year, and she could easily imagine him looking right at home on some sandy California beach with a surfboard under his arm, heading out into the crashing waves, if it weren't for that predatory look in his eyes. Despite his outrageous good looks, there was simply no mistaking McConnell for anything other than what he was: a soldier with a bad-ass attitude who could cut down anything that stood in his way, whether it was human…or something more.

And vampires had always been his specialty.

While the group of girls staggered away, leaving Raine behind, he took a step closer, crowding in on her, those piercing eyes watching her like a hawk. She sensed that he was judging her reaction, waiting to see if she would flinch from his nearness, like she always had in the past.

But not this time. Tonight, she was too angry to be afraid, her emotions in chaos, and she lifted her chin higher, glaring up at him. From one instant to the next, the heat in his eyes changed, becoming softer, hotter— but while the heat was familiar, those green eyes were now burning with something Raine had never seen in the human before. For a fraction of a second, his gaze dipped to her mouth as she licked her bottom lip, and something inside her flickered with a strange, forgotten kind of awareness, as if parts of her psyche that had long been buried in darkness were slowly fighting their way back into the light. Her pulse raced…not with fury, but with something that felt impossibly like arousal, even while a sliver of uneasiness crept through her system, coiling coldly in her stomach.

Can't forget that he's a killer. Can't forget what he's done. All the bloodshed. All the pain…

Yes, when they'd first met, she'd been able to see what had happened to his family all those years ago, gleaning more than a few pertinent, painful glimpses of his memories. She could understand his rage. But it didn't mean she wasn't wary of him. Since the return of the Casus, he might have defected from the Collective Army to fight with the Watchmen, but that didn't erase all the years he'd spent hunting vampires and slaughtering them. A militant organization of human mercenaries devoted to purging the world of all preternatural life, the Collective Army had been in existence since the Casus had first begun the mass killing sprees that had led to their imprisonment. But in an ironic twist, the Army was now working in coordination with the Casus, which had prompted Seth McConnell's departure.

Now, he was one of the good guys. But how long would it last? Despite the kindness he'd shown her, Raine still didn't trust him. And considering all the twisted, complicated issues that stood between them, she sure as hell didn't have any business being attracted to him.

"Come on," he growled, his deep voice nearly drowned out by the synthesized beat of the music. Before she could protest, he curled his long fingers around her arm, pulling her through the nearby doorway that led into one of the bar areas of the club. The high-ceilinged room was no more private than the one before, but at least the music was muffled enough that they could talk.

Only, Raine didn't want to stand there and have a conversation. She wanted to run. To hide. To get as far away from him as she could!

And for one brief moment of madness, she wanted to throw her arms around his neck…breathe in that rich masculine scent and simply hold him close, as if that was exactly where he belonged. In her arms. Against her body…

And I've lost my freaking mind, she silently groaned, wondering what was wrong with her. No other man had even remotely sparked her interest in the past months—so why in the hell did she find McConnell so damn appealing?

Needing to put some space between them, before she made a fool of herself, Raine jerked out of his hold and took an unsteady step back, coming up hard against the wall behind her. But he didn't take the hint. Instead, he took another step closer, so that she had to crane her head back to hold that hot green stare. With a shaky breath, Raine concentrated on trying to get inside his mind, but all she could pick up was a hazy blur of shadows and white noise, as if he'd thrown up some kind of mental block. Which meant she was just going to have to get her answers the "normal" way…and talk to him.

"This doesn't make any sense," she choked out, fighting to keep her voice as level as possible. "What are you doing in Paris?" She knew she sounded rude and abrasive, but didn't see that she had any choice, since she needed him to keep his distance.

He didn't give her an answer—just took a slow, deep breath, his head tilting a little to the side, the green of his eyes turning darker—and for a fraction of a second, Raine thought she caught an image from his mind. An image that showed the two of them together, his tall, powerful body pressed tight against hers, pinning her to the wall. His lean hips were wedged between her thighs, her legs wrapped possessively around his waist, while his strong hands held her head, keeping her still as he ravaged her mouth, kissing her long and hard and impossibly deep.

Gritting her teeth, Raine forced the provocative image from her mind, furious with herself for letting the human get to her so easily. He hadn't said more than two words to her, and already she was shaking with nerves, imagining things that didn't exist. She knew damn well that the vision wasn't real. That it had come from *her* thoughts, and not his. But that wasn't even the part that had her so irritated. No, it was the fact that they'd both been steamy and naked, not a stitch of clothing between them—and while Seth McConnell looked good in jeans, the bastard had looked even better *out* of them.

And that's really something I could have gone without thinking about.

A second demand to know exactly what he was doing there had just settled on the tip of her tongue, when his gaze dipped to the gleaming metallic cross hanging around her neck, the ancient weapon resting just between her breasts. "If you're here for the Marker," she told him, wondering why there was a bitter edge of disappointment to her words, "you needn't have bothered, McConnell. When I'm finished with the cross, I have every intention of returning it to your friends."

"I figured as much." His voice was rough, even huskier than she remembered it. "But the Marker isn't the reason I'm here."

Her brow scrunched with confusion. "It isn't?"

With a slow shake of his head, the soldier locked his piercing gaze with hers. "You are."

CHAPTER TWO

AS SHE STARED UP at him with those big, dark eyes, Seth figured the little crossbreed couldn't have looked more panicked if she'd found his blade at her neck, ready to open her throat. "*I'm* the reason you're here?" she croaked, a quiver moving through her slender frame, while a flush of color burned in her high cheekbones and across the delicate bridge of her nose. "But…that doesn't make any sense."

Pushing his hands in his pockets, he forced out a gruff explanation. "I'm here to protect you."

"*Protect me?*" Her nostrils flared, hands fisting tightly at her sides. "Have you lost your bloody mind, McConnell?"

Ever since Seth had discovered Raine's absence from the compound in England, he'd been asking himself that exact same question. His actions were not only illogical, they were impulsive and reckless. There were a thousand and one other things he *should* have been doing at that moment, and yet, there he was, following after Raine Spenser like some kind of lovelorn hero intent on rescuing his damsel in distress.

Only, he was a far cry from hero material.

And she sure as hell didn't look like she wanted to be rescued.

But it didn't matter. Seth knew he should have been refocusing on his hunt for Ross Westmore—Westmore was the man working to bring back the Casus, as well as the one who'd held Raine captive at the beginning of the year—but from the moment he'd learned that Raine had left the safety of Harrow House to visit her parents in Rome, then set out on her own again, he'd panicked. All he'd been able to think about was finding her. Keeping her safe. Keeping her *close*.

Not that she was his to look after. They weren't involved. Hell, they barely knew each other—and what they *did* know wasn't much to build on.

She was a half-blooded vampire who wanted nothing to do with men.

And he was an ex-hunter who had spent the past twenty years of his life slaughtering every vampire he could get his hands on.

And since she was also part psychic, Raine had no doubt been able to see each and every one of those killings the first time she'd ever laid eyes on him. But even knowing he was the last person in the world she would want to have close to her, he hadn't been able to stop thinking about tracking her down and getting her someplace safe. And it didn't end there, because after he got her out of danger, he wanted to get the crazy little vamp someplace private. Someplace where he could do things he knew damn well he would never be able to do outside the realms of his imagination. Things like touching her. Kissing her...

It was probably wrong in more ways than he could count, but Seth had been drawn to this woman from the moment he'd first carried her small body out of Westmore's compound, when she hadn't even been conscious. Over the weeks that he'd known her, that interest had grown into an uncomfortable attraction, and now that attraction had damn near become an obsession. A stupid, dangerous one that had sent him running from Harrow House a month ago, only to leave him burning with lust for a woman who had seemed to go out of her way to avoid him.

Despite everything he couldn't stop wanting her—though *want* didn't actually come anywhere close to describing this strange desire that only seemed to be growing stronger each day. What he really wanted was to possess her in some kind of primal act of dominance, the need reminding him of the way the shifters he now called friends acted with their women. Seth wanted to get her under him and go at it until their bodies were slick and steaming and they were barely able to breathe. Wanted to lose himself in her until he'd somehow managed to ease this infuriating ache that continually grew, spreading, until it now filled every cell of his body.

So yeah, he had the mother of all hard-ons for the vamp, jonesing for her like an addict. And yet, at the same time, there was a part of him that wanted to stay away from her out of sheer self-preservation. All of which meant that, somewhere along the way, he'd clearly lost his damn mind, the war no doubt screwing with his head. From the moment the Casus had started to return, everything had been turned upside down on him, until he didn't even know who he was anymore.

And since he'd met Raine Spenser, everything had really gone to hell.

As her shoulders pulled back, pressing her breasts against the thin material of her sweater, her gaze locked with his, burning with a fury Seth had never seen in her before. The last time he'd been near her, she'd been closed down, as if an off switch had been flicked inside her chest. But now she vibrated with anger and power, that wild gaze nearly stealing his breath. Yeah, it only added to his current state of idiocy, but there was no point in lying about it. Her eyes were the pale, pure gray of the Deschanel vampires, but with threads of dark Alacea blue woven through, and he found them unbelievably beautiful. As unique as the woman herself.

Seth studied her face and her eyes, searching for the signs of trauma that had been there when he'd first met her back in February, but was unable to find them. Lowering his gaze, he noted the changes in her body, as well, and it was clear, even to his human eyes, that she was finally…mending. She looked different than she had a month ago, fuller, healthier, no longer the starved little waif she'd been when he'd carried her out of that miserable compound. And in the weeks that had followed, her health had only deteriorated, her body growing weaker, instead of recovering.

Obviously, something had happened to turn all that around.

"You look…stronger," he said in a low voice, when what he was really thinking was that she looked good enough to eat. Sexually, that is. It seemed an important distinction, considering this was a woman who had a *thing* for blood.

"What is it you want, McConnell?"

He cocked his head a little to the side as he held her stare. "First of all, you know my first name, so use it. And why ask the question when you already know the answer? Can't you just read my mind?"

"Believe it or not," she snapped, her tone one he'd never heard her use before, "I have better things to do than go digging around inside that thick skull of yours."

Seth accepted her answer with a quiet shrug, wondering if her mother was right. When he'd talked to Simone Spenser earlier that day in Rome, the woman had been surprisingly open with him, taking him into her confidence, when he'd honestly expected her to slam the door in his face the second she laid eyes on him. But instead, they'd talked for nearly an hour, and she'd told him she believed Raine's mental powers were still decreasing due to the trauma she'd suffered, and Simone was afraid that if Raine didn't come to terms with what she'd been through, she might lose her psychic abilities for good. Seth had hoped the woman was wrong, but surely Raine would have used her powers to discover his intentions if she'd been able to.

And if her powers *were* still weakening, then she was in even more danger than he'd first assumed. Whatever she was up to in Paris, he had no doubt that it was dangerous work. Though the others figured she'd simply wanted the cross for protection, since the Markers acted as a talisman to those who wore them, Seth believed there was only one reason she would have risked the wrath of the Watchmen…and that was to kill a Casus. She might have made a quick trip to Rome to see her family, but the real reason she'd left Harrow House with one of the ancient crosses was because she was going on the hunt.

"It shouldn't be so hard to figure out why I'm here, Raine. Did you really think we were just going to let you run off and get slaughtered?"

One slim brow arched with derision. "Look around, McConnell. I don't see anyone else stalking me."

"The others would have come after you as soon as they realized you were no longer with your parents, but all hell's started to break loose, which is why I was called back to England. I only found out that you were no longer at Harrow House when I returned to the compound. No one had even told me you were gone."

Annoyance filled her expression. "My comings and goings should hardly be any concern of yours, so why would they bother to tell you anything?"

"Because they knew I expected them to protect you," he growled, fisting his hands in his pockets. "The second you set foot outside of Harrow House, I should have been notified."

"There was nothing to worry about. They knew I was with my parents."

"I don't care if you'd gone to visit the bloody Prime Minister," he shot back, his blood running cold at the thought of her being alone and unprotected. "They should have told me that you'd left."

"And so you just came on your own? Without anyone else?" It was clear from her tone that she was hoping for a way to ditch him.

"Garrick was with me until this afternoon, but he got a call from his parents and had to head home." Before their defection, Trevor Garrick had been Seth's second-in-command when they'd both been a part of the Collective Army. He was a hell of a friend, and an even better soldier, which was why Seth continued to put his trust in him.

"Well, you should have gone with him. Whatever you came here for, you're wasting your time."

Ignoring the assholes bumping into him as they pushed their way toward the crowded bar, Seth crossed his arms over his chest. "I'll be the judge of that," he muttered, no doubt sounding like an asshole himself, and a surly one at that. But damn it, he *was* surly.

Her chin lifted a fraction higher, her husky voice thick with anger and something that sounded close to panic. "How did you even know I was in Paris?"

"I paid a visit to your parents." For safety purposes, her family had been staying at the Watchmen compound in Rome ever since Raine had been rescued, so it had been easy for Seth to find them.

Her color drained at his words. "If you hurt them—"

"Don't be ridiculous." His lip curled in an offended sneer. "Of course I didn't hurt them. Despite what you seem to think, I'm not in the habit of murdering innocent people, even if they are vampires." At least, not lately.

That little notch was back between her brows. "Then how did you get them to tell you where to find me?"

For a brief moment, the corner of his mouth twitched, but he fought back the smile, knowing it would only piss her off. And she was already prickly enough as it was. "Actually, that part was pretty simple. Your mother likes me."

Her eyes went round and she had to open her mouth twice before she was able to say, "That's not funny, McConnell."

He gave her a believe-what-you-will kind of shrug, ticked that she kept refusing to use his first name. "I'm just stating the facts, Raine."

"No. You're lying," she snarled, the gray of her eyes beginning to glow with an unholy light that should have freaked the hell out of him, but the surge of blood to his groin said otherwise.

"I'm not lying," he replied in a low voice, making sure he was shielding her from anyone who might catch sight of that strange silver gaze. "After we talked for a while, she told me you were in Paris and gave me the name of your hotel."

"My mother wouldn't do that," she argued, and it didn't take a genius to see that she didn't want to believe him. "It doesn't make any sense. Her Alacea powers are incredibly strong. She would have been able to use those powers to read you…to see into your past." Her voice was rising with each word, a testament to her distress. "You actually expect me to believe that my own mother would send a vampire killer after me?"

"If you don't believe me, call her," he suggested.

She crossed her arms over her chest, mirroring his own stance, and forced her response through tightly clenched teeth. "I will."

Seth's mouth had just started to tip with a slow, wry smile, when she added, "Even if you're telling me the truth about my family, that still doesn't explain what you're doing here, in this club. How did you know I was here?"

Well, shit. To be honest, he'd been hoping to avoid this part of the conversation, but the woman was like a pit bull with a bone. Scraping his fingers through his rain-damp hair, he blew out an exasperated breath and told her the truth. "I don't actually know."

"How can you not know? You're here, aren't you? You had to find me somehow!"

"Hell, I'd explain it if I could, but I can't. I knew you were in the city, but I didn't have any idea where. I started at the hotel your mother gave me and just…kept walking the streets, looking for you. I'd finally decided to head back to your hotel, and wait you out there, when I saw you walking across the street out front and heading into this place."

Disbelief filled her gaze. "So you just happened to

run into me? In a city the size of Paris? Do you realize how...*improbable* that is?"

He shrugged his shoulders again. "What can I say?" he muttered, feeling almost embarrassed by the strange coincidence. Trying to make light of it, he added, "Maybe the fates were looking to bring us together."

"The fates?" Shock widened her eyes, while anger darkened them. "Isn't that a little fantastical for a man like you?"

Seth arched a brow at her snarly tone, enjoying the way her cheeks burned with color as her temper rose, the fierce emotion a welcome relief to the pale fear she'd worn the last time he'd seen her. "You think I could still be close-minded, after all the crazy crap I've witnessed? I might not understand most of it, but I know the world works in mysterious ways."

"Great," she snapped, the panic in her eyes growing sharper. "So now the fates are conspiring against me?"

Suddenly feeling like a jackass for riling her, he softened his tone. "I'm here to help you, Raine. I didn't come to cause you any trouble."

"Well, I haven't asked for any help, and better yet, I don't want any. Especially not from you!"

That quickly, his guilt vanished. "In case you didn't notice," he growled, "I didn't ask."

She muttered something under her breath that he couldn't quite make out, but it was clear she didn't trust him.

"And to be honest," he added, "I'm surprised you didn't see me coming."

With a delicate snort, she said, "My powers are hardly working right, remember?"

Yeah, he did. But he also couldn't help recalling that when she started to…well, *care* about someone, the less she could see them. In fact, she could barely read her loved ones at all, which is why she wouldn't have known that he'd visited her parents unless she'd talked to them directly.

But before his brain could run away with that intriguing thought, she said, "You still haven't told me why the others gave you this ridiculous job."

Seth shook his head. "That's not how it happened."

"No?"

"They didn't send me after you. I came on my own."

That seemed to throw her a little, though he could tell she was trying to keep it from showing. "Well, now you can just turn around and go back. I have things I need to do, and they don't involve you."

"It's strange you would say that," he muttered, his muscles bunching with a renewed wave of tension.

"Why?"

"Because I thought we had an understanding."

"What kind of understanding?" she asked, her voice laden with suspicion.

He ground out his response, wishing they weren't having this argument in the loud nightclub, surrounded by drunken idiots. "The kind where you didn't do anything stupid, putting yourself in danger again, after I helped save your ass."

The thought of exactly *what* he and the others had saved her from had Seth's gut coiling, a trickle of sweat snaking down his spine beneath the soft cotton of his shirt. The woman had been through hell during her captivity at Westmore's compound, both physically and mentally. She'd been raped by groups of those vile monsters, beaten repeatedly and shown the slaughtered pieces of her younger sister's body. And yet, she'd somehow survived, refusing to let them break her completely.

She'd looked away from him when he'd finished laying into her, her expression a beguiling cross between mutinous and contrite. Time stretched out, marked only by the staccato rhythm of their breaths and the muffled electronic pulse of the music, and then she suddenly gave herself a little shake. "I've said thank you," she told him, locking her gaze with his again. "Several times, in fact. But what you did for me after the escape does not mean that you have any say in what I do now."

Like *hell* it didn't. "Whatever you're getting into, I'm not letting you do this alone, Raine."

Anger burned in the depths of her eyes. "At the risk of repeating myself, you don't have any choice, McConnell."

"Don't be so sure about that," he drawled with a heavy dose of pure, masculine arrogance, knowing damn well his words and tone were going to piss her off even more. And for some dumbass reason, that temper of hers was really setting him off, to the point that he couldn't help wondering what she'd do if he tried to kiss her.

When his gaze dipped to her mouth, she drew a swift

breath, her voice almost guttural as she warned, "Try it, soldier boy, and I'll rip your bloody throat out."

Excitement vibrated along his nerve endings, bringing a fresh surge of heat beneath his skin. He'd thought she was fascinating before, but now... Christ, his head was spinning from trying to figure her out. She was so much harder than she'd been the last time he'd seen her. Angrier. Even more complex. But still as beautiful as ever. He couldn't stop staring at the plush shape of her lower lip, loving the crease that ran down its center. He was entranced by the color, the curves, the texture....

Gotta taste her, he thought, his breathing heavy, head dangerously thick with lust that he fucking knew was going to land him in a shitload of trouble. But he couldn't wait, months' worth of hunger suddenly bearing down on him, impossible to resist. His nostrils flared as he drew in a deep breath of her scent, and before he could think better of it, Seth crowded in on her, flattening one hand against the wall at her back, caging her in, her other side blocked by the broad back of a male who was chatting up some redhead beside them. As he started to lower his head, the music faded away, the annoying crowd forgotten, his pulse roaring as he drew close. Closer...

Then she lifted her knee and nailed him right in the nuts.

Pain doubled him over, his stomach twisting as a violent wave of nausea swept through him, and he went to his knees, hard, using everything he had to keep from blacking out. She'd used considerable more force than he would have thought a woman her size was capable of, but then, the Deschanel were known for being exceptionally strong.

When his vision finally cleared, Seth sucked in a rough gulp of air and lifted his head, ready to give her absolute hell…

But the maddening little crossbreed was already gone.

CHAPTER THREE

TWO MORE SECONDS. Just two…and his mouth would have been on mine. Those firm lips. Warm, clever tongue…

As the disturbing words whispered through Raine's mind, she made her way down a deserted, moonlit street, lost in a daze, the rain pelting against her cold face, already blocks away from the club. She couldn't believe that Seth McConnell had come after her. Could believe even less that he cared enough to worry about what happened to her. After all, she'd seen the gruesome killings he'd made against her kind in the name of the Collective Army.

But when he'd been staring at her in the nightclub, none of that had mattered. His eyes had burned with that same hot, soft glow that she remembered from the days after he'd helped rescue her from Westmore back in early February, and she'd practically melted.

The compound had been located in the middle of the Deschanel Wasteland, a cold, desolate realm where exiled vampires were sent for punishment, as well as one of the deadliest places on earth. The journey had been hard, and yet, McConnell had cared for her the entire way, watching her with that same burning look whenever he'd cut open his arm and collected a cup of his blood for her to drink. And even though it wasn't anywhere near as sweet as it would have been from his vein—which he'd made clear was *not* an option—his taste had still been enough to…concern her. It'd been too good. Too…right, somehow. Almost as if his flavor was the perfect match for her most primal hungers.

Jarred by her unsettling thoughts, she stopped to prop her shoulder against a darkened storefront so that she could close her eyes for a moment. She felt raw inside, and it was obvious his presence had put a chink in her carefully constructed armor. If she wasn't careful, he could take her apart, piece by piece, and she'd find herself in that chilling suck of pain again. Consumed by guilt and regret. Living in agony with nothing but that stark, tearing cold filling her up inside.

Only her anger could make her burn.

Anger…or McConnell.

Damn it, she would *not* think about it…about *him*. She couldn't. Not if she wanted to keep what little sanity she still had left. She'd been doing her best to put him out of her mind for weeks now, so God only knew she should be getting good at it. In fact, she'd been trying so hard not to think about him, she hadn't even realized he was in the club until he'd gotten right on her. Of course, he had a lot of natural mental guards for a human and they were difficult for her to get through. It'd been that way ever since Kellan Scott, the Lycan she'd been imprisoned with at Westmore's compound, had explained to the soldier exactly how her powers worked. Powers that were weakening every day…and Raine had to face the fact that she might never be at full strength again. The deep trances she'd gone into whenever the Casus had raped her had left severe wounds within her mind—ones she knew damn well might never be fully healed.

As it was, she was left in a strange state of limbo, able to lust…and yet, burdened by shame for taking what she knew the Deschanel would have seen as the coward's way out.

Coward or not, she was already able to feel desire. Hell, who was she trying to fool? She might be wary of having a man's weight crushing her down, unsure of exactly how she would react—but there was no doubt that she wanted Seth McConnell with a hunger none of her past attractions had ever come anywhere close to matching. She'd been fighting hard not to admit it, but she wanted him in ways that didn't make sense. In ways she couldn't even explain.

Despite how she felt about his past, about the man that he'd been and the things that he'd done, for some inexplicable reason, McConnell had been her only point of light in the days following her rescue. A fact that her battered, unstable emotions hadn't been able to handle, and so she'd cut that connection, doing her best to avoid him once they'd reached the safety of Harrow House. And by doing so, she'd left herself with no other choice but to sink deeper into the darkness that had taken root in her soul, until she no longer knew herself. Until only her hatred and her quest for revenge had been the things that could save her.

But just because she *couldn't* allow herself to get close

to him, didn't mean that he didn't fascinate her. The guy might have been a trained killer, but he'd always been gentle with her. He was also dangerously easy on the eyes, with a slow, sexy smile and a rumbling, husky kind of laugh that could have melted metal. And no matter how badly she might have wanted to, she couldn't deny that his strength, as well as his intellect, impressed her. He had no supernatural powers, and yet, she'd seen him spar with the shifters back at Harrow House, knocking them on their asses more than once. And he'd been able to find her. She didn't believe in fate. No, she laid the credit at McConnell's feet, though she would never admit it to his face. But he had incredible instincts for a human, and he'd honed them to a fine point during all his years as a hunter. Somehow, he'd tracked her down in a city of millions, and she knew she was going to have to be careful if she was going to keep away from him.

Speaking of careful…

As she cast a wary eye over her silent surroundings, it occurred to her that she was crazy to have let her guard down. And the chilling words that were suddenly rasped over her shoulder were testament to that fact.

"Well, if it isn't the little psychic bitch. Westmore's gonna kiss my ass when I drag you back to him."

Shit.

As she turned around, Raine came face-to-face with Andre Carlson, the Casus she'd followed into the club, his ice-blue eyes burning with malice. He watched her with a mocking expression, no doubt thinking she was the dumbest female on the planet. After all, taking him by surprise was one thing—while going head-to-head with the bastard was something else entirely.

"But first," he drawled, "I think we'll have some fun. You ready to play like it's old times, sweetheart?"

Damn it, she'd been so stupid! Mooning over the soldier when she should have been focused on where she was…and *who* was with her. It was inexcusable. She knew better! After all, wasn't being careless what had landed her in Westmore's compound in the first place?

"I asked you a question, whore."

She'd slipped the Marker inside her sweater as she'd left the club, wanting to feel it pressed against her skin, as if the metal could somehow bring her a measure of comfort. It burned against her chest, thrumming with power, as though it was eager to take the monster down. But she had to be careful. The Dark Markers were not only the keys that opened the spellbound, heavily fortified gate to Meridian, they also formed a map that would lead to the Casus's hidden prison. If the Watchmen were going to succeed in their plan to enter Meridian and destroy the Casus once and for all, then they would need each cross.

"Are you deaf?" he growled. "I'm talking to you."

"Sorry. I spaced out there for a second," she murmured, surprised by the calmness of her tone. "I was just imagining Westmore's lips on your ass. Bet you love it when he does that, huh?"

He hit her so hard that her head cracked to the side, though her reaction was more from shock than the force of the blow. Thanks to the cross's protection, his fist slid right over her skin, but the idiot was so angry, he didn't even notice. "Such a filthy little mouth," he snarled, grasping her chin. "You've gotten bitchy since your escape."

She smiled so wide her teeth were bared…as well as the fangs that had already descended. "Then why don't you try to teach me a lesson?"

"We will."

We? What the…

Before she could react, strong hands grabbed her upper arms, and Raine realized her error in judgment was even worse than she'd thought. Facing off against one Casus was dangerous enough, but two would be all but impossible. Not that she was afraid of dying. But damn it, she still had three more monsters she intended to hunt down and drop, before finally going after Westmore.

"Let's get this started," the newcomer purred in her ear, and as he pulled her against the front of his body, bile rose in her throat at the feel of his erection digging into her lower back.

Do something! Fight back!

Right. Time to stop standing there, waiting for a miracle to happen. If she was going to get out of this, she'd have to do it herself. Using the second Casus's hold on her arms as leverage, she swung her right leg into the air, aiming a powerful kick into the side of Carlson's jaw, the satisfying crack of breaking bone fueling her aggression. The bastard crumpled to the ground, a low groan spilling from his lips as he spat out three teeth.

"Now that just wasn't nice," the second one snickered.

He turned, pinning her against the nearest wall. "Looks like you need to be taught some manners."

"And here I was thinking that I'd rather just kill you instead." Gritting her teeth, Raine pushed onto the tip of her toes and slammed her head back, a thick crunch filling the night as the back of her head connected with his nose. He'd underestimated her, thinking she wouldn't fight back, just like the first one she'd killed two days ago in Spain. But she was no longer the victim. She was the one who wanted blood, damn it—and she was going to take it.

As the Casus released her right arm to grab his mangled nose, she dipped and twisted, the front of her sweater catching on something and tearing as she wrenched herself out of his hold. With a feral growl, he swung his fist, the blow catching her on the cheekbone, but like Carlson's first punch, his fist simply skidded across her face, leaving her unharmed.

"What the fuck is going on?" he demanded in confusion, just as she countered with her own jab, her fist connecting with his mouth and splitting his lip.

"Are you really that stupid?" Carlson muttered, finally moving back to his feet. His jaw was swelling, slurring his words, but Raine could still understand him. "She's wearing one of the Markers, you blind idiot."

The Casus's ice-blue gaze dipped to the metallic cross now visible through her torn sweater, his lip curling with disgust. "How the hell did she get that?"

"I stole it," Raine offered with a sharp smile, releasing her talons. She could have turned and ran, and would have likely been able to get away. But she'd come to Paris with a plan and she wasn't leaving until she'd seen it through.

"What do we do?" he asked his comrade.

"We take her. Just because we can't hurt her doesn't mean we can't capture her."

Oh, hell, no.

She'd been there, done that, and there was no way she was going back again.

They came at her hard and fast, and Raine fought wildly. But it wasn't enough, and she suddenly realized they were just biding their time, waiting for her to wear herself down.

Knowing she had to go on the offensive, she reached for the cross hanging around her neck and pulled it over her head. Gripping the warm metal in the palm of her right hand, she tightened her fingers around the ancient weapon and felt the familiar, excruciating burn of heat as it began to transform her arm into an instrument of death. One that was called an Arm of Fire, because of the way molten flames would engulf her entire limb, from fingers to shoulder, when she found her target. Once her arm was glowing with the power of the cross, she had to punch her way through the back of the monster's neck, at the base of his skull, and then her arm would erupt into flames, those flames spreading through the creature's body, torching him from the inside out. It was the only way to truly destroy a Casus, sending its soul on a one-way trip to hell.

In Spain, she had made sure her prey was too weak

to fight back before using the Marker, but this time was going to have to be different.

"Who's ready to play with me now?" she rasped, while they snarled at her glowing arm. They were clearly frightened, knowing she now had the power to kill them. They weren't, however, frightened enough to run.

I'm just going to have to change that.

Together, they rushed her, demonic growls tearing up from their throats, the moonlight glinting against the jagged fangs now filling their mouths. Carlson delivered a powerful roundhouse that caught her on the shoulder, and while the cross protected her from the bruising force of the blow, it was still enough to knock her down. Her knees hit hard against the gritty asphalt, but she kept rolling, coming up in a low crouch. The second Casus came at her and she hissed, baring her fangs as she sprang forward, slicing her talons across his throat. Blood sprayed, but it wasn't enough to take him down, the host's body able to endure more than a human could while it was possessed by one of the shades. As she tried to get behind him, where she could drive her burning hand into his neck, he grabbed hold of her left arm, slamming her into the ground. Raine hit the asphalt so hard that her breath left her lungs, but she immediately started to twist and kick when she felt Carlson wrap his long fingers around one of her ankles.

"Now get her off the ground!" he barked at his partner. Together they hoisted her into the air, Carlson holding her ankles, while the other held her by one arm.

Ohmygod, she thought. *I've failed!*

A cold fear twisted through Raine's system as the reality of the situation spread over her. Her eyes filled with hot, blistering tears of outrage, while her mind filled with a torrent of strange questions that revolved around McConnell. Would he try to rescue her a second time? Or would he simply wash his hands of her, once and for all?

The Casus began carrying her down the deserted street, and she screamed so loud she was surprised the glass storefronts lining the road didn't shatter from the harrowing noise. Her heart raced, beating faster and harder, raw panic searing her veins, and she suddenly found herself throwing the Marker onto the ground. Without the cross in her palm, she was able to release the deadly talons on her right hand, and she lifted her arm over her head, clawing at the Casus's forearm, trading the cross's protection for the chance to get free. Dark satisfaction poured through her veins as her fingers sank into his flesh, digging all the way down to the bone, until his hot blood poured over her hand. He roared with fury, releasing her arm, and her upper body crashed to the ground, pain radiating through her skull with the force of a hammer as it cracked against the asphalt.

The bastard who held her legs—the one named Carlson, who she'd come there to kill—suddenly let them go, and with a low, mocking spill of laughter, he smiled down at her. "You dropped the Marker," he rumbled, reaching down and undoing the top button on his jeans. "Without its protection, you're fucking helpless. Just like you were before."

Raine was still disoriented from the blow to her head, but she managed to roll over and start crawling. She had no idea where she was trying to go—only knew that she had to get away. She had made it no more than a few feet when there was a sharp tug on her hair, reminding her of every time this asshole had attacked her at Westmore's compound. Her throat closed with fear as her head was wrenched back, a fresh surge of pain radiating through her skull.

"Where the hell do you think you're going?" he asked with another low laugh, flinging her onto her back. He came down on her with all his weight, straddling her waist, and she tried to claw at him with her talons, but he backhanded her so hard that she went numb, stars flickering across her vision.

Then he hit her again, this time with his fist, smashing her lips against her teeth and breaking the skin, the scent of her blood instantly filling the air.

"Damn," he groaned, his graveled voice thick with hunger. "You have no idea how good that—*oomph!*"

One second Carlson was sitting on top of her, and in the next he was gone, a furious roar jerking from his chest as something crashed heavily into his body, tackling him to the ground. Scrambling into a sitting position, Raine pushed her hair out of her face just in time to see McConnell pin the Casus facedown against the road, wrench back the hand Carlson had just used to hit her, then twist and torque, breaking his arm so badly that the bone broke clean through the skin. The monster's howl of pain filled the air, the look on the human's face one of dark, violent rage. The other Casus finally pulled himself to his feet, his body shuddering as he began to make the change into his true Casus form, but McConnell grabbed the gun tucked into the back of his jeans and drilled three bullets into the male's chest.

Then he lowered the gleaming automatic weapon to the back of Carlson's skull.

"No!" Raine screamed, her sharp cry echoing through the night, but she was too late. The shot rang out, silencing the bastard's howls, his blood flowing out over the road like a dark, inky stain.

"I can't believe you did that!" she seethed, watching as McConnell rose to his feet and stalked toward her, the moonlight shimmering against the metallic surface of the gun before he tucked it back into his jeans. He crouched down beside her, his expression impossible to read as he ran his sharp gaze over her battered face. For once, she didn't flinch from his nearness—until he started to reach forward, as if he would push back the tangled fall of her hair.

"Don't! Do *not* touch my hair!" she growled, scurrying back from him like a crab. It seemed crazy, but that was the only thing she remembered clearly from her torture, and she couldn't stand the thought of a man's hands in her hair. *"Never touch my hair!"*

He lifted his hands to show her he understood and moved back to his full height, taking a step back to give her some space. Even though Raine knew his blood-thirsty anger wasn't for her, but the ones who'd hurt her, the murderous look in his dark eyes still made her shiver with fear.

"It's okay, Raine." His husky voice was low and calm, as if he were trying to soothe a frightened animal. And that's no doubt what she looked like to him, with her fangs extended and her talons dripping blood. "You know I'm not going to hurt you."

"I told you to leave me alone," she muttered, wiping the blood from her mouth with the back of her wrist in a stiff, uncoordinated motion. "What are you doing here?"

Silence, and then a rough, graveled response. "They had you once. I won't let them have you again."

"I didn't need your help. And I don't want it!" She barely managed to push herself to her feet, having to use the storefront behind her for support. "I don't want you here!"

Great, she thought, the instant the words had left her mouth. *Now I sound like a petulant child throwing a tantrum.*

Instead of shouting back at her, like she was sure he wanted to do, McConnell took a deep breath, no doubt trying to control his rage. But he still sounded pissed when he jerked his chin toward the fallen Casus and asked, "Are they the reason you're in Paris? Were you hunting these assholes by yourself?"

She gave a jerky nod, then retracted her talons and fangs. "The last one you killed—Carlson. He was the one I came for. But I wanted him killed with a Marker, not a gun!"

"I don't fucking believe it." Obviously losing a bit of the hold on his fury, he ground the words out, his voice more guttural than she'd ever heard it. "What the hell, Raine? Are you trying to get yourself killed? You got a bloody death wish?"

"If I did," she shouted, "you'd be just the man to handle it, wouldn't you?"

He flinched, looking as if she'd struck him, and a sliver of shame immediately sliced through her insides, making her cringe. In all the weeks she'd known him, they'd never once discussed his past. They'd never discussed anything, simply suffering the heavy silences that were always wedged between them like soundproof sheets of glass. But now that glass had been shattered.

He spent a few moments scrubbing his hands down his face, then finally said, "I'm trying to come up with a logical reason for why you'd be willing to take this kind of risk, but I can't. So you're going to have to explain it to me."

Raine lifted her brows. "You've talked to my mother, McConnell. If she told you I was here, surely she told you the reason why."

"Actually," he muttered, crossing those big arms over his chest, "all she gave me was your location. Said I had to figure out the rest on my own."

A tight smile caught at the corner of her mouth and she had to choke down a lump of emotion. "Well, that sounds like my mother."

"We're not leaving until you tell me why you're here, Raine."

Knowing that she had to give him some kind of explanation, or he really *would* make her stay there all night, she squared her shoulders and got on with it. "It's just some unfinished business that I'm taking care of. It doesn't concern either you or your friends, so there's no need for you to get involved. I plan on handling this on my own. Then, when I'm done, I'll make sure the Marker is returned to the Watchmen."

He slid a hard look toward the bodies that were still bleeding out on the street, rubbing a scarred hand over his mouth—and she knew the instant he thought he had it figured out, that dark green gaze whipping back to her face, sharp and bright. "Christ, he was one of the bastards from the compound, wasn't he? One of the ones who raped you?"

It was her turn to flinch in reaction, and he cursed something ugly and rough as he turned, stalked across the quiet street, then brutally punched his hand into a brick storefront. The violent blow instantly split the skin across his knuckles, the hot scent of his blood making her mouth water.

The soldier's harsh breaths filled the air and he lifted his arms, his head hanging forward as he braced his big hands against the dark bricks. "You're going after the ones who hurt you." The thick, guttural words weren't a question. He believed he had it right. "How many are there?"

She hadn't meant to answer his question, or correct him, but she did. As if the words were being pulled from her against her will, she heard herself offering him a quiet explanation. "I'm going after the five who killed my sister. I've already killed one in Madrid. Carlson was meant to be the second. But now you've sent his shade back to Meridian."

He turned, propping his shoulders against the wall, his hands hanging loose at his sides as he locked that piercing gaze with hers. "Was he one of the ones who attacked you or not?"

"It doesn't matter," she forced through her clenched teeth, shaking. "He killed Rietta. That's all I care about."

For a moment he said nothing, simply holding her stare, and then he spoke in another soft, quiet rasp. "I know you suffered through hell in that place, Raine, but what you're doing…" He flexed his hands at his sides, his expression grim. "It won't change anything. Not for you, and not for your sister."

She could tell from his tone that he spoke from personal experience, but she didn't ask for him to elaborate, knowing that the more distance she could keep between them, the better. She was already too drawn to him as it was.

And she already had a good guess at the answer. After all, she knew he'd lost his family at the age of fifteen to a rogue nest of vampires. Surely that was the impetus for the killing spree he'd gone on afterward, slaughtering every Deschanel he could find, whether they were young or old.

"It's not just about revenge," she told him. "When I'm done with the Casus, I'll find Westmore, and I'll find the three Markers he has. It's my fault he has two of them and I intend to get them back. Your friends won't be able to get into Meridian without them."

Thanks to a journal that had been found in Westmore's compound, they now knew that there were twelve Dark Markers in all. In order to keep them from falling into the wrong hands, the powerful crosses had been hidden in various locations all over the world. The Watchmen had been able to find eight of them, but Westmore had stolen one, and with Raine's help he'd been able to find two more before the Watchmen could get their hands on them.

"We only have two more to find," the human rumbled, "and then we plan to go after Westmore and get the other three crosses. So it's all going to be taken care of, Raine. This isn't something you need to be involved in. No one blames you for what happened. Hell, they'd have all done the same thing."

"I doubt that," she muttered, her stomach churning. "And it doesn't matter. I'm the one who did it, and I'll fix it. Just as soon as I've dealt with the ones who killed Rietta."

He moved away from the wall and toward the "host" body that Carlson had inhabited, nudging it over with a push from one of his heavy boots. "I know he hurt your sister, but… Was he also one of the ones who touched you?" he asked her in a raw voice, keeping his gaze locked on the body.

"Honestly, McConnell." A tired, weary sigh. "What does it matter?"

"Just tell me." The softness of his voice sent chills across the surface of her body. "I need to know. *Did. He. Rape. You?*"

She relented with a husky, "Yes," then watched, stunned, as he pulled the gun back out and fired five shots into the male's groin, turning it into a bloodied, shredded mess. Then he replaced the gun, turned and hammered his fist against the wall for a second time… then a third, the heavy, choppy force of his breaths echoing through the night. It was a shocking display of visceral aggression, one he didn't seem capable of controlling, reminding her of a Lycan's rage, raw and animalistic. And she'd have been lying through her teeth if she'd said she didn't find it hot as hell.

When he finally turned toward her again, the look in his unholy green eyes made her chest feel tight, as if she couldn't get enough oxygen. "Have you talked to anyone about it? About what happened to you?"

She panted, fighting down a rise of nausea, hating that he was thinking about it…that he even *knew* about it.

"Are you going to answer me?"

She shook her head, wrapping her arms across the front of her body, as if they could form some kind of shield. "There's nothing to say."

"I could help find someone," he told her, the gentleness of his tone nearly her undoing. "It doesn't have to be me. A counselor. Someone who's trained to—"

"Damn it, this has nothing to do with you!" She flung the words at him, using them like weapons. But he didn't back down.

"It does now. Someone's got to look out for you."

She reeled, thankful for the wall at her back, his tone scaring the hell out of her. "Whatever you're thinking, don't. You need to just turn and walk away, McConnell. Go back to the others."

He scowled, his expression sharp with disbelief. "And just let you get yourself killed?"

"This…this isn't going to happen," she suddenly stammered, hating her weakness. Hating that part of her that wanted to cling to him…rely on him. She had to be strong, damn it. She wasn't going to be that little victim that everyone had tiptoed around back at the Watchmen compound. The one they treated like blown glass. "I'm leaving now," she said, pushing away from the storefront, "and I'm going alone."

"Like hell you are. Where *you* go, *I* go. You want to go on a killing spree? Fine," he ground out through his clenched teeth, walking toward her. "But I'm going with you."

She shook her head again, trying to make sense of what was happening. "You can't be serious. Is this some kind of sick joke?"

He stopped a few feet in front of her, a muscle pulsing hard in his jaw, his eyes so dark they looked black in the silver glow of moonlight. "I'm not joking, Raine. I meant what I said."

"Yeah, well, you won't be able to keep up. I'll ditch you the first chance I get. And now that I know you're out there, I won't be so easy for you to find."

"You're not going anywhere without me," he countered, the calmness of his tone bringing a fresh wave of panic.

"Are you insane?" she snapped. "You don't even like vampires! You've spent your entire life killing them!"

"But I spent a hell of a lot of time making sure your little ass made it to England, where you would be safe. I'm not going to let you just run off and fuck that up."

"You can't stop me," she growled, knowing her eyes must be glowing with rage.

"You're wrong," he argued, working his jaw. "You owe me, Raine."

"I don't owe you anything!" she shouted, her panic spreading, spearing through her system. She knew, from the look on his face, that something bad was coming. But never in a million years could she have guessed what he said next.

"According to the sacred laws of the Deschanel, you damn well *do* owe me."

The sacred laws? No! He wouldn't dare!

"Don't even think about it," she warned him, unable to control the tremor in her voice, her throat tightening with rage and fear, her eyes burning with tears.

"Are you going to be reasonable?" A quiet, composed demand that made her want to hit him.

"You self-righteous jackass!" she screamed, shoving hard at his chest, not caring who heard or what attention they drew. But the bastard didn't even budge. "I am *not* your problem!"

"You are now," he said in a rough voice, his long fingers wrapping around her wrists as she pounded against his chest. "Because I'm claiming a Blood Oath from you, Raine Spenser. And until I free you from it, your stubborn little ass is mine."

CHAPTER FOUR

A small town on the outskirts of Venice, Italy

Ross Westmore was a man who liked to win, no matter the cost.

The vices that shaped most males meant little to him. He didn't care about money or sex or fame. But the power that came with victory…*that* was what made him tick. What drove him to succeed, no matter who or what he had to destroy in the process. He knew the Watchmen were scratching their heads, trying to come up with a logical explanation for why he was fighting so hard to free the Casus, and that right there was the answer. *Power.*

And he wasn't alone. Most of the Kraven shared his thirst for power, simply because it was something they'd always been denied. The offspring of female Deschanel vampires who were raped by Casus males before their imprisonment, the Kraven had been kept a secret by the Deschanel clan for centuries. Considered a sign of weakness, they were treated little better than slaves by the vampires, and the Kraven were tired of it. Tired enough to abandon their stations within the vampire clan and follow Westmore in his quest to break the Casus out of Meridian.

Then, once the Casus had been freed and embraced the Kraven as their brethren, Westmore and the others of his kind would no longer be considered an embarrassing abomination. As the Kraven and Casus bloodlines mixed, they would become more powerful than any creature the world had ever known—and Westmore would be considered a hero.

Hell, I'll probably be considered a god, he thought, walking onto his balcony through an open set of double doors, a cool breeze rushing against his face while the lights of Venice flickered in the distance. *And what could be more powerful than that?*

But to make his plans a reality, he needed the Dark Markers. Only the ancient crosses could set the chain of events into motion that would free the Casus from their impenetrable prison. He'd been so close to achieving his goal in January, with the psychic under his command, only to have his dream snatched away from him. Now he seethed with frustration, longing to strike out against the Watchmen with the full force of his army. But he had to be smart...patient. Those were the traits that had gotten him to this point, and they were the traits that would lead him to success.

Westmore couldn't afford another failure. There had been too many of those already. Thanks to the archives the Watchmen had stolen from his compound in the Wasteland, they knew the Markers were the only way to find and enter Meridian. They might not know how to assemble the Markers into the map that would lead to the Casus's prison, or how to use them as keys, but they weren't idiots. They would figure it out.

And they knew the crosses could be used to kill the Casus shades, destroying everything he'd worked for.

Which meant his only option was to gain possession of the Dark Markers at the earliest opportunity.

"Or…is it?" he mused out loud, one hand shoved deep in his pocket, while the other slowly stroked his jaw, his gaze focused on the moonlit canal that ran beside his building as he thought back to the scene he had watched play out there a few hours earlier. A flock of mature gulls had been challenging some younger birds for a fishing boat's evening catch. Eventually, the older gulls accepted defeat, leaving the younger ones to brave the wrath of the fishermen as they swooped in for the fish that'd been piled in baskets at the edge of the dock. The younger gulls had flown their bounty to the rooftop of a lower building where they gathered to eat, ignoring the presence of the older gulls, no longer seeing them as a threat. And it was then that the older gulls launched the second wave of their attack, with a strength and viciousness that caught the younger birds by surprise. Their earlier retreat had obviously been a ruse, one designed to give the younger gulls a false sense of security while they did the hard work and collected the food.

When they had appeared to give up, Westmore had thought the older gulls were pathetic, but as they deftly overran the younger birds and dined on their spoils, he'd changed his mind, thinking they were rather genius.

There they'd been, eating like kings, and with a minimal amount of effort. Could the answer he was looking for really be that simple?

A husky rumble of laughter started to break from his throat, only to be cut short when the doors to his bedchamber opened behind him, and he knew it would be Seton. He'd allowed no one else to know his location.

"Is there a problem?" he drawled, the politeness of his tone no doubt alerting the Casus to his displeasure at the interruption. Not that Seton would care.

"The psychic vamp we had at the compound is causing trouble. She killed Carlson and Rogers barely an hour ago in Paris."

At the mention of Raine, myriad emotions buffeted the Kraven's system, each one more staggering than the first. There was fury, of course, as well as frustration. But most of all, there was…longing. Such a strange emotion, considering its focus was for another person, and not his coveted power. But Westmore couldn't deny its existence.

He wanted her back. Wanted her to be *his,* so that he could do with her as he pleased…and make her pay for leaving him.

"Are you sure it was her?" he asked, his tone no longer relaxed, the bitterness that flavored his words impossible to hide.

"I'm sure. Stevens was meant to meet up with Carlson at the Gare d'Austerlitz before heading to Austria. When he didn't show, Stevens started searching the part of town where Carlson had been staying, and found both Carlson and Rogers. The psychic's blood was at the scene, and she hadn't been alone. He could smell a human with her."

Westmore absorbed the news with stoic silence, his back to the Casus as he turned toward the stunning view once more, the distant lights of the city flickering like jewels that'd been tossed across the land with a careless hand, their glittering glow reminding him of the psychic's eyes. He'd spent countless nights trying to sort out what drew him to the female. Her intelligence? Her beauty? Yes, both had called to him. But mostly it was the power that thrived inside her. It was evident in every word that she spoke, every breath that slipped past her lips, and he wanted to possess it. Claim ownership over it.

But to do that, he needed Raine back in his clutches.

"Do you know who the human could be?" Seton asked, interrupting his thoughts for the second time that night.

"I know who it is," he murmured, resting his hands on the railing, while his insides coiled with fury at the idea of Raine working with the human male. "Spark mentioned him the last time we talked. He's a Collective soldier who defected at the beginning of the war, only to join forces with the Watchmen."

"Is he the one who helped them attack your hideout in Colorado? McConnell?"

"One and the same. When he left the Collective, most of his unit followed him. He was also with the Watchmen who helped rescue the psychic from the Wasteland."

"Troublesome fucker, isn't he?" Seton gave a harsh laugh. "I hope he's there when we make a grab for the crosses. It would be fun to go up against a human who actually knew how to fight back."

Westmore nodded absently, his mind wandering back to his memory of the gulls, intrigued by the compelling idea taking shape in his thoughts. Obviously, there was no point in attacking the Watchmen now. Without Raine, he had no way of reaching the last Markers on his own. And he needed them all if he was going to form the map to Meridian and open the gate.

So maybe all he really needed was to play the loser, like the older gulls, then bide his time until the last possible moment—and hit those bloody shifters when they least expected it, stealing their victory right out from under their noses.

It was a bold move, but perhaps his best shot at success. And he truly loved the touch of irony. Could just imagine the look on the shifters' faces when they realized they'd been fooled.

Knowing exactly how he wanted this to play out, he turned and leaned his back against the balcony railing, his arms crossed over his chest as he locked his gaze with Seton's. "Send Spark after her."

A flash of surprise flared in the Casus's ice-blue eyes. "But the psychic can read her. They'll know she's coming, and Spark will end up dead."

"Do I look as if I care?" he asked with a sharp smile. "We won't need the assassin once the gate to Meridian has been broken. At that point, all she'll become is a meal for one of your brothers. Might as well use her while we can."

"I guess that's true," Seton allowed, pushing his ink-black hair back from his scarred face, the dark strands such a sharp contrast to the paleness of his skin. "So what's your plan?"

He had no intention of sharing his plans with Seton. In truth, for his idea to work, he needed this particular Casus to know as little as possible, so he simply said, "We know that Bryce was killed in Spain a few days ago, and now Carlson. It's obvious Raine is seeking revenge against those who've wronged her."

Seton's grin was a sadistic cross between pride and humor. "If she's coming after every Casus who fucked her, it's going to be a long-ass list."

"I actually think she's going after the five men who killed her sister, which would mean Rogers was simply in the wrong place at the wrong time."

"Should we warn the others?"

"No. She's *reading* them, which means she'll know. So we simply locate the remaining three and have them watched. When she's spotted, send Spark. The assassin will act as a diversion, drawing their focus, so that you can complete the job."

In order to pull off his plan without making the Watch-men suspicious, Westmore had to sacrifice a few pawns. He was taking a calculated risk in sending the Casus, since Seton rarely lost a fight, but the opportunity was perfect. He just hoped McConnell and his new friends were up to the challenge.

Of course, he didn't like knowing he would have to wait longer to have Raine back in his grasp, but it would be worth it in the end. Who knew? Maybe she'd accompany the Watchmen to Meridian, and after the Casus had defeated the shifters, he could make sure that McConnell's last memory of this world was an image of Westmore sinking between Raine's silky thighs.

"Why not just send me after her?" Seton asked, pulling his mind back to the conversation. "Why involve the assassin?"

"Why the concern?" He gave the male a long, piercing look. "Are you protective of Spark?"

The Casus snorted. "Hardly. But the assassin is human. She could screw it up. She's—"

"A complication I no longer need. She might be human, but she's a powerful woman. One who expects compensation for her work. But with the psychic able to monitor her every move, she's no good to me. Might as well use her as a diversion." He regarded the Casus with a challenging smirk. "Unless you have a problem with following orders?"

For a moment, Seton looked as if he'd enjoy nothing more than raking his claws across Westmore's face. He didn't like being treated as a subordinate and his anger was evident in the hard lines of his expression. An anger Westmore knew would play well into his plans.

"Consider it done," Seton said in a graveled voice, then turned and stalked across the lavish room, leaving Westmore standing on the balcony alone, with nothing but his thoughts and mounting hungers.

"And, Seton," he called out, just before the Casus reached the door.

"Yeah?"

A slow, wicked smile curved the Kraven's mouth. "I have important plans for the psychic. So no matter what happens, make sure she stays alive."

CHAPTER FIVE

THE RAIN CAME down in a slow, endless pour, as if tears were being quietly spilled from heaven. There were no blinding strikes of lightning or crashing rumbles of thunder to mirror the tension in the air. Just that soft, wet rain that kept spilling and spilling, as if it would never end.

With tired eyes, Seth ignored the pain in his bandaged right hand and stared through the rain-spattered window of the train, watching the French countryside move by in a hypnotic blur. He was thinking about the war and the fight they'd had against the Casus just hours before. About what the others were doing back at Harrow House, hoping the latest lead they were following had actually helped them translate a section of a journal they'd found at Westmore's compound. The Watchmen called it the "death" journal, since it contained instructions on how to kill a variety of species, many of which were no longer even in existence. But the one passage they needed most—the passage they believed explained how a Death-Walker could be killed—was written in some archaic language they couldn't read. And considering the way things were going down, it was information they were definitely going to need.

The Death-Walkers were a pain in the ass, and one that would have to be dealt with, just as soon as they'd taken care of the Casus. Thanks to a vampire named Gideon Granger, who was now working with the Watchmen, Seth and the others had learned what the Death-Walkers were back in December, after the creatures had made their first attack. According to Gideon, every time a Dark Marker was used to send a Casus's soul into hell, a doorway was opened into the part of hell that held the tainted souls of the clans, and one of those souls was able to escape. These creatures were the Death-Walkers, and their time in hell had left them seriously screwed up in the head. All they cared about was creating chaos among the clans, hoping to pull the world into a never-ending battle of blood and misery that they could sit back and enjoy. And they were pulling humans right into the middle of the bloodshed by turning them into the Infettato, or the Infected. The Infettato were humans who had been bitten by the Death-Walkers, their bodies turned into mindless, zombielike eating machines that were controlled by their makers. The Watchmen had their hands full trying to keep the Infettato from becoming public knowledge and starting widespread panic among the humans, but that job was becoming more difficult with each week that went by.

So yeah, it was pretty natural for him to be sitting there, mulling all that shit through his mind. But mostly he was thinking about the woman sitting beside him, who was obviously trying to pretend he didn't exist.

She'd changed her damaged, blood-spattered clothes

when they'd made it back to her hotel room in Paris. The blue sweater and jeans she'd pulled on were nothing fancy, but he couldn't stop staring at the way the soft cashmere clung to the slope of her shoulders and the tantalizing curve of her breasts.

"You know," he finally said in a low voice, "you're going to have to talk to me sooner or later."

She turned her head to the side, staring across the aisle, toward the empty seats that sat across from them, still doing her best to ignore him. But Seth knew he was getting to her. Her hands were clenched, her jaw held hard and tight, as if she was choking back the curses she longed to hurl his way. She was, without any doubt, still furious with him for claiming that Oath. But he didn't regret what he'd done.

The muted light in the train car glittered against the cross that they'd retrieved before leaving the scene of the fight, and Seth was thankful for that small piece of protection hanging around her neck, though it wasn't enough. He wanted her back at Harrow House.

Obviously unable to hold back any longer, she turned toward him in a sudden burst of energy that sent the long waves of her hair falling over one shoulder. "Just out of curiosity, how old was the Deschanel you tortured for the information about a Blood Oath?"

Seth lifted his brows. "What makes you think the information wasn't given freely?"

Her beautiful eyes glittered with fury and distrust. "There's not a chance in hell a vamp would have simply offered up that kind of intel. Blood Oaths are one of our most closely held secrets, meant to be used only among our kind, because of the power they give to another. So what exactly did you do to garner such an admission? Threaten to kill a child? Or was it a father? Did you threaten his family? Or did you simply torture the poor bastard until he broke?"

"I'm not doing this with you, Raine. If you want answers, get them yourself. They're all right here," he said, tapping his temple.

She gave a delicate snort. "Too ashamed to own up to your sins, McConnell?"

"You know, you weren't nearly this bitchy when we were escaping from the Wasteland. Is there a reason for the change in attitude?" he asked, hating how easily she could get under his skin. "Have I done something to piss you off?"

Her lip curled, those brilliant eyes burning with a rage that only made them more stunning. "What about binding yourself to me with some archaic Court covenant? I think that would be enough to irritate any woman."

"Before tonight," he growled.

She ground her teeth together, shaking her head with a stiff, sharp movement.

"Then why aren't you treating me like you did before? You were skittish around me while we were making our way to England, but you were never openly angry. You never acted like a bitch."

"I was half-dead and trying to heal," she muttered. "I didn't have the energy to get pissed at you. I just tolerated your presence."

He wanted to argue, but knew that what she'd said was true. After being held in Westmore's compound for several weeks, she'd been in bad shape when he'd found her, and her condition had only worsened in the days that followed. Her friend Chloe, who'd also been held as a prisoner and was now engaged to Kellan Scott, had thought that maybe it was the psychic's guilt that kept eating away at her, wearing her body down. After all, Raine had made it out of the compound when her sister hadn't. And her mother had alluded to similar thoughts when they'd discussed her failing psychic abilities.

But if guilt had been wearing her down, what had prompted the physical change in her? What was making her grow stronger?

"Speaking of healing," he murmured, figuring it was a good time to steer the conversation in another direction, since he was only going to keep getting slammed. "How is your arm?" She'd been caught in an explosion during their escape from the compound back in early February and her right arm had been badly burned.

"It's finally healed," she replied grudgingly, though she did push back her sleeve to show him the pale skin. There was the faintest shadow of a scar visible on her forearm, but nothing you would notice unless you were looking for it.

Lifting his gaze to her face, Seth eyed the rapidly fading bruises and scrapes the Casus had made earlier that night. "Your face is already healing from where that bastard hit you tonight. Why are you healing so quickly now, when you couldn't before?"

She pulled her sleeve back down and shrugged. "I've got a few theories, but nothing concrete."

A scowl wove between his brows. "And nothing you're going to share, huh?"

"Wow. You're pretty good at this mind reading yourself," she drawled. "And this is the norm for me. We vampires heal quickly, but then, I'm sure you already know that."

Wanting to keep her talking, Seth chose to ignore the sarcasm and kept digging for information. "So your Deschanel abilities are working at full capacity, but your Alacea ones are still on the fritz?"

"Yep." She shifted in her seat, keeping her gaze focused on anything but him, while he just kept staring at her, unable to look away.

"If your psychic powers are as weak as you keep claiming they are, then how are you managing to track down the Casus?"

Sliding him a dark glare, she said, "I'm managing. That's all you need to know."

Refusing to give up, he fired another round of questions. "If you can read them, can they lead us to Westmore? Is that how you plan to find him and get the Markers back?"

She shook her head, but offered no other explanation.

"Come on, Raine. I saved your ass tonight. You owe me this much, at least."

She took a deep breath, her golden hair catching the soft streams of light from overhead as she turned her head away from him, staring out that far window again. "Westmore must have anticipated that I would go after the Casus, or assumed I would send someone else to do the job." She was starting to sound more tired than pissed, and he took that as a good sign. "That's the most logical explanation for why he's scattered the bastards across Europe. As far as I've been able to tell, he hasn't allowed them anywhere near him since he left the Wasteland, his location for the moment completely secret. But I'm assuming he's in Europe. Otherwise, he wouldn't be keeping the Casus on this continent, where they'll be within easy reach if he needs them."

"What about his security?"

"I don't know. If he has anyone with him, it's someone I can't read."

Well, shit. He didn't like the sound of that. It just meant there was another asshole out there who could sneak up on her at any time.

"If Westmore learns that you're the one going after the Casus, Raine, then it stands to reason that he'll try to set a trap for you." He tried to school his expression as she brought her gaze back to his, but it wasn't easy. "You know he wants you back."

"That's likely, yes."

Her I-couldn't-care-less tone drove him mad. "And you're willing to take that risk?" he growled.

"I am." Her chin lifted. "But they won't be taking me alive a second time."

Now *that* was something he really didn't like the sound of. "What's your plan?"

She gave a soft, bitter laugh. "Who said I had a plan?"

His nostrils flared. "You're actually trying to irritate me, aren't you?"

Another low slide of laughter, and she looked away, staring at the back of the seat in front of her. The train car was empty but for an elderly couple six rows back, their soft snoring keeping perfect time with the rhythm of the wheels racing down the track. "All I know is that I won't let them take me alive," she finally said, her hands rubbing down her denim-covered thighs. "Since I'm only half-Deschanel, I'm easier to kill than most of my kind. I'll take my own life before letting them lock me up a second time. I just… I couldn't go through it again."

"If that's true, then why didn't you kill yourself tonight?"

She stiffened, as if his question had caught her off guard, before slanting him a slow, mocking smile. "Disappointed?"

Seth narrowed his eyes. "I'd hardly be wasting my time trying to keep you alive if I wanted you dead, Raine. I'm just trying to understand you."

IT WAS HIS TONE, more than the words themselves, that rattled something inside her. Something Raine had thought safely buried, where she wanted it. A strange desire to want to connect with someone on a level that went deeper than mere friendship, or even sex.

Realizing he was still waiting for a response, she managed to say, "I guess I was still hoping that something would happen. That something would stop them."

"You got lucky." His hands clenched into fists on the armrests of his seat, and she could sense his internal struggle as he forced himself to relax, his voice a bit rougher as he said, "I might not have found you."

The train made its next scheduled stop, then resumed its long trek, and she was thankful for the interruption, not wanting to think about how close it had been with the Casus…or how much she owed the soldier for bailing her out. After a few tense moments of silence, she turned toward him again. "When you found me in the club, you said all hell was breaking loose for the Watchmen. I've only been gone a week. What's happened?"

Some of his tension eased, and the corner of his mouth twitched, as if he was fighting back a smile. "Actually, they won't be the Watchmen much longer. Kierland's finally put his master plan into action."

She knew that Kierland Scott, a gorgeous auburn-haired Lycan, was regarded as the leader of the Watchmen unit currently stationed at Harrow House, and that he was also one of Seth's friends—but she had no idea what the human meant by a "master plan."

"What are you talking about?"

With a frown, he asked, "Didn't anyone at Harrow House tell you about the meetings?"

"No one at Harrow House would tell me anything." As soon as the words left her mouth, she winced, thinking she sounded like a bitter old hag. But damn it, she'd hated the way all conversation had ceased the second she walked into a room at the Watchmen compound, as if they were afraid of saying the wrong thing in front of her. With a wry tilt to her mouth, she leaned her head back against the seat and closed her eyes as she went on to say, "And I'd obviously be lying if I said it hadn't been extremely annoying."

He gave a rough bark of laughter, the deep, gritty timbre spilling deliciously through her veins. "Yeah, I can understand how that could grate on a person's nerves. But the condensed version goes something like this. The Watchmen have known for some time that the Consortium leaders are failing to do their job. So they've decided to make a break from the organization."

She didn't need him to explain who the Consortium leaders were. Anyone who was a part of the ancient clans—the nonhuman races who walked the earth—knew that the Consortium was a kind of preternatural United Nations, its purpose to keep peace among the clans and ensure the secret of their existence from the human world. The Watchmen reported directly to the Consortium, serving as their eyes and ears around the world. But it appeared the organization was no longer viable, the Consortium's policies plagued by indecision and bureaucracy.

"Kierland's convinced the other Watchmen units to break with the Consortium and form a new organization?" she asked, assuring herself that she was only staring at him so intently because she was interested in the conversation…and not because he looked incredibly gorgeous sitting there in the soft glow of light, the golden stubble on his cheeks and jaw bringing the rugged angles of his face into sharper definition.

He nodded in response to her question, saying, "He didn't have much choice. The Consortium's refusal to take action against the Casus has stripped them of respect. They're now viewed as a bunch of frightened old men, too bogged down in politics to be effective."

"So what's this new group called?"

His mouth twitched again, and this time a crooked grin took shape. "That's still under debate. Kellan suggested the X-Men, but it was quickly turned down. Aiden said the spandex would ride up his ass."

That sounded exactly like something Ade, a tiger-shifter with a seriously sarcastic sense of humor, would say, and a soft burst of laughter slipped free, before she choked off the throaty sound, stunned that he'd been able to make her lower her guard. She fidgeted in her seat, unnerved by the way he was watching her, the heat in his eyes so warm she could feel a simmer beginning beneath her skin, her primal instincts reacting powerfully to the raw force of his masculinity, whether she wanted them to or not.

Needing conversation to steer her mind away from her body's frustrating reactions, Raine broke eye contact and coughed. "So, um…what will you do when this is over?"

"You mean your hunt?"

Shaking her head, she wet her lips with a nervous swipe of her tongue. "The war."

Even though she was now watching her fingers trace

the grain of denim across the top of a thigh, she could feel the heat of his stare against her profile, the intensity of his gaze nearly as compelling as the deep rumble of his voice. "I'll continue to work with Kierland and the others."

"You mean hunting?" Impossible to ignore the way her stomach twisted at the thought.

"I mean *helping,*" he corrected her, that deep voice edged with irritation. "I have experience, good or bad, Raine, that can be useful to the Watchmen." From the corner of her eye, she watched as he turned his head to the side, his jaw like carved marble as he stared out the window into the starless night. "It's time for the Collective to come to an end. But some things out there still need to be dealt with, and the Consortium can't be trusted. Not after what they've allowed to happen with the Casus. Christ, who knows what other nightmares they've turned a blind eye to or hidden from the Watchmen? So there's a helluva lot of work that will need to be done, even when the war is over."

"Sounds intense."

"I'm sure it will be." His tone turned wry as he pulled a hand down his face and drawled, "But then, it probably doesn't get more intense than this. Protecting a headstrong Deschanel on the hunt for blood is about as intense as it gets."

She laughed, and his head came back around, his sharp green gaze locking hard on hers. At his questioning look, she said, "I'm sorry. It's just ironic."

He didn't look angry, merely curious. "What is?"

She rolled a shoulder, as well as her eyes. "The way you spent over half your life killing vampires, and now you're determined to protect one. Talk about a change of heart."

Though she could sense his tension level was still high, another one of those slow, crooked smiles lifted the corner of his mouth. "Who knows? Maybe it's penance for my sins."

She sensed the deeper meaning to his words, and couldn't stop herself from probing for more detail, needing to understand him in a way she couldn't explain. Yeah, she could have fobbed it off to curiosity, but she'd have been lying, because it went deeper than that. Deeper than she was willing to admit. "So then you think that what you did while with the Collective was wrong?"

He leaned his head back against the headrest and closed his eyes, arms crossed over his chest. For a moment, she didn't think he would answer, but then he finally said, "You've seen inside my head, Raine. If you're looking for an answer to that question, I'm sure it was in there."

"To be honest, I didn't spend a lot of time evaluating your emotions." Her tone was dry. "I was a little too horrified by all the murder and mayhem lingering around in there."

A hard, husky laugh surged up from his chest, and he rolled his head toward her, his voice a delicious rasp of sound as he said, "I'll answer your question if you answer one of mine."

Her pulse picked up a little, but then it always did

that whenever he was giving her one of those intense stares that said she had his complete and undivided attention. The train could have slid off the tracks and pitched straight into a ravine, and he wouldn't have looked away. But she didn't feel threatened by the predatory look. She felt nervous...flushed.

"Okay," she agreed, figuring whatever he asked would be worth it, if it meant she could delve a little deeper into his psyche. Though she'd been resolved not to pry into his private life earlier in the night, they were now stuck with each other, thanks to that bloody Oath—and she never had been the type who could walk away from a puzzle until it was finished.

"Why you?" he asked her, lifting his head off the back of the seat.

"What do you mean?"

"Why does Westmore need *you* so badly? What's different about your power?" His dark gaze moved slowly over her face, feature by feature, and she could feel a rush of heat burning in each place that it touched. "I don't know much about the Alacea," he admitted, staring at her mouth, before lifting his gaze back to her eyes. "They don't commit a lot of crimes, so we're not told much about them in the Collective. Do you all have the same powers?"

"Um...no. The Alacea are eclectic. Some can see into another's thoughts, some can't. Some can use their gifts on command, while others struggle for control. There's no rhyme or reason to the way power is distributed, and it's not uncommon for different powers to be held by different members of a family. But usually only one form of sight is given, whether that's into the past, the present or the future. Even in those rare cases where an Alacea *does* have two forms of sight, one is often much weaker than the other."

"I know you can see into the past, as well as the present. So then your powers are…unique?"

"I guess you could say that. Especially since reading the present is the most uncommon of the three. But only my family knows that I have, or *had*, two strong forms of sight."

"Then how did Westmore know you were what he needed?"

"He'd been searching for someone like me for months," she explained, a bad taste filling her mouth as she thought of the man who had destroyed her life. "He had sent scouts out roaming the earth, spying on every psychic they could find. They could read our powers, and it turned out that I was exactly what he was looking for. It wasn't the future that interested him, but the past…and especially the present, since he needed me to keep an eye on Saige Buchanan as she deciphered the maps."

Saige was engaged to a shape-shifter named Michael Quinn, who was one of the Watchmen back at Harrow House. The woman was also a part of the Merrick clan, which had close ties to the war and were mortal enemy of the Casus. All three of the Buchanan siblings were working with the Watchmen, and they also each possessed a unique gift that had helped in the search for the Dark Markers.

Saige's particular gift enabled her to "hear" objects, and she'd used this strange talent to decipher the encrypted maps that led to the places where the Dark Markers had been hidden. By using her Alacea powers, Raine had been able to "watch" as Saige deciphered the maps, and had then passed that information on to Westmore, enabling him to send the Casus after the crosses.

The one time she'd tried to lie about a Marker's location, he'd had Rietta killed to teach her a lesson.

It was clear that Seth wanted to keep questioning her, but the conductor's voice came over the intercom, announcing the next station stop at the German border, which was where they were getting off. Raine stood and grabbed her backpack from the overhead compartment, then stepped aside so that Seth could unfold his long body from the row of seats. He grabbed his own bag, and they exited the train a few moments later, the platform nearly empty since it was the middle of the night.

"You can grab a taxi and head on over to the Marriott," she told him, hiking her bag higher onto her shoulder. "I'll meet you there in about an hour."

"Meet me there?" he rumbled, taking hold of her arm as he ground to a halt. "Just where the hell do you think you're going?"

She could have lied, but decided to give him the brutal truth. If he didn't like it, maybe he'd save them both from this complicated mess and go back to England. "I need to eat."

"You told me you'd already eaten before we boarded the train in Paris."

Raine made sure no one was close enough to overhear them, then said, "I need blood, McConnell. Not food."

Surprise flickered in his gaze, before melting into a slow, glittering burn of anger. "Like *hell*," he snarled, the low words nearly carried away by the cool wind whipping down the platform. "Is this some kind of stunt meant to piss me off?"

Sighing, she said, "I'm not jacking you around. Real food only does *part* of the job for me. I need blood to keep up my strength, and that fight tonight zapped more than I'd planned on losing. Plain and simple, I need more of the red stuff."

"You're not going anywhere," he muttered as he set off through the station, dragging her behind him as he headed toward the taxis.

"You'd rather I starve?"

He cut her a blistering glare from the corner of his eye. "You are *not* going off into the night to find some guy to fuck for food."

Well, that was certainly blunt. And while it probably didn't make a lot of sense, she actually liked that he didn't censor everything that came out of his mouth when he was with her, the way his friends had, always afraid they would say something to upset her. Yes, she'd had horrific, ungodly things done to her, but she wasn't going to fall apart at the sound of a swear word. It had been part of the reason she was so itchy to get away from Harrow House.

Pulling in a deep breath through her nose, she ran her tongue over her teeth and casually said, "For your information, McConnell, I don't have sex with my food."

"Just…don't say anything." His voice was harder than before, his grip on her arm a fraction tighter, though she could tell he was trying not to hurt her. "I hate being lied to."

"I'm not lying," she argued, then kept silent as he pushed her into the back of a taxi and climbed in beside her. She stared out the window while he gave the name of the hotel to the driver through the sliding window, before slamming it shut, providing them a modicum of privacy, while the night's darkness provided them a bit more. From the corner of her eye, she watched as he popped his jaw, a muscle pulsing hard in his temple. He looked…bleak, and she decided to give him the explanation he didn't deserve. "I wasn't looking for some*one* to feed from," she said quietly. "I was going to find the local blood bank."

His head whipped toward her so fast, she was surprised he hadn't given himself whiplash. "Is that what you've been doing? Breaking into blood banks?"

With a shrug, she said, "It's easier than it sounds. An internet connection can usually get me the information that I need, such as the name of the bank's supervisor. Then it's just a matter of locking into their thoughts, if I'm able to, and searching for the access codes to the alarms."

"Clever." His voice was soft…and there was maybe just a tad of admiration in his tone.

"I, uh, try to keep it simple."

"Simple, but still too dangerous. It stops now."

Her mouth flattened into a thin line of frustration. "You're being unreasonable. And you're also not the boss of me."

Wow. And wasn't it great that she now sounded like a bratty preteen?

"I'm not going to starve you, Raine. If you need blood, you can have more of mine." She flinched in reaction, but he didn't notice, his attention already focused on the knife he'd pulled from his back pocket. She knew exactly what he was going to do, this same scenario playing out time and again while they'd made their way across the Wasteland. The human had made it more than clear that he would *never* give her his vein. Instead, he lowered his window and emptied out the water bottle he'd pulled from his pack, then made a shallow cut in his strong, corded forearm and collected the blood in the empty container.

Christ, that smells good, she thought, as the rich, drugging scent reached her nostrils, making her head spin. *And so unforgivably wrong.*

But it wouldn't stop her from taking what he offered. She couldn't. Once that mouthwatering scent hit her nose, she was hooked. Now she needed it too badly.

He scowled as he handed the bottle into her trembling hand, those green eyes shadowed with grim, angry emotion. Part of her wanted to throw the blood in his judgmental face, but she greedily clutched the bottle in her cold fingers. Just before the rim touched her lips, her eyes flicked to the knife he still gripped in his hand

and she smirked. "You'd rather die than do this the easy way, wouldn't you?"

"I'm sure the knife hurts a helluva lot less than your teeth."

"It's too bad you'll never know for sure," she murmured, and she could feel him watching her with piercing intensity as she lowered her lashes and drank deeply, letting the warm, succulent liquid flow down her throat, spreading through her body, slipping deeper…and deeper….

And all the while, she tried not to think about the past or the future…or how badly she wanted to sink her fangs into Seth McConnell's masculine throat.

CHAPTER SIX

Saarbrücken, Germany
4:00 a.m.

IF HELL EXISTED on earth, then Seth had no doubt that he'd found it. They'd checked into their hotel a half hour ago, and all that'd been available was a room with a king-size bed, which meant he'd be cramping it on the love seat for the remainder of the night. But that wasn't the hellish part. No, the part that had him twisted into knots, pacing the room from one side to the other, was the fact that he was alone with the vamp.

Strange, that in all the time he'd known her, they'd never once been behind a locked door together. Always before, there had been friends nearby. Watching. Listening. Ready to be there if she needed them.

Knowing damn well that he made her nervous, Seth was relieved, if not a little annoyed, when she sat down in the middle of the bed with her backpack, pulled the wavy mass of her long hair over one shoulder, whipped out her laptop and began typing away, doing God only knew what—and completely ignoring his presence. Of course, it gave him the opportunity to simply watch her, his gaze never wavering from the delicate angles of her face as he paced…and paced, the carpet no doubt wearing thin beneath the soles of his boots.

Though he hated to admit it, she looked better for the blood he'd given her, color blooming in her cheeks with a soft, youthful glow. A glow he couldn't help but feel strangely proud for putting there. He'd used the first-aid kit he always traveled with—in his line of work, the thing was constantly needed—and wrapped a bandage around his arm, but the shallow cut still throbbed, reminding him of those quiet, intense moments in the back of the taxi. As he'd watched her drinking his blood, it'd been impossible to control his body's reactions. His heart had hammered like a bitch, his cock hardening to the point he felt light-headed. Though his mind obviously had trouble coming to terms with her "liquid" diet, his body had no trouble reacting to the provocative idea of her taking sustenance from him.

Or was he simply experiencing relief at the fact that he'd been able to keep her from going out and finding her meal elsewhere? After all, he knew the Deschanel were hardly without means. They had "feeders" in every city of the world—men and women who gave of their blood freely. Most were from clans who were allies of the Deschanel, though he'd heard of humans filling the prestigious positions. They were more than well compensated for their work, often earning millions a year.

And it wasn't always their blood that they offered, but their bodies, as well.

If what Raine had said about finding a blood bank was true, then there had to be a reason, and Seth couldn't help but think that she didn't want to get close enough to anyone to feed directly from their vein. But if that was true, then why did she take such exception to the fact that he refused to allow her to bite *him?*

And why am I asking myself this question, when I already know the answer? It's obviously a matter of pride. She knows I won't ever allow it, so she makes those comments simply to irritate me.

Or…was it something else entirely? Could she honestly—

No! Damn it, that's enough!

Knowing he was only going to twist himself into knots if he didn't get his mind on to a different subject, he said, "So who are we hunting in Germany? Seton?"

She stiffened with a little gasp, her expression so rigid she looked ready to crack as she set her laptop aside. "How do you know about Seton?" she demanded, pressing her back and shoulders against the headboard. "Were you gossiping with the others? God, you're all like a bunch of schoolkids!"

Seth knew, from talking to Kellan and Chloe, that Seton was the Casus bastard who'd overseen Raine's punishments while the group had been imprisoned, carrying them out at Westmore's command.

"We weren't gossiping," he muttered, raking his fingers through his hair like he did when he was tense, which seemed to be his usual state these days. "I was just…worried. I wanted to gather as much information as I could."

Her nostrils flared. "My private life is none of your

goddamn business, McConnell. You have no right gathering *information* about me, and you can't shove me under a microscope just because you feel like it. I'm not the subject of one of your Collective hunts!"

Narrowing his eyes, he quietly said, "I'm not hunting you, Raine. I claimed that Oath because I'm trying to help."

"Oh, right." Breathless laughter shook her chest, while a flat smile twisted the corner of her mouth. "How can I keep forgetting that the vampire killer has had a change of heart?"

Seth stopped pacing at the foot of the bed, his muscles corded with strain as he held her furious stare. "Damn it, what do you want to hear?" His voice was getting harder…grittier, the words ripping out of him against his will, scratching like barbs in his throat. "You want to hear that I'm sorry for what I've done? That there's a part of me that feels like a monster for all the Deschanel that I've cut down in cold blood? Then fine, I do. It's a screwed-up feeling, but it's one I've got to live with. You happy now?"

"Why feel sorry?" The gray of her eyes turned silver, glittering like streaks of lightning. "We vampires all deserve it, right?"

"A lot of them did." He shoved his hands in his pockets and locked his jaw, forcing the graveled words out. "Others…I can't be so sure."

His husky admission had obviously surprised her. Her mouth dropped open a little, her tawny brows pulling together over eyes that were stormy with disbelief, and he actually felt his face start to flush with heat.

What the hell am I doing?

Clearing his throat, Seth turned and stalked toward the window. He braced one hand high on the frame and stared out at the pinkening skyline, the sun finally making its early-morning climb, fighting its way against the darkness, while he wondered why he couldn't just keep his mouth shut around her. Yeah, he'd lived with things he knew were wrong during his years with the Collective, but he'd made excuses, not wanting to admit that his entire life was built on a steaming pile of hatred and prejudice. But that didn't mean she was going to understand…or forgive him.

"What's going on, McConnell?" He could hear the thread of confusion in her soft words. "You still owe me an answer to that question I asked you on the train. Do you honestly regret all the blood you've shed in the name of the Collective Army?"

"Not all of it," he muttered, rubbing his free hand against his stubbled jaw. "But revenge is an ugly thing, Raine. Be ready for what it does to you. Because if you give in to it, you might not like what you become."

For a moment all he could hear was the soughing sound of her breaths, but he could feel the stormy heat of her gaze burning against his back, and he steeled himself for her response, knowing damn well that he wasn't going to like it. "I'm sure that's true, but it doesn't matter. I'm willing to sell a piece of my soul if it means making the Casus pay for their sins."

"A piece?" A wry laugh slid bitterly from his lips, and he dropped his head forward, his fingers digging into the wooden window frame with so much force, he was amazed it didn't crack. "More like the whole fucking package."

"You don't think a man like Seton should pay for his sins?"

"I'm not saying that." Of course the bastard needed to pay. Just thinking about the son of a bitch made him want to rip something apart with his bare hands—but he didn't want Raine being a part of that. She'd already been through enough ugly crap to last a lifetime. "All I'm saying is that you shouldn't have to kill yourself to make it happen. Even if it is only a part. You've already suffered enough."

"Yeah, well, I happen to believe that it's his turn to suffer."

"So then it *is* Seton we're here for?" he asked, looking over his shoulder.

She shook her head, and he could see the exhaustion in her eyes that she was trying so hard to conceal. "Not yet. I'm saving him for the end. I figure he and Westmore will be together, so I'll be able to take them out at the same time."

"Can you read him?"

"No. And he knows it."

AT HIS QUESTIONING LOOK, Raine wet her lips, forcing herself to hold his gaze as she explained. "When they were torturing me, I was asked questions. Ones that I couldn't always answer with a lie. I admitted I couldn't read Westmore…or Seton."

"Why is that?"

"I don't know. Bad luck? I hated them the most? Whatever the reason, they're blank to me."

"So it's not only your loved ones you can't see?" he asked in a gritty rasp, his eyes darkening. "It's also the people you despise?"

"Sometimes," she murmured, pulling her knees into her chest and wrapping her arms around them.

He looked back out the window, his posture rigid, and Raine realized what he was thinking. She could no longer read him, so the logical conclusion was that it was because she hated him. It was on the tip of her tongue to tell him that wasn't true, but she bit back the words, knowing no good could come from it. Better to let him think what he would. She was already too drawn to him, slipping deeper into dangerous territory with each second that went by.

She shivered, rubbing her hands down her arms, her skin suddenly too tight for her body, and was actually grateful for the distraction when he came right out with his unspoken question, even though it was going to mean admitting things she'd rather have kept to herself.

"Why do you think you can no longer read me?" He took a deep breath, the hand he'd braced at the edge of the window clenching into a powerful fist. "Is it because you hate me after seeing the things I've done in the past?"

"I don't know why I can't read you, McConnell. But

it isn't because of hatred. I might find it…difficult to accept you, and the things you've done definitely make me angry, but…even though I know that I *should,* I don't hate you for them." She lowered her gaze, staring at the swirling pattern of the bedspread, and made an admission that should have made her burn with shame. "To be honest," she said in a quiet voice, "if I were in your place, I probably would have done the same things. That wouldn't have made them right, but I don't think it would have stopped me."

He turned as she lifted her gaze, his expression mirroring his surprise. "You really believe that?"

With a stiff shrug of her shoulder, she said, "Aren't I doing something similar now?"

"Yeah, but the Casus are a bunch of evil bastards who deserve to die."

"And after what happened to your family, you felt the same way about vamps, didn't you?"

"I did. But do you know what I finally learned?" His voice got rougher, and she could feel the raw force of his emotions blasting against her like a hot wind. "I learned that I can't hate every vampire for what was done to my family. And no matter how many kills you make, Raine, you won't be able to change what happened to yours."

"I know that," she told him, more than a little shocked by the honesty of their conversation. For two people who hadn't known each other long, and who had so many reasons to be enemies, they spoke with a candor that was more than a little unsettling. "I'm not trying to change what happened. I'm just trying to find a way to live with it, the same as you did."

He swore under his breath, and began pacing again, his bristling, restless energy seeming too much for the room to contain. "If not Seton, then who are we here for, Raine? If we're going to do this thing, I need to understand the plan."

"There are three more that I want, before Westmore. Seton will be the last of those three, and to find him I'm going to have to find the Kraven. But the next one I'm going after is named Schultz. He's here in Germany."

"And what about Spark?" he asked, shoving his fingers through his hair so hard that it would have hurt if the blond strands hadn't been cut so close to his scalp.

Spark was a Collective assassin who was working with Westmore. The female soldier had once targeted Raine for attack during her imprisonment, but Kellan had managed to turn the assassin's attention on him instead…and had taken a gruesome beating for it. Just thinking about it made Raine feel sick to her stomach.

Forcing the words past the knot of guilt in her throat, she managed to say, "Spark might be a bitch, but she had nothing to do with Rietta's death."

"But she nearly got you raped again." His tone was so graveled it reminded her of a Lycan. "Kellan told me what happened."

"But this isn't about me. It's about what they did to my sister."

"Even so, I still think we need to be careful where Spark's concerned. She's been holed up in Budapest for months now, but we'll know if she moves. The Granger brothers are still running personal surveillance on her."

Ashe and Gideon Granger were two Deschanel vampires who were working with the Watchmen, same as Seth. Watching Spark was a simple assignment for guys of their experience, considering they were *Förmyndares*—specially trained vampires who protected the Deschanel clan—but the brothers had personal reasons for wanting to get their hands on Westmore and had hoped the assassin would eventually lead them to the Kraven leader.

The Grangers were also wonderfully gorgeous, and infinitely more suited to a woman like her, but Raine wasn't interested in them. Despite their outrageous appeal, it was McConnell who'd held her attention from the very beginning—which meant she obviously had something wrong with her wiring. Yeah, she had no doubt that he'd make some woman incredibly happy one day—but that woman sure as hell wouldn't be a vampire.

The soldier came to a stop at the foot of the bed and pushed his hands into his pockets again, his gaze locked with hers, and Raine was thankful that he hadn't been able to read the direction of her thoughts. "Do you think Westmore knows we bugged her?" he asked, still thinking about Spark.

Before they'd escaped the Wasteland, the Watchmen had managed to capture the assassin. They'd let her get away, but only after they'd tagged the backpack that she always carried with an electronic tracking device. To cover their plan, they'd told her she was being released so that she could deliver a message to Westmore, demanding that he show in two weeks' time at the Eiffel Tower, ready to hand over the three Dark Markers in his possession. The Kraven leader hadn't shown, but then, they hadn't expected him to. But they were disappointed that the assassin obviously hadn't been allowed to join Westmore at his new hiding place, which would have led Seth and his friends right to him.

"It's more likely that he's worried I'd be able to get a read on her and tell the Watchmen where he's hiding," she said in response to his question. "Like I told you before, I'm sure that's why the Casus haven't been allowed to join him."

"Could you read her if you needed to?"

"I don't know. It's doubtful. I'm using everything I have just to keep tabs on the Casus I'm going after. The easiest way to think of my power at the moment is like a battery. Every glimpse I steal is draining that battery, and nothing seems capable of recharging it."

Nothing except for this seething need for revenge burning inside her, which was the only reason she'd been able to clue in to those Casus she was hunting—but she kept that truth to herself.

Lifting his bandaged right hand, he rubbed at the muscles at the back of his neck, and asked, "If it's difficult for you to see the ones you hate most, like Westmore and Seton, then why can you see the Casus?"

"Every threat doesn't become a blind spot. You're looking for logical explanations, but I don't have any.

This isn't science, McConnell. It's the supernatural. You can't apply human reasoning."

"But you have a theory, don't you?" The way he looked at her with those piercing eyes, and the sureness of his tone, made her feel as if *he* was the one who read minds.

"If I had to guess," she murmured, tugging her knees closer to her chest, "it would be because the orders were coming from Westmore and Seton. The others were just their sheep."

"So you're blind to those you sense as a direct threat?"

"Sometimes." With a wry half smile, she said, "It's a twisted system, isn't it?"

"Yeah." He kept rubbing at the back of his neck, as if trying to work out a knot. "But I would never… I'm not a threat, damn it."

"Why does it bother you so much?" she asked, more than a little confused by his reaction. "I thought you'd be pleased to know that for the most part, you're completely blank to me now."

He blew out another ragged breath of air and finally stopped rubbing his neck, shoving his bandaged hand back in his pocket. "I'm not saying I want you wandering around in my head," he growled, the rough words thick with frustration. "But I don't want to be something you fear, either." As if he sensed her desire to break eye contact, his dark gaze locked tighter with hers, making it impossible for her to look away. "I want you to trust me, Raine."

A little warning bell started to sound from somewhere deep inside her mind, but she ignored it, too fascinated to back down now. "Why?"

A grim burst of laughter spilled over, and he leaned his head back onto his broad shoulders, staring up at the corrugated ceiling. "Hell if I know."

"You're lost, aren't you?" she said softly, suddenly feeling as if she was sensing him on a level that went beyond her powers, and it was unnerving. She didn't want to share that kind of emotional connection with the human, instinctively interpreting his tones and expressions and body language, almost as if she were his lover. It was too…intimate. Too real.

"What's that supposed to mean?" he asked, a notch forming between his brows as he lowered his head.

With a nervous shrug, she said, "Your life has been turned upside down. You now work with your enemies. You fight against men who were once your friends. I might not be able to read you clearly, but I can sense the conflict within you. And I'd be willing to bet that sometimes you must feel as if you're trapped inside some kind of dream."

Quietly, he said, "Is that how you feel?"

Her mouth twitched, and she knew the small smile touching her lips looked bitter. "If so, then I've been trapped in a nightmare for months. If I could, I'd wake up and find that this entire year never happened."

"I've felt that same way before," he told her, his rough voice resonating through her body like an emotion, and she knew he was thinking about the months that had followed his family's death.

"I know you have," she whispered, before taking a deep breath and hardening her tone. "But I'm not your ticket to redemption, McConnell. If you're thinking you can save me from myself and absolve your sins, it's not going to work. You should cut your losses now and let me finish this on my own."

His eyes narrowed, but before he could say anything in response, his phone rang. After checking the display, he took the call, and without so much as a word to her, he walked out onto the room's shallow balcony, shutting the double doors behind him. Raine leaned back against the headboard, trying to hear his conversation, but all she could make out was the deep rumble of his voice. So she settled for simply watching him instead, allowing herself a moment to appreciate those broad, muscular shoulders and the long, powerful lines of his body. He had to be at least a few inches over six feet, which was tall for a human, the years he'd spent honing his body into a lethal weapon looking damn good on him, even if it did give him the dangerous air of a predator. She didn't imagine, though, that he'd ever had any trouble finding women who were willing to play the part of his prey.

And why on earth does that thought make me want to track down said women and scratch their bloody eyes out?

She was still mulling over an answer when he slipped the phone in his pocket and came back into the room. A groove had woven its way between his brows again, and she waited for him to tell her what had happened. But the words never came. Instead, he just started that restless pacing again, looking as if he were a million miles away, completely lost in his thoughts.

"Is there something wrong?" she finally asked, unable to take it anymore.

"Everything's fine," he replied, his tone flat, and she knew he was lying.

"Damn it, don't do that."

He slid her a shadowed look. "Do what?"

"Keep things from me. Considering you've attached yourself to me, against my will, the least you can do is be honest."

He didn't look happy about it, but he gave her the explanation she'd demanded. "You know that Westmore has been sending scouts sniffing around Harrow House for months now, trying to get under our defenses, right?"

She nodded.

"The part you didn't know is that since he hasn't had any success, he's taken several Watchmen who belong to other compounds and held them hostage, demanding you in exchange."

"And no one ever told me?" She pressed one hand to her throat, feeling as if the oxygen had suddenly been sucked out of the room. "This is insane. Why didn't anyone tell me what was happening?"

He stopped pacing and propped his shoulder against the wall. "They didn't tell you because there's nothing you could have done," he muttered. "But this proves that your family has done the right thing by remaining at the compound in Rome. It also proves how dangerous it was for you to leave Harrow House."

Not wanting to rehash that particular argument, she asked, "What happened to the Watchmen who were captured?"

His expression tightened. "My unit was able to recover one of the shifters. He was being kept at an old Collective safe house in Austria."

"And the others?"

He shook his head. "They didn't make it."

Her throat was so dry she couldn't even swallow. "What about the Watchman you rescued?"

"He just passed away. That's what Kellan was calling to tell me."

"Jesus… All that because of me?" Her voice cracked, and she lowered her gaze to the bed, feeling as if she'd been scraped raw inside. "No wonder no one followed me to Rome last week. Your friends must have been relieved when I finally left their home."

"It wasn't like that and you know it. The only reason Kierland didn't drag you right back when you left Harrow House was because he figured it might be safer for you in Rome with your family. But you snuck away from there as well and for some reason your parents covered for you. Kierland only found out that you'd left the compound the day before yesterday, and your mother refused to tell him where you'd gone."

Lifting her gaze back to his, she said, "So you decided to take action and went to see my parents in person."

He gave her one of those nearly imperceptible nods,

the masculine arrogance of the gesture reminding her of the shifters he now called friends. God, no wonder he got along with the testosterone beasties so well. Despite the differences in their DNA, they were remarkably similar, both in attitude and determination.

Realizing he was carefully studying her facial features, she started to blush. "What is it?"

"You look a lot like your mother. But you have your dad's chin."

"I have his stubborn streak, as well."

His head tilted a little to the side. "Why *did* your parents cover for you, Raine? It's obvious, after meeting them, that they love you."

The heat in her face burned brighter. "I wasn't exactly honest with them about what I'm doing. I told them that the Deschanel Court had ordered me to hunt down the Casus, but that the elders didn't want the Watchmen involved. They think I'm working with the *Förmyndares*."

His eyes went wide. "Christ. Couldn't your mother tell you were lying to her?"

"No," she admitted with a sad kind of smile. "She can't read me."

"Can she see the future?" he asked, his gaze sharpening as he suddenly straightened away from the wall. "Not for you, but for others?"

She rolled her shoulder, wishing she could get inside his mind and find out what the hell he was thinking. "Sometimes she has…flashes," she explained, "but it's nothing she can control. Now tell me why you want to know."

He was back to rubbing that golden stubble along his jaw. "I just had the feeling that she wasn't all that surprised when I showed up."

She couldn't help but laugh. "So you think my mom didn't protest my sneaking away from the compound because she believed you were coming to play the part of my rescuer?"

"I think she knows how seriously I take your protection." His tone was gruff, and with a small jolt of surprise, Raine realized he wasn't joking.

"Don't say things like that," she said shakily, unable to control the shiver that coursed through her body. "It makes me nervous, because I can't figure out what you're after."

"I'm not after anything, Raine. I just want you to be safe." He cut a quick look toward the window, then headed over and lowered the blinds, blocking out the early-morning rays of sunshine that were creeping in. "We should get some rest while we can. That nine o'clock train to Berlin you want to catch doesn't leave us much time to sleep."

She pulled her lower lip through her teeth, silently debating what to do, then spoke in a nervous rush before she could change her mind. "You don't have to use the couch. It's about three feet too short for you. You can lie on the bed, so long as you keep to your side of it."

He turned toward her slowly, his brows arched. "You sure that wouldn't bother you?"

She nodded, but the way he was staring at her made her fidget. "What?"

"You're just not acting like I'd expected," he said carefully, pushing his big hands back in his pockets. "You're much calmer."

It wasn't easy, but she forced a casual shrug. "I know you won't force yourself on me. So as long as you don't try anything stupid or accidentally touch my hair, I won't panic."

His eyes got that soft, hot glow that always ramped up her pulse. "And what if I lose my head a little and try to kiss you again?"

"Then I'll lay you flat," she drawled, moving off the bed and setting her laptop on the bedside table. "Just like the last time."

"Just for a kiss? You're a bloodthirsty little thing, aren't you?"

"You have no idea," she muttered under her breath, slipping off her socks and then climbing into the bed with her jeans and T-shirt still on. "We vamps are as bloodthirsty as it gets."

He came closer, and she turned her head on the pillow, thinking he looked even taller when she was lying down, his shoulders even broader. "You know, I might be a lowly human," he teased, one of those crooked grins crossing his mouth, "but I'm not a weakling."

"Neither am I. Not anymore." She rolled over, giving him her back, and for a moment, nothing happened. Then the mattress sagged under his weight as he sat down on the other side of the bed, no doubt removing his boots, and she reached out to turn off the lamp, before softly adding, "So try not to forget it."

RAINE KNEW SHE WAS dreaming, but she didn't care. All she cared about was keeping more of this feeling, because it was too good to just give up. Too comforting and warm, easing the tight knot in her chest. Turning her muscles to jelly. No tension…no stress. Just an easy, exquisite sense of simply being.

She stood looking into the window of a house, watching a teenage boy play a board game with a little girl who looked like she was his sister. The boy was probably around fifteen or sixteen, well into the age where girls and cars were the only things that mattered. He should have been in hell sitting there on a pink carpet with a laughing little girl who couldn't have been more than six, but amazingly, he looked as if he was enjoying himself, his green eyes shining whenever he said something that made the child erupt into another fit of giggles.

While the little girl rolled the dice, the boy lifted his hand, shoving his golden hair back from his face, and the casual gesture made Raine gasp, her own hands lifting, pressing flat against the chilly windowpane as she tried to get a clearer look. The gesture was so familiar, she suddenly knew *exactly* who she was watching. This was a teenage Seth. But what did it mean? Had she managed to slip into his dreams while they were sleeping? Or was she simply seeing one of his memories? A memory from his childhood, when he'd played with his little sister. A sister he'd lose not long after this moment, judging by his age in the dream. Raine quickly spun away from the window, unable to watch anymore. All those warm, cozy feelings had just been destroyed, a cold, sharp ache left in their place.

"I don't want to see this," she croaked, knowing she had to leave. She had no idea where she was going, but she started to run down the moonlit street. The trees swayed with the violent breeze, pulling in closer at her sides, until the road became little more than a path, the wind and leaves whipping against her body with stinging bursts of pain. Stark howls began to sound in the distance, reminding her of the Casus, and she cried out, afraid, using every last ounce of strength to run harder... faster. She looked back over her shoulder, terrified of what she might find, but there was nothing but a deep, impenetrable darkness, like staring into the bottom of a well.

"Must go faster," she whispered, but when she looked forward again, she ran into a wall. An unyielding, towering wall of hot, masculine muscle. Panic gripped her tighter, until she lifted her gaze and found it was an adult McConnell holding her in his arms, crushing her against his hard chest.

Seth.

With her next gasping breath, his warm, mouthwatering scent filled her head, and desire surged through her with so much force she felt stunned, as if she'd been dealt a violent blow.

God, she might not trust this man, but she couldn't deny that she wanted him physically. Every part of him.

His tall, muscle-hard body. His strength and his power. As well as that intoxicating rush of blood pulsing through his veins.

Unable to control her actions, Raine felt herself lifting onto her tiptoes, her hands curling around the back of his neck, his skin hot and silky beneath her palms and lips as she touched her mouth to the side of his throat. He made a low, masculine sound of approval, his arms locking tight around her waist as he crushed her against him, his heavy erection pressing into her stomach, making her achy and wet. Raine tasted the saltiness of his flesh with a flick of her tongue, consumed by visceral hunger, and in the next instant she sank her fangs deep into his jugular, the scalding wash of his blood so good she immediately started to come. His throat muffled her sharp cry as she pulsed and throbbed and shattered, the orgasm so strong she could feel the pleasure rushing through every part of her body, bursting in every cell.

He growled her name, so she sucked harder, drinking more of him down, knowing she'd need to stop in a few seconds. He said her name a little more gruffly, and she somehow found the strength to pull her fangs free, swiping her tongue over the tiny puncture wounds. Her head lolled back as his hands gripped her ass, lifting and grinding her against the thick ridge of his cock, the friction so good she was building up to another devastating release, and she couldn't control the feral, provocative sounds breaking from her throat, wanting him so badly she thought she might go out of her mind if she didn't get him inside her.

"Goddamn it, Raine! Wake up!"

She gasped at the sudden roar of her name, instantly ripped from the erotic depths of her dream as she opened her eyes and found McConnell standing beside the bed, his bandaged hand braced on the headboard, the other buried in her pillow, so that he was kind of leaning over her without making her feel crowded. She knew she was bright red, blushing, her heart hammering so loudly even his human senses must have been able to pick up the erratic sound.

"You okay?" he asked, giving her one of those hard, penetrating stares that made her feel like he could see right inside her.

"I'm fine," she rasped, wetting her lips, wondering what the *hell* had just happened.

"I know you need more rest, but you were moaning in your sleep. I thought maybe you were having a nightmare."

Was he messing with her? Oh, God, she hadn't called out his name, had she?

"It was nothing," she muttered, realizing she'd been thrashing so badly she'd kicked off the covers, the cool air making her shiver.

"Didn't sound like nothing," he murmured, the barest hint of a smile suddenly playing over his mouth as he lowered his gaze to the hammering beat of her pulse at the hollow of her throat. Then his gaze dipped lower, trailing over her body, touching on her breasts…stomach…legs, his smile lifting the corner of his mouth when he caught sight of her pink toenails.

"Can you please move?" she croaked, sounding like she'd swallowed a frog. "I need to get up."

His gaze slowly made its way back to hers, leaving a flush of heat in its wake. "You don't have to rush," he said huskily. "You can sleep a little more."

"What time is it?"

"Only eight."

Her eyes went wide. "Then there's no time for sleep."

"Sure there is," he murmured, and her embarrassment quickly morphed into irritation. She knew damn well he would have liked nothing better than to keep her from reaching Berlin.

Scooting her way to the other side of the bed, she said, "I'm leaving this hotel room in twenty minutes, McConnell. You can either come with me or stay here. The choice is up to you."

He straightened to his full height as his smile slipped away, leaving his expression guarded. "Are you sure you'll be okay in the sunlight?"

Though the Deschanel could be badly burned by the sun, they could go out into the light of day without suffering any serious injuries, so long as they'd recently taken blood from a species who wasn't sensitive to sunshine.

"I'll be fine," she said, climbing off the bed. "I had enough of your blood last night to do the trick."

He gave a curt nod and started to head toward his bag, which was still sitting on the dresser, but stopped and turned back to her when she said his name.

"What do you want to do?" she asked, crossing her arms over her chest. "And I don't mean what do you think you *should* do, because of that misguided notion you have of protecting me. What do you *want* to do?"

For a moment, he only stood there, giving her another one of those dark, predatory stares. Then he quietly said, "Questions like that put me in a hell of a situation, Raine, since I don't want to lie to you. But on the other hand, I don't think you're ready for the truth." His eyes got darker. "So for now, I guess I'll be helping you kill a Casus."

CHAPTER SEVEN

Berlin, Germany

RAINE COULDN'T BELIEVE what she'd done. She'd actually slept beside a former Collective hunter and had a freaking sex dream about him. A dream in which she came harder than she ever had before. What in God's name was wrong with her?

And being charmed by the way he'd stared at her toenail polish? Come on. She was so freaking pathetic! Not to mention severely frustrated by the part of her that wanted to stop by a spa and get the full works, just to see how he would react after she'd been all glammed up.

And that wasn't even all of it. There was also that intense way he had of looking at her, as if he was reading her as easily as a book. And then that damn predatory stare when he'd teased her about what he "wanted" to do, as if the answer was something…sexual.

Whoa! Not going there. No way in hell.

They'd spent most of the day making their way across Germany by train, since it was the fastest way to travel when trying to avoid airport security. And considering the number of weapons McConnell was carrying, avoiding law enforcement and government agencies seemed like the safest way to go. After finally reaching Berlin, they'd grabbed a quick dinner, left their bags at a local hotel and were now back on the Casus's trail, making their way through some of the historic city's seedy back streets.

McConnell kept close to her side, armed to the hilt, his presence an irresistible comfort—though she'd have cut out her own tongue before admitting it to him. She couldn't afford to let him know how deeply he affected her.

Then came all those other complicated issues, like guilt and anger and fear. Yes, she could understand why his life had taken the course that it had. But that didn't mean she could just forget the fact that he'd lived most of his life as a killer.

And aren't you being a judgmental little bitch?

The husky words came from somewhere deep inside her, and she felt like saying, *Hey, it takes one to know one.* But damn it, she didn't want to start having conversations with herself. Especially ones that were bound to lead someplace deep within her scarred psyche that she figured was best left alone. Untouched and unexplored.

"Have your parents lived in Italy long?" he asked, his deep voice pulling her from her thoughts. "I noticed they both have accents, but they were hard to place."

She was thankful for the interruption, if not a little surprised. Despite the hours they'd spent in each other's company that day, their conversations had been limited by the crowds of people that had surrounded them. But there was no one around now, and they were free to say what they wanted. Which, she supposed, could be a good thing…or a bad one, depending on the topic. But since the subject of her family seemed safe enough, she said, "Their accents are a cross between Russian and South African. I was actually born in Johannesburg."

"Then why don't you have a similar accent? You speak perfect English, like Ashe, only not as British sounding."

"That's because I spent most of my childhood in Britain and Canada, as well as the South Pacific. My parents have always thought it's important to move a family around, so that children are exposed to different cultures and places."

"Did you like moving around so much?" he asked, the glittering lights of a neon billboard painting his face with iridescent streaks of color. Pink streamed across his brow and his left eye, followed by blue, purple and then green. He should have looked ridiculous sporting the rainbow splashes, but it seemed that nothing could take away from his raw masculinity. And yet, he didn't act like a macho jerk, which was one of his most attractive qualities. In Raine's experience, it was the true men who were comfortable in their skin. Who didn't constantly go around with a chip on their shoulder. The others were just posers, like Westmore.

Not wanting to waste time thinking about that Kraven monster, she finally answered the soldier's question. "Actually, I loved it. So much that I chose a career that kept me moving."

"A career?"

It was obvious that she'd surprised him, and she couldn't help but smile. "What? You thought I just sat around reading minds and dropping fang?"

He glanced down at her with a bemused expression. "To be honest, I'm not sure what I thought." They walked past a group of teenagers drinking beer on the front stoop of a run-down apartment building, McConnell's dangerous vibe probably the only thing that kept the kids from mouthing off. "So what do you do?" he asked her, once they were alone again.

It was impossible to hide the pride in her voice as she said, "I'm an environmentalist. For the past two years, I've been working for charities that are investigating the effects of deforestation."

"Sounds interesting."

"It is to me," she murmured, beginning to wonder if she sounded like a science geek. "But, um, I guess it's hardly the kind of thing that would interest a guy like you."

Tension slowly crept into his posture, the cotton of his shirt stretching tight across his broad shoulders. "You know, Raine, I might not have a fancy degree, but that doesn't mean that I'm an idiot or that I don't understand the importance of the environment and ecological preservation."

"I'm sorry. That didn't come out right. I wasn't trying to say that you're not intelligent," she said in a rush, practically stammering her way through the awkward explanation. "I just thought it would probably sound boring to a guy who travels the world…um, doing what you do."

"Yeah, well, believe it or not," he muttered, "I happen to be interested in other things besides killing and maiming."

Okay. Definitely time to change the subject. "Well, I told you about my childhood, so now it's your turn. Even though your accent is clearly American, it's hard to place the regional dialect. So where were you raised?"

She watched him from the corner of her eye as he popped his jaw, and realized he was definitely still irritated with her. "Didn't you see that when you went traipsing through my memories?"

Raine was starting to get the feeling that he was testing her whenever he made a glib comment like that, as if he was trying to discover just what she *had* seen. "Like I told you before," she murmured, "I got caught up on certain things."

For a moment there was nothing but the distant sounds of traffic and their footsteps on the cracked pavement as they made their way down the street, and then he blew out a rough breath and finally answered her question. "I was raised in Southern California."

"Wow. So you really were a surf bum?"

He snorted, shaking his head. "Hardly. My family lived up in the mountains behind L.A." Sliding her a wry grin, he added, "Never was much for the beach. Always had a thing about sharks."

Raine rolled her eyes. "Let me guess. You didn't like their teeth."

"Do you know anyone who does?" he rumbled, arching a brow.

Shrugging, she said, "Some people think they're beautiful creatures."

This time, he was the one who did the eye rolling. "They could look like mermaids, but it wouldn't mean I wanted anywhere close to their mouths."

Watching him from beneath her lashes, Raine couldn't help but think about how sweet it would be to sink *her* teeth into him. To feel his flesh close in tightly around her fangs and drink directly from his vein. It was a dangerous thought—but not nearly as dangerous as the one that came after it, because she was suddenly wondering what it would feel like to feed from him while he was buried deep inside her. While that wonderfully strong, muscular body was holding her down, moving over hers, filling her with hard, heavy lunges that got faster…harder…deeper, at the same time that hot blood was pumping over her tongue, sliding down her throat like honey.

He probably didn't believe her, but she hadn't been lying when she'd told him that she'd never "eaten" during sex before. She'd never seen the two things as something that should be mixed, kinda like alcohol and operating heavy machinery. One wrong move, and disaster could strike, since there was a strong chance that her psychic abilities could cause her to form a powerful link with her lover. And that was before taking into account the fact that the Deschanel rarely mixed feeding and sex with other species because of the dangers that could be involved if the coupling was purely physical. You could feed before sex, or after—but doing the deed while you were literally doing "the deed" could lead to all sorts of disaster.

Still, Raine would have been lying if she'd said she didn't think it sounded sexy as hell. Which meant she definitely didn't need to be thinking about it.

"We should probably stop talking," she grumbled, casting a quick look over her shoulder to make sure they weren't being followed. "We need to concentrate."

"Believe it or not, I can do two things at the same time," he drawled, reaching beneath the hem of his shirt and grabbing the gun he'd tucked into the back of his jeans.

"Why do simple things like that always sound dirty when you say them?" she asked, watching as he checked the clip on the weapon.

The corner of his mouth kicked up with a grin. "I can't help it if your mind's in the gutter."

Hah! If he only knew. She was so far in the gutter she had one foot in the sewer.

"You mentioned something this afternoon about flying into Paris yesterday, but how did you get all those weapons through security?" she asked, eyeing the gun.

"I didn't have to travel with them. I stopped by the Watchmen compound in Paris before coming after you. They loaded me up."

"Convenient."

"Yeah, it was great," Seth lied. In truth, there were still those who questioned his loyalty to the Watchmen, and one particular lion-shifter in the Paris compound had been a major pain in his ass. The guy's name was Remy, and he hadn't liked having a former Collective officer in his home. Not that Seth could blame the guy. It was going to take years for many of the shifters to accept him—and in the end, no matter how diligently he tried to prove his loyalty, a hell of a lot of them would still eye him with suspicion.

Same as the little crossbreed walking beside him.

"You got a read on the Casus yet?" he asked her, tucking his gun back into the waistband of his jeans. He also had a knife strapped to his left calf and another Sig holstered on his ankle, as well as a switchblade in his pocket.

"He's just gone into a local bar," she replied, the thread of steel in her soft voice sending an uneasy feeling through his system. It didn't fit, like watching a toddler holding a handgun. "The name of the place is the Highwayman. It's only about two blocks away."

They walked those two blocks in silence, so that she could keep her focus on the Casus, while Seth kept his attention focused on their surroundings…as well as her. Though he knew it was liable to drive him crazy, he couldn't stop thinking about the soft moans she'd made during her nap, or the hot blush that had covered her cheeks when he'd woken her. Her breath had been shallow, her nipples drawn into tight buds beneath the thin cotton of her shirt, and he'd wanted her in a way that he hadn't thought possible. It was as if he *needed* her on some primal, instinctual level that went deeper than lust, and he couldn't explain it.

Yeah, she was pretty. But pretty women weren't all that hard to find and he didn't go around acting like a jackass with any of them, ready to lick the ground for a chance to be close to them. He just enjoyed them and moved on, never missing them once they were gone. But he'd missed the hell out of the psychic when he'd left Harrow House, and they hadn't even been involved with each other.

Did he feel protective of her? Obviously. Any man who was a man would want to protect someone who'd gone through that kind of hell. But that still didn't explain this pull he felt toward her. There was something more than attraction and protectiveness to the draw. Something that kept her constantly in his thoughts. A question he needed to find the answer to.

And he was starting to feel that if he didn't get inside her, he was going to go out of his damned mind.

"The bar is just around the next corner," she murmured, and Seth reached down to grab her hand, which earned him a startled look of surprise.

"It's better if we go in looking like a couple," he told her, his voice a bit gruffer than he'd expected, but the feel of her small hand in his had thrown him a helluva lot more than he'd been prepared for.

"Um, good idea."

"And don't take this the wrong way, but you might want to slut it up a bit."

She snorted. "Nice try, McConnell."

"I'm serious," he murmured, throwing a pointed look at her conservative sweater. "I'm betting the local women don't normally come here without showing a little skin, and we're looking to blend in."

"Fine," she muttered, slipping her sweater over her head to reveal the sexy little…he searched his mind for what to call it. Not a tank top. Camisole? Yeah, that sounded right. It was soft and sleeveless, with tiny little buttons that ran up the front, the neckline dipping deep enough to show a healthy dose of cleavage. And while he wasn't thrilled about the barflies getting an eyeful, he was more interested in making sure this little operation went as smoothly as possible.

After tying the sweater around her waist, she reached up and pulled off the knit cap that covered her hair, the heavy mass falling in long, lustrous waves around her shoulders as she tucked the cap into one of her back pockets. Seth grabbed her hand again and led her inside, where they found the bar packed to the rafters, the stench of smoke and sweat so thick it coated their skin. Without a doubt, this was a place to drown in misery, the men rough-edged, while the women looked just as he'd predicted, with flat eyes and whiskey-flavored smiles. Raine might have been showing a bit more skin than she would normally reveal, but she still stood out like a shiny new penny, and so he kept his body in front of hers as he hustled her past a row of pool tables and into the back corner of the bar.

"You see him?" he asked, leaning his elbow on the high counter that wound its way around the walls, the surface scarred and littered with empty bottles and overflowing ashtrays. He had to raise his voice a little to be heard over the blaring strains of an old country music song, but he wasn't going to complain. Not when it gave him an excuse to lower his face close to hers.

Raine wet her lips as she looked over the crowd, then lowered her gaze and gave a little nod. "Yeah. He's the one at the far end of the bar. Shaggy black hair and a goatee."

Despite the mass of people, Seth was tall enough to see over most of the other customers, giving him a clear view of the Casus as the guy downed what looked like a shot of tequila. It was difficult to fight against his natural instincts, but he managed to hold himself in check.

As if the human-looking monster sensed their presence, he turned on his stool and started spreading a slow look over the crowd. Seth swung toward Raine, using his body to block the Casus's view of her. "I think he knows we're here."

"That's not possible. I'm masking my scent, so he couldn't know that it's me."

With a shrug, he said, "Maybe he's just picking up a bad vibe. Can you get any kind of read on him?"

She closed her eyes and drew in a slow breath of the smoky air, her attention focused completely inward. "He doesn't know anything about the two Casus you killed in Paris, or the one I killed in Spain, but he's got a bad feeling that something's going down. Something he doesn't know about. Seton was meant to contact him today, on his cell phone, and he never did. Now he's nervous. Feels like maybe he's being set up."

"Does he know we're here?"

He watched those long, golden lashes lift, revealing luminous eyes that were dark with emotion. "He's looking for something out of place, but hasn't found it yet. He's wondering if someone is tailing him—if they're going to come after him when he leaves. If we're not careful, he's going to plant his ass on that stool all night."

"Then we'll blend in," he rasped, and before she had time to react, Seth grabbed hold of the high counter on either side of her body, caging her in. She blinked as he leaned in close, her eyes going wide as he lowered his face over hers. "Don't panic," he whispered, and in the next instant, he brushed her mouth with his. The soft, fleeting contact wasn't nearly enough, and he found himself slanting his mouth over hers, seeking more of that succulent warmth, her taste hitting his system like a drug. She made a muffled sound of surprise, but didn't try to claw his eyes out, so he kissed her a little harder, thrusting his tongue against hers, his hands leaving the bar to snake slowly around her back, carefully avoiding the golden tips of her hair.

"What the hell are you doing?" she suddenly growled, ripping her mouth from his as she braced her hands against his chest, her nails digging into his rigid muscles.

"Looks like I'm losing my head again," he muttered, before going in for a deeper, wetter kiss, unable to get enough of those plush lips or the sweet, slick well that lay within. If he was only going to get this one shot, Seth figured he might as well make it count. He could feel the heat of her skin through the thin camisole, his callused palms snagging on the delicate material, while his cock hardened to the point of pain as she finally stroked her tongue against his.

Somehow finding the strength to pull back, Seth swept his gaze over their surroundings as he grabbed hold of her hand and all but dragged her through the nearest doorway, into what was some kind of dimly lit storeroom used for cleaning supplies.

"Are you out of your freaking mind?" she demanded, staring up at him as if he'd lost his grip on reality. "I didn't come here for a make-out session. I'm on a hunt!"

Seth slammed the door shut and moved closer, crowding her against a bare patch of wall beside a shelving unit. "You wanna get made here?" he asked roughly, bracing his hands against the cracked plaster on either side of her head. "Or do you want him to stay relaxed until he heads for a place we can take him down?"

"Obviously the second," she huffed. "But I don't see—"

"Then just shut up and kiss me," he muttered, cutting her off with the touch of his mouth against hers. It was hell on his system, but he forced himself to be gentle, his hands curling into tight fists as the kiss spiraled into some kind of moist, intimate exchange that damn near blew the top of his head off. Neurons had to be melting down, his wiring so fried he was surprised steam wasn't coming out his ears.

"Why?" A soft, breathy thread of sound, so unlike her usual snippy tone, the sexy way her soft lips were moving against his making him sweat. "Why are you doing this?"

"Because it's a helluva lot better than arguing," he growled back, shocked by the tremor in his thick words. But Christ, he'd never felt anything like this in his life. Her taste was addictive, the warm silk of her mouth too sweet to be real. He could have easily kept kissing her for hours, days, but any second now they were going to run out of time. She was going to be torn away from him when reality reared its big, ugly head, and he'd be left sucking wind. Writhing in a shitload of frustration.

Which meant he had to get as much of her as he could, while he still had the chance.

As his mouth worked over hers, Seth placed his battered right hand against the side of her throat, his thumb settling against the rushing beat of her pulse. She moaned a thick, hungry kind of sound as he dragged his hand lower, sliding beneath the edge of the chemise, seeking out the exquisitely soft skin that lay beneath. His palm smoothed over the gentle swell of her breast just as she pushed her hips forward, rubbing against the aching ridge of his denim-bound cock. Her head fell back as she panted for breath, eyes closed, lost in sensation…and something clicked inside him. It was so simple, and yet, the reverberations of that little click were huge. Mind-shattering. Life-changing.

With his breath jerking between his parted lips, Seth stared down at her, lost in the dazzling, heart-pounding details, thinking she was the most beautiful thing he'd ever seen. He touched his mouth to the bloom of color burning in the elegant curve of her cheek, the tender action completely at odds with the way he shoved aside the fragile silk of her bra. He had his mouth on her before she could draw her next breath, lapping his tongue against a hard, rosy nipple, the earthy, feminine taste of her skin no doubt doing some kind of internal damage to his organs, considering he felt like a twisting, snarling mass of need. He greedily sucked that tender bud between his lips, teasing it with his teeth, and would have worried he was being too rough with her if she hadn't arched her back higher, grinding herself against his mouth and his cock, her nails biting into his shoulders as she held him to her.

"You are so fucking beautiful," he rasped, baring her other breast with a shaky hand, his other hand sliding to her lower back, inside the waistband of her jeans…then inside her panties, while he licked her nipple with teasing flicks of his tongue, making it shiny and wet. He gripped the silky curve of her ass, sliding his fingers lower, seeking that moist, humid heat between her thighs. He was desperate to feel her come in his hand, clenching around his fingers, before he tore those fucking clothes off her and felt her coming around his cock. But the moment he grazed her slick flesh, she flinched, stiffening in his arms, and he quickly withdrew his hand.

"No!" she snapped, shoving at his chest so hard that he stumbled back, her eyes wild with panic. "I can't…I can't do that. Not with you."

"Jesus, Raine." He speared his hands through his hair,

curving his fingers over his skull. "What the hell did I do?"

"I should…I should have stopped you sooner," she stammered, panting, her hands shaking as she wrenched her bra and top back into place. She kept her face averted, no longer looking him in the eye. "I just…I don't want this."

Seth scrubbed his hands down his face, then dropped his arms. "Maybe not now," he told her, the rough words scraping his throat. "But there will come a time when you want a man again."

"Yes, but he'll be someone I feel comfortable with." She lifted her face, locking her gaze with his. "He'll be someone I can trust."

Anger followed fast on the heels of concern. "You can trust *me*."

"Knowing the things you've done?" she asked, with a brittle thread of laughter.

Feeling like he'd just been sucker-punched, Seth narrowed his eyes. "I would never hurt you," he growled, his hands flexing at his sides as he fought the need to pull her back into his arms, knowing it would only make things worse. "Damn it, you know that."

"And what about guilt?" Her voice was dangerously soft, those dark eyes burning with challenge. "Think about it, McConnell. Do you really believe I could ever want a man who cringes at the idea of being with a vampire? One who can't stand the thought of letting me feed from his vein?"

CHAPTER EIGHT

FORGET ANGER. Fury poured through Seth's veins like a hot, slick acid, his jaw aching as he ground his teeth together. He couldn't believe it was all going to come down to this. That his blood would be the thing she used to keep him at a distance.

"Let me get this straight," he bit out. "Are you actually saying that I can't fu—can't *be* with you unless I'm willing to let you drop fang on me?"

"I'm saying that even if I weren't a mess, which I am, I don't want to be with a man who's ashamed of what I am!"

"I'm *not* ashamed," he argued, unable to recall the last time he'd been this pissed.

"You can lie all you want, but it isn't going to change the truth."

Seth turned away from her as he rubbed a hand over his eyes, the taste in his mouth almost too bitter to swallow. "We'll finish this conversation later," he rasped, after he'd taken a few deep breaths and finally trusted himself to speak. "Right now, I want you to stay focused."

"Then keep your damn hands to yourself, because he's finally leaving."

"Good. But I'm warning you, Raine. Do *not* do

anything stupid." He slid her a hard look as he placed his hand on the door latch. "You'll listen to me and do what I say."

"Like hell. I don't take orders from you," she snapped, pulling the Marker from her pocket. "So just stay out of my way and try not to get hurt."

They made their way out of the bar, the street eerily silent, while a violent rumbling of thunder could be heard in the distance, the air damp with the thick scent of an approaching storm. Raine jerked her chin to the right, indicating the direction the Casus had taken, and Seth started to reach for his gun, but stopped short at her look of outrage.

"You shoot only if there's no other choice!" she said in a low, angry slide of words.

He didn't even bother to respond, not trusting what he would say at that moment.

With the Marker held in her right hand, its power already making her arm glow, Raine started walking more quickly, then broke into a light jog. "Come on," she told him, turning into the small alley on their right. "He just turned a few blocks up ahead of us. If we hurry, we can get ahead of him and cut him off."

Keeping close to her side, he asked, "Is he on a main road?" As much as Seth wanted to see the bastard pay, he didn't want to fight a battle in the midst of innocent bystanders.

"He's actually heading into one of the local parks. This is our best shot. There's no one else around."

"Just stay sharp," he growled. "And whatever you do, don't let him rile you."

They ran the rest of the way, the rolling thunder masking the sounds of their boots striking the ground as a light rain began to fall, helping to cover their scent. Within minutes they'd made their way to the far side of the park, a winding path snaking its way through the rolling hills and patches of lush, dense foliage. The path was illuminated by a series of softly glowing antique streetlamps that cast out a flickering wash of light, the moonlight snarled by the swiftly moving storm clouds.

Raine came to a stop in the center of the path and stared at the point where it disappeared around a bend in the trees. "He'll be coming around that curve in the next twenty seconds."

A violent crack of lightning smashed into the ground a quarter mile to the east of their position, illuminating the night with glittering sparks of light, and it was in that moment that the Casus came into view, his pale, ice-blue eyes widening with shock when he caught sight of them.

"Whoa," he called out, his curious gaze shifting from one to the other as he continued to move toward them. "What's this?"

"I'll tell you what this is." Raine's voice lashed out like a weapon, cutting and sharp. "This is your last minute on earth before crashing straight into hell."

Stopping about fifteen feet away, the Casus ran a quick glance over her glowing arm, then lifted his gaze and smirked. "Don't be so sure of yourself, sweetheart."

"You should listen to her," Seth warned him.

The guy sniffed at the air, then gave him a slow smile. "Is that right, human? And here I was thinking that you should learn not to mess with things that are scarier than you are."

"You don't scare anybody," Raine shot back. "And since I know you haven't heard, I'm thrilled to be the one to tell you that Bryce and Carlson are already dead."

"Is that what this is about?" he asked with a gritty laugh, flicking his eyes over Raine before locking his pale gaze with Seth's. Those eerie, frozen chips of ice-blue darkened with surprise. "You're coming after me because I fucked the bitch?"

"This is for my sister!" Raine shouted, her voice cracking at the end. "The one you tortured. She was just a girl!"

"The little teenager? I remember her," he drawled, his mouth curving as he stroked a hand over his goatee. "She was as sweet as she looked."

"You're a pig!" Raine choked out, shaking with fury, the storm drawing closer with loud, bellowing roars of thunder. The air tasted electric, charged with rage, their faces misted with cool drops of rain. They had only minutes before the full deluge was going to hit, and Seth wondered which storm would strike first: the one moving in with the weather front…or the one Raine was about to create.

Another rusty laugh shook the Casus's chest as he took in Raine's reaction to his cruel words, but Seth was beginning to think the guy's cockiness was just an act. Raine had said that Schultz was nervous in the bar, and even though Seth didn't have Raine's exceptional Deschanel senses, he could have sworn he could smell the bastard's fear.

"You know, if you wanted the girl to live," the Casus murmured, keeping one eye on Seth as he spoke to Raine, "you shouldn't have lied to Westmore about where the Markers were hidden. He had no choice but to punish you."

Seth knew exactly what the asshole was trying to do. The Casus wanted to push her until she lost control and attacked him in a blind rage, abandoning caution in exchange for fury. And it was working. She was glowing all over now, sparking with anger, the raging emotion pulsing off her slim, shaking body with so much heat he was surprised she wasn't steaming.

For a moment, all Seth could do was stare. Hardly the time to be left with his jaw hanging, but *damn*. A guy had his limits. She was over-the-top gorgeous, glowing with a soft metallic light, so beautiful she hurt his eyes. And yet, there was something all wrong with the picture. It was the fury, the rage. Yeah, he liked seeing her all charged and glowy, but as trite as it sounded, Seth wanted her vibing with happiness. With pleasure. He didn't want her revved up with some seething need for revenge, knowing damn well how dangerous it could be. And he suddenly understood what had prompted the changes in her body. She was riding a hard, dangerous high fueled by hatred, the emotion making her feel stronger, even as it was slowly eating away at her soul.

"If Westmore was angry about what I did, then he should have punished *me*," Raine snarled at Schultz. "Not Rietta!"

"I don't think so." The bastard's voice dropped as his smile spread wider. "I think knowing your little sister was taking your beating hurt you a helluva lot worse than if you'd been in her place. And we did everything we could to make it last, just so we could listen to her scream."

Raine immediately gave a shriek of outrage, and the dam on her restraint broke, shattering like glass. Before Seth could grab her, she launched herself at the Casus, striking out at him with so much speed she was little more than a blur of color as she used the talons on her free hand to slash at Schultz's face. Seth was already running toward them, a guttural roar on his lips, when the Casus released his long, sinister-looking claws to strike back, but she was too fast, twisting to avoid what could have been a potentially deadly blow, if it weren't for the cross in her right hand. But she wasn't so lucky the second time, and after getting nailed with a nose-cracking jab to his face, Schultz managed to catch her in the ribs with his foot, the powerful kick sending her sprawling over the ground.

"I'm fresh off an afternoon kill," he growled down at her, jagged fangs beginning to fill the human mouth of his host body. "So don't think this is going to be easy, bitch."

He started to go in for another kick as she was moving back to her feet, but Seth threw himself between them, taking the brunt of the blow on his thigh. The air left his lungs in a hard burst as he hit the ground, rolling, his body already moving into position for his counterstrike. Whipping his leg around, he caught the Casus across his lower back, pitching him forward, and Raine delivered a powerful kick right to the bastard's chin. Schultz snarled with fury while Raine hissed back at him, baring her fangs—and in the next instant, Seth watched on in horror as they crashed together, their bodies locked in brutal combat. Unable to tear them apart, Seth shouted for Raine to back off, but she wouldn't listen, her eyes glowing a hot, gleaming silver as she fought. When she smashed her boot into the asshole's jaw and sent him sprawling, Seth was finally able to get between them. He grabbed hold of Schultz's neck, wrestling him facedown against the path. "Now!" he shouted, using all his weight to hold the bastard down. The Casus's body shuddered, bone and muscle expanding, his spine becoming bumpy and ridged as he began to transform into his true shape, and Seth roared, "Goddamn it, do it now!"

Thankfully, Raine didn't waste any more time. She sank to her knees on the ground beside the Casus and slammed the hand holding the Marker into the back of his neck, right at the base of his skull. A sizzling, crackling pop filled the air as her hand sank deep, the monster's body bucking so badly Seth had to fight to retain his hold. Lightning slammed into the ground again, closer this time, illuminating the night with surreal, metallic streaks of light, just as the skies opened, sheets of rain falling hard and fast, hissing like oil in a hot pan as the drops splashed onto Raine's glowing arm.

She cried out as her hand sank deeper, that sizzling sound growing louder as the scent of burning flesh filled the air. Her face contorted with pain, eyes closed, teeth clenched, and Seth couldn't take it. Couldn't stand seeing her in so much agony.

Releasing his hold on one of the Casus's arms, he started to reach back for his gun. But he was already too late.

JUST AS HER ARM erupted into bright, fiery bursts of flame, Raine threw back her head and screamed…and screamed…and screamed, until it felt like her throat would implode.

She'd thought she'd be prepared this time, after killing Bryce this same way, but the pain was just as sharp and excruciating. Tears poured from her closed eyes, and she could tell from the blast of heat and Seth's rough curses that the fire was spreading through the Casus's body now. A bright, orange glow burned against her thin eyelids as Schultz's body was torched from the inside out, the ground beginning to shake with deep, rumbling shocks, as if an earthquake was mounting beneath them.

"Raine, come on." Seth's voice was pleading, his strong, calloused hands suddenly settling on her shoulders, trying to pull her off the monster. "Damn it, let go of him! That's enough!"

She hissed, baring her fangs, knowing damn well that she couldn't let go until Schultz was nothing more than a smoldering pile of ashes. The pain in her arm intensified, as if her skin were being stripped from the straining limb, and she screamed louder, the stark sound clashing against Seth's furious roar just as a red, pulsing wave of rage swept through her, impossible to contain. She was pissed at the Casus and the past. Pissed at Seth for trying to stop her. For kissing her. For showing her that she could still feel pleasure, when all she deserved to feel was loneliness and pain. The wave grew, blasting through her, consuming her, turning black and oily and thick, and just as Schultz's body erupted in a violent, deafening blast, she opened her eyes and launched herself at the human with everything she had, the force of the explosion slamming them through the air.

He went down hard, landing on his back, and before he could so much as grind out another outraged curse, Raine was straddling his waist, pinning him to the ground. Her fangs grew longer as she crouched over him, hissing, her talons digging into his flesh. All her hatred and rage had been transferred to the soldier who was pressing his big hands against her chest, holding her away from him.

"Raine, goddamn it, stop!" The force of his words finally punched through that electrifying haze, and she blinked, shaking her head, trying to figure out what the hell was happening. "It's over, okay? The bastard's dead. I'm not going to hurt you."

She blinked again, wetting her lips, and started to move off him, when she realized her talons were buried deep in his shoulders. "Oh…God," she choked out, a sharp hiss rushing through his compressed lips as she retracted her talons, jerking her hands from his body. "What…what did I…?"

"It's okay," he told her, his voice thick with something she couldn't quite place. He didn't sound angry or afraid. Just worried…and something more. Something she wanted to understand more fully, but was too confused to focus on. "You just got a little carried away, but it's okay."

Her gaze was locked on his bloodied shoulders, and she jerked herself out of her stupor, scrambling to her feet. "I could have killed you!"

A dry note edged into his careful words as he sat up. "Raine, I'm not as easy to kill as you seem to think. Everything is *fine*."

"No, it's not." Her own voice was shredded, the painful sound making the muscles in his face tighten. "You should never have rescued me," she said brokenly, stepping back until she came up against one of the broad tree trunks, her hands rubbing up and down her rain-spattered arms. Despite the flames that had engulfed her arm only moments before, her skin was unharmed, thanks to the protective powers of the cross. "You should have left me with Westmore. I'm too dangerous. Too unstable."

"Damn it, will you just shut up?" He was all masculine power and grace as he moved to his feet, stalking toward her, while the wind and rain rushed against him. He didn't stop until he was towering over her, so close she could scent the heat of his body. See the droplets of rain collecting on his thick lashes. "You haven't done anything wrong!"

"Stop lying!"

A muscle pulsed in his jaw. "I'm not," he ground out, all but smashing the words with his molars.

"You are," she screeched, no doubt sounding like a madwoman. Feeling like one, as well. "And I'm so sick of the lies. Every time I turn around, someone is lying to me, thinking it's going to make things better. But it doesn't make anything better. It just pisses me off!"

His chest heaved as he sucked in air, then blasted her with a gritty response. "You want the truth, Raine? Fine. I'll give it to you. Yeah, you're hurting and you're angry. I get that. I even understand it. Revenge is your new drug of choice, and you'll do whatever it takes to get it. I'm not happy about it, but…"

"But what?"

He shook his head, flinging away the meandering drops of water dripping down his gorgeous face—and his voice dropped as he said, "But in case you hadn't noticed, it's not scaring me off."

Her mouth trembled so hard, she could barely get her reply out. "What the hell does that mean?"

"It means that I want you. I've been fighting the way I feel about you for months and I'm tired of it," he growled, grabbing hold of her hand and tugging her past the scorched patch of ground where Schultz's body had fried. He paused only long enough to scoop up the smoldering Marker and hand it to her, then took off again, his path taking them back to where their hotel was located.

Raine stared at the rigid set of his shoulders, wanting

to latch on to them and hold them for support, but she couldn't allow herself that kind of weakness. Instead, she simply muttered, "The Oath might bind me to you for the moment, McConnell, but it doesn't give you rights over my body."

"Don't worry, Raine." He sounded tired, and supremely insulted. Not that she blamed him. "I've never forced myself on a woman, and I sure as hell don't intend to start now."

It wasn't easy, but she managed to keep her voice even as she said, "Then you should know that it's never going to happen between us. The bar…that was a mistake. One I don't intend to repeat."

The moonlight glinted against his blond hair as he gave a sharp, decisive nod. "Then consider this fair warning that I intend to change your mind."

"You're crazy," she muttered, pocketing the Marker.

He snorted. "Tell me something I don't know. I haven't been able to think straight since I met you."

It wasn't easy, considering she was still shaken by what she'd done, but she managed to stamp down hard on the spark of warmth brought on by those husky words. Wetting her lips, she said, "Whatever you do, it isn't going to change the fact that I don't want you."

"And who's the liar now?" She couldn't see his face, but she was willing to bet the Marker in her pocket that one of those crooked smiles was twitching at the corner of his mouth.

"If you're determined to do this," she said, glaring at the back of his head, "then we're at war, McConnell."

"If that's how you want it, honey." His white teeth flashed as he looked back over his injured shoulder, the dark cotton of his shirt tattered and stained with blood, the soft green of his eyes glittering with a dark, provocative promise. "But if I were you, I'd seriously think about letting me win."

Her eyes went wide, and the arrogant ass winked at her before looking forward again, leaving her to think about what he'd said. Thinking…and imagining all the ways that a man like Seth McConnell could drive a woman out of her mind with pleasure. If the brief taste she'd had was anything to go by, the guy was seriously gifted.

And Raine couldn't help but fear that she was *seriously* screwed.

CHAPTER NINE

HOT WATER POUNDED down on the back of her head, the thick, billowing steam blanketing her from the rest of the world, and Raine figured she just might stay there in the shower all night. The idea sounded infinitely better than actually walking out of the hotel's bathroom and facing McConnell again.

Not yet. Just need a little more time alone…

She was still freaked. Still shaken. Not only by what had happened after she'd killed Schultz, but by what had come before. That erotic little interlude in the bar had basically blown every brain cell she possessed, while turning her body into a hot, melty glow of sexual need, just like in her dream.

She'd been stunned by the powerful rush of pleasure that had burned through her when McConnell's warm mouth had been on hers…on her breasts, his body hard and thick with hunger. It'd been unlike anything she'd ever known. Mind-blowing. Breathtaking. And it wasn't like she could blame the rush on inexperience. Raine had never been one to play the field, but she knew how pleasure worked. She'd even been in two committed relationships. Neither had worked out, but she'd remained friends with her exes. They were nice, mellow scholarly types who she'd worked with. Nothing like Seth McConnell, who was pushy and arrogant and as alpha as they came.

When he'd kissed her, it'd been so intense. And every time she thought about it, her legs got that shaky feeling again, which was why she kept trying to put it out of her mind.

Once they'd reached the hotel, Seth had tried to get her to relax, asking her if she wanted some food, coffee—hell, he'd even offered more of his blood—but she'd relied on nonverbal communication, simply shaking her head each time he asked her a question, her throat too quivery for speech. He must have decided to give up, because he said nothing when she finally came out of the bathroom after her shower. Dressed in ratty sweats and a navy tank, she pulled her damp hair over one shoulder, using her brush to work out the tangles as she moved about the room and watched him from the corner of her eye, too restless to sit down. He was tapping away on a weathered laptop as he sat on the queen-size bed, his back to the headboard, wearing only his jeans. Couldn't be comfortable to sleep in the damn things, but she knew he'd kept them on to stop her from freaking out. Either that, or he was wearing cartoon boxers that he didn't want her to see. The whimsical thought almost made her smile, but then she focused on the raw puncture wounds in his broad shoulders, and her humor faded. The marks were angry and red against his smooth skin. A visceral reminder of just how mental she'd become.

I can't believe I hurt him like that, she thought, ripping the brush through her hair so viciously she was probably going to give herself a bald patch. She could believe even less that he wasn't angry with her about it. Instead, he'd done nothing but try to reassure her, telling her it was okay, and her throat did that tight, trembling thing again.

Setting down the brush, Raine forced herself to crawl into her side of the bed and snuggle beneath the covers, keeping her back to him. She listened to him tapping at the keys, and despite her tension, she enjoyed the warmth of his scent as it wrapped around her. Within a few moments, she found herself drifting into that warm, heavy fall that led to deep sleep, which was strange, considering she'd barely slept for months, usually just putting herself into one of the light trance states, or *Transsis,* that Alacea used when they needed rest but were short on time. It didn't make any sense, but she felt safe with him. Despite the outrageous claims he kept making about being attracted to her, she knew he wouldn't attack her, and so Raine snuggled deeper into her pillow, exhausted clear down to her bones.

Just need to put everything out of my mind for a while. Just need to…sleep.

Heavy waves of darkness rolled over her, her body sinking into sleep as if it was a warm, comforting cloud that had wrapped her in its arms, holding her tight and close. The feeling was so good, Raine wanted it to sink down into every cell of her body, penetrating her, until she could experience that delicious warmth everywhere. So sweet. So perfect.

She didn't know how much time had passed, when that cloud suddenly said her name, its voice a gravelly rasp of sound, and her eyelids twitched as she realized the cloud's comforting arms had strong, powerful muscles. Her cheek was pressed against what felt like a broad, solid chest, the deep, resonating beat of a heart thudding beneath her ear while a big hand stroked gently down her spine, and comprehension struggled to find its way through the tangled layers of sleep.

She had a horrible suspicion she was lying in McConnell's arms, and as she forced her heavy eyelids to lift, suspicion became a humiliating reality.

"Holy shit," she croaked, pushing against his chest as she scrambled away from him, quickly retreating to her side of the bed. She wished she could dredge up an ounce of outrage, but she'd clearly been the one who'd crawled into his arms, plastering her body against his. "I'm so s-sorry," she stammered, completely mortified. "I don't know what I was… I don't understand why I—"

"'S'okay," he rumbled, his deep voice rough with sleep as he rolled to his back and stretched like a big, muscular cat, muscles flexing beneath acres of golden, hair-dusted skin. "You were dreaming," he added, scratching lazily at his chest, silvery streams of moonlight sneaking through the blinds to reveal the rugged contours of his body, as well as the multitude of scars that were a testament to his profession. He had the sheet wrapped around his waist, his chest deliciously bare, the six-pack abs damn near making her drool.

"Yeah," she murmured, not even sure what they were talking about. His moonlit body had melted her brain.

Sitting up, he propped his back against the generic pine headboard, the sheet falling away as he raised his left leg, the worn denim of his jeans hugging the rigid muscles in his powerful thigh. Of course, his arms were just as spectacular. His biceps bulged as he lifted his arms, shoving his hands through his short hair, and she wondered if he still did that out of habit, the gesture reminding her of the dream with his sister, when the teenage Seth had shoved his shaggy hair back from his brow.

"Since we're up, I think we should talk about what you said tonight," he rumbled in a low voice, staring into the shadows. "I'm not ashamed of you, Raine. Far from it. I think you're an amazing woman, no matter what bloody species you are. And I know there are things about me that…upset you. The truth is that some of them I can work on, and some will probably never change. The attack on my family—" he rubbed his hand across his jaw and exhaled a rough breath "—it colors the way I look at a lot of things. But I meant what I said in the park."

She pushed back the sheet and sat up near the foot of the bed, knees drawn into her chest with her arms wrapped around them, needing at least that small bit of space between their bodies. His profile was stark, that rugged jaw like granite, the soft shafts of light picking up the golden glint of stubble. "The attack… It was bad, wasn't it?"

"Yeah…it was bad." She could see the movement of his throat as he swallowed.

"And that's why you joined the Collective."

It wasn't a question—just a statement of fact—but he nodded in response, rubbed his jaw again and explained. "They started working on my recruitment while I was in one of their hospitals. Delivered their spiel while I was still hooked up to tubes, not even able to breathe on my own."

She felt like something had reached in and grabbed hold of her heart, squeezing it in a deathly grip. "I…I didn't know you'd been hospitalized."

He turned his head, locking that beautiful green gaze with hers, and she felt a jolt all the way down to her soul. Just from a look. "You didn't see that part in my memories?" he asked with surprise.

She shook her head. "No. I saw that your family had been killed. Their suffering and loss was always at the edge of your consciousness whenever you made a kill. At least, the ones that I saw. But I didn't go back to the actual event. I guess I always assumed that you had shown up after the attack, and found them as they were dying."

He gave a raw, pained laugh and lowered his head into his hand. "Oh, I was definitely there."

"I'm sorry." Her voice was soft, thick. "I guess it's no wonder that you hate the Deschanel."

He pushed that strong hand back through his hair again and took a deep breath, before locking his gaze back on hers, those dark eyes swirling with shadows and heat. "You're right, Raine. I hated them for a long time. For years, I could hardly feel any other emotion. But what I'm trying to tell you is that I'm starting to see things differently. I know that sounds trite, but it's true. I think I've suspected for a while now that there was something wrong with the path that I'd chosen, but it was hard to break out of the cycle. Every time I questioned myself, I'd come across a truly fallen vampire who'd hurt others, and I'd feel justified for leading the life I had. Then this shit started with the Casus, and I finally got out. And since then, I've come to realize that there are vampires out there who aren't all that different from me. Who are fighting for the same things I am."

"I know. Your friendship with the Grangers has been a surprise to you, but one you're willing to accept. Because you're changing? Because they're *Förmyndares?* You don't know. You've been thinking a lot about the decisions you've made. I could sense that in you from the beginning. Your confusion and your willingness to look at the choices you've made in life." Her cheeks burned with heat, but she forced herself to say it all. "But to be involved with a vampire sexually or romantically or whatever you want to call it? Do you really think you could do something like that, Seth?"

IT WAS THE FIRST TIME she'd ever called him by his first name, and his reaction was instantaneous. A burning, white-hot need to reach out and grab hold of her, crushing her against his body. Rolling her beneath him. Gathering her close and hard and tight.

"You're the main reason for this change, Raine. Not the Grangers. And it's not just any vampire I'm interested in. I want *you*," he told her, holding that stormy, lightning-on-a-midnight-sea stare. Her color was high, her lips rosy and full, all that honey-colored hair falling in long, lustrous waves around her slender shoulders. Hell, even her ears were precious. Small, pale, delicate. If he'd ever seen a more beautiful woman, it'd been wiped from his memory.

"This isn't right," she whispered, her eyes wide with panic, and he knew he was getting to her. It wasn't him that she feared, but the idea of giving something between them a chance. Of making herself vulnerable, when she'd only just started clawing her way out of the nightmare that had nearly destroyed her. He wasn't so blind that he couldn't understand her reasoning, but damn it, he couldn't just let this go without fighting for it.

"Why? Give me one good, solid reason, Raine."

"I can give you dozens," she snapped, then she almost immediately cringed. "God, I'm sorry," she whispered, lowering her gaze. "I don't mean to be a bitch. You've done nothing but try to keep me safe, and I appreciate that. Even though the Oath pissed me off, I know you only did it because you thought it was right. I just…I don't see how this could work. It's bad enough when one person is weighed down with baggage, but we both are."

"Raine, look at me." He waited until she finally followed the soft command, then went on. "None of that shit matters if you want me. And I think you do." Hunger roughened his words, his body reacting the same damn way that it always did around her, his cock thickening against his fly. "I've felt the way you respond to me."

Her face burned hotter. "Yes, I want you. But that doesn't mean that I'm happy about it. The truth is that it frustrates the hell out of me. You're a complication that I can't afford. So whatever's going on here, it needs to stop. We're not good for each other."

"How can you be so sure about that?" he demanded, hooking his arm around his bent knee as he leaned forward. "Have you ever thought that we might be exactly what the other needs?"

She wet her lips with a nervous flick of her tongue. "I don't see how that could be possible."

"Why not?"

"You scare me, for one."

Seth snorted. "Bullshit. At first, maybe. But I don't really believe that anymore. And I don't believe you're buying it, either. What scares you is the idea of taking a chance."

For a split second, it looked as if she would argue, but then her mouth compressed into a hard, flat line. "Even if you're right, what about the fact that I don't trust you? And without trust, who knows how I might react if we had sex? You saw what happened tonight. I could hurt you."

His laugh was low and husky. "You might be a little bad-ass, Raine, but I can take care of myself."

She was starting to look desperate. Sounded it, too. "I have fangs."

"I noticed," he said dryly, wondering how many times this subject was going to get thrown in his face. "But let's not hash through the vein thing again."

"That's just it," she huffed, flinging up her arms in frustration. "You can't give me what I need, and I know I couldn't give you what you need."

Okay. He really didn't like the sound of *that*. "What are you talking about?"

She broke eye contact and looked away, chewing nervously on the fleshy pad of her lower lip. "The truth is that I lied to you, McConnell."

He figured he was probably going to be pissed about the lie—but for the moment he was more pissed about the fact that she was back to using his last name. "What about?"

"I told you before that all I'd seen of your memories was your killings," she said, pulling her knees in closer to her chest. "But that isn't true."

An uneasy feeling slithered through his insides. "Spit it out, Raine."

SHE SLID HIM A QUICK glance from the corner of her eye, then looked away again, staring across the shadowed expanse of the hotel room. "I, um, I actually saw you with a few women."

"I thought you only focused on the killings."

With a shrug, she said, "It's not my fault if the first thing you did after most of your hunts was go out and get laid."

He pushed his thumb and forefinger into his eyes, then muttered an eloquent, "Shit."

"You're quite aggressive," she added, watching him from beneath her lashes. "I mean, for a human male."

His head shot up with a snap, eyes narrowed with a sharp, measuring gaze. "Know a lot about our sexual styles, do you?"

"A little," she admitted with another shrug. "To be honest, I've only ever dated human men."

His surprise was obvious. "Why's that?"

"It's no great mystery. Most of the men I work with are human."

A frown wove its way between his brows. "Did they know what you are?"

"No."

His voice got deeper, sounding a bit rougher to her ears. "Then I assume you didn't feed from them."

A wry smile touched the corner of her mouth. "Obviously."

"And they weren't…aggressive?"

"They were nice guys, but they were also hard-core academics. You're intelligent, highly so, but for a human you're also very in tune with your senses and your appetites. It probably comes from all the years you've spent as a hunter."

"My latent animal instincts?" he asked, arching a brow.

"Something like that," she agreed. "I'm guessing that's why you fit in with the Watchmen so well."

His head tilted a bit to the side as he studied her

expression, her eyes. "And so you think…what? That I wouldn't be able to control myself with you?"

It wasn't easy, but Raine forced herself to give him the truth. "I think you'd want a certain level of intensity that I wouldn't be able to handle. Not with a man who has your past. Not after everything that's happened. It's too much."

"You know, for someone who keeps claiming to understand," he argued, the gruff words thick with frustration, "you sure as hell seem to enjoy throwing the things I've done back in my face."

"Just because I understand your reasons doesn't mean I can handle your actions."

He leaned his head back against the headboard, scrubbing his hands down his face. "Jesus, Raine. Haven't you ever had regrets?"

Regrets? God, did she ever. Her mistakes had caused so much pain. If she hadn't been so stubbornly determined to prove her independence, she would have accepted the private security her parents had wanted her to have in South America, and her sister wouldn't have paid the price for her stupidity. Rietta had come to visit her while on Christmas break, and when Westmore's men had attacked, she'd tried to get her to safety, but the young girl had been picked up not long after. And then Raine had gotten her killed.

"Of course I have regrets," she whispered, "but it doesn't change anything between us."

He exhaled another rough breath, then ran a shaky hand over his eyes. "Look, I know I've made mistakes, and I'm man enough to own up to them. But I also know that a lot of the things I've done were necessary. So I've got to live with the good and the bad, Raine. I've got to accept that everything can't be seen in black and white."

God, he was good. She felt like he had her cornered, and she had to fight harder for air, her chest lifting with the panting force of her breaths. "That's not fair, McConnell. You're trying to simplify a situation that can't be reduced to basics."

"Sure it can." The husky words crept lazily through the shadows, but were edged with steel. "You just don't want to come out from behind all your excuses and face reality. You want to keep hiding, holding me at a distance, too afraid to let something good happen to you. God forbid, when you're getting such a rush from this revenge business."

"You're being such a bastard!" she flung back at him, hating that he was turning this all around on her. "What is your problem, McConnell? Why are you doing this? Why me? You could have any woman you want. Easily."

"How many times do I have to say it? I don't want any other woman. I want *you*."

She floundered, unable to understand why. "Are you… Is this some kind of game?"

"No game. I just want to find a way to make you smile." The rough intensity of his voice made her shiver. "Not one of those baring-your-teeth-at-an-enemy smiles, either. I want to see the real thing, Raine. I want to see you smile because you can't help yourself. Because you're fucking happy, for once."

"I don't even know what to say to that," she rasped, shaking from the inside out.

"You don't have to say anything," he told her. "But there's something that's been drawing us together from the start. I just want to follow it through. See where it leads."

"Come on, McConnell." Her laughter was breathless, her pulse so loud it was roaring in her ears. "Where do you think it's going to go? Sex is the only option, and I don't think screaming orgasms are going to solve our problems."

His eyes burned with that hot, familiar glow. "They might not solve anything, but God knows I'd enjoy them. I can't think of anything that would be sweeter than making you come. Except maybe making you come with a smile. When I make that happen, I'll consider myself the luckiest man alive."

For a moment, Raine didn't know what to say, her heart hammering, her breath all jammed up in her throat. She was so tempted, but knew she had to find a way to resist him. To keep her distance. "You're just not thinking straight." Her voice was cold, hard. "It's like I told you before, I'm not some shot at redemption for you to grab on to."

He looked away from her, and there was a twitch in his left brow. But he didn't shout at her. He didn't even look angry. Just…disappointed. "You know what? You need to think up some new arguments, Raine. It's getting old hearing the same ones, over and over again." He snatched up the shirt he'd left on his bedside table and jerked it over his head, then slid his long legs over the side of the mattress and moved to his feet. "But you have no right to get pissed just because I'm giving you that honesty you so *sweetly* demanded tonight."

"Where are you going?" she asked, as he headed around the foot of the bed.

"I need a cold shower," he replied, his tone flat, and anger flared through her system like it did whenever she didn't know how to feel these days. Which seemed to be often.

"Then why did you put your shirt on?" she snapped, twisting around on the crumpled bedding so that she could follow him with her eyes, his ass looking absolutely deluxe in the worn denim. But then, everything on Mc-Connell looked good. And by good she meant freaking mouthwatering.

He didn't bother to respond to her, simply shutting the door to the bathroom behind him, and she just sat there huddled on the mattress, staring at that closed door as the hotel's ancient water pipes began to rattle and hum. Taking a deep breath, she worked to get a handle on her raw emotions, unable to decide if she was going to curse or cry.

But he was right. She *did* want him. Even now, she couldn't stop thinking about him standing beneath that hot spray of water, his long body naked and wet and slippery. Was he hoping she would join him? Was he taking himself in one of his big, bruised hands, his head back, muscles coiling and flexing beneath all that slick skin, wishing it was actually *her* hand holding him?

Oh…God.

Knowing she was twenty different kinds of fool, Raine had just slipped off the bed and started to move toward the bathroom door, unsure whether she was going to keep yelling at him…or simply throw herself into his arms, when a vision suddenly flashed into her mind. It was hazy and distorted, like watching something on a TV channel with bad reception, but she could make out the woman's beautiful face, killer bod and dark red hair.

"Damn it," she moaned, holding her head in her hands, knowing damn well that she was "watching" Spark. The kill Raine had made that night must have been some kind of boost to her Alacea powers, because she could see the assassin moving around a hotel room, the location impossible to determine. Spark was checking her weapons, the gleaming pieces of deadly metal set out on a low coffee table, and Raine struggled to get into the human's mind, but there was too much interference. All she could make out was her own name. The assassin was thinking about her, which probably meant that Spark had been given a new assignment.

McConnell was right. They're coming after me.

If she continued on her current course, the odds were high that they would find her. Then it would become a race to see who could succeed first: her or them. And if she stayed with McConnell, he would be in even more danger than he was now.

To be *on* the hunt was one thing, but she couldn't allow McConnell to become one of the hunted. Which meant there was only one thing to do.

Raine had already resigned herself to losing her own life—but she wasn't willing to throw the human's away so easily. And if she was doing this to protect him, then it wasn't breaking the Oath. Or at least that's what she told herself. The Court might look at it differently, but she doubted Seth was going to walk before the Deschanel elders to lodge an official complaint.

Steeling herself to the decision, Raine threw on her jeans, sweater and boots, then stuffed her sweats and the tank into her bag. Doing a quick glance around the room to make sure she'd gotten everything, she spotted his pocket knife sitting on the bedside table—the same one he used whenever he cut open his arm to collect blood for her—and quickly rushed over to grab it, sliding the knife into her pocket. It was petty to steal something of the human's, but damn it, she needed it. If she was never going to see him again, she wanted something to remind her of him. Something tangible and real that she could hold in her hand.

Don't go, a voice whispered inside her mind. *Stay with him.*

The voice of temptation? Must be, because staying was exactly what she wanted to do. But it was only going to benefit *her.* There was nothing good in this for McConnell. Even if she didn't get him killed, he'd probably come to hate himself for getting involved with a vamp. So she was doing the right thing by leaving.

She knew that. Believed it.

But as she shut the door to their room behind her, Raine wished it didn't feel so wrong.

CHAPTER TEN

STRANGE, HOW THE SENSE of relief, of freedom, that Raine had assumed she would feel after running never came. It'd been nearly an hour since she'd bailed on Mc-Connell, but she felt even more trapped than before, as if there was a rush of darkness closing in on her, squashing her down. With every step she took, she became more certain that she'd made a critical error in judgment. After all, she knew that Seth's fighting skills were legendary. He might be human, but he was a human that the other species feared. So, then why had she run? Was she just using her vision of Spark as an excuse to put distance between her and McConnell because she didn't trust herself? Didn't trust that she'd stick to her bloodthirsty agenda if she allowed herself to keep falling for the complicated, compelling soldier. And she was *definitely* falling for him.

Had she turned away from McConnell because she knew it would have been impossible to hold on to the hatred fueling her strength if she allowed that "something good" he'd talked about to happen to her? Was that why, since the moment he'd tracked her down in Paris, she'd been doing her best to throw all those obstacles between them, lobbing them like emotional grenades?

Raine didn't know the answer—but the reason didn't matter, when the result was the same. She had run…and now she was on her own, just like she'd been before. But it didn't feel the same. The night seemed darker, the air colder. And she was…damn it, she was lonely.

She missed McConnell.

But you made this bed, she muttered to herself. *It was your choice. So stop complaining.*

Determined to follow that grim advice, Raine kept walking, block after block, moving from neighborhood to neighborhood.

Since she wasn't wearing a watch or carrying a cell phone, she wasn't sure of the time, but finally decided to head back to one of the main roads and grab a taxi to the airport, hoping distance from the human might help her to think more clearly. Taking a deep breath, she'd just started to turn around, when something suddenly crashed into her consciousness, like a knife that'd been hurled from the shadows. Or more like a mental wrecking ball, the episode significantly more intense than when she'd "seen" Spark in the hotel room. Dropping to her knees on the cold sidewalk, Raine held her head in her hands, while a boy's voice called out to her, begging for help.

Scared, that small voice whispered. *Don't want to… Not again… Isn't there anyone who can help me?*

Lowering her hands, Raine forced herself to her feet and turned in a slow circle as she cast out her senses, searching for a clue that would lead her to the boy. She stumbled forward, but his voice became weaker, so she headed back the other way, her feet moving faster as the voice became louder in her mind.

His name was Thomas and he was almost twelve, she realized, hiking her backpack higher on her shoulder as she threw herself headfirst into the psychic pull that was drawing her toward him. *Into him.* He was a stranger, someone she'd never met before, and yet, his mind was open to her in a way that reminded Raine of how her powers had worked before Westmore had captured her. She could see him so clearly. So much fear and pain and loneliness.

He wasn't a human child, but a Deschanel vampire, like Raine's father. He was also an orphan, his parents killed by the Collective during a family vacation when he was only five. Thomas had managed to survive because his mother had forced him to hide beneath a pile of dirty towels in the hotel's laundry room before the Collective had found her. His memories of his parents were hazy, but Raine could see that they'd been from warring families, and after their deaths his relatives had shunned the young boy. He'd lived on the streets ever since, scrounging for food, his Deschanel strength the only thing that had kept him alive, whereas a human child would never have made it.

Following those wrenching, silent pleas for help, Raine wove deeper into the heart of the city, no longer paying attention to the street names, her entire being focused on following the sound of Thomas's voice.

And then she found him.

She was standing in a small, cramped alley set between

two run-down apartment buildings and blocked by a high, barbed-wire fence at the back. Two foul-smelling Dumpsters were wedged against the fence, the boy hiding between them, his back to the rusty metal. There was barely enough room for his slender body in the narrow space, a single shaft of moonlight illuminating his frail form…and the object of his panic.

Lying on the ground before the Dumpsters was the unconscious body of a homeless woman in her late twenties, her mouth hanging open, clothes as tattered as Thomas's, her chest moving with slow, shallow breaths. Looking into the boy's mind, Raine could see that he'd been napping in that small space, only to awaken and find the drunken woman blocking his exit. And that's when the hunger had slammed into him, scraping him raw inside. He'd been trying to fight it for hours, not wanting to hurt her. But it was so hard…and he was so hungry and cold. He knew her blood could warm his belly for a little while, that it could take away the pain twisting his guts into knots, but he was trying so hard to fight it.

I don't want to be a monster, he whispered to himself, over and over. *Don't want to be a killer.*

The child was so focused on the sleeping woman, on fighting his internal battle, he hadn't even noticed Raine was there. Keeping her voice as gentle as possible, she said, "Thomas, don't be scared. I'm not going to hurt you."

He jerked at the sound of her voice, pressing harder against the fence at his back, his eyes huge in the silvery moonlight as he stared up at her. Those big gray eyes

reminded Raine of her little brother, Luke, and she wondered if this was how Luke had looked when he'd been
Westmore's prisoner. Had he been this frightened? This
pale?

After Westmore had taken Raine and Rietta hostage,
her parents had sent Luke into hiding with relatives,
hoping to protect him. But Westmore had managed to
find the boy, and after Rietta had been killed, Westmore
had threatened to torture Luke, as well, if Raine didn't
tell him the location of the next Marker. But she'd had
no information to give him, since Saige Buchanan hadn't
yet decoded the next map, and so Raine had tempted the
Kraven with information that he wanted about a rogue
Casus named Gregory DeKreznick. Then she'd refused to
share what she knew until he'd released her brother—and
it had worked. Luke was now in Rome with her parents,
and though he was still traumatized by Rietta's loss and
his own captivity, he was slowly returning to normal,
acting more like a carefree little boy every day.

Raine only hoped there was a way to save Thomas,
as well.

"Who are you?" the child croaked, shaking, his teeth
chattering as she lowered her backpack to the ground and
slowly inched forward, moving deeper into the alley.

"My name is Raine, and I'm part vampire, like you,
and part psychic," she told him, crouching down until she
could grab the homeless woman's ankle and pull her to
the side, wedging her against one of the buildings. With
that done, she edged closer to Thomas, giving him a
tentative smile. "My psychic powers help me to see inside

your mind, so I know what you've been through…and what you're afraid of. I want to help you."

"You…can't," he whispered, his hunger rising, fighting against the hope that wanted to bloom inside him.

"If you trust me, I *can* help. I promise."

He trembled, his talons releasing at the tips of his small fingers, moonlight glinting against his white fangs. "Can't control it."

"You *can*, Thomas." She made her voice firm, sensing that she was losing him, his gaze flicking between her and the woman. "You just don't know the way yet. But you can learn."

Bitterness and fear graveled his words, making them nearly impossible to understand. "And who's gonna teach me?" he asked, blinking tears from his eyes as he glared up at her. "You're just a girl."

"But I'm a girl who knows some powerful people," she said, unfazed by his insult. She knew only too well how boys at his age felt about *girls*. "I'll help find you a home. Somewhere you can be safe, where you can learn how to control the hunger."

"I've…tried." The words were nothing more than a low, hoarse scrape of sound, his eyes fluttering from exhaustion. "But it's too hard."

She winced as she caught images of the way he'd been living. He'd tried to feed mostly from stray animals, but there had been a few times in recent months when his cravings had become too strong and he'd struck out against a human. The child was lucky the Collective had been busy for the past year aiding the Casus; if they'd found him, they would have executed him. And then there were the *Förmyndares*. As protectors of the Deschanel, the *Förmyndares* were formidable soldiers who were quick to cull out any rogue vampires who threatened to expose the existence of the clan.

But the child wasn't a rogue. He was just…untrained. Lost.

Moving a little closer to the frightened boy, Raine said, "I know it's been difficult and scary, Thomas, but you don't have to do this alone. Can you trust me to help you? I promise I won't let anyone hurt you."

It was painful to see the longing in his pale eyes. He wanted so badly to believe her, and she held her breath as he struggled to make a decision. When a few moments had passed and he finally shuffled forward and reached for her hand, she grabbed hold of it as if he was the one offering *her* a lifeline.

"That's it," she coaxed, giving his small fingers a reassuring squeeze. "It's going to be okay. I promise." But no sooner had the words left her mouth, than Raine tensed with shock, unable to believe the scent that had just reached her nose. Spinning around, she found Mc-Connell standing at the end of the alley. His face was in shadow, making it impossible to read his expression, but she knew damn well that he was pissed. Every muscle on his tall, powerful body looked hard with aggression, his scent a raw, visceral mix of fury and frustration, combined with the subtlest hint of relief that he'd found her.

"Thomas," she whispered, keeping her eyes on

McConnell as she spoke to the boy, "I want you to stay behind me. A friend of mine is here, so don't panic. I just need to talk to him. Okay?"

She sensed his worried nod and felt him lean to her side as he cast a wary look toward McConnell, then immediately did as she said, pressing in close to her back. His thin body was freezing, reminding her that Deschanel males ran cold once they began puberty, until the time when they finally found their lifemate.

Fear made her heart pound as she realized that if she didn't successfully handle the situation with McConnell, Thomas might never live that long. The soldier might have tolerated her and the Grangers, knowing they weren't killers. But the child had committed acts that McConnell would most likely see as criminal. As murders that required punishment.

"What are you doing here, Raine?" The human's voice was deep and rough, his muscular chest rising and falling with the heavy force of his breaths. A fine sheen of sweat glistened on his brow, telling her how quickly he'd been moving as he'd tracked her down.

"I'll explain everything," she told him, holding up her free hand to warn him back, "but you need to stay where you are."

"Who the fuck is the kid?" The sharp words cut through the night like a knife, and she could feel Thomas edging closer to her back, the boy no doubt sensing the threat that the soldier could pose to them both.

"I mean it, McConnell. Don't come any closer. You're scaring him."

"Is he the reason you ran out on me?" he rasped, dropping his bag on the ground before taking a step toward them. His voice shook with rage. "Do you know this kid?"

"I'll answer your questions, but first, I want to know how you found me."

"Believe me," he snarled, shaking his head, "I wish I knew."

She struggled to keep her voice calm, but it wasn't easy. Raine felt as if she was trapped between two wild animals, the night air thick with the scent of looming disaster. "Did you put one of Kellan's tags on me?" she asked, thinking that one of the Lycan's tracking devices could have been sewn into the lining of her backpack, same as Seth and his friends had done with Spark's.

He scraped his palm over his jaw and glared back at her. "No tags, Raine. I just went where my gut told me to go."

"That's impossible," she argued. "You're only human!"

His eyes narrowed at her tone, the tiny lines that fanned out at their corners only adding to his rugged appeal. "A human who managed to find your ass."

"I'm sorry," she whispered, knowing she'd insulted him. "I didn't mean it like that. It's just that…none of this makes any sense."

"Neither does your running away. You're lucky I'm not counting this as a breach of the Oath. Otherwise, your ass would be in some serious trouble."

"I'm sorry that I…ran out, but I sensed Thomas and

knew that he needed help," she lied, leaving out the part about Spark. He was already pissed enough as it was. If she started telling him she was afraid of getting him killed, his pride was only going to crank that anger up even higher, and she needed him to stay calm. "I didn't think you would understand, so I came on my own to find him."

His gaze flicked to the unconscious woman sprawled at the side of the alley, then back to her. "And what exactly did you find him doing?" he asked, taking another step closer as he sniffed the air. "He smells like he's covered in dried blood, Raine."

Taking his hand from hers, Thomas crouched down by her side, huddling close to her knees, his top lip curled back over his fangs as he growled at the male he was seeing more and more as a dangerous threat.

"I'm warning you, Seth, back off." She lowered her hand to Thomas's head, petting his dark hair as she tried to soothe him. "He's scared. He needs help."

He watched the way she stroked the boy's dark locks, then glanced down at Thomas's bared fangs, before locking that burning gaze back on hers. "Jesus, Raine. He looks feral. He could attack you." His voice was ragged, the look in his beautiful green eyes tearing at something soft in her chest. Something she didn't seem able to protect from him.

"He isn't going to hurt me, I promise. But he's frightened. The blood hunger onsets with the early stages of puberty in males, and it's imperative that parents teach their sons how to maintain control. But Thomas has been an orphan since he was five. There's been no one to help him."

"And how do you know this isn't a trap?" he demanded, his big hands fisting at his sides as he obviously struggled to do as she said and stay back, when it was clear he wanted to barge forward and grab hold of her, wrenching her to safety. "For all we know, he could be working for Westmore!"

"He's not," she said, shaking her head. "I swear it, McConnell. I can read him clearly and he's not working with anyone. He's just a frightened boy who needs someone to help him."

"You trust him that easily?" he asked in a low voice, and she winced, knowing damn well that the soldier had been trying so hard to earn her trust, and here she was giving it out freely to a stranger. She didn't blame him for looking...*irritated* with her. Surely that wasn't pain lurking in his dark eyes. Just because he wanted a fling with her didn't mean that he cared. She was just projecting her own stupid emotions on to the human, which was only going to make the situation a thousand times worse than it already was.

And yet, he had come after her. Again. That had to mean something, right?

Determined to find a way to soothe his anger, Raine said, "If you could see into his thoughts, Seth, I know you would understand."

"I seriously doubt that," he muttered, running a shaky hand over his face. "Just because he's a kid doesn't mean he isn't a killer, Raine."

She shivered at the coldness of his tone, and couldn't help but wonder if the soldier had ever hunted a child of Thomas's age. Had he been that ruthless? That cold?

She didn't want to believe it—but damn it, she knew how intensely his hatred had burned in the years following his family's murder. Just because she hadn't witnessed such an event in his memories didn't mean that it hadn't happened.

And if he'd done it once, was he capable of doing it again?

Her heart raced, panic flooding through her system as he came even closer, making Thomas growl. The child's heart raced, too, his fear and panic flooding through her, as if she were experiencing those raw emotions as her own, and she reacted without even thinking, releasing the talons on her right hand and lunging forward to swipe at the human's chest. McConnell stopped instantly, stumbling back a step, his eyes going wide with shock as he lowered his gaze to the hand she'd dropped by her side. Looking down, her stomach lurched when she saw the sharp talons dripping with blood.

Ohmygod… What have I done? she thought, jerking her gaze to his chest while something inside of her screamed in horror, the shattering sound locked deep within, unable to escape. McConnell's shirt was shredded, his skin sliced open in five long cuts, the sight of his seeping blood making her feel ill.

Dizzy with confusion, Raine lifted her watery gaze to his face as a hard sob broke free and jerked from her throat.

His dark eyes burned with fury, as well as pain.

But the part that cut the deepest was the stark, heart-wrenching look of betrayal that he couldn't disguise.

SINCE HE DIDN'T TRUST himself to speak, much less move, Seth held his body locked in place, his jaw clamped against the angry curses burning to be said.

"I'm sorry," she whispered, her big eyes tormented and bright in the ethereal moonlight. "I didn't mean to…to hurt you. But I can feel his fear like it's my own." She wet her lips, her jaw trembling. "I can't…I *won't* let you kill him. It's not right. Whatever he's had to do to survive, it wasn't his fault. He's just a child."

Seth didn't like the situation, but he understood what she was saying. If the child *had* killed, there was nothing to be done. It would be like punishing a shark for hunting. It was just a vampire's natural instinct to seek blood.

Still, he couldn't say for certain how he would have handled the situation a year ago. All he knew was that he couldn't mete out death to the boy now. Not when those silver eyes were staring up at him, reminding him so much of Raine. Not even when his chest was burning with pain, his blood dripping down onto his stomach, soaking into his clothes. He wanted so badly to be furious, taking comfort in the familiar feeling, instead of this emotional minefield he found himself treading with the crossbreed—but he couldn't be angry. The kid couldn't help the way he'd been born, any more than Seth could control the fact he was human. Before the boy was punished for making the wrong choices, he needed to be shown what the *right* choices were.

"I wasn't going to kill him," he ground out. "I just wanted to be close enough to help you handle him. He doesn't look strong enough to stand on his own, much less walk."

She swallowed, appearing at a loss for words, and he looked down at the scrawny kid, recognizing the fear in his eyes. It reminded him of the way his baby sister, Alicia, had looked the night she'd been killed, and the bands that had been squeezing his chest seemed to relax a little. "You sure he won't hurt you?" he asked, looking at Raine again.

She nodded, her face paling as she slid another glance over the wounds she'd left in his chest, and he knew she was in shock.

"I need to make a few calls," he muttered. "Will you wait for me here?"

She nodded again, and he turned, heading back to the street, where he figured he had a better shot at getting reception on his phone. After retrieving his bag, he quickly slapped some bandages over the scratches on his chest, then pulled out a fresh shirt and changed, stuffing his ruined one into a nearby trash bin as he made his calls. Only a few minutes had passed when he returned to the alley, his bag hooked over his shoulder. Raine was crouched down beside the boy, using a hand wipe from her backpack to clean his dirty face, the child's gray eyes huge with adoration as he stared up at her. Seth noticed that his feet were grubby and bare, and something twisted in his chest as he thought of the boy living on the streets alone, with no one to care for him.

They both tensed as Seth approached, but he held out his hands, saying, "I'm not gonna hurt you, kid. I'm just going to help you up, okay?"

The boy shook with a slight tremor, edging closer to Raine. "Thomas, it's okay," she told him, her voice soothing and warm. "You can trust him."

Looking as if he was sticking his hand into a tiger's cage, the kid took a deep breath and reached for Seth's hand. As he pulled the boy to his feet, Seth looked at Raine and said, "He's freezing."

"He's too young to borrow warmth," she explained in a low voice. "Someone Thomas's age shouldn't be outside when it's cold."

Seth frowned as he pulled his jacket out of his bag, remembering that unmated Deschanel males could only "borrow" heat through sex, until they finally found their lifemate and began "the burning." Wrapping the jacket around the kid's shoulders, he picked him up, holding him against his chest. Both Raine's and the boy's eyes went wide, but it took only a moment for the child to snuggle against him, burrowing into his heat.

"Come on," he grunted, jerking his chin toward the street.

As she hooked her own bag over her shoulder, she sent a worried glance toward the homeless woman. "What do we do? We can't just leave her there."

"I put in a call to one of the local shelters. They're

sending someone over. Which means we need to get lost."

"Where are we going?" she asked, following him out of the alley.

"The Granger brothers just got to town," he said in a low voice, heading right when they reached the street. "We're taking the kid to Gideon."

"I don't understand," she murmured, and Seth figured he'd have had to be deaf to miss the skepticism in her tone.

With a sigh, he said, "I'm not lying, Raine. Spark moved locations, so they followed her here to Berlin. He called me just before I left the hotel."

"Well, I guess that makes sense."

"What does?"

"Nothing," she mumbled. "Are you going to have any trouble going up against her?"

Like *hell* he would. Spark was a royal bitch, and one he unfortunately had a past with. What was even worse was that Raine knew he'd slept with the assassin, since the woman had tried to embarrass Seth by telling his new friends about it after they'd captured her in the Wasteland.

Running his tongue over his teeth, he said, "Spark isn't going to be an issue."

"And what about Gideon? Do you trust him?" she asked, slanting a worried look toward Thomas, who appeared to have already fallen fast asleep. Seth thought the kid might even be drooling on him, a soft snore spilling quietly from his open mouth. "As a *Förmyndare,* how is he going to handle the situation?"

"I don't know what a *Förmyndare* would do, but as a *friend* of ours he's going to take the boy someplace safe. And if it makes you feel any better, he sounded as concerned as you are. I don't get the impression that he and Ashe are in the habit of punishing those who need help."

"Thank you," she said, touching his arm with her fingertips, and he swore he could feel that sizzling point of contact all the way down to the soles of his feet.

"Don't thank me. I'm not the one saving his life," he muttered, irritated at how easily she could make him react to her, when she obviously didn't want to be with him. Hell, she'd run away in the middle of the night. How much clearer did she have to make it before he got the hint and gave up trying to convince her to take a chance on him?

They walked the rest of the way in silence, until they reached the Hilton where he'd arranged to have Gideon get them a room. The vampire was waiting for them beside a sleek black Audi in the hotel parking lot, the key cards to their room in one hand, his other hand in the pocket of what looked like a designer pair of slacks, the vampire's shirt fitting his broad shoulders as if it'd been hand-tailored. His sable hair was windblown, a light stubble shadowing his hard jaw. It was strange, how the guy could look like he'd just stepped off the pages of a fashion mag, and yet, still manage a deadly air, the look in his eyes too hard to belong to anyone but a trained hunter.

Gideon said hello to Raine, only a trace of his Scandinavian accent shaping the husky greeting, then turned his attention to the boy in Seth's arms. "Is he unconscious?"

Shaking his head, he said, "Just exhausted."

"I've made arrangements for the boy to stay with a family I've known since I was a child. They'll take good care of him."

"I can't thank you enough for doing this," Raine said, her soft voice thick with emotion.

"It's not a problem," the vampire told her with an easy smile, his appreciative gaze doing a quick flick over her body, before he shot a curious look toward Seth, then headed around the gleaming sports car and opened the passenger side door. Seth laid the boy down in the soft leather seat, and together the three of them moved to the front of the car, so they could talk without waking him.

As Gideon casually took a seat on the hood, Seth asked him, "Where exactly does this family live that you're taking him to?"

A wry grin played at the corner of the vamp's mouth. "I'm afraid that's on a need-to-know basis, McConnell."

"And I don't need to know?" The words were sharper than he'd meant them to be, but his patience had dried up a long time ago.

"I'm not trying to start shit with you, man. I just want to keep the boy safe."

Though a low burn of rage poured through him, coiling in his muscles, Seth fought back the urge to throw a punch. He was still pissed enough about Raine running out on him that it would have felt good to go a round with the *Förmyndare,* but he knew they didn't have the time. So he settled for simply telling him off. "You're being a prick, Granger."

"And you're acting like a cocky son of a bitch," Gideon drawled. "As usual."

Raine rolled her eyes. "I'm going to let you two keep trading insults and say goodbye to Thomas."

Seth watched her return to the passenger side of the car, while Gideon watched *him.* He tried to school his expression, giving nothing away, but the vamp wasn't an idiot. The Deschanel waited until Raine had crouched down beside the boy's seat, before saying, "So you and Raine, huh?" He flashed Seth a sly smile. "Anything going on between you two?"

"None of your goddamn business."

The vampire's dark brows lifted with interest, his gray eyes gleaming. "Ah, so it's like that, is it?"

Seth glared. "I like you, Gideon. I really do. So just shut up before I'm tempted to kill you."

The guy's laugh was rough as he climbed off the hood and slapped Seth's shoulder. "I like you, too, man. And that's why I'm going to give you a little advice."

Seth ground his jaw, but knew there was no point in

fighting against the inevitable. The vampire was going to meddle, whether he wanted him to or not.

And the bastard was clearly enjoying himself, his light gaze glittering as he lowered his voice and said, "Sometimes female Deschanel don't come easily, no matter how good a time they're having. But…there *is* one surefire way to get them going." He gave Seth a measuring gaze, then added, "That is, if you can handle it."

Seth held his breath as he waited for the vamp to finish, something in Gideon's expression warning him that he wasn't going to like what was coming. When a few seconds had ticked by, he lost his patience and barked, "Well, what the hell is it?"

Gideon gave a throaty chuckle, then turned and headed toward the driver's side of the car. But Seth caught the vampire's drawled words as they drifted over the guy's shoulder, and his insides went cold.

"If you wanna make her come, just give her your vein."

CHAPTER ELEVEN

An hour later...

RAINE HAD NEVER been the restless sort, until now. Maybe McConnell's pacing was rubbing off on her, because as she waited for him to finish the phone calls he was making out on the balcony, she could *not* sit still. Thankfully, their new hotel room was bigger than the last, with two double beds and plenty of floor space. When she'd asked Seth why he'd changed hotels, he'd told her that he suspected Westmore's men might have been watching Schultz, seeing as how Spark had rushed to Berlin. And if they *had* been at the bar when Raine caught up with the Casus, she and McConnell could have been followed back to the hotel.

Raine had snuck out a service entrance when she'd run out on him, which had hopefully prevented her from being followed. McConnell had done the same when he'd come after her, which meant that, for the moment, they were off the radar.

Of course, as soon as she clued in on the next Casus's location—a particularly slimy Casus named Wentworth—they would probably be walking into a trap, since she assumed Wentworth would be under surveillance, as well. But she wasn't going to try to run again. A selfish decision, no doubt—but she couldn't leave him.

And yet, just because she'd had a change of heart didn't mean Seth would stick around. After the way she'd clawed at him, she wouldn't be surprised if he finally decided to bail. The moment they'd entered the room, she'd immediately taken a shower, desperate to wash off the scent of his blood, still unable to believe what she'd done. God, how many times was she going to attack the poor guy before he'd had enough and washed his hands of her?

And why does it hurt so much to think of that happening?

It frightened her to admit it, but Raine didn't want him to leave. Not that she knew exactly *what* she wanted… but she needed the time to figure it out. Time to figure out precisely what was going on between them.

McConnell had told her, point-blank, that he wanted her. There was a part of her that still doubted the truth of that statement—after all, he truly could get *any* woman he wanted—and she thought he might simply be trying to distract her from going through with the hunt in an effort to protect her. If so, it didn't make him a bad guy. He was just trying to save her life. But…there was also a part of her that was starting to believe he really *did* want her. She could hear it in his voice when he spoke to her, see the hunger in his eyes. It didn't make much sense, considering she was no great prize—but Raine knew she hadn't been imagining those things.

And then there was the way that he treated her. The restraint he'd shown when dealing with her. He could have fought back the two times she'd struck out at him and easily taken her down. But he hadn't and she'd have been lying if she'd said she wasn't a little in awe of him.

So what the hell was she going to do about it?

Before she even realized what she was doing, Raine found herself picking up her backpack and heading into the bathroom again, the air still steamy from her shower. She set the pack on the counter and rooted around inside for the cosmetics the ladies back at Harrow House had given her, despite her assertions that she didn't need them. She'd thought her new friends were crazy at the time, considering she couldn't have cared less what she looked like, but now she was grateful. And while it only took a few minutes, the effect was…shocking. She applied a light tinted moisturizer, some smoky liner, lip gloss, and used a bit of styling gel in her hair to give the wavy locks that tousled, just-rolled-out-of-bed-with-Jude-Law kind of look. All in all, it wasn't bad, she figured, considering how out of practice she was. Her eyes looked huge with the smoky liner, her mouth glossy and full. Maybe even kissable.

Yes, it was ridiculous to be putting on makeup in the middle of the night, but heck, it was almost morning at this point. And she liked the results. Felt a little more confident now that she didn't look like a washed-out ghost—a look she'd been cultivating for months, just wanting to disappear into the scenery. But not anymore.

Taking a deep breath, Raine picked up her bag and

walked out of the bathroom to find McConnell sitting at the foot of the bed nearest the balcony, his elbows braced on his parted knees, just staring at some distant spot on the ugly beige carpet. He turned his head toward her as she cleared her throat, then immediately jerked to his feet, his eyes going wide as he studied her face, her hair. His mouth dropped open a little, his breathing sounding a little rougher as he continued to stare…and she could hear the heaviness of his heartbeats, his pulse rapidly gaining speed.

Not knowing what else to do, Raine set her backpack on the floor and went to him, stopping when she stood only a foot or so away. He'd taken his shirt off and put fresh bandages over the wounds on his chest, the scent of an antiseptic sharp against the mouthwatering scent of his body. She wanted to lean forward and place a tender kiss against the white bandages, then the healing wounds in his shoulders, but was too nervous. Too ashamed. Instead, she reached into her back pocket and pulled out his knife, offering it to him. "I wanted to give this back to you."

His brows drew together as he took the knife from her hand. "How did you—"

Taking another quick breath for courage, she said, "I took it when I left."

He shook his head a little, clearly confused, his eyes lowered to half-mast as he held her stare. "Why?"

"Because I wanted to have something of yours." She coughed, then forced herself to go on. "It wasn't an easy decision for me. Um, leaving you, that is. I didn't…I didn't want to go. But I don't like knowing that your life is in danger because of me."

The instant the words left her mouth, she knew she'd said the wrong thing.

"Jesus, Raine." He towered over her, so big and muscular and deliciously male. And so impossibly angry with her. "What's it going to take to prove to you that I'm strong enough to protect you?"

"I know you can protect me. That's not the issue."

He turned away from her, walking across the room, tension radiating off his back as he stood before the balcony's sliding glass door, staring out at the city's flickering skyline. It was the first time Raine had ever seen his naked back, and she felt like she'd been punched in the chest, her breath rattling from her lungs as she wheezed, *"Ohmygod."*

"What?" he grunted, sending her a dark look over his shoulder.

"Your back," she whispered, staring at the multitude of scars that marred his skin. She had no doubt that they'd been made by rogue Deschanel. When a bite was accepted willingly, a Deschanel could heal the wound by swiping their tongue across the punctures. It was only when the wounds were left to fester that they remained permanent.

He stiffened, as if only just realizing that he hadn't put his shirt back on. "Haven't you seen them before?" he demanded in a rough voice, heading over to the bag he'd left sitting beside the bed.

"How could I?" she asked, watching as he took a

T-shirt out of the bag and pulled it over his head. "You always put a shirt on if you're going to walk around in front of me."

He hooked one thumb in his front pocket, his head angled forward as he used his other hand to rub the muscles in the back of his neck. "But if you've seen my memories, wouldn't you have seen…my body in them?"

"I see your memories from your viewpoint, McConnell. So your back isn't visible."

"Guess that makes sense," he muttered, sliding her a shuttered look from the corner of his eye.

"Why are they…?"

"Only on my back?" His mouth twisted with a bitter smile. "Because a vamp generally sneaks up on you from behind."

"Guess that makes sense," she murmured, echoing his words, hoping to make him laugh. But he didn't soften, and she knew he wasn't going to make this easy for her. Which meant she was just going to have to forge on and battle her way against his anger. "Seth, I've been doing a lot of thinking tonight, and I want…I want you to know that I trust you."

He turned toward her, his hard gaze locking with hers as he crossed his powerful arms over his chest. "So saving your life didn't mean anything to you, but it matters that I helped the kid?"

"What you did tonight," she murmured, nervously tucking her hair behind an ear, "I know that couldn't have been easy. But you did it, anyway. It was…amazing."

"Yeah, well, we assholes do what we can," he muttered, looking away, and then immediately bringing that smoldering green gaze right back to her face, as if he couldn't help himself.

"You're not an asshole," she said softly.

A low, bitter sound tore from his chest. "Sure I am. If I wasn't, you wouldn't have risked eternal shame by breaking your Oath and leaving."

"I thought I was doing the right thing," she told him, moving a few steps closer to where he stood beside the bed.

"Don't we all," he said, pulling a hand down his face.

"Seth, about tonight." She dared to take another step closer to him, the deep glow of the lamp on the dresser behind her reflected in the molten depths of his eyes, the green so hot it reminded her of wild jungle fauna. "I told myself that I was running because I didn't want to put you in danger, but the truth is that—" A brusque knock sounded at their door, cutting her off, and she sent him a questioning look. "Were you expecting anyone?"

"Not unless it's the grim reaper coming to slay my ass," he offered dryly, heading past her and toward the door. He looked through the peephole, cursed something gritty under his breath, then ripped open the door. A second later, Ashe Granger, Gideon's brother, walked into the room, looking every bit the gorgeous bad-ass that Raine remembered him from their travels across the Wasteland. His clothes were all black, his dark hair still incredibly short and the gleam in his silver eyes impossibly wicked.

"What are you doing here?" Seth growled, sounding anything but friendly as he closed the door behind the unwanted visitor.

The vampire's curious gaze shifted between them, and he grinned. "Just wanted to stop by and say hi."

Seth snorted. "And who's watching Spark while you're out socializing?"

"A cousin of ours who's in town," he offered casually, his six-foot-plus height making it easy for him to hitch his hip on the edge of the dresser. "I wanted a break from watching the redhead, so I put Liam on guard duty for a while."

"Is Thomas okay?" Raine asked, drawing the vamp's attention.

"I just talked to Gideon a few minutes ago. He said the kid hasn't stopped chatting his ear off." Looking at Seth again, he asked, "How did you find them, anyway? The boy told Gideon that Raine was alone when she found him, but that you tracked them down. Did you tag her?"

"I would have," he muttered, cutting her a dark look before returning his gaze to Granger, "but I never thought she'd be stupid enough to run."

Ashe watched him carefully, a curious tilt to his head as he said, "If you didn't tag her, then how did you know where she was?"

"I don't know how," he rasped, rolling his shoulder. "I just…found her."

Ashe scratched his chin and "hmm'd" under his breath.

She and Seth looked at each other, then back at the vamp. "What does that mean?" they asked in perfect unison.

Ashe appeared lost in thought. "Nothing."

Seth popped his jaw, then said, "I hate to sound like a dick, Ashe, but I'm low on patience tonight. So spit it out or get the hell out of here."

The vampire's mouth twisted with a smile and he held up his hands. "Sorry, man. I'm not trying to be a pain in the ass. I was just thinking about something that I learned during my *Förmyndare* training." He crossed his arms over his broad chest and went on. "According to Deschanel lore, there have been cases in history where a human male forms a bond with an unmated Deschanel female. The bonds are based on protection, and he becomes her guardian, willing to risk life and limb to ensure her safety. They call it a *Sangra* bond, and in such cases the human male supposedly develops the ability to find the female, tracking her over long distances."

Seth shook his head. "I've never heard of anything like that before."

The vampire shrugged. "Like I said, it was during my training, when all the secrets of our clan are revealed. And it's not exactly something that the Deschanel want advertised, since they frown upon humans and vamps breeding."

"But you said the bonds were based on protection," Raine murmured. "Not…breeding."

"Honey, when a man wants to protect something that badly, there's a reason for it," he drawled, sliding a knowing smile toward Seth. "Usually means the bastard wants to nail her so badly he can't see straight. That kind of hunger causes all his latent primal instincts to kick into high gear, which accounts for his ability to track her."

A heavy silence settled between them, electricity practically crackling in the air, while Raine's mind reeled. She couldn't believe her physical reaction to the provocative news, her pulse racing, chest tight, while inside she went soft and warm. Desire coursed through her veins, making her burn, while a shivery burst of chills fluttered over the surface of her skin.

"But who knows if it's true?" Ashe murmured. "So much of the Deschanel lore is just that—fiction." His voice was deep and rich. "You can't always believe everything you hear."

Seth paced his way to the sliding doors, rubbing the back of his neck again. "I just talked to Kierland a little while ago," he rumbled, deftly changing the subject. "He said there's been another Infettato attack."

The vampire muttered a sharp curse, then asked, "Where was this one?"

"Russia. Aiden and Quinn are going to head out and try to handle the situation. There's also a local Watchmen unit who's going to help them."

They talked for a bit longer about the threat of exposure posed by the Infettato, and then Ashe moved to his feet. "Okay, I'll get out of here and let you both grab some sleep. We should plan to meet again in the morning, so give me a call when you're up."

They said their goodbyes, and Raine locked the door behind him. When she turned back toward Seth, he looked as confused as she was by Granger's strange revelations. "Do you think that what he said is true?" she asked.

He lifted his shoulders, the muscles in his chest drawing her eye as the cotton of his shirt pulled tight across his firm pecs. Knowing damn well how dangerous it was to ogle him, since it always made her feel a little dazed, Raine set her jaw and forced her gaze back to his face, a sliver of wariness shooting up her spine at the intense, predatory way he was watching her.

Just because she'd decided not to run didn't mean she planned to jump into bed with him, and her nerves had her babbling. "Personally, I think it sounds crazy. Not to mention impossible."

His rough, breathless bark of laughter caught her off guard. "Impossible. Improbable. Christ, that seems to be the hallmark of our relationship."

"We're not in a relationship," she argued, knowing she had to preserve as much emotional distance as she could.

"Sure we are," he rasped, his head tilting a fraction to the side as he stared at her. "It might be dysfunctional as hell, Raine, but you can't argue that there's something going on between us."

"You're freaking me out," she whispered, wrapping her arms around her middle.

"Good. 'Cause I'm feeling pretty freaked out myself."

"If you're trying to sweet-talk me, McConnell, then you have a lot to learn about women."

He gave another rough burst of laughter, sliding her one of those killer grins that always made her a little weak in the knees. "Trust me, honey. When I decide to sweet-talk you, you'll know."

Raine just stared back at him, too turned on to do anything else. And he knew it, the knowledge burning like embers in the hot depths of his eyes as he took a step toward her.

"Granger had it right, by the way," he said in a dark, rumbling drawl.

"Had what right?" she asked, wetting her lips, unable to break away from his smoldering gaze.

"I want you. In my bed. Under me." They were rich, husky words that stroked her like a physical touch, and even though she was wary, she still wanted to curl into them, rubbing her face against their warmth. "Hell, I'll take you any way I can have you, Raine."

"This is insane," she whispered through trembling lips, knowing she had to find some way to resist, because she was too close to making what would surely be a mistake.

God, how could it not be? She needed her hatred to keep her strong for her hunt, and he was only just leaving that part of his life behind, trying to look to the future. A future she wouldn't be a part of.

"I've heard Kellan and the others talk about your reputation," she murmured, grasping at straws, even though she could feel the quicksand of an inevitable downfall sucking at her heels.

"Hell, they *all* have reputations." He flicked the lamp on the dresser down to its lowest setting as he walked past it, the light becoming nothing but a soft, shadowy glow.

"But they're particularly impressed by yours. For a human to be in the same league as a shifter? That's a big deal, Seth."

"Have I had a lot of women? Yeah, there have been more than a few," he admitted, closing the space between them while she kept retreating, until she found herself pressed up against the door. "But do I want any of those women now? Not even a little," he rasped, his eyes burning with a wicked gleam that told her he knew she was losing ground. "The only woman I want is standing right in front of me."

"Then it's a guilt thing," she said, sounding pathetically desperate even to her own ears.

He snorted. "What? Making you happy and keeping you coming is going to change my past? The buzzer's sounding on that one, Raine. Try again."

"But you hate vampires!" she shouted, no doubt waking the humans who were sleeping in the neighboring rooms. "Just because you feel bad about some of the ones you've killed doesn't mean you don't still hate the race!"

"I'm done with the hatred," he told her, so close now that she could feel the delicious warmth of his heat as it pressed against her. "There's another emotion burning inside me now. Has been ever since I met you. I can't stop it, Raine. Can't control it. And I'm tired of fucking trying."

She trembled, stammering, "We c-can't."

"Why not? We're both single. Both adults. Who's it gonna hurt?"

"Damn it, don't do this," she pleaded. "Please, Seth."

His nostrils flared as he drew in a deep breath, and she could sense his visceral struggle to hold himself back from her. "You say that, Raine, but do you have any idea how you're looking at me right now?"

"And what about the way you look at me?" she demanded, feeling as if a part of her was battering against some invisible wall that separated them, doing everything it could to break it down, while the other part just wanted to hide behind its safety. "You might not hate me, Seth. I…I believe that. But you *do* feel guilty about wanting me."

Frustration flared off him, vibing and hot. "That's not—"

"Just listen to me! I'm not…I'm not blaming you. But we can't pretend this is going to work."

"It could," he growled, "if you were willing to take a chance!"

And just like that, the wall started cracking, on the

verge of shattering into a million fractured pieces. "How can I take a chance on anything when I'm broken?" she snapped, tears streaming from her eyes in a hot, salty rush. "God, don't you see that? I wouldn't be any good for you like this!"

"You're not broken," he ground out in a thick, graveled voice. "You're hurting, and I want to be the man you let get close enough to make it better. Damn it, Raine. I just want to get close to you." He started to reach for her, but she flinched, and he dropped his hands to his sides, his muscles bunched with tension, his breaths ragged. So easily, he could have reached out and overpowered her.

But he didn't. Instead, he forced his body back a step. Giving her space. Giving her the distance she'd demanded.

"Tell me to leave you alone," he rasped, "and I will. Just say the words, Raine."

She swallowed, pulling in a shaky breath…and tried. But nothing would come out, her voice frozen in her throat. And she knew why.

She didn't want him to leave. Didn't want to be alone. What she wanted was Seth, regardless of the consequences. For however long it lasted, she just wanted to wrap herself around him and hold on, taking every ounce of pleasure from the experience that she could get.

But she couldn't just give in. Couldn't reach for what she wanted, because she no longer knew how.

"Damn you!" she shouted, slapping him across his face as frustration poured out of her in a violent, uncontrollable wave of rage. "You're driving me crazy!" she cried, pounding her fists against his chest again…and again, until he finally snagged her wrists, manacling the delicate bones in his long fingers as he forced her arms over her head, pinning them against the door. His face was a rigid mask of hunger and lust, and she could feel how badly he wanted to pull her against him, his need blasting against her, driving hers higher, until there was simply no other choice but to give in.

"Please," she whispered, hoping he could read what she wanted in her eyes, since she couldn't get anything else out.

He held her stare, his breaths coming a little harder…a little faster. His burning gaze flicked to the hammering beat of her pulse at the base of her throat, then the tight tips of her breasts beneath her thin sweater, before shooting back to her flushed face.

Then he groaned two soft, husky words that completely melted her down.

"Be. Sure."

CHAPTER TWELVE

BE SURE...

Raine knew exactly what Seth was saying: that once he started, he wouldn't be stopping. She closed her eyes, trying to think past the lust, but it was impossible. She would just have to steel her heart against him while she slaked her hunger, without letting him sway her from her course, because there was no other choice.

Raine could no longer pretend she didn't *have* to know what it was like to be with him, the carnal need as necessary as the air in her lungs. She was shaking so badly she could barely manage a nod, but that was thankfully all it took to get him going. One second she was wishing for him, and in the next, his strong arms were wrapping around her, crushing her against his bandaged chest. His hands roamed her back, then slid lower, gripping her ass, while his mouth did deliciously wicked things to hers that made her go hot and wet in *all* the right places.

Eager to finally touch his magnificent body, Raine slipped her hands inside the back of his waistband... and encountered only warm bare skin, not a stitch of boxers or briefs to be found. As if he'd read her mind, he said, "After you left, I was in a hurry. Didn't bother with anything but the jeans."

"Sorry," she whispered, not knowing what else to say.

"God, you have no idea how badly you scared me," he rumbled, running his mouth along the sensitive edge of her jaw. "When I realized you were gone, I…Christ, I don't think I've ever been that terrified."

"Just kiss me," she rasped, too needy to sort out what she should say. She just wanted to feel. To take and give pleasure back in return. Needing to touch him, she tried to push one hand into the front of his jeans, but he snagged her wrist, dragging it away from his body as he drew back his head.

Reading the question in her eyes, he forced out a gritty explanation. "Can't take that."

"But I want to touch you."

His eyes crinkled sexily at the corners as he stared down at her. "You touch me, and this is going to be over before we even get started. No way in hell am I letting that happen."

He didn't give her another chance to argue. Instead, he kept her busy as she struggled to keep up with his devastating kisses, his mouth eating at the breathless sounds she made, while his hands made short work of her clothes. Her sweater was ripped over her head, her jeans unbuttoned and unzipped so quickly, she barely had time to register the actions before he was pushing her back on the nearest bed and ripping the denim from her legs.

He took off his shirt as she lay there panting, wearing only her bra and panties, as well as a head-to-toe blush that covered every inch of her skin. But he didn't seem to mind, his hot gaze leaving a scorching trail of heat in its wake as he looked her over, while Raine could only stare, wide-eyed and dazed, at the blatant proof of his desire. The top button on his fly had popped open, revealing the heavy, glistening head of his cock. She wished he'd left the light burning brighter, so that she could see that purely masculine sign of need more clearly, without the soft darkness obscuring the details. But she knew it was better this way, the shadows helping her to relax.

"So beautiful." The words were soft and thick, as if he were simply speaking his thoughts out loud, his big hands shaking as he grasped her hips, pushing her farther across the bed. Then he pulled off her silky panties and trailed those deliciously rough hands up the insides of her thighs, shoving them apart. As he forced her legs indecently wide, pressing her knees into the bedding, a dark, primitive sound tore from his chest, his eyes dilating with hunger when he dipped his gaze from the pale ringlets on her mound to the soft, pink folds nestled beneath.

Raine vibrated with nervous energy, her breath jerking in sharp, shallow pants as she watched him crawl onto the bed with her, settling between her legs, that pale, golden glow of light playing seductively over the rugged contours of his body. Over those broad, muscular shoulders and strong, corded arms, his biceps bulging beneath his gleaming skin. He was like some wild, beautiful animal crouched over its prey, but she wasn't afraid. She wanted him too badly. And though it surprised her, she truly did trust him.

"Seth," she whispered unsteadily, simply wanting to say his name. To feel it on her lips.

"Wanted this for so long," he murmured, the rough, lust-thick words making her shiver as he drew his big hands back along her trembling thighs, until they framed her sex. He used his thumbs to spread her open and his lids lowered, the thick lashes leaving spiky shadows on his carved cheeks as he licked his lips. Then he leaned forward…and tasted her wet flesh with a deep, voluptuous stroke of his tongue.

"Seth!" she said again, this time as a deep, throaty cry, and he gave a feral growl in response.

Though she sensed he was trying hard to control his aggressive sexuality, determined not to frighten her, there was no gentle easing into the explicitly intimate, erotic act. He touched her as though he had every right to her body, lapping his tongue over her melting sex as if he was devouring something sweet. Her back arched hard, heels digging into the mattress, while choked, husky cries fought to break from her throat. She fisted the sheets, her head thrashing, while her body struggled to make sense of the shocking sensations. All she could feel were those hot, wet licks and the rough bursts of his breath as he ate at her with a raw, savage avidity. Even as he became more frenzied, his control slipping, his skill was unlike anything she could have ever imagined. It was like he was inside her mind, sensing her pleasure. He knew exactly where to linger. Where to be soft. When to be rough.

His fingers gripped her thighs so hard she knew she'd

be bruised, but she didn't care, needing that strong anchor to push up against, her hips rolling…and rolling. She'd never been this lost to sensation in her life—but this was *Seth* doing these incredible things to her body, his tongue lashing her clit, thrusting hungrily inside her, and she couldn't fight it.

"Don't stop!" she cried, pushing her fingers through the damp strands of his hair as she tried to hold him to her. "It's too good… *Ah, God!*"

"Come for me," he demanded, his lips moving against her clit as he spoke. "I want you to come in my mouth, Raine. I want to feel it. Taste it."

Tears leaked from the corners of her closed eyelids, streaming in hot trails down her cheeks, a broken sob spilling from her lips as the tension within her pulled tighter…and tighter…and then finally broke. She came in a hard, shocking rush, the deep pulses clenching around his tongue as he thrust it into her again and again, while he thrummed her clit with his thumb. He stayed at her until her body finally quieted, her muscles heavy and lax, legs sprawled shamelessly wide as he lapped with hungry strokes, rumbling wicked things about her taste.

And then he was rising over her, bracing his weight on one hand as he used the other to rip down the cups of her bra. His fingers glistened with her juices, his lips parted for his ragged breaths as he rubbed that warm moisture into her nipples, then lowered his head and took one shiny tip into his mouth. He suckled hungrily, *greedily,* the pressure just shy of pain, but the pleasure so intense Raine didn't care. She just wanted more, and her hands roamed his shoulders and arms, squeezing the solid muscles and corded bands of sinew as they flexed beneath the sweat-slick heat of his skin.

He left both nipples throbbing as he suddenly reared back, that hot gaze seeming to touch her everywhere at once. He stared into her eyes, then at her mouth, her breasts, before settling another blistering look on her sex. Then he locked his jaw as he ripped open his fly and took hold of his shaft, a low growl in his throat as he rubbed the taut, swollen crown through her drenched folds.

"Just do it," she groaned, digging her nails into his hips as she tried to drag him inside her. "I want this, Seth. I *need* it!"

"Birth…control?" he ground out, the muscles in his arm flexing as he gripped himself even tighter. "Can't risk…don't want to hurt you."

She knew he probably thought she was still too weak to carry a child—but she wasn't. And while it was clearly stark-barking mad to even be contemplating the idea, considering the circumstances of their relationship, she couldn't deny that there was something oddly compelling about the thought of carrying McConnell's babe. Would it have his amazing eyes? That golden hair that was shades lighter than her own?

And my brain has clearly been fried by lust. Only thing to do now is enjoy it.

"It's okay," she panted, so desperate she could barely form the words. "Alacea can only get pregnant during the two days before our cycle, so we're safe."

He gave a firm nod that sent a bead of sweat snaking down his nose, the hammering beat of his heart filling her head, while his decadent scent poured over her senses, driving her wild. She couldn't believe this was really going to happen. *And there are no bad memories. No pain or fear. Just this insatiable craving for him...*

She'd wanted this so badly, and now that the moment was here, it was even better than she'd imagined, her pulse rushing so swiftly she should have been light-headed. She was so excited she couldn't stop her fangs from releasing with a sharp burst of heat, suddenly slipping beneath the curve of her upper lip—and that's when disaster struck.

Though he tried not to show it, she caught the look of disgust in Seth's eyes before he dropped his gaze to her breasts. And just like that, the sweet burn of desire coursing through her veins turned cold, like ice.

God, she was so stupid. She'd gotten so wrapped up in her own issues, she'd forgotten about his.

He was still the most gorgeous, masculine thing she'd ever set eyes on, and she knew that he wanted her. But Raine couldn't ignore the fact that there was still a part of him that loathed being with her, and she felt herself lifting her hands to hold him back as he settled deeper between her thighs. "No. I...I can't do this," she stammered, pushing him away. "Please, stop."

His gaze immediately shot to her face, a frown wedged deep between his brows. "What's wrong?"

Her stomach twisted so hard, she thought she might be sick, and she tore her gaze from his as she wiggled out from beneath him. "Believe it or not, I don't like being looked at like I'm some kind of parasite."

He flinched as if she'd slapped him, but didn't try to deny it. Rolling to his back, he scrubbed his hands down his face and muttered, "Shit. I'm sorry."

"Don't apologize," she said in a choked voice, moving into a sitting position at the edge of the bed. "That just makes it worse."

"Raine—" he started to say, but she cut him off.

"Do you really think there's anything you could say right now to make this better?" she asked in a tight rush, her hands fisting the sheets at her sides.

He exhaled roughly, then said, "You know, just because a guy wants to get involved with a doctor doesn't mean he'd let her operate on him."

Her head whipped to the side as she glared at him over her shoulder. "It's not my profession, Seth! It's a *part* of me. Of who I am." A fact she'd foolishly overlooked when this erotic interlude had started, because she'd wanted him so badly.

"And you don't think I'd change the way I am if I could?" he growled, sitting up and shoving his hands through his hair, his frustration evident in the harsh lines of his expression. "Damn it. I'm not trying to hurt you."

"I know that." Her voice was soft, her anger slipping away as a sad sense of acceptance took its place. "I'm not blaming you, Seth."

He pulled back his shoulders, his green eyes shadowed and bleak. "Sure as hell feels like you're blaming me."

"I'm not. But you have to be reasonable. How would this work?" she asked, shaking her head. "I can't go into a relationship trying to hide what I am. Not even for an affair."

He opened his mouth, ready to say God only knew what, but was interrupted by the ringing of his cell phone. Blowing out a sharp breath of irritation, he moved off the bed and zipped up his jeans as he headed toward the dresser, where he'd left the phone. He answered the call, then looked at her, saying, "It's Ashe. I'm putting him on speaker."

The vampire's voice crackled from the phone. "Guys, we've got a problem. Gid and I just found out we're not the only ones running surveillance on Spark. Liam, our cousin, spotted a Casus who's watching her, too. The guy's holed up in the room right next to ours. Said he's a big bastard, with a scar that runs along the right side of his face."

"It's Seton," she murmured, scrambling for her clothes. "He's here."

"How do you know?" Seth asked, giving her a sharp look. "I thought you couldn't read him."

"I can't." She pulled on her panties, then her jeans. "But I'm the one who gave him the scar. And I can read Spark."

He turned the lamp on high, flooding the room with light. "Since when?"

"Since earlier tonight." She didn't look at him as she pulled her sweater over her head, but could feel the force of his anger as it blasted against her.

"You knew she was in town, didn't you?" His voice was raw. "You knew before you ran."

She nodded, saying, "But I wasn't reading her as clearly as I am now." Settling her gaze on the phone, where Ashe was still listening, she said, "Spark doesn't know that Seton's in town, but she did get a call from him earlier today. He told her he was delivering orders from Westmore."

"What were the orders?"

"To come to Berlin and find me."

"Was it a kill order?" Ashe asked.

"No," she answered. "She's meant to take me in alive."

"So then why would Seton come to Berlin, as well?"

"I'm not sure. But I can tell you that Spark is suspicious. She knows there's a good chance that I can use my powers to read her. She thinks they're setting her up. Figures they're using her as a decoy to distract us, so that a backup team can swoop in and close the deal."

"They're trying to draw you out," Seth growled, a muscle pulsing in his hard jaw.

"Well, we know where they are," Ashe said. "Our best bet is to strike now. But we'll have to move fast. I'll have Liam keep an eye on Spark and tell Gideon to stick to Seton."

"And where are you going?"

"I'm coming back to the hotel to get the two of you. I'll text you from the lobby when I get there."

The line went dead and Seth slid the phone into one

pocket, then pulled the knife she'd given him out of the other. "What are you doing?" she asked, watching as he opened the blade.

"We don't have much time, but you need to feed before going into something like this."

She didn't argue. Not when it meant getting more of his blood. Call her a junkie, but she was already strung out on his taste, unable to say no, needing the feel and warmth of him in her mouth. He sliced into the same cut that he'd made before, reopening the wound, then collected the blood in one of the hotel's glasses. She took it without looking at his face, but knew he watched her as she drank, the flavor somehow even richer than it'd been before. When she'd finished, she took the cup to the bathroom and rinsed it out, leaving it sitting by the sink, and came back to find him opening his first-aid kit.

"You don't need another bandage," she told him, her voice shaky with nerves as she crossed the room to him. She was helpless to ignore the idea that had just sprung into her mind, determined to see it through.

"I'd rather not bleed all over myself," he replied dryly.

"Just trust me," she whispered, taking hold of his strong wrist, loving the way the golden hair on his arm crinkled against her palm. He flinched as she lifted his corded forearm to her face, his pulse racing, the scent of the warm blood easing from the wound making her mouth water. But she stayed in control, determined to show him she could be trusted. That she wasn't going to attack him in a fit of bloodlust and savage his arm.

Instead, she slowly swiped her tongue over the shallow cut, the biological composition of her saliva acting as a coagulant and healing agent.

"There," she whispered a moment later, lowering his arm as she released her hold on him. "All better."

"Thanks."

The gruffness of his tone made her shiver, and she lifted her gaze to find him staring down at her, the look in his dark eyes impossible to read. Their bodies seemed to sway closer together, and they stayed that way for what felt like forever, searching for answers in each other's eyes, until the sudden vibrating of his phone broke them apart.

"That's probably Ashe," she whispered, while he pulled out the phone, glanced at the text and nodded. They grabbed their things, planning to leave them in Ashe's car, and left the room. The elevator was empty as they took it down, but she knew Seth was on the lookout for trouble. He'd loaded himself up with weapons, two guns and several knives hidden under his clothes, his big, muscular body vibing with tension. Just before the doors started to open, he reached down and pressed the button to keep them closed.

"What's wrong?" she asked, wondering if he'd sensed something. He might not have possessed supernatural senses, but she trusted his instincts.

He popped his jaw, keeping his gaze locked on the doors as he said, "When this is over, we're finishing that conversation."

She didn't need to ask which one. Raine knew exactly

what he wanted to talk about. But she wasn't going to change her mind. She might want him so much it hurt, but she couldn't pretend to be something she wasn't. If she tried, anything she felt for him would turn to resentment, and she'd be left with one more regret to add to a list that was already far too long.

"I don't think there's much left to talk about," she told him, forcing herself to sound firm. Strong.

But he turned his head slowly, looking right at her, and his green eyes promised her she was wrong. That he *would* get his way. Ignoring the voice in the back of her mind whispering that she was running like a coward, Raine opened her mouth, ready to argue, but he released the button and the doors opened onto a chaotic scene that looked like something out of a war movie. Smoke billowed in thick clouds, obscuring the lobby, the acrid stench of chemicals filling the air, while the hotel staff ran around shouting panicked orders for evacuation, the blaring wail of an alarm suddenly vibrating through the building.

Raine couldn't see anything, but she knew what had happened, her powers flooding her mind with sudden bursts of information so quickly it made her dizzy.

"It's Spark," she shouted, reaching out for McConnell just as he grabbed her arm and jerked her into his side, a gun in his free hand. "She's already here!"

CHAPTER THIRTEEN

THOUGH HE WANTED to pull Raine back into the elevator and get her the hell out of there, Seth fought the impulse, knowing it was probably what Spark had planned. If she'd paid for hired guns to help her, odds were high that men would be waiting for them on the upper floors of the hotel, as well as the other exits. Their best shot was to fight their way out of the lobby, where Granger would be waiting for them—but he didn't have a goddamn clue what they were up against, the fog so thick he couldn't see more than a few feet in front of him.

"Why isn't the smoke burning our eyes?" Raine asked him as he pulled her off the elevator and pushed her behind him, keeping the wall at her back. Her voice was remarkably calm, considering the circumstances, and while he hated the risks she continually took with her life, he couldn't help but be thankful that she wasn't one of those women who panicked at the first sign of trouble.

Turning his head to the side so that she could hear him over the wailing alarm and the panicked hotel staff who were now screaming about the exits being blocked by gunmen, he said, "Spark's used a Collective creation called fog bombs. They're meant to be used for cover, without the debilitating effects of actual smoke."

"She's waiting for us near the doors," Raine said. "And she's not alone. She has five armed men with her that she's worked with before. They're expecting us to try to fight our way past them, and she's given them orders to shoot you on sight. There are more gunmen covering the other exits." She paused, no doubt listening to the thoughts streaming into her mind, then added, "She had someone follow Gideon here earlier tonight. That's how she found us."

"If you can read her so clearly now, why didn't you know she was coming?"

Though Seth wasn't looking at her, his gaze focused on their foggy surroundings, he could feel her rolling her eyes. "My powers aren't a sure thing, McConnell. It's probably best not to rely on them."

"Can you get a read on Ashe?"

"He was waiting for us near the elevators when the blasts went off. He's slipped behind the reservations desk—and he's getting ready to shout for you."

Sure enough, the vampire's deep voice rang out a second later, and Seth pulled her along behind him as they made their way through the thick mist. "Raine says Spark is covering the entrance," Seth said, as soon as they'd bunkered down behind the desk with the vampire, three of the hotel's employees huddled nearby, clearly terrified. "And she's not alone. She has five guys with her in the lobby and more are covering the rest of the hotel."

"How did she find you?" the vampire asked, his expression grim as he cast a sharp look toward the shell-shocked humans. Seth figured Granger would have had more sympathy if they were women…but probably couldn't wrap his head around the fact that three grown men were frozen stiff with fear. Not that Seth could understand them, either—but then he knew he no longer thought like the average human male.

Answering the vampire's question, Raine said, "She had Gideon followed when he came here to pick up Thomas."

Ashe muttered a raw curse, his pale eyes burning with fury. "I just talked to Liam. He's still watching the redhead that we *thought* was Spark through her hotel room window. Spark must have known Gid and I were tailing her and set up a decoy."

"Does Gideon have Seton?" Seth asked, slipping his bag off his shoulder.

The Deschanel shook his head. "I talked to him right after I got off the phone with Liam. Seton took off a few minutes ago, but Gideon lost him."

"Shit," he growled, knowing damn well that their chances of finding the bastard again were slim. Seton wasn't going to make it easy for them by showing his face until he was ready to make a move against Raine.

Either that, or the Casus was going to use this cluster-fuck as the perfect opportunity to sneak in and grab her. Which meant Seth had to get her out of there as soon as possible, every moment putting her in greater jeopardy.

Scooting closer to his side, Raine asked, "How long is this fog going to last?"

"Another ten minutes or so, but the cops will probably get here before then," he told her, hating the worry he could see in her eyes. He wished they were anywhere but there. Wished they were someplace quiet and calm, where they could finish what they'd started up in that hotel room. It made him feel like shit for reacting the way that he had to her fangs, his shame so thick he could taste it, and he'd have kicked his own ass if he could only reach the damn thing. She'd been so warm and trusting, and he'd repaid her by acting like a complete jackass.

He couldn't believe he'd just thrown it away. Not when everything had been so perfect. Christ, his head was still reeling from the way she'd come for him, his mouth still watering for more of her taste…and his dick was just in downright hell.

"What should we do?" she asked him, and it was with a surreal sense of pride that he realized she was willing to let him make the call. That she finally trusted him to protect her.

Not giving a shit what Ashe thought of it, Seth leaned over and gripped the back of her bare neck, her long hair tucked up tight under her black cap. Holding her steady, he planted a hard kiss against the heady softness of her mouth, then forced himself to let her go.

"I'm going to handle this," he told her, his voice hard with command. "I want you to stay here."

Her eyes shot wide with panic. "What are you going to do?"

"I'm not sure," he admitted, "but I'll think of something." He slid Ashe a questioning look, and though the vampire didn't appear happy about being given guard duty, he relented with a sharp nod. Looking back at Raine, Seth said, "Whatever happens, you don't leave Granger's side."

He didn't give her time to argue, but immediately vaulted up onto the high counter. Knowing exactly how Spark worked, he figured she'd have her men fanned out in front of her, while she used their bodies to shield her position. Which meant he'd have to take out the thugs before he could get to the assassin.

As another canister was released, Spark shouted at the top of her lungs, and he could tell from the direction of her voice that she was near the entrance, just as Raine had said. "You know we have the advantage!" she called out over the alarm and screaming crowd that was gathering in the lobby, the hotel's guests apparently being herded into the spacious, high-ceilinged room. "And you know I have no qualms about shooting one of these innocent bystanders. How does one dead hotel guest for every minute that you make me wait sound to you?" she asked, and he could hear the smile in her husky voice. *Crazy bitch*. She always had gotten a kick out of killing.

"If you don't want anyone to get hurt," she added, "you'll go ahead and turn yourself in, McConnell!"

A shot rang out from somewhere in the hotel, increasing the crowd's panic, and he knew he had to act fast. Pulling up a mental image of the lobby from his memories, Seth tilted his head back. Though he couldn't see the wires in the thick smokelike fog, he jumped, the fingers of his right hand just managing to snag one of the thick cables he recalled being strung across the ceiling as part of some modern light fixture. With his Sig in his left hand, Seth hooked his feet around the cable and started to shimmy across the lobby, careful not to crush any of the small bulbs hanging from the wire, while the fog obscured him from view down below.

Within seconds, he was hanging directly over Spark and her men, their forms just visible in the hazy mist. With his knees hooked over the cable, Seth slowly lowered his upper body, his abs flexed tight as he swiftly formulated his plan of attack. In a flash, he used his right hand to reach around the head of the gunman standing directly beneath him. He grasped the guy's chin and gave it a violent yank, instantly breaking his neck, while shooting the man standing beside him in the head. Then he drilled bullets into the other three, and pulled back up to the cable before he was even spotted.

Now the gunmen were lying dead on the tiled floor, one with a broken neck and the other four with gunshots to the center of their foreheads, while Spark spun in a circle, gun raised, trying to determine where the attack had come from.

"Come on, McConnell. Show your face," she shouted over the screaming crowd, the gunshots only increasing their distress.

Knowing he had only seconds before she looked up and spotted him, he holstered the Sig and reached for one of the "tranq" poppers he'd shoved in his pocket before leaving the room. The high-dosage sedative had been created by the Collective and was dispensed from a small syringe that fit in the palm of his hand. The instant Spark moved beneath him, Seth lowered his upper body again, jabbing the short needle into her jugular. A second later, she slumped to the floor in an unconscious heap.

After dropping deftly to his feet, Seth tucked her gun into the back of his jeans, then quickly opened the hotel's front doors. As the fog began to dissipate, spilling into the cold night air, he picked Spark up, slinging her body over his shoulder as he forged his way back to the reservations desk, eager to make sure Raine was all right. With the main doorway clear, panicked guests and hotel staff rushed for the exit, knocking into him as they scrambled past, but he pushed forward, scowling as he picked out the sounds of fighting coming from up ahead.

As he drew closer, Seth could hear Ashe's feral curses, the visibility finally improving enough that he could see the vampire in violent hand-to-hand combat with three more of the hired thugs who worked for Spark. With the fog quickly thinning, he watched the vampire make short work of the humans. The bodies of several other gunmen were scattered across the floor, having already been dispatched by the vamp, and he realized Ashe had clearly had his back, keeping the men from crossing the lobby while Seth had been dealing with those at the entrance. He was just about to offer his thanks when he caught sight of the vampire's grim expression…and knew something had happened to Raine. Racing toward the reservations desk, he found the area empty but for another fallen gunman and their bags.

"Where the fuck is she?" he growled, tossing Spark's body on the counter as he spun toward the vampire.

Ashe used the back of his wrist to wipe the bloodied corner of his mouth. "She's gone."

"What do you mean, gone?" His voice was deceptively soft, his chest so tight he could barely breathe, while panic seared through his veins like an acid, stripping him raw inside.

"I mean she took off while I was in the middle of dealing with these assholes," he muttered, jerking his chin toward the bodies that littered the ground. "I told her to stay put, but your woman listens for shit, McConnell."

"You were supposed to be watching her!" he roared, his hands curling into fists as he advanced on the vampire.

"I was!" Ashe roared right back at him. "But I was trying to keep four of those bastards from grabbing her when she bailed. What the hell was I supposed to do? Chain her to me?"

Knowing he was only wasting precious time arguing with the vampire, Seth took a deep breath and worked hard to get a hold on his anger. "Did she tell you where she was going?"

Ashe scowled. "She shouted something at me as she flew past, claiming to have spotted Seton in the crowd. Then she took off after him."

"Oh, Christ." His pulse was roaring in his ears, rage and fear practically turning him inside out.

"There's more," Ashe muttered. "She said that you'd be able to find her. Said to make it quick."

Seth was so furious he wanted to kill something—but he knew he needed to focus on Raine. On hooking into that weird connection they had going, so that he could find her before it was too late.

Have to find her. That's all that matters, because I...

Before he could finish the thought, Gideon came tearing into the lobby, looking as if he'd run the entire way across town. "I had to ditch my car," he told them, his chest heaving between each word. "Street's blocked by two fire engines that crashed into each other on their way here. The wreck took out three cop cars, but more will be on their way as soon as the road's been cleared."

Ashe looked at Seth. "Can you get a read on where she is?"

"Not yet," he snarled, knowing damn well that Seton was going to attack her the second he got the chance.

"I'll be wanting to hear about what went down here," Gideon rumbled, casting a quick glance over the bodies that littered the floor, "but I get the feeling we're in the middle of another crisis. So someone give me the short version."

Ashe quickly filled Gideon in on the recent events while Seth tried to focus. The thought of her being hurt was enough to break him and bring him to his knees, but he didn't have time to indulge in any of that self-

pity bullshit. Exhaling a ragged breath, Seth struggled
to think past the panic. "She isn't far," he said a moment
later…doing everything he could to calm his mind
enough that he could follow that mysterious "pull" that
existed between them.

Gideon scratched the stubble on his jaw and glanced
toward the front of the hotel, where masses of people
were still milling about in confusion, trying to figure
out what had happened. "He wouldn't take her up to a
room," he murmured. "He knows the authorities are on
their way." Even then, sirens could be heard drawing
closer. "He wouldn't risk getting caught like that."

"The basement," Seth suddenly barked, sensing in
his gut that he was right. Looking at Gideon, he asked,
"Can you grab our bags from behind the desk and get
Spark out of here?"

The vamp grimaced with disgust, but was already
tossing the assassin over his shoulder as Seth set off
for the stairwell with Ashe right on his heels. Together,
they ran down the stairs, the air dank and cool as they
entered the weathered underground level of the hotel.
While the rest of the building had obviously undergone
modern renovations, the basement had been left virtu-
ally untouched, looking like something out of the past
century.

"Where to now?" Ashe asked him.

"She's close." Seth moved deeper into the dimly lit
space, weaving through metal shelving units and supply
boxes that'd been stacked nearly to the ceiling. "I don't
get it," he finally muttered, placing his palms against a

dark paneled wall. "I can feel her, but there's nothing here. It's just a goddamn dead end."

"Maybe not." Ashe ran his hands along the paneling, feeling for something between the grooves. "Here we go," he rasped, just as there was a soft click…and a section of the paneling popped open.

Too impatient to wait, Seth ripped the paneling out of the way, revealing a narrow hallway that led to what looked like some kind of thick metal door, the light filtering in from behind him glinting against its dull surface. "What the hell is this place?" he asked, moving into the hallway.

"I'm betting it's an old Stasi interrogation room," Ashe murmured, the sounds of the hotel's generators rattling through the walls.

"How would a guy like Seton even know it was here?" he asked, trying to open the door the instant they reached it. But it was locked. He pressed his ear to the cold metal, but the door was too thick to hear anything from inside the room. Still, he knew she was in there. The knowledge filled every cell of his body, and his muscles seemed to expand with rage, coiling beneath his skin.

As he pulled his gun and stepped back, getting ready to blast the lock to hell and back, Ashe answered his question, saying, "Seton wouldn't know about it, considering he's been locked away for the past millennium and only managed to escape within the past year. But that body he's taken over comes with a lifetime full of memories. His human host could have been a war historian. Hell, he could have been the builder who did the renovations on this place. Anything's possible," he added, just as Seth fired the shot.

The bullet ripped through the lock, shattering it into pieces. Seth immediately kicked in the door and rushed into the room, too furious to consider that Seton might have a gun of his own.

So much for control…

But if the Casus had a gun, he never got the chance to fire off a shot because he was too busy handling Raine. He had her backed against a wooden table in the center of the room, both of them bloody and shouting as she struggled to fight him off. With a red, visceral haze of fury filling his vision, Seth headed straight for the Casus, a guttural roar tearing from his chest as Seton shoved Raine to the side, her head cracking loudly on the edge of the table. In the next instant, Seth slammed into him, taking the guy to the ground. They rolled across the gritty floor, punches flying as blood spattered. This bastard had touched *his* woman—had hurt her—and Seth wanted his blood with a primal fury unlike anything he'd ever known. He snarled as he grappled against the Casus's supernatural strength, finally landing a shot that broke Seton's jaw. Then he hit him again…and again, until the son of a bitch finally lost consciousness.

Blood pooled beneath Seton's head, his lips split, nose broken, both eyes swollen shut. A part of Seth wanted to keep smashing the asshole into the floor, the bloodthirsty rage like a narcotic in his veins, but he managed to stop himself as he caught sight of Raine's Marker. It was wrapped around Seton's wrist, the cord broken where he'd obviously cut it away from her neck. Seth yanked the Marker free, shoved three "tranq" poppers into the side of Seton's throat, then pulled himself to his feet and turned, using his shoulder to wipe the blood off his mouth as he made his way back to Raine.

Ashe had gotten her off the floor and set her on the edge of the table, the single bulb hanging from the ceiling casting a pale light over them as the vampire used his sleeve to blot the blood dripping from her nose. Though she was holding her head up, it swayed, her gaze unfocused. Seth made a low sound as he watched Ashe place a hand on the back of her neck to hold her steady, the gesture too possessive for his liking.

"Move back, Granger."

With a breathless laugh, Ashe stepped away, allowing Seth to move between her legs, putting his own hand on the back of her neck. He whispered her name, but her eyes rolled back in her head, the lids sliding closed, as if she'd passed out.

"What about Seton?" Ashe asked.

"What about him?" he snarled, wishing Raine would open her eyes and look at him. He couldn't handle her being hurt.

"I'm just hoping you didn't kill him, considering he's the best lead we've got for finding Westmore."

Her cap had fallen off, her long hair streaming over one shoulder, and Seth gritted his teeth, hating that he was going to have to touch it, knowing how much it bothered her. But he needed to check her head, worried that she'd injured it when she'd hit the edge of the table.

As he ran his fingers over her skull, he answered Ashe's question, saying, "I didn't kill him, but he won't be waking up anytime soon. I dosed him with sedatives."

The Deschanel's tone was dry. "I was wondering how we were going to keep him from turning fully Casus on us, so I guess that works."

"We'll give him another dose before we leave, just to be safe," he rasped, his heart pounding as he found a lump just behind her left ear that was the size of an egg... and still swelling. Jesus. No wonder she was out of it.

"Speaking of leaving," the vampire murmured, "you'll need to give her your wrist before we go."

He cut the vamp a sharp look. "Why?"

"She needs blood."

A gritty laugh jerked from his chest at how easily Ashe could drawl such a statement, as if he'd just said, *She looks like she needs a pickup. We should grab her some Starbucks.*

"I don't know what blood is going to do for a lump on her head," he muttered. "And she just took my blood before we left our room."

"If she's got a concussion, fresh blood will help her heal more quickly. And since we need to let things calm down a bit upstairs before we sneak out of here, we've got the time."

"But I don't feed her from my vein," he growled, the rough words thick with frustration. "I collect it for her in a cup."

The vampire's surprise was obvious. His lips parted, and he looked like he wanted to say something, but changed his mind. Instead, his dark brows drew into a tight frown as he started to roll back the sleeve on his bloodstained shirt, muttering something under his breath about how they weren't exactly standing in a housewares department. And he was right. The only thing left inside that miserable room, besides themselves, was the table, lightbulb and Seton.

"Can I drip it in her mouth?" Seth asked, feeling like a fucking idiot.

"If she was conscious. But considering she's out of it, if we want to make sure she swallows, we have to get her to bite."

When the vampire reached out, taking hold of Raine's arm to hold her steady, Seth reluctantly stepped away, unable to believe he was going to let this happen. But what choice did he have? He wouldn't be able to stomach giving her his own vein, and she needed the blood.

But it was hell to watch. As Ashe lifted his wrist to her soft lips, Seth locked his jaw so hard he was surprised it didn't crack.

"Come on, honey," Ashe murmured, stroking his skin against her lips, coaxing her to feed. "That's it," he crooned, looking as if he was trying hard to hide his pleasure when she moaned, then sank her fangs into his flesh and started sucking. She moaned louder, grasping the vampire's arm to hold it tighter against her mouth… and the temperature in the musty room seemed to rise, higher…and higher, a drop of sweat snaking down Seth's spine. A hard shudder racked the vampire's tall frame and he looked away, as though he didn't want Seth to see his expression.

"Careful, vamp." Seth's voice was a low, sinister rasp, his jealousy and frustration like a physical force in his body, punching against his skin as it struggled to break free.

Ashe didn't say anything in response—but Seth could have sworn the vamp's shoulders were shaking slightly, as if he was holding back a laugh. Bloody smart-ass.

Keeping his narrow gaze locked on Raine's face, Seth watched as color bloomed in her cheeks, the bruises already fading…her busted lip mending before his eyes. Ashe's blood apparently packed a hell of a punch, which was the only thing that kept him from acting like a caveman and knocking the bastard out of the way.

After what had to be at least thirty seconds of strong, hungry feeding, Raine finally opened her eyes, that storm-dark gaze immediately connecting with Seth's. Her eyes shot wide and she pulled back from Ashe's arm with an audible gasp, as if only just realizing that she'd been enjoying another man's taste in front of him.

"Um…thanks," she whispered to the vampire, wiping her damp mouth with the backs of her fingers.

Seth was still seething with frustration, but it didn't stop him from moving in front of her the instant Ashe stepped away, a hoarse, "No problem," falling from the vampire's lips as he headed over to where Seton lay bleeding on the floor.

Unable to control the trembling in his hands, Seth shoved them in his pockets and popped his jaw. He opened his mouth, swallowed, his throat uncomfortably tight as he finally managed to grind out the words he needed to say. "What the hell were you thinking?"

She blinked, as if taken back by his question, then frowned. "I was doing what I came here to do, Seth. And I'd have had him, too, if he hadn't gotten lucky with the Marker."

"We're meant to be doing this together," he growled. "But every time I turn my back, you fucking disappear."

"I didn't have any choice," she shot back, her own anger mounting. "When I saw Seton, it looked like he was slinking away and I couldn't risk losing him. You were busy with Spark and Ashe had his hands full. So I did what I had to. It's not like I planned for it to happen. It just did."

"You know what, Raine? You wouldn't have told me even if you *had* planned it."

"Only because I know you would have tried to stop me, and he's our best chance at finding Westmore. The opportunity was there, so I took it. But I didn't mean to worry you. I didn't think you'd—"

"What? That I'd care?" he rasped, the ragged words hoarse with emotion. A muscle pulsed in his jaw, and he fisted his hands inside his pockets. "Christ, Raine, I don't want to lose you, but I can feel you slipping away from me, and there's nothing I can do to stop it. When are you going to realize you don't have to keep holding on to that fucking hatred of yours so tightly? You could let it go, if you'd just open your eyes and see what's right in front of you!"

"*Seth.*" Her face instantly softened, the gray of her eyes seeming to shine like silver. "I know I've been saying this a lot lately, but I'm sorry."

"Sorry you scared ten years off my life?" he muttered, running a shaky hand down his face.

"Yes."

Seth took a deep breath, then quietly asked her, "Were you…are you trying to kill yourself, Raine? Do you want to die? Is that what this is all about?"

"No." She gave a little shake of her head and lifted her shoulders. "I just… I guess I wasn't as worried as I normally would have been. I mean…if something went wrong, I knew you weren't going to be far behind us. That you would come for me."

In that moment, he was torn between wanting to kiss her…and needing to throttle her crazy little ass for taking such a dangerous risk. "And what if I hadn't been able to get here in time? How do you think that would have made me feel? I'd have spent the rest of my life knowing I hadn't been able to keep you safe."

"But you did."

He glared at her bruised, blood-smeared face. "Barely."

"Please don't be angry with me," she pleaded, wetting her lips. "I know I worried you, but I was afraid he was going to get away and we'd be left second-guessing where he was. But now we can use him to find Westmore." The husky words vibrated with excitement. "I thought you'd think this was a good thing, Seth. I thought you wanted Westmore as badly as I do."

"Yeah, I want Westmore." His voice was flinty, and she flinched at the sound of it. "I just wasn't willing to see you raped or killed to get him."

Figuring there was nothing left to say, Seth had just started to turn away from her when she slipped off the table and grabbed his arm. "If you don't want to talk to me any more, that's fine. But can you at least tell me what the plan is when we leave here? It's not like we can check into a new hotel carrying an unconscious man."

"Actually, I think I can help with that," Ashe offered from the other side of the room, proving that he'd been listening to every word they'd said. "There's a *Förmyndare* safe house not far from here that isn't in use. It'll give us the perfect place to…*question* the Casus."

Oh, Christ. How much stranger can this get?

A breathless laugh shook Seth's chest, the situation too surreal to take in. A year ago, getting anywhere near a *Förmyndare* safe house would have meant certain death for a guy who was part of the Collective Army. And now he was being *invited* to stay at one.

Despite his shitty mood, a grim smile curved his mouth as he thought of all the demons who were surely shivering from the cold at that moment, ice forming on their gnarled horns, snowflakes glistening on their lashes…

Because hell had surely just frozen over.

An hour later...
A small town on the outskirts of Venice, Italy

KNEELING BEFORE a bloodstained altar that he'd built in the closet of his suite, Westmore carved a crescent into the palm of his hand, dripping the blood into the bowl that sat before him. The flickering lights of the thick candles that surrounded him cast maniacal shadows against the gleaming metal of the altar, but not even the candles' rich scent could disguise the grisly odor of the entrails coiled in the bottom of the bowl, along with other various body parts. Some animal. Some human.

He waited with sharp impatience, eager to impart his news, his eyes sliding closed as he began to chant the ritual words he'd found written in the pages of the archives.

"It's going according to plan," he murmured a moment later, when a shadowy face finally filled his mind. It was Anthony Calder's shade, the Casus leader's ice-blue eyes glowing within the monstrous contours of his wolf-shaped head.

"They've taken Seton?" the Casus asked, the words garbled by his fang-filled muzzle. The shades were eternally trapped in their true form, until they could escape from Meridian and come back to this world.

"My sources have just confirmed his capture. He's now a prisoner of our enemies. Soon, he'll break and give them this location. Then the Watchmen will come to retrieve the Markers, and it will be time for the next step."

Calder's eerie gaze narrowed with warning. "You'd better know what you're doing, Westmore. It's a risky plan."

Brimming with confidence, the Kraven allowed a slow, arrogant smile to curve his mouth. "But the best ones always are."

CHAPTER FOURTEEN

A FEW DAYS AGO, Raine would have never believed it could happen, but now that she was separated from him—she'd come to Italy with Ashe, while Seth had remained behind in Germany—she was missing the human. A lot.

After they'd made it out of the hotel early that morning, they'd met up with Gideon and headed for the remote *Förmyndare* safe house located a half hour out of the city. The men had locked Spark in a cell and taken Seton to the basement for questioning about Westmore's location, while Raine had tried to nap on an upstairs sofa, without much luck. Despite her exhaustion, she'd wanted her chance to question Seton, as well—only Seth wouldn't hear of it.

She knew he was still pissed at her for going after the Casus on her own, but his anger hadn't affected his protective instincts. So she'd been left upstairs to doze…and worry…and think about the human. About how badly she wished things could be different between them. How badly she wanted to hold him. Be close to him. She just… she didn't see how that could ever be possible, given their circumstances. And so she'd tossed and turned…

and seethed with frustration, instead of the hatred that had been her constant companion for so many weeks.

Just after 9:00 a.m., Ashe had come upstairs to tell her that Seton had finally cracked and given them an address just outside of Venice. Though she'd had her doubts, the information had obviously been valid, considering she and Ashe had finally spotted the Kraven a little while ago, when he'd stepped out onto the balcony of said address with a mug in his hand. They'd had a clear view of him standing there in the golden afternoon sunshine from a table at the café across the street from the luxury flats, their table hidden beneath the café's dark green awning.

Raine had thought this moment would feel so satisfying…but it wasn't the same without Seth. When she'd been told that he would remain behind with Gideon and the prisoners while she went to Italy with Ashe, it'd been impossible not to feel as if the soldier was trying to get rid of her—and though a cold rage had been her first reaction, she was at the point now that she just wanted to see him again.

The knot behind her ear had healed, as well as the bruises Seton had left on her face—but the rift between her and Seth seemed deeper than ever. He hadn't even asked to talk to her the few times Ashe had spoken to him on the phone. It was like he'd turned her over to the vamp, and while she found Ashe charming, he wasn't the one that she wanted.

Damn it, she *wanted* McConnell, no matter how illogical it was. No matter how problematic. And she couldn't stop the raw ache that bloomed within her chest whenever she considered the possibility that it might never happen. Though she'd been fighting against that very thing, Raine couldn't help but fear that all the fight had simply left her when it came to that particular breathtaking male.

And he's going to be here any minute now, she thought, shivering with nerves and excitement.

Once she and Ashe had confirmed that the address in Italy checked out with Seton's confession, and they'd talked to people in the building who recognized Westmore's description, Seth and Gideon had headed down to join them. But since commercial air travel wasn't possible, considering they'd had to bring the prisoners with them, in case they were needed for further questioning, Gideon had managed to swing it so that they could transport Spark and Seton on a private plane... and land at a private airstrip. The plane had set down an hour ago, and they'd taken the prisoners to another *Förmyndare* safe house, along with Liam Granger, who had said he could stick around for as long as his cousins needed him. When Gideon had called to let his brother know that the prisoners were secure, Ashe had told him that they'd finally spotted Westmore, and so Gideon had grabbed Seth and the two were currently on their way to the café.

Fidgeting in her chair, Raine leaned forward to check the time on the historic clock tower just visible at the end of the street, wishing they would hurry up and get there.

And yeah, she knew it was a bad sign that she was

more excited about Seth's arrival than she was about finding Westmore. *What am I doing? I need to get my head on straight.* No matter how twisted up she was over the intoxicating human male, she had to remember her true purpose for being there. Had to remember the reasons that were driving her to succeed with her hunt… at any cost.

Yes, she'd told McConnell that she wasn't trying to kill herself, and that was the truth. But she was also willing to do whatever it took to succeed…even if the price was her life.

The only problem was that before, the idea of paying that particular price hadn't seemed too much of a sacrifice. And now…now Raine couldn't pretend that there wasn't something making her want to stay. To survive. It had screamed through her skull when she'd run after Seton, furious that she was willing to take such a risk, when there was suddenly something worth living for.

She didn't have a clue what that *something* was—but every part of her was insisting that it was something she could only find with McConnell. Urging her to find a way to undo the damage she'd done. But she didn't know how. Not when things were still so freaking complicated between them.

"Nice place the Kraven's got," Ashe murmured, the deep rumble of his voice, with its slightly British tones, instantly pulling Raine from her troublesome thoughts. He slouched back in his chair, his dark glasses concealing his eyes, somehow managing to look both gorgeous and dangerous at the same time. A compelling, seductive type of dangerous that no doubt had women falling at his feet wherever he went. It was said among the clans that the complex nature of the Deschanel was a delicate balance between the light and dark aspects of the world, and the Granger brothers were prime examples.

After taking a deep swallow of his coffee, he went on. "Westmore must have been saving his pennies for a long-ass time to afford such a prime piece of real estate. Either that, or the Collective bought it for him. And according to Seton, the guy's got it fitted out with top of the line security."

"What is a Kraven's life span, anyway?" she asked, never having paid much attention to the rumors she'd heard about the strange, secret race.

He gave a rough sigh. "Hell, who knows? Some of the first Kraven ever born are said to still be living, though their minds deteriorate over time. They can only breed within their own race, and not many of the offspring survive. We're not even sure how old Westmore is or who his parents are. Gideon's done a lot of research on him in the Deschanel Court and hasn't been able to uncover anything that would explain his obsession with the Casus."

Before she could ask another question, the café's buxom waitress stopped by their table, interrupting the conversation…again. She had been vying for the vampire's attention since they'd arrived. *Can I get you anything,* signore? *More espresso,* signore? When Raine knew what she'd really been saying was, *Would you like to sleep with me,* signore? *I'll do anything you want,* signore….

"So you and Seth, huh?" he rumbled, once he'd finally managed to send the dimpled waitress on her way. "I honestly never thought I'd see the day when a Deschanel hooked up with a former vampire hunter, but Seth's a great guy. I think he'll be good for you."

Raine sent him an exasperated look. "We're not a couple, Granger."

The vampire gave a gruff bark of laughter, his sensual mouth curved with a cocky smile. "Is he aware of that?" he asked in a slow drawl, and she had no doubt that if she could have seen his eyes, they'd be glittering with humor.

"A relationship would be…impossible." She washed the bad-tasting words down with a mouthful of coffee and tried to stop glancing at the doorway that led into the café.

"Hell, if there's one thing I've learned, it's that nothing is ever impossible. Especially when it comes to a man who's found his focus."

"His *focus?*" Her gaze flicked to Ashe's dark lenses. "I don't understand."

"That one thing he needs. That he can*not* do without."

"It isn't like that," she argued, but instead of sounding adamant, her voice had gone kind of soft and dreamy. "You're…wrong," she whispered, hating how badly she wished the vamp was *right*.

"I'm not wrong, Raine." His smile was lopsided. "But you can tell yourself that if it's easier."

"I can't be his…his focus, or whatever you're calling it. McConnell *hates* vampires."

His shoulders lifted in one of those rolling kind of shrugs that only a guy with a killer bod could pull off, muscles rippling beneath the dark cotton of his shirt. "Hey, things change."

"No, they don't." She sounded tired now, not to mention embarrassingly bitter. "At least, not for the better."

Again the waitress returned to their table, and this time Ashe ordered them two more coffees, along with an assortment of pastries, his easy smile damn near giving the woman heart palpitations. Raine stared at the gorgeous vamp from the other side of the table, wondering why she couldn't have fallen for him instead of the soldier. He was funny, sexy and exceptionally easy on the eyes. Everything would be so much simpler if she could just look at him and feel that breathtaking *spark* that lit her up whenever McConnell walked into a room. Ashe wouldn't have made her yearn for things she couldn't have. Wouldn't have twisted her into emotional knots. She could have used him for a fling…and happily let herself be used in return.

Leaning his head back, his gaze apparently focused on the café's rustic awning, he said, "I can't believe I'm saying this, but don't even think about it."

She laughed softly, and didn't bother to deny the direction her thoughts had been taking. "Too pathetic?" she asked.

He ran his tongue over his white teeth as he lowered his head. "No…and that's the problem. I'd happily take you, and no doubt end up keeping you. Then the soldier would have my head for it."

Her mouth twitched with a grin. "Wow. I never thought I'd see the day that a *Förmyndare* was afraid of a Collective soldier."

He gave a deep, husky laugh, then slid her a wry smile. "I'm not too arrogant to be smart. There aren't many humans I'd be wary of in a fight, but Seth is at the top of that list." His head tilted a bit to the side, and even though Raine couldn't see his eyes, she knew he was watching her. "But, if you really wanted me, I'd take my chances. Problem is, I'm not the one you want, sweetheart. You're just running from the inevitable."

"And how do you know what I want?" She didn't like feeling so transparent.

His voice gentled. "I can see it in your eyes. Every single time you look at him."

"Then I must be a masochist," she said in a strained voice, "falling for a guy who hates what I am."

"McConnell doesn't hate you, Raine. And you're wrong about things not changing. I don't think his hangups about blood will last after seeing the way he watched you feed from my wrist. The poor guy damn near turned green with envy." He took another drink of his coffee, then scratched his jaw as he said, "What's happening between the two of you might not be expected, but I can't say that I'm surprised."

Her forehead scrunched with confusion. "You aren't?"

"Naw. The human was weird about you from the beginning. After your rescue from that compound, we were all worried about you, but he…well, you could tell it was personal for McConnell."

"I think you're exaggerating," she murmured, even though she knew he was right.

"You know," Ashe drawled, "you were weird about him, as well."

She blinked with surprise, then frowned. "I was not."

"Yeah?" He paused as their coffees and pastries were delivered, but the second the waitress walked away, he said, "Then tell me why you refused to feed from any of the other males in our group. The idea drove Seth crazy, but he was willing to deal with it in order to make you better."

Breathlessly, she asked, "How do you know that?"

"Because when you were at your worst, he all but begged me to force you to take my vein," he told her. "He only gave up when Juliana explained that her blood was just as potent as any that we could give you, and you were already feeding from her."

Juliana Sabin was one of the Deschanel who'd been exiled to the Wasteland, along with her family. She was also the reason they'd been able to make it out of that horrid place, and they all owed her a tremendous amount of gratitude. Not that Ashe would ever admit it, considering he and the little vamp constantly bickered.

"I didn't know," she said in a hoarse voice, wondering what Seth's behavior had meant. "I just didn't want to get that close to a man after what had happened."

Ashe gave her a gentle smile. "But you let McConnell get close to you."

She wet her lips, then spoke in a husky rush. "Maybe that was only because I knew what he was—a man who hated vampires. Maybe I knew there wasn't a chance he'd ever be tempted to touch me."

His chest shook with a breathless laugh. "Yeah, and maybe I'm a fucking fairy princess. Face it, Spenser. You would have had to be blind not to notice the way he looked at you. But even then, you trusted him."

"And if I did?" she snapped, her emotions in chaos. "What the hell does it mean?"

"Only you know the answer to that one. But I'd figure it out fast. A guy gets a certain look about him when he's at the end of his patience." As if summoned by his words, Seth and Gideon walked through the café door, onto the patio. Ashe took one look at the soldier's face and smiled. "And, honey, McConnell's definitely got *that* look."

As they headed toward the table, both men appeared exhausted, their eyes tired and dark, but she could see what Ashe was talking about. Seth's expression seemed particularly grim, as if he was stuck in a difficult situation with no viable solution. But he was still the sexiest, most mouthwatering thing she'd ever set eyes on. The dark smudges beneath his hard gaze only accentuated the mesmerizing green of his eyes, the gilded stubble on his jaw glinting in the Italian sunshine, begging for the touch of her fingers. And that firm mouth…God, she wanted to kiss him so badly she could hardly sit still, the desire to taste his lips like a physical need pulsing through her body.

For the first time since they'd met, Raine suddenly found herself asking why they couldn't have met *earlier,* before she'd been broken into pieces. Before the parts of her that had known how to seek happiness and pleasure had been scarred with hatred and this consuming need for revenge.

And yet, she'd *enjoyed* what had happened between them in that hotel room in Berlin. But honestly, who was she trying to fool? She enjoyed it every time he touched her. Every time he kissed her… But being beneath him, with his wicked mouth turning her inside out with ecstasy—*that* had been the best. And she'd wanted more. She'd wanted it all, everything he could give her…everything he could do to her. At least that's what she'd wanted right up until the moment her fangs had released and she'd caught his heartbreaking look. Though Raine had known it would hurt to find herself in such a horrid situation, the pain that flooded through her body had been shocking, as if someone had reached into her chest and squeezed, leaving her heart bloody and pulverized.

God, she thought, shivering with confusion. *I am such a mess.*

Just before Gideon and Seth reached the table, she said, "By the way, I happen to know that I'm not the one you want, either. So, no, you wouldn't have really been tempted, Ashe. But it was nice of you to say so."

The vampire tensed at the soft words, and she knew he was wondering just how much she knew about his personal life—but he didn't have time to question her before his brother was slapping his shoulder and taking the seat on his right, while Seth dropped into the one on his left.

Seth gave her a gruff hello, then started relaying the new information that he and Gideon had been able to get out of Seton about the security on Westmore's apartment, acting as if he wasn't at all affected by her presence. But Raine knew he wasn't as calm as he seemed. She could hear the rush of his pulse, his heart beating hard and fast, his body burning with feral waves of heat. And then there was the way that he kept flexing those big, scarred hands on the arms of his chair, as if he was trying to keep them from fisting...or grabbing on to something. *To someone...*

Though Raine knew it was wrong, she would have given anything at that moment to be able to read his mind, but he remained stubbornly blocked to her. It was so frustrating, never being able to see into the ones she most wanted to read, and her muscles cramped with frustration.

"I can't believe this is the place," he muttered, taking a long swig of the beer he'd carried outside with him, obviously having picked up the icy bottle at the café's bar. "Garrick and I were in this town three weeks ago, looking for Westmore, but the trail stopped cold. Then we heard he was seen in Budapest, so we headed that way."

"Speaking of Garrick," Ashe murmured, "what's going on with him? Kierland told me he'd had some kind of family emergency."

"His dad had a heart attack, so he had to head home. When I talked to him this morning, he said the doctors didn't think his dad was gonna make it."

"That's terrible," she said, feeling awful for Garrick.

"Yeah. His dad's a good guy. I'm hoping he pulls through."

Raine could tell by the tone of Seth's voice that he was genuinely worried. Her fingers itched to reach out and stroke his arm, offering comfort, but she fought the impulse, feeling too unsure of herself. Impossible not to second-guess everything she thought…everything she *felt,* since all of it was still so new and unfamiliar.

Of course, it didn't help that his mere presence had her on the knife's edge of desire, her senses drenched in him, as if she was absorbing the sensual data through her skin. She felt trapped, restless, her foot tapping as she tried to just calm the hell down.

"So," Gideon said around a mouthful of pastry, nodding toward Westmore's building. "How hard do you guys think it's gonna be to get to the Kraven?"

"I think it might be easier than you think," Raine offered. "I haven't been able to pick up anyone on the top floor, so I think Seton was telling the truth when he said that Westmore's alone. Which means that if we can get past his security, we'll have a clear shot at him, as well as the Markers."

"I don't like it," Seth muttered. "It doesn't feel right. He's too paranoid to just be hanging out on his own."

Gideon shrugged. "But he doesn't have much choice, does he? Not when he knows what Raine can do."

Ashe spoke up, saying, "We're going to need to move fast. He's bound to be growing anxious, considering he hasn't heard from Seton. If we don't move tonight, he might try to run, and we can't risk losing him *or* the Markers."

They talked a bit longer, and decided that the brothers would stay and keep an eye on Westmore, while Seth took Raine to a local bed and breakfast so they could grab a few hours of sleep. Then they would meet up again later and make their plans for the night. After saying goodbye, Raine followed Seth out of the café, using the rear exit to avoid being seen by the Kraven if he was watching the street. Once outside, Seth directed her to a gleaming black Jeep.

Neither of them said much as he steered the car through the narrow streets, the tension between them so thick it felt heavy in her lungs, like the humid Mediterranean air. When he finally pulled to a stop in front of a small white villa located at the end of a shaded lane and surrounded by a thick, wild garden of flowers, she asked, "Is this the bed-and-breakfast?"

He cut the engine and ran his tongue over his teeth, staring through the front windshield. "No. This is the safe house where we left Seton and Spark."

"I thought we were going to a B and B," she said, her tone tense. "I don't want to stay here." The idea of sleeping under the same roof as Seton made her skin crawl.

"We're not staying here, Raine."

Panic started to creep through her system. "What's going on?"

"Seton told us the truth about Westmore's location, which means he's probably told us the truth about the security systems, as well. We've gotten what we needed from him."

She could tell from his tone that something wasn't right, and she whispered his name. *"Seth?"*

"We won't be here long, I promise," he said, getting out of the car. A moment later, he introduced her to Liam, who'd walked out to meet them on the front porch. She could easily see the guy's resemblance to the Granger brothers, though Liam was a good bit younger, with lighter hair. As they followed Liam inside the villa, he gave Seth an update on Spark and Seton, explaining that they were due for another round of sedatives if he wanted to keep them knocked out. Seth thanked the vampire for keeping an eye on things, then turned to Raine. "I need to go downstairs for a moment. Just wait here with Liam."

He didn't wait for her response, turning and heading down a narrow stairway tucked into a corner of the room. Unfortunately, Raine had never been all that great at following orders, and as soon as Liam stepped out onto the front porch to make a call—no doubt wanting to let the Grangers know that Seth had returned to the safe house—she followed the soldier down the stairs.

It didn't take her long to find the room where Seton and Spark were confined. They were both in cuffs, chained to metal chairs that had been placed back-to-back in the center of the floor, so that they couldn't see each other. Cells lined the sides of the room, dismal but clean. And for the moment, empty. There were no other prisoners but for the two sitting on those chairs.

Seth stood in front of Seton, his arms crossed as he stared down at the sneering Casus. She hadn't made a sound, and yet somehow the human knew she was there, lurking in the doorway. "Raine," he said in a low voice, "go back upstairs."

"No."

At the sound of her voice, Seton turned his head to the side, his mouth curling with a slow, cruel smile. "Do you want to know something sweet, honey? Westmore told me a little secret before I left. Seems the next time he gets his hands on you, he's finally going to treat himself to a piece of psychic pie. 'Bout time he had a taste. I know he's gonna get such a kick outta that little power charge inside you."

A guttural sound tore from Seth's throat that reminded her of a Lycan, and he slammed his fist into the Casus's face, splitting tissue, the monster's blood flowing hot and free. But it didn't shut him up. Seton spit out two teeth, then grinned. "You can do whatever you want to me, human. But it won't change the fact that she'll be the last girl I fucked when I die." He slid Raine a sharp smile. "And when I come back again, she'll be the first."

"Not if we do this right," Seth growled, slanting a dark look toward Raine. He came toward her, holding out his hand as he said, "Give me the Marker."

Her eyes went huge as she stared back at him, hardly believing what he'd said.

His deep voice vibrated with command. "Now, Raine."

Her fingers felt numb as she took the cross from her pocket and placed it in his outstretched hand. She couldn't believe he was actually going to use the Marker to destroy the Casus, her lungs tight as she watched him palm the metallic cross in his right hand and head back toward Seton. She could believe even less that she wasn't arguing with him about the right being hers. Yes, she'd needed to be the one meting out punishment for all that Rietta had suffered at the hands of these sadistic bastards, but…it felt somehow *right* that McConnell was working with her. Helping her to carry the load.

But will it change me? Will I weaken if I share this with him? she thought with a frown, suddenly wanting to reach out and snatch the Marker back from him. But it was too late. His muscular arm was already glowing, his veins bulging beneath the golden sheen of his skin as he gripped the Marker in a tight hold.

Wearing a fierce look of determination, he grabbed the back of Seton's chair and pulled it away from the one that held Spark, giving him room to get behind the Casus. Fisting his left hand in Seton's hair, he wrenched the

Casus's head forward, exposing the base of his skull as he snarled, "You're going to hell, you son of a bitch."

Though he didn't try to fight for his escape, Seton's ice-blue eyes burned with hatred as he stared across the room at Raine. "And once Calder gets his hands on you, hunter—well, let's just say that you'll be joining me there."

"What do you mean?" Raine demanded. Seton's words had been more than just an idle threat. It sounded like they actually had a *plan* for Seth. But before the Casus could answer her question, Seth slammed his hand into the back of Seton's neck, jerking a guttural cry from the monster's throat. Within seconds, Seth's arm was engulfed in flames, those flames spreading rapidly through the Casus's body.

When Seton had been reduced to nothing more than a smoldering pile of ash, Seth took a step back, his body drenched with sweat, every muscle coiled and ready for battle, his expression one of grim intent as he turned his attention to Spark. The assassin blinked as he moved in front of her, and it was the only time Raine had ever seen the female's face drained of color, her green eyes wide with fear.

"Don't," Spark whispered, shaking her head.

Seth ground his jaw as he pocketed the Marker...then drew his gun. Raine tried to read the look in his eyes, but they were hidden by his lowered lashes.

"Please!" Spark gasped, straining against her bonds. "I'm begging you, don't! I don't want to go to hell!"

"It's where you belong," he muttered, releasing the gun's safety.

"That's not true." The assassin's voice cracked as she stared up at him. "You don't…you don't know what made me this way. You don't know what was done to me. Why I became what I am."

"Excuses at this point are pointless, Spark. You could have helped Raine when she was in Westmore's compound, but you didn't. You were willing to let them rape her again…and again, rather than disobey your fucking orders!"

"And why should I have helped her?" she cried, her voice choked with tears. "No one ever helped *me!*"

"You were raped?" Raine asked, stepping into the room. Seth glared at her, his look warning her to stay back, but she ignored him.

Spark lowered her head, quivering, looking smaller than she ever had before. More fragile. Breakable. Then she gave a stiff, jerky nod.

If Raine had thought the information would soften Seth's resolve, she'd have been wrong. "Your past doesn't excuse the choices you've made, Spark."

"Doesn't it?" the assassin whispered, glaring up at him, her pale face streaked with tears. "I've been intimate with you, McConnell. And I've read your file at the Collective headquarters. You know something about being tortured, don't you? Know how it can fuck with your mind."

He managed to blank his expression—but not before Raine caught a glimpse of the pain that stabbed through him, and he seemed to pale beneath the flush of anger burning along the crests of his cheekbones. He popped his jaw, his nostrils flaring as he drew in a slow, deep breath, his gaze locked on some distant point on the floor. She swallowed, needing to help him…to know what he was hiding, but she couldn't read him now any more than she could before. So she shifted her attention to someone she *could* read…and focused on Spark.

It took a moment to push her way through the assassin's anger and fear, but Raine finally managed to seek out those memories that she'd always purposefully avoided, knowing how badly it would hurt to see Seth and this woman together. But in that moment determination drove her, and she sought out those things she needed to know…searching until she found them. There was no order to the chaos. Just violent blasts of images and words. She saw the cruel, brutal scarring that covered his groin, her heart breaking as she found the information Spark had discovered in his file. He'd been tortured by the rogue Deschanel who had attacked his family, the scarring caused by fangs that had torn into his sexual organs again…and again.

It was impossible to imagine how painful the horrific experience must have been for him. Raine felt herself swaying and had to reach out, bracing her hand against the wall, her stomach churning as she tried to process the gruesome images Spark had seen in the file. Photos of the young McConnell that had been taken at the scene of the attack. Others after he'd reached the hospital and the Collective doctors had fought to put his broken body back together again.

God, no wonder the man couldn't stand the sight of her fangs.

And she couldn't help but remember the way he'd dimmed the lights in that hotel room in Berlin. How he'd kept her from grabbing his cock. He hadn't wanted her to know.

Spark finally spoke again, breaking the stifling silence. "I'm no different than you, McConnell. And considering your little girlfriend is on the hunt for blood, I'm no different than her, either."

He exhaled a rough breath, then slowly brought his gaze back to the assassin. "What happened to you was wrong, if you're even telling the truth. But it doesn't matter. You couldn't be more different from Raine if you tried. She only hurts those who destroyed an innocent life. You hurt those who *were* innocent."

"And you didn't?"

"I hope I didn't. But if I did, at least I acted thinking I was meting out justice. You actually did it for fun. You let your hatred consume you. You let it win, Spark."

"Don't me call that," she spat, struggling harder against her bonds. "My name is Elizabeth!"

He didn't respond as he lifted the gun, and Raine shouted, "Seth—*don't!*"

He slanted her a shuttered look. "She deserves to die."

"She deserves to be *punished*—but I don't want

her blood on your hands. Just…lock her up. Let the Watchmen decide what to do with her."

"She deserves more than that, damn it."

"I'm begging you, Seth. Please. For me."

He looked back at Spark, and she and Raine both flinched, thinking he would pull the trigger. But he didn't. Instead, he slowly lowered the gun to his side.

"Oh, God. Thank you," the assassin whispered, every ounce of her cocky arrogance gone.

"Don't thank me," he muttered. "Thank Raine. I did this for her." Then he turned and walked past her, out of the room, and Raine quickly followed him. He told a wide-eyed Liam to put Spark in a cell, then headed outside. A burst of lightning cracked in the distance as they stepped onto the porch, a violent storm blowing in, and he stopped to reach into his pocket, pulling out the Marker. Without a word, he handed the cross back to her.

"He could have given us more information," she said softly, staring at his stark profile. "Why did you kill him, Seth?"

"Because he hurt you."

She shivered as he walked down the porch steps, realizing he wasn't going to say anything more. That those four little words were the entire sum of his justification. It felt so…odd, the way they could have such an impact.

Even stranger that he seemed to be saying something more.

CHAPTER FIFTEEN

THE SOLDIER HAD KILLED for her. Brutally. Without mercy or hesitation.

Raine figured she should have been horrified by such a primitive act, but that would have been a human reaction. And she wasn't human. She was a Desch-lacea, and as such, she recognized both the purpose and meaning in what Seth had done.

He'd also listened to her plea to spare the assassin, which seemed equally poignant, and Raine's determination to keep her distance from him was unraveling like a spool of thread. God, how could she stay away when all she wanted was to be close to him?

They'd made the drive to the quaint bed-and-breakfast he'd chosen in silence, but even now, he kept stealing glances at her from the other side of the suite's bedroom, as if trying to gauge her mood. He probably thought she was upset by the things Seton had said about her, but that wasn't the reason she felt twisted with worry. Yeah, the Casus's words had been disturbing and unpleasant, to say the least—but she was more upset by what Seton had said about Seth…and by what she'd seen in Spark's memories. By what Spark had read in

Seth's file. The things that had been done to him when he was only a boy.

"Can we talk now?" she asked him, unable to take the heavy silence a moment more.

He pulled a hand down his weary face, seeming to give the question some thought. Eventually, he muttered, "I'm still pissed about last night, Raine. I don't think you'd much enjoy my conversation at the moment."

Compelled to see this through, she said, "Then let's talk about last night."

He eyed her with a shrewd, measuring gaze, then gave one of those Lycan-like nods. "Okay. Just out of morbid curiosity, how did you plan to handle things with Seton back in Berlin if I couldn't find you? Did you plan on using your talons to slit your wrists? Enrage him to the point that he lost control and killed you himself?"

She turned and walked to one of the room's windows, which had been left open, a set of rustic wooden shutters with tilted slats allowing a cool breeze to flow into the room, along with the warm, rich scents of the flower-filled garden. "I wouldn't have needed to do either of those things. There are different levels of trances that an Alacea can slip into. If I'd wanted to, I could have simply put myself into one of the deepest levels. Without another Alacea there to bring me back, I wouldn't have survived." She pushed her hands into the pockets of her cargo pants and turned to face him. "But despite what I said to you on the night you found me, I wouldn't have killed myself, Seth. Not when Westmore is still breathing…and the Markers are still in his possession."

"It's interesting you should bring that up," he rasped, "since I've been thinking about it."

"Thinking about what?"

"About how you planned to kill Westmore and get those Markers. I mean, you can't read him or Seton, so it's not like you could track them, the way you've been tracking the other Casus. If we hadn't managed to capture Seton and get him to talk, I think there's only one way you could have planned to get to them. You were going to let them capture you, weren't you?"

"I could have," she murmured, admitting nothing. "But what would I have done about the Markers?"

"Kellan told me that some of his homemade tracking chips have gone missing. If I looked through your things, I think I'd find them."

The guy was good, she'd give him that. But she didn't like how easily he could get into her head, and she lifted her brow with a cynical arch. "Is this the part where you call me stupid and suicidal again?"

He shoved both hands through his short hair, his shoulders and arms thick with bunched muscle. "I'm not going to yell at you." They were tight, controlled words, as if he was making an effort to sound calm. "I just…I don't understand why you're so willing to throw your life away. I know you went through hell, that you miss your sister, but…Christ, Raine, you *survived*. Why can't you just take a step back and let me help you?"

"I *am* letting you help me."

He stared at her through narrowed eyes, his gaze searching, his tension evident in the grim lines of his expression. "I want you to stop taking stupid risks with your life."

"I don't consider them stupid, Seth. I see them as necessary." A slight smile touched her lips, her voice softer as she said, "And despite how pissed I was at you when you claimed that Oath from me, I appreciate the fact that you're with me now."

"You're just never going to stop, are you?" He gave a tired sigh and slumped back against the antique armoire that stood behind him, a high four-poster bed looming off to her left. "I swear I've never known a woman who's as crazy as you are, Raine. Or who's as brave."

As soon as the husky words left his mouth, she could feel the color bleed out of her face. "Please, don't say that."

"Why not?" he muttered, rolling his shoulder. "It might drive me bat shit, but it's true."

To her horror, tears filled her eyes, the back of her throat burning as she sniffed.

"Wait a minute. *Now* you cry?" His brows drew together and he shook his head. "What the hell did I say that was so bad?"

"I don't want to talk about it," she whispered, wondering if she'd ever felt like such an idiot.

"Jesus, Raine. C'mon." His voice was raw. "You've gotta give me something."

She sobbed harder, unable to control the tears, her mouth trembling as she covered it with her hand. Choking back a sharp curse, he pushed away from the armoire and started toward her, the rustic floorboards creaking beneath his feet, while the hazy beams of watery sunlight sneaking through the weathered shutters painted his body in iridescent stripes of gold. He looked so big and solid and strong, she just wanted to crawl inside him and hide away from the world. Just wanted to lose herself in pleasure and sex, slaking her body's hunger for him again…and again, but now she knew that she couldn't. Not when he thought she was something she wasn't.

"Don't," she choked out, when he tried to reach for her. "I don't trust myself with you."

"Bullshit. You trusted me to find you, Raine. To get you back."

She lifted her head, staring up at him through a salty veil of tears. "That's different."

"And *that's* just more bullshit. Trust is trust."

"Seth, I…" She broke off, too afraid to say that she was falling for him. That she couldn't stop thinking about him. Couldn't stop *wanting* him. The entire time she'd been traveling to Italy with Ashe, all she'd been able to think about was what had happened between her and Seth in that damn hotel room in Berlin, the erotic memories playing constant havoc on her body and emotions.

Swallowing down the lump of regret in her throat, she forced herself to say, "There are things you don't know about me. Things that would make a difference between us. And that's why I…I don't think we should do this."

"Damn it, Raine. I'm not going to put a move on you." His chest rose and fell with his jagged breaths. "I just want to hold you. I want to find a way to help make things right."

"There's nothing you can do."

His heavy-lidded gaze burned with determination. "You're wrong. I'll hold you and I'll make it better. There may be a lot of things I can't do, *but I can do this*." The dark intensity of his voice made her shiver, a wave of heat crawling up her chest, burning beneath her skin. "I can be there for you, if you'll just let me."

"Why are you doing this? It doesn't…it doesn't make any sense."

He lifted his hand as if he was going to curl it around the back of her neck, then paused, his sharp gaze falling to her hair. He studied her face, reading the tension there, and slowly lowered his hand, fisting it at his side. "When I first found you at Westmore's compound, I knew you were going to be important to me." The husky words were rough and low. "I couldn't explain it, and I didn't know how, but I *knew* it was true. And now? Now, I'm just trying to figure it out. But you keep pushing me away."

Her frustration flared. "I only push you away because I don't know what else to do."

"And you think I do?" A bitter snort. Then a hard roll of his shoulders. "This…whatever the hell is going on between us…this kind of shit is *not* normal for me, Raine."

Softly, she said, "I know that."

"Then help me deal with it," he pleaded, a deep notch etched between his brows.

Her heart turned over in her chest, and if it weren't for her guilt, she would have thrown herself at his feet and begged him for a chance at…anything. Whatever she could get. But she couldn't change who she was or the things she'd done. Couldn't let go of her fear…or her shame. "We're too different, Seth."

"Who gives a fuck? Yeah, we have shit to work through, but what couple doesn't?" The green of his eyes burned with the savage force of his frustration. "Damn it, Raine, you're brave enough to give us a chance. I know you are."

She wet her trembling lips. "That's just it. I'm not brave at all."

"Like hell you aren't. I don't know anyone else, man or woman, who could have gone through what you went through without letting those bastards break them."

"God, don't say that." She couldn't hold back a fresh surge of tears. "You have no idea how wrong you are."

"I'm not wrong. It's the truth."

"No, it's *not* the truth. The truth is that I cheated!" she shouted, completely losing it as she cried harder. He seemed stricken by the tears pouring down her cheeks, a guttural curse on his lips as he finally grabbed hold of her, pulling her against his chest and wrapping those powerful arms around her in a strong, possessive embrace.

"I know you don't want to be held, but I need to hold you," he growled, his heartbeat pounding beneath her ear as she relented and tucked her head under his chin, pulling in a dizzying breath of his scent. "So while I'm doing it, why don't you explain what you mean by cheating?"

She shook her head, trembling, her hands fisted on his hips. "It's too embarrassing."

"Raine, what happened to you," he rasped, pressing a tender kiss against the part in her hair, "it's not something to be embarrassed about."

"I know that. I mean—it's not like I could have stopped them. But I…"

"Go on," he coaxed, holding her tighter.

"I'm ashamed of how I handled it," she confessed, her voice cracking at the end.

"What do you mean, honey?"

She blew out a shuddering breath and let her tears soak into the warm cotton of his shirt, then quietly said, "I used my Alacea powers to go into an Aldori trance. Basically, it means that I…I went away. I separated my mind from my body. I don't really remember the rapes. Just bits and pieces, like when they would pull my hair."

"And this trance is what you're ashamed of?" he asked in a deep, husky rumble.

"Yes." She ground her teeth so hard that it hurt. "It's awful, isn't it? I mean, what kind of coward would just hide like that?"

"Raine, you did the right thing."

She stiffened with shock, pulling back from his chest so that she could see his face, though he kept his arms looped around her. "How can you say that?"

"Because it saved you."

"But at what price? It was so…cowardly. So weak."

A muscle pulsed in his jaw, his voice a ragged slash

of sound. "Christ, Raine. What you did isn't something to be ashamed of. It made you a survivor."

"You have no idea how the Deschanel would look at this," she whispered. "They consider running or hiding the ultimate sign of weakness, and would rather die than turn away from a confrontation."

He made a thick sound of disgust. "I don't give a shit how the vampires look at it. I'm only thankful that you were smart enough to save yourself."

"Yeah, I saved myself," she croaked. "But I got my sister killed."

His gaze softened with compassion. "Rietta's death is not your fault, Raine."

"You're wrong," she argued, dropping her forehead against his chest. "When I went deeper into a trance, I couldn't make the best decisions. One time I…I lied to them about the location of a cross, which was stupid, since it was obvious they'd realize I lied when they didn't find a Marker and no Watchmen showed up searching for it. When that's exactly what happened, they killed Rietta to teach me a lesson." Her voice was strangely hollow, the eerie sound so hoarse she was surprised he could even hear her. But she knew he was listening, his muscles twitching in reaction to her words. "So I tried to stop going into the trances after that, but as soon as they'd pull my hair, it was like my mind had trained itself to go under. And when I came to, I'd be lying on the floor, bleeding, unable to remember what had happened."

"Oh, angel," he murmured, as he crushed her against him, lowering his head over hers in a sheltering embrace.

"I know it had to hurt like hell when you found out what had happened, but you found a way to survive, Raine. That's what matters. They would have killed Rietta, anyway, because they had no reason to keep her. And your brother, as well, if you hadn't been able to use your sight on Gregory to save him."

Fisting her hands in the front of his shirt, she said, "It didn't just hurt, Seth. It's like the guilt is eating me alive. I hid from their torture, and cost Rietta her life. And what makes it even worse is that she didn't even have that choice. She was too young to put herself into a trance of that depth, which meant that she couldn't hide like I did. Everything she suffered was because of *me*. There's no way you can understand how that makes me feel."

His laugh was sudden and harsh. "I understand better than you think."

She lifted her face so that she could see his eyes. "What do you mean?"

His mouth twitched with a humorless smile as he released his hold on her and took a step back, shoving his hands in his pockets. "There are things you don't know about the night my family was attacked."

"I looked into Spark's mind at the safe house and I saw what she'd read in your file," she admitted in a soft voice, blinking to clear the tears from her eyes. "They tortured you, didn't they?"

"Yeah." He coughed to clear his throat, his gaze shifting to the side as he muttered, "But what I never told anyone is that I was the reason they'd come after us in the first place. The rogues had seen me in the woods near our house, fighting another kid from my school who'd been picking on my best friend. The guy was older than me, and bigger, too, but I kept at the fight until I finally knocked him out, and the vamps thought it'd be fun to feed from a human who didn't know when to stop. And just like they expected, I fought them as hard as I could when they attacked us. I didn't have a clue what I was doing, but I managed to hurt a few of them before they strung me up to a tree in our backyard. And still, I kept on fighting."

A violent clap of thunder rattled the shutters as he paused to exhale a rough breath. His corded throat worked as he swallowed, and then he went on, his voice graveled and raw as he said, "So they made it a game. There was a female in the group, and she wanted me to fuck her, while the men...did things to me. She said if I didn't, they would kill my little sister—who was the only one left alive at that point—as slow and as painfully as they could." His eyelids flickered at the memory, and Raine pulled in a deep breath, trying to brace herself for what she knew was coming. "I remember when they dragged her out into the yard," he rasped, his voice tight with pain. "She was so scared, and I...I wanted so badly to stop myself and just give in. To do anything they wanted and save her. But I...couldn't. I just kept fighting, so furious I couldn't control myself. And then I had to watch them kill her."

"*Seth,*" she whispered, her voice thick with tears. "I'm so sorry."

He made a hoarse, bitter sound and dropped his head back on his shoulders. "And when they'd finished killing her, they went ahead and had their way with me. By the time the Collective showed up, I was barely alive. It turned out that they'd been hunting the rogues, but got there too late for my family and me. I spent days unconscious, and when I finally woke up in one of the Collective's hospitals, the first thought that went through my mind was that if I hadn't fought, my sister might have been spared."

Raine couldn't believe she hadn't seen this in his memories, but then, it was probably buried so deep, she would have had to go looking for it. "You know that's not true, Seth. Rogues aren't predictable. They're driven purely by instinct—by *hunger*."

"But I'll never know for sure, will I?" he asked, lowering his shadowed gaze back to hers.

God, she'd been such a bitch to him from the very beginning, always throwing *her* issues in his face, when he'd lived with his own nightmares and tragedies. Shame seared through her veins, making her ill. She couldn't stand to see him in pain. Couldn't stand to have him compare his actions to her own, when he had nothing to feel guilty for. "Seth, what you did…you didn't have a choice. You couldn't control what was a natural reaction. You fought because you wanted to make the ones who had hurt your family pay for their crimes. But I *did* have a choice. I chose to avoid what happened to me, and ended up causing pain to someone I loved."

"You don't think I'd have done the same thing and

gone into a trance if I'd had the option?" he asked. "Because believe me, I remember more than I want."

She shook her head vehemently. "I think you would
have fought till the end."

"Raine, fighting isn't always the answer. My sister
fought, and all it got her was more pain. If she could have
done what you did, I'd have begged her to do it. So just
trust me when I tell you that you did the right thing."

"How can you be so sure?" she whispered, undone
by the way he was staring down at her, as if she was the
most amazing thing he'd ever seen.

"Because if you hadn't," he said huskily, his face tightening with emotion, "I might have lost you before I even
found you."

"God, Seth. You have to stop saying things like
that."

His nostrils flared as he drew in a sharp breath. "Why?
I think it's exactly what you need to hear."

Wrapping her arms around her middle, she said, "But
I can't handle it. Not now, when there's so much going
on. I'm on overload."

"I know things have been hell for you, but you don't
have to go through this alone, Raine. That's what I've
been trying to tell you all along. If you just need someone
to hold you, to be your friend, I can *be* that person." His
voice dropped, and there was a dangerous glint in his
gaze as he added, "But I'm not going to lie and pretend
that I'm not dying to fuck you—because I am."

A breathless burst of laughter caught her off guard,

and she used the back of her wrist to wipe her nose. "Well, that's blunt."

"Just trying to be honest." His tone was light, but his green eyes burned with a hard, molten glow.

"I could still freak out on you, Seth. I could even try to hurt you again."

"And I'm a big boy, Raine. I can take care of myself."

She stared back at him through a teary haze…so tempted she could feel the violent, potent force of desire pulsing in every cell of her body. It throbbed in her earlobes and on the backs of her knees. In the sensitive creases of her elbows and in her nipples…and deeper within, where she felt heavy and warm and achingly empty.

"And more importantly," he added, "I would never hurt *you*. Despite what you've seen in my memories, I *can* be gentle." A playful, sexy grin touched his mouth. "Hell, I'd even let you be on top."

Her heart thundered as she nervously wet her lips. "Is…is that what you want?"

"The truth?" he murmured, lifting his hand. He cupped her jaw as she nodded, watching the movement of his thumb as he rubbed the callused pad across her lower lip, pressing it into the center crease. "The truth is that I'd rather take you under me, but I don't think you're ready for that. And you might never be ready for it," he said, lifting his gaze, looking her right in the eye. "But I want you any way I can have you."

As Raine stared up at him, she knew she was falling under his spell, bound by desire. By *need*. It was impossible to stop the avalanche of hunger gaining momentum within her. It was like a wild force of nature tearing through her. Uncontainable. Uncontrollable.

She couldn't let him change the course she'd set. Her guilt wouldn't let her. But that didn't mean she couldn't enjoy what time with him she had. Hell, why was she even fighting it anymore? She didn't need to see the future to know that she and this man were going to end up in bed together. It seemed inevitable, like the changing tides and winds and the spinning of the world. An inexorable truth that wouldn't be denied, no matter how many obstacles stood in their way.

"I want you, too," she said in a breathless rush, grabbing his shoulders, wanting it to happen before she could freak out and change her mind. "So just hurry."

He gave a harsh growl, the primal sound vibrating through her as he claimed her mouth with a dark, devastating kiss. It was hot and deliciously *hungry,* cranking her desire up to a feverish, scorching level, her body shuddering with the desperate need to have him against her. *Inside her.*

"Christ, the things I want to do to you," he said, still cupping her jaw with one hand, while the other swept low on her hips, pulling her against him, the thick ridge of his denim-bound erection pressing against her stomach.

"I want to do things to you, too," she whispered, nipping his bottom lip. But as she tried to slip her fingers inside the top of his jeans, he quickly snagged her wrist and broke the kiss.

"Before we go any further," he ground out, holding her puzzled stare, "there's something I need to tell you."

CHAPTER SIXTEEN

"It's okay," Raine whispered, stroking the hot color in his cheek with her free hand. "I already know about the scars."

She could feel his body tense as he squinted down at her. "You saw it in my mind? What they did to me?"

"No. But I caught a few glimpses from Spark this afternoon."

He closed his eyes, his color draining. "Damn it," he growled, breaking away from her and heading toward the window. She turned around, watching as he braced both hands high on the window frame, his arms and shoulders corded with strain. "I never should have touched that woman."

"Why did you?" Heat rose beneath her skin as she said, "I don't mean to pry, and I know it's none of my business, but she doesn't seem like the type you normally hook up with."

His tone was gruff as he explained. "It was two years ago, on the anniversary of my family's death. I got… hell, I probably drank enough to kill me. Got lucky that it didn't. But when I finally sobered up, I found myself in a hotel room with her. I couldn't even tell you what had happened. I don't remember."

"Well, at least you didn't do anything crazy, like tattoo her name across your backside," she murmured, relieved when his shoulders shook with silent laughter. Raine knew he would turn around soon…hopefully picking up where they'd just left off, so she quickly turned the lights out, sinking the room into shadows as muted shafts of fading sunshine slipped through the shutters. She needed those shadows to cover the evidence of her own physical scars, desperate to do whatever she could to keep the past from intruding on this moment.

With her heart hammering from excitement, Raine bent down to take off her shoes. When she straightened, Seth was pulling off his shirt as he came toward her, and she damn near drooled as she stared at his broad chest. He was no longer wearing any bandages, and even the angry, healing welts that she'd made with her talons seemed incredibly sexy, though she hated the fact that she'd caused him pain.

While his expression was nothing short of severe, all hard lines and rugged angles, it was pure lust that burned in his eyes as he reached for her and crushed her against him, his mouth taking hers in a raw, dominating kiss. He made a thick sound in the back of his throat, the kiss turning explosive as his big hands roamed her figure, stroking roughly over her back and hips, before curving around her ass.

"Need you," he snarled in a low, gravelly rumble, hoisting her against the front of his body as he took her down to that massive, four-poster bed. He didn't give her any time to panic, ravaging her mouth with those deep,

drugging kisses as he came down over her, grasping the hem of her fitted black T-shirt and shoving it above her breasts. As he ripped the shirt over her head, he took a swollen, silk-covered nipple between his teeth, his breath choppy and rough as the dusky shadows deepened, church bells ringing out crisply somewhere in the distance, while the thunder still bellowed and rolled. Her bra quickly followed her T-shirt, his hot mouth closing hungrily over a hard peak and suckling strong enough that it arched her back. A sharp cry spilled from her lips as Raine gripped his powerful shoulders, his skin warm beneath her palms as he growled and moved to her other breast. His talented lips and tongue created a hot, exquisite suction that had her gasping, her nails digging into his firm flesh, her body eager to feel his rippling muscles pressed against her.

Just live in the moment, she thought, her hips lifting… begging…seeking. *Just live in the now.*

"I want you naked." Her voice was shaky and hoarse, her pulse rushing so hard it was a chaotic roar in her ears. He fed another visceral growl into her mouth as they rolled across the mattress, ripping at each other's buttons and zippers, desperate to reach hot, bare skin. Raine made guttural sounds that she'd never heard herself make before, driven by a primal, violent desperation to get him inside her—to feel his hard, thick body filling her up and possessing her.

The storm raged, lightning crashing outside, shaking the shutters as he braced himself above her on his elbows, his hips wedged tight between her spread thighs.

He rolled his hips, rubbing his cock against her slippery flesh, and her belly hollowed out with a sharp breath, her muscles trembling. But she wasn't afraid. She was on fire, needing him so badly she wanted to scream.

"I won't go inside you yet." His voice was husky and dark, his body shuddering as he struggled for control. "I just want to feel you."

"It's wonderful," she whispered, the care he was taking bringing tears to her eyes. The guy was too freaking good to be true—but damn it, she didn't want careful. Not now, when his acceptance of her darkest, most shameful secrets had burned its way through her worries and fears, turning them to ash. All she wanted was for Seth McConnell to lose his control. To see this magnificent male reduced to the same gnawing desperation that was pumping through her veins, driving her insane.

Reaching between them, Raine wrapped her hand around his shaft, startled again by how big he was. But she wanted him too much to worry.

"Is it okay if I touch you like this?" she asked, suddenly realizing that he'd gone completely still, not even breathing, his face turned away so that she couldn't see his expression.

"Anything," he growled, and his hips punched forward, forcing her hand to slide down the length of that hot, thick staff. "Just…just not your mouth."

Oh… Though she'd never really gone for the whole oral sex thing, at that moment Raine wanted so badly to go down on him. She wanted to give him pleasure and feel that warm, silken skin against her lips. Wanted that taut, slick head pushing against her tongue. But she didn't want to do anything that was going to bring back his own horrific memories, so she satisfied herself with touching him instead. The thick ridges of scar tissue pressed against her palm, her heart breaking as she thought of how much it must have hurt when the rogue vampires had tortured him with their bites. God, no wonder he equated feeding with pain—and she could no longer blame him for his reaction when he'd seen her fangs. His memories still haunted him, and she'd have been lying if she said she didn't understand.

"Damn it, Raine. I can't wait." He swiftly pulled out of her hold, his voice raspier than she'd ever heard it. "Have to get inside you. *Now*."

"Then roll over so I can be on top." Though she wasn't afraid, she didn't want to take any chances. If she could be on top, she'd be in control....

As he reached down and pushed two long fingers inside her, preparing her for his body, he rubbed his lips across her flushed cheek, nuzzling the warmth of her skin. "You're not going to freak."

"You sound awfully sure of that."

"I *am* sure of it." He put his face above hers, so that he could watch her eyes as he did something wicked with his fingers that made her shiver and gasp. "I plan to keep you so busy coming, you won't be able to think about anything but how good it feels."

Her chest shook with a soft laugh as she ran her palms down his back, then over his tight ass. "You are so cocky, McConnell."

His eyes crinkled sexily at the corners as he stared down at her. "Only some parts of me."

"Well, I like *all* parts of you," she told him, smoothing her hands up his sides, his muscles sharply defined and packed with strength.

There was no panic or fear. The only thoughts in her mind were how much she wanted him…how much she needed him.

"And if it means I get to be with you," he growled, already rolling to his back and pulling her over his chest, her thighs straddling his waist, "I'll stand on my head and sing opera. You name it. I don't care. I'll do it."

He sounded so desperate, so eager, that Raine couldn't help but grin down at him, a youthful excitement coursing through her veins that reminded her of the sharp-edged, heart-pounding anticipation she'd felt as a child whenever she'd known something wonderful was about to happen.

She scooted back a little, so that she was poised above him, and let her head fall back as she closed her eyes, giving herself over to the devastating sensations that were surging inside her. There was so much warmth and happiness. Something was burning within her—an emotion more powerful than anything she'd ever known, and she clung to it as she felt him reach down and grasp that thick shaft, angling it upward, so that the blunt tip was pressing a hot, slick kiss against the opening of her body.

The moment was simply…*perfect*. Thunder rumbled and crashed beyond the windows, the room steamy and richly scented with the wild, cleansing scents of rain and flowers and Seth—an intimate cocoon removed from the harsh realities of the war and their future. She knew this stolen moment would be ripped away from her before she was ready, and so Raine clung to the perfection of it, lost to its provocative beauty, determined to fight for it for as long as she could.

"You ready?" he rasped, the brutal edge of need in his rough voice making her melt for him, her body a soft, molten glow, eager for everything he could give her. He shuddered beneath her, a visceral bite to his words as he demanded, "Damn it, Raine, are you ready for me?"

SETH STARED UP at her as she slowly lowered her head and opened her eyes, the gray striations flashing like lightning against a sky of dark Alacea blue—and then she whispered, "Oh, yeah."

The instant the words left her lips, he started pushing into her, using both hands to grasp her hips. He lowered his gaze, his jaw clenched as he watched the broad crown penetrate that delicate opening, his eyes nearly rolling back in his head at how perfectly she gripped him. *Hot. Slick. Tighter than anything I've ever had.*

Christ, she was so narrow inside. *So small.* It made him ill to think of how badly the Casus must have hurt her.

Maybe he was a bastard for pushing her to do this, but damn it, he wanted to make her feel good. Wanted to show her that she didn't have to let those sadistic monsters win. That her life could be hers again.

And yeah, he wanted to fuck her more than he'd wanted anything in…well, in forever.

But he was going to take this slow, even if it killed him. If it took an hour for her tender little sex to take him, then he'd grit his teeth and enjoy every goddamn second of it.

Still keeping one hand on her hip, he reached up just as she'd taken the engorged head completely inside her, careful not to touch that long, golden hair as he grasped the back of her neck and pulled her down to him. Her tight nipples pressed against his chest, pulling a raw sound from his throat as he took her mouth, her lips soft and sweet and deliciously full. Flicking his tongue across that sexy crease in her bottom lip, he shuddered as he thought of how it would feel to have her plush mouth wrapped around him—hating that it was something he'd never be able to enjoy. But he was enjoying *this,* the throaty sounds she made as her spine curved in perfect grace and her body took him a little deeper, nearly doing him in. Determined not to embarrass himself, Seth sucked in a deep breath and fought to keep it together. But it was damn near impossible. He'd been on the edge for too long, craving this woman for months.

Just don't lose it, he silently snarled. But, damn it, she was killing him, her body melting around him in a tight, slick hold that felt better than anything he'd ever imagined. He was shaking, fighting to keep control… determined to make it good for her. Then he lifted his gaze from the place where they were joined to find her watching him with those beautiful, soul-deep eyes…the smallest shadow of a smile on her lush mouth…and he nearly died. No one had ever looked at him like that… as if she could see right inside him. As if she *knew* him, inside and out.

"Seth," she panted, a gasp spilling from her lips as he tightened his grip on her hips and sat up, rubbing his tongue across one of those ripe, pink nipples. With her arms wrapped around his head, holding him to her, she whispered, "You know what I said the other night about not being able to handle your aggressive side?"

"Yeah?" He moved to her other breast, loving how she tasted…how she felt against his lips and tongue.

"I was wrong. I need more," she said on a breathless moan, suddenly jamming her hips down, and despite the grip he had on her, she managed to take in another thick inch. "Stop holding back."

"Damn it, Raine." He lifted his head, giving her a hot look of warning. "Don't do that again. I'm going to be gentle with you even if it kills me."

"Well, it's killing me," she snapped, struggling against his hold.

"You'll survive," he barked, trying to keep a grip on her slick skin as she bounced on him, forcing another inch inside her…then another. "Goddamn it, stop that!"

"No." She leaned forward, biting down hard on the cord between his neck and shoulder, exacting just enough pressure to make him feel the burn without breaking the skin…and got exactly what she'd demanded. Undone by that primal act of aggression, Seth cursed as he swiftly

rolled over, reversing the position of their bodies, her eyes glowing with triumph as she found herself pinned beneath him. The little crossbreed was playing with fire, pushing him, and he only prayed she wasn't going to get burned.

"Spread your legs wider," he said. The instant she did, he gave a rough, guttural roar as his hips instinctively punched forward, shoving over half his length inside her. And as a sharp tingle began running along the length of his cock, like a warm electric vibration, he understood what Seton had been talking about. It must have been an Alacea thing, because he'd never heard of this happening with the Deschanel—and it was going to completely break him.

"Goddamn it," he snarled, his body burning as he stretched her arms over her head. He couldn't stop himself as he pulled back his hips, then slammed back inside, going all the way to the hilt, the heavy penetration jerking a sharp cry from her throat. "I was trying to be gentle with you!"

"I don't need gentle," she gasped, writhing beneath him, her storm-dark eyes burning with satisfaction. "I need *this*. I need you to let go!"

"Shit," he growled, completely losing it. He pressed her hands into the pillow as he began riding her with deep, jarring thrusts, grinding against her at the end of each hammering downstroke, desperate to feel her hot, slick flesh clasping every throbbing inch of him. "It's insane."

"What is?"

"You. *This.*" He struggled to say something that made sense, but his friggin' brain was fried.

Not that sex didn't normally feel good. The whole point of it, after all, was pleasure. But this…being inside Raine, it was surreal. So damn intense he didn't want it to end, and he found himself slowing his pace, determined to make it last. But even though he'd eased off the speed, he was still riding her with heavy lunges. The slick, wet sounds of their bodies coming together filled the air, while the heady scent of her skin filled his head, those damn little electric vibrations nearly stopping his heart. He placed a kiss on her shoulder, then the side of her throat, letting his tongue rest against the heavy beat of her pulse. If he'd had fangs, Seth knew in that moment that he would have wanted them to pierce that pale skin and lay claim to the rich blood pumping within. A bizarre thought for a guy like him, but one he couldn't deny.

"You okay?" he asked, releasing her hands so that he could brace his weight on one arm, his other hand sliding down her side.

"I'M BRILLIANT," RAINE told him, loving the way his hard muscles bunched beneath his skin as he moved over her, *inside her.* She wanted to bite him so badly she was drooling. Wanted to lick him. *Everywhere.* "Honestly, Seth, I'm great. Stop worrying."

He touched his mouth to her shoulder again. "Don't want to hurt you."

She loved how his phrases were becoming shorter, gruffer, as if he had to concentrate to get the words out.

He was getting close—but he was holding himself back… waiting for her, and she knew she had to be honest with him.

"Just so you know," she gasped, "I don't ever come during sex."

He drove himself deep and held, pulsing inside her, his green eyes narrowed…dark with determination. "You will with me."

"But it's… There could be a problem."

"What kind of problem?" he asked, brushing the pad of his thumb over her nipple, his body buried so deep in hers she could feel the throbbing rhythm of his heartbeat.

"Um, I don't really want to…"

"It's okay, Raine. You can tell me anything." He pushed deeper, wedging himself inside her until his slick hips were pressed tight against her inner thighs. "Gideon told me that it's not always easy for female Deschanel to orgasm without first taking a man's vein. Is that why?"

"Not really. I mean…that didn't seem to be a problem the last time we were…intimate." She chewed on her lower lip, then said, "But something will happen if I come when you're inside me. Something I've heard can be unsettling for some males."

His head tilted a bit to the side, curiosity mixing with the lust on his gorgeous face as the last streams of sunlight began to fade, the rain falling softly against the tiled roof and splattering against the shutters. "What kind of something?"

"It's an Alacea thing. When our powers reach a

certain level of maturity, we, um, kinda become…sexually charged."

"I know." His eyes burned. "I can already feel that charge just from being inside you."

"But if I orgasm, that sensation is going to be even more…intense."

"Then go for it, sweetheart." A sexy, lopsided grin touched his mouth. "There's not a damn thing you could do to scare me away."

He curled his hand around the back of her knee, pressing it toward her chest so that he could grind into her body at a deeper angle…and her eyes nearly rolled back in her head.

"You like that, Raine?" As Seth stared down at her, gauging her reaction, her head shot back and her fangs dropped, glinting beneath the sensual curve of her upper lip. "I guess you do," he growled, more than a little surprised with himself, since he was finding it incredibly sexy that he'd just made those sharp little fangs release.

"I'm sorry!" She turned her face to the side, her body stiffening beneath him.

"Don't be sorry." He kissed her temple, then the corner of a closed eye, unable to get enough of how her tender sex clung to his shaft, trying to hold him inside. "You have no idea how much I hated seeing you feed from Granger," he confessed, touching his mouth to the sensitive skin beneath her ear, her breath quickening as he shifted his body a little higher over hers, increasing the pressure on her clit. "Not because you needed the blood, but because he was giving you something that I *can't*. But I can give you other things, Raine. I can make you feel good, if you'll let me."

"I don't know how," she told him, her voice trembling and soft.

"Just stop fighting it. Let yourself go, and let your body have what it wants."

She blinked up at him, looking drunk on lust, her face glowing and flushed and beautiful. "But my body just wants *you*."

"Then we're good here," he managed to get out between his ragged breaths, satisfaction surging thickly through his veins as he started moving inside her again. "Because, honey, you've got me."

RAINE TRIED TO SAY something in response, to tell him how wonderfully amazing he was, but all she could manage was a garbled jumble of *God… More… Yes!* Each time he drove himself back into her, she gave a sobbing cry of pleasure, her inner muscles clenching, on the very edge of release. He reached between them, grinding his callused thumb against the top of her cleft, his rugged face close to hers…those piercing eyes watching the pressure build…and build. It drew tighter, making her wild, her head thrashing on the pillow, and just when Raine thought it was going to break her, she finally crashed, hurtling into that blinding darkness so hard that for a moment she couldn't even breathe, her lungs locked in a tight, clenching vise.

"That's it," he groaned, the powering thrusts getting harder...*deeper*. As the pleasure seared through her, unleashing the full charge of her Alacea powers, he shouted, "That feels so damn good, Raine!"

Sweat glistened on his skin as he braced himself on his straightened arms and slammed into her, pumping hard and fast. She lifted her arms over her head, surrendering to him completely as he threw back his head and roared with the explosive force of his release, jetting into her with scalding blasts of heat that went on...and on, before finally collapsing over her, just managing to catch his weight on his elbows.

"Shit." He pressed his forehead against hers, fighting to catch his breath. "I didn't hurt you, did I?"

She wet her lips and searched for her voice. "Mmm... not at all."

His hips rolled as he kept moving inside her with shallow strokes, as if he couldn't stand to leave her. Not that she was complaining, her inner muscles clutching at him greedily. Despite the fullness, it felt so right to have him there. So *complete*...

"I want you again," he said in a dark rumble, kissing her temple, his cock already getting thicker...harder, his stamina as primal and animalistic as Raine had known it would be. "Can you—"

The husky words were interrupted by sudden knocking on the outer door to their room, and they both tensed. Seth raised his head and placed a finger over her lips, signaling her to stay quiet, obviously planning to ignore whoever was there. With his dark gaze locked hard on hers, he gave her a thick thrust, his cock lodged so deep inside her she could feel him pulsing against her womb. She shivered, gasping, and he replaced his finger with his mouth, swallowing the sounds she made as he forced his hips tighter against hers….

But the intruder wasn't going to be denied.

"It's Ashe," a deep voice shouted from the hallway. "Open up. We need to talk."

CHAPTER SEVENTEEN

"Congratulations, McConnell."

His head was still hazy with pleasure, and for a moment Seth thought the vamp was congratulating him for finally getting Raine into bed. But before he could ask the *Förmyndare* what he meant, Ashe said, "Kierland called me when the meeting was over. Seems—"

"What meeting?" he asked, cutting the vampire off. He still didn't have a clue what the guy was talking about.

Ashe pushed past him and into the small sitting room, his hair and clothes damp from the rain. "See, if you hadn't been so busy frying Seton—which we'll be discussing later, by the way—you'd have answered your phone when Kierland tried to call to tell you that a meeting was going down back at Harrow House. Members from every Watchmen unit who've decided to join forces with us were there for it." He sat down on the small love seat, spread his long arms across the back and lifted his brows. "And here's the kicker, McConnell. You've been voted the new security chief of the Justice League."

Disbelief…followed swiftly by…well, more disbelief.

With a grimace, Seth said, "Please tell me that's a joke."

The vampire stroked his shadowed jaw and smirked. "Just the Justice League part. They're still trying to come up with a decent name. But the security chief thing is as real as it gets."

Tension crept into his muscles, and there was a heavy dose of skepticism in his voice when he spoke. "You expect me to believe that a bunch of shape-shifters voted a former Collective Officer as their security chief?"

Ashe shrugged, a husky laugh rumbling up from his chest. "Hey, you know how persuasive those Scott boys can be. Aiden said they made you sound like a saint."

"I think I'd have paid money to hear *that*," Raine murmured, closing the bedroom door behind her as she walked into the cramped sitting room. She'd thrown on jeans and a sweater, her hair falling in wild waves over her shoulders, her delicate feet cute and bare. There was a wild stain of color in her cheeks, giving her a healthy glow, her mouth still a little swollen and red from Seth's kisses. All in all, she looked like a woman who'd been thoroughly tumbled, and he had to shove his hands in his pockets to keep from reaching for her...and dragging her right back to their bed, the vampire be damned.

Despite the surprising news that Ashe had just delivered, Seth couldn't help but resent the interruption. He wanted to be back in bed with Raine, his body still aching and hard, needing more of her. Luckily, the shirt he'd pulled on with his jeans had covered his hard-on when he'd answered the door...and was still doing the job.

"I hear that congratulations are in order," she said to him, her arms crossed over her chest as she walked to his side. "And just so you know, I'm not at all surprised by their vote."

A wry smile twisted the corner of his mouth. "Well, that makes one of us, because I sure as hell am."

She laughed, shaking her head. "Honestly, McConnell, you don't have to look so shell-shocked. They would have been idiots to give it to anyone else. You'll be perfect in the position."

"All things considered," he rumbled, lowering his voice, "I liked the position we were just in."

She blushed, casting a quick look toward Ashe, but the vampire was in the middle of answering a call on his cell phone. "There'll be no living with you now, will there?" she asked, as she returned her gaze to his face, a soft smile on her lips.

Wait a minute. Is she actually...smiling at me?

He shook his head a little, worried he might be imagining it, his brain possibly more fried than he'd realized. But sure enough, that soft smile was still in place. A genuine, happy smile that made his heart pound so hard, he thought the bloody thing might burst through his chest.

"Seth?" She was suddenly studying his expression with concern, her head cocked a little to the side. "What's wrong?"

In that moment, he felt like a tongue-tied youth, his ears going hot as he swallowed the lump lodged in his throat and shoved his hands deeper in his pockets.

"Nothing's wrong." His voice was gruff with emotion. "It's just that you're so damn beautiful, Raine. I don't know if I've ever told you that before, but you are."

Her eyes went a little wide, that sweet smile turning embarrassed. "I think the sex must have gone to your head."

"And I think the sex was so good it nearly killed me," he shot back, careful to keep his voice soft. "So good, I'm thinking I might just keep you in bed twenty-four hours a day."

She laughed, as if he was joking—but Seth personally thought it sounded like a hell of a plan. He'd never felt anything like being inside Raine, and all he could think about was getting her beneath him again. He just had to get rid of the damn vampire first.

Intending to do just that, Seth opened his mouth, ready to tell Granger that he needed to get lost, when the vamp spoke up, his conversation with whoever had called apparently finished. "I have more news," Ashe said, drawing their attention as he moved to his feet and slipped the cell phone back in his pocket. "Westmore left the apartment building and Gid's followed him to the opera house in Venice. He's going to stay there and keep an eye on him, while the three of us break into that penthouse apartment and grab the Markers."

"And what about Westmore?" Raine asked.

The vampire's pale gaze locked with hers. "Once we've got those crosses in our possession, then the four of us can bring in the Kraven. Gideon will stay with him until we're ready."

"What do you mean 'bring him in'?" Anger radiated from her slender frame, her shoulders back, twin splotches of hectic color burning in her cheeks. "That bastard needs to *die*. Not become some freaking prisoner!"

"And he will," the vampire told her, his lord-of-the-manor tone something that Seth figured was only going to piss her off even more. "But we need to question him first, which we can do at the safe house."

"And I say screw the safe house. I want him taken out *now*."

She ripped her angry gaze away from the vamp and looked at Seth, as if expecting him to back her up. But he couldn't. Not when it meant her diving headfirst into danger again. Damn it, he'd reached his limit! He didn't even want her going with them to break into that bloody apartment. He just wanted her to be safe.

Looking at Ashe, he asked, "Will you give us a minute?"

"Sure," the Deschanel murmured, his pale gaze moving between them, no doubt trying to figure out how this was going to play out. "I'll be waiting out in the car."

As soon as the vampire had shut the door behind him, Seth walked back into the bedroom, flicked on the lights and headed toward his bag, which he'd left on a low chest at the side of the bed. He took out one of his guns, tucking it into the back of jeans, then strapped on his ankle holster and slipped a few other items into his pockets. "I'll make a deal with you," he said, as Raine walked into the room.

"I'm listening."

"I'll help you track down that last Casus you're after as soon as we're done here—but just give me this one, Raine. I want you to let me deal with Westmore on my own."

"What do you mean?" she asked warily, taking a seat on the side of the bed.

Seth looked down at her, begging her with his eyes to just listen to him. "If you promise to stay here, I give you my word that I'll make sure that son of a bitch is dead before the night is over."

She stared back at him for a long, breathless moment, her small hands fisting in the sheets, then finally said, "I'm sorry, Seth, but I can't do that."

He ground his jaw, knowing damn well what he had to do. "Can't?" he grated, closing the space between them. "Or won't?"

She licked her lips as she craned her head back, her beautiful eyes soulful and dark. "Please try to understand. I *need* to be there."

"And I need to know that you're safe," he muttered, reaching down and snagging a metal cuff around her wrist. Before she'd even realized what was happening, he'd hooked the other cuff through a section of the heavy, old-fashioned radiator that was mounted on the wall, beside the bed's headboard. Despite Raine's above average strength, the radiator was sturdy enough that she wouldn't be able to break free.

"What the hell are you doing?" she cried, tugging violently at the cuff, her eyes wide with betrayal as he stepped away.

"I'm making sure your stubborn little ass stays alive. And don't bother trying to break them," he rasped, jerking his chin toward the cuffs. "They were made to hold a full-grown Deschanel male."

"Damn it, you can't do this!" she shouted, the gray of her eyes burning with a hot, angry glow.

"No. I don't *want* to do this, but I can. And you're not leaving me any choice." His deep voice was thick with frustration and his own blistering anger. "Going up against those dumbass Casus is one thing, but at least you can read them. Westmore isn't only one of your blind spots, he's also tricky as hell, and I'm not comfortable with the way he's just up and left his apartment. We could be walking into a goddamn trap, and I can't risk anything happening to you!"

Her nostrils flared as she pulled in a deep breath—no doubt preparing to scream for help at the top of her lungs—until he said, "You can make as much noise as you want, Raine, but it isn't going to make a difference. This place is owned by a vampire couple who are friends of the Grangers. They won't be calling the cops to help you."

She exhaled with a sharp hiss, her fangs dropping as she snarled, "You son of a bitch!"

"Hate me if you want," he said, "but I'm doing this because I care about you."

"Care about me?" She made a thick sound of disbelief.

"If you cared about me at all, McConnell, then you'd take off these damned cuffs!"

He pulled a hand down his weary face, then finished getting ready to leave, putting on his socks and boots. As he slipped into his jacket, he gnashed his teeth, hating that what had started out as the best damn night of his life had now been reduced to *this*.

"For what it's worth, I'm trying to do what I think is right," he said in a low voice, wanting to kiss her good-bye, but knowing damn well that she'd probably just try to take a bite out of him. "I have to do whatever I can to protect you, Raine. To keep you alive. I know that's not what you want, or what you've asked for, but it's the way it is."

She refused to look at him, her face lowered and turned to the side, hidden behind the heavy fall of all that long, beautiful hair. She didn't wish him good luck or tell him to be safe. She just sat there and seethed, the trust she'd put in him earlier now buried beneath the crushing weight of her rage.

With a heavy sigh, Seth finally turned and walked out of the room, locking the door behind him.

THE WAITING WAS the worst part. Even though she was pissed as hell at the soldier, Raine couldn't stop worrying about him. He and Ashe had been gone for nearly two hours now, and every moment felt like an excruciating year, her imagination going wild with one horrid scenario after another.

Knowing she was going to drive herself mad if she

didn't stop the mental torture, she decided to use the time and her powers to check in on Thomas, and was able to see that the boy was settling in well with his new family in Germany. With that done, she turned her focus on locating Wentworth, and finally managed to find him in Florence. In fact, the information had come to her with amazing ease, and she couldn't help but wonder what had brought about the change, considering she'd been trying to get a read on the Casus ever since she'd killed Schultz in Berlin.

Was her power getting stronger? And if so, why?

Was it something physical? Environmental? Or could it be something else?

Something like…what had happened between her and Seth?

Yeah, they'd gone at it like bunnies…and it'd been the best sex of her life. *Possibly even the best sex that ever existed.* But she still didn't know where they stood with each other. And how could she? Their future was so uncertain, so many external factors working against them.

He might have won this time, but she had no intention of giving up her hunt. Still, she wasn't going to rant and scream at him when he returned. She'd started to feel that she probably owed McConnell at least this one pass, after everything that he'd done for her…and everything that she'd put him through.

When another hour had passed and they finally returned, she knew from Seth's expression that something had gone wrong with their plan. "What happened?" she asked, pulling her knees into her chest as she sat with her back propped against the headboard, her left arm stretched out at her side, still dangling from the cuff.

He slid a wary gaze toward her, looking surprised by the fact that she sounded so calm.

"Well?" she prompted, raising her brows. "Are you going to give me an answer, or do I have to guess?"

He took his jacket off as he came toward the bed, draping it over the footboard before propping his shoulder against one of the thick bedposts. Rubbing one of those battle-scarred hands over his tired eyes, he said, "Ashe and I managed to get the Markers from the apartment. In fact, it was pretty damn easy. But…" He lowered his hand, locking that dark gaze with hers. "Westmore got away from Gideon."

Her eyes shot wide with surprise. "How?"

"Gid had a clear view of him at the opera house, but then the bloody fire alarm went off and they had to evacuate. He lost Westmore in all the confusion. Gid headed back over to the apartment and is watching it again, but Westmore hasn't returned. We're thinking maybe we triggered some kind of silent alarm, which means he knows we've got the Markers."

Raine took a moment to sort out her feelings, confused by her reaction to the news. She should have been experiencing a sharp stab of disappointment that the Kraven leader was still free, but instead, all she could focus on was the intense burn of relief still surging through her veins at the fact that McConnell had made it back to her safely. That he hadn't been killed. That she hadn't lost him.

"Well, at least you got the Markers," she murmured. "I bet Kierland and the others are pleased."

He narrowed his eyes, looking as if he was trying to figure something out. Something complex and confusing, like one of those annoying riddles they put on the crossword page in the newspaper.

"What?" she asked him.

"It's just...I thought you'd be more upset about Westmore."

She shrugged her shoulders—or at least as much as she could with one arm still shackled to the radiator. "I'm not thrilled that he got away, but we'll have another chance at him. Considering how easy it was for you and Ashe to get the Markers, I doubt the burglary caught him by surprise. I think the wily little bastard probably has a plan. No way in hell is he just giving up and letting us destroy everything he's worked for."

"You think he set us up?" he asked, taking a key from his pocket as he came closer and unhooked the cuffs.

"I think he's playing some kind of twisted game," she said, rubbing her wrist as she watched him slip the cuffs back into his bag. "It's possible that he's tagged the Markers with tracking chips."

Her worries that he wouldn't take her seriously evaporated as he turned around and headed into the sitting room, where Ashe was waiting. As she climbed off the bed, she heard Seth repeating her words.

Raine came into the room just in time to catch Ashe's

vicious scowl as he leaned forward from his place on the love seat, his focus on the three Markers that were lying on the small coffee table in front of him. "If that's true, then how do we get them out?"

"Depends on how deeply he imbedded them," Seth replied, his voice tense. "We might risk damaging the Markers if we screw around with them."

"But if he's bugged them," the vampire muttered, "then he'll be following us, mirroring our every move, until he finally tries to take every last damn one of them."

Raine picked up one of the Markers, turning it over in her hand. "Then we'll just have to be ready. As long as we know he's tracking us, we can't be taken by surprise."

They talked for a moment about how Gideon and Liam would remain in the town, keeping an eye on the apartment, as well as Spark, and then Ashe collected the two Markers on the table, taking the one that Raine offered back to him as he moved to his feet. "I've got to go and get my things from the safe house," he said, shifting his gaze to Seth. "Then I'll meet you guys back here and we can head out. I told Kierland we should make it back to Harrow House by tomorrow. Apparently, they've been lucky with these last few crosses and now Saige is getting close to having the last map decoded, so we're going to need all the Markers in one location as soon as possible."

While Seth saw the vampire out, Raine headed into the bedroom to collect her things. Though she should have been buzzing with restless energy, she felt a kind of calm acceptance of what was to come, the end of the war finally nearing. Seth came into the room behind her and leaned his shoulders against the wall, arms crossed over his broad chest, a guarded expression on his face as he watched her move around the room.

"Are you looking forward to going back to Harrow House?" he asked in a low slide of words.

She didn't look at him as she responded. "I'm not going back just yet."

There was a sharp curse, followed by a guttural command: "You're done, Raine."

"You said you would help me go after Wentworth. Was that a lie?" she asked, dropping her open bag on the bed as she looked over at him.

"No, it wasn't a lie." His breath roughened and he dropped his arms, flexing his hands at his sides, his expression grim. "I guess I was stupidly hoping that you'd be reasonable once we had the Markers."

"But there's still one cross to find. And I can't return this one until I've killed Wentworth," she said, pulling the Marker she'd taken from Harrow House from her pocket.

A scowl creased his brow. "I thought you didn't know where he was."

"I was finally able to get a read on him while you were gone and he's close, Seth. In Florence. We're talking only a few hours by train, and my parents have a new villa there that we can stay in." She took a quick breath, then rushed on. "I can't just let him get away. If I'm lucky, I'll take him down fast and have this Marker back to the

Watchmen before they find the last one…and everyone will be happy."

"Really?" His eyes narrowed to hot, angry slits. "Because I'm thinking that you're pushing your luck, and the odds are high that you're going to end up dead."

Softly, she said, "And like I told you before, I'm willing to accept those odds."

Frustration flattened his mouth, but he took a deep breath, obviously trying to figure out the best way to handle her. "Your hatred's like a drug," he rasped a moment later, his deep voice thick with emotion. "Trust me, I know the feeling, Raine. But the problem with any addiction is that it keeps eating at you, long after you've gotten your fix."

"But without the hatred, I'll be left with nothing but the guilt." She gave a breathless laugh that was flavored with bitterness. "And between the two, I'll take the hatred any day."

"Damn it, you have nothing to feel guilty about."

"I wish I could agree with you, Seth. But I can't."

"You mean you *won't*."

His expression was so tortured, she couldn't help but feel like a bitch. But damn it, she couldn't give in, no matter how tempted she was to just tell him what he wanted to hear. This was something she *had* to do. If she ever wanted to have any kind of normal life again, then she had to know that she'd done everything she could to avenge her sister's death.

Throwing in the last of her things, Raine closed the pack and lifted it over her shoulder. "You can either come with me or head back with Ashe," she told him, forcing herself to meet that furious green gaze. "But either way, I'm finishing what I started."

Harrow House
The Lake District, England

HAVING WORKED HIS ASS off in a grueling session down in the manor's gym, Noah Winston was feeling remarkably mellow as he walked out of his bathroom and headed for his dresser with a towel wrapped around his waist. Of course, the instant he caught sight of his reflection in the dresser's mirror, he winced, his body pulling tight with a familiar tension. His eyes seemed lighter each time he saw them, looking more and more like a Casus each day. That pale shade of ice-blue color continually mocked him with the knowledge that his hours were numbered, as well as those of his family.

Tick…tick…tick…

And then there were the nightmares. The disturbing dreams of him hunting and killing, feeding on human flesh and drinking his victim's blood. It'd gotten to the point that he was afraid to fucking fall asleep, every night's dreams worse than the last.

Of course, his behavior hadn't gone unnoticed. He knew the others thought he was acting strange—but hell, it's not like it should have been hard for them to understand. As a member of one of the strongest Casus bloodlines in existence, Noah had reason to be cranky. A millennium ago, one of those Casus bastards had raped a human female who miraculously survived…and went on to give birth to a child, and so his bloodline had begun. A bloodline tainted with Casus blood.

And while the Winstons weren't the only humans with Casus blood flowing through their veins, such bloodlines certainly weren't common. They were, however, in hot demand at the moment, since it was these cursed lines that were used as host bodies by the Casus shades.

Considering how worried he was about his family, the only thing keeping Noah sane at the moment was the search for the Markers and his work on the death journal, which they hoped would provide them with a way to destroy the Death-Walkers once the Casus had been killed and the Walkers had escaped from hell. Noah had written several letters asking for information and mailed them to Louisiana, hoping the crazy Broussard family he'd grown up with could give him some answers about the strange language used in the part of the journal they believed referred to the Death-Walkers. He'd had to mail letters, since he knew the Broussards, who lived out in the bayou, refused to have anything to do with computers or telephones. But he didn't know if anyone had received his inquiries. They certainly hadn't bothered to reply. The last time he'd talked to his youngest brother in San Francisco, who was staying at Noah's condo, there'd still been no response.

Either the letters Noah mailed had been ignored…or they'd simply been thrown away without being opened— and considering how the Broussard family felt about him, he supposed neither scenario would have been all that surprising.

A heavy fist knocked on his bedroom door, but he pretended he didn't hear it, not in the mood for company as he ripped open a drawer and pulled out a pair of sweats. Unfortunately, Kellan Scott never waited for an invitation to enter—but just came right on in, a satisfied smile on the bastard's face, which was about the only expression the Lycan ever wore these days. The guy reeked of romantic bliss, and though Noah tried to be happy for his friends, he couldn't help but feel that everyone at Harrow House was finding a bit of heaven in the midst of all this hell...except for him.

"I've got some bad news, and I've got some good news," Kellan drawled, propping his shoulder against the wall as Noah pulled on the sweats, then hooked the towel around his neck. "Ashe called to say that Westmore got away, but they managed to get the Markers."

"Did Saige finish the map yet?" he asked, using one end of the towel to dry his hair.

"No, but she's nearly got it."

"And what about the Marker that the psychic took off with?" He tossed the towel on top of his overflowing hamper, then turned and crossed his arms over his chest, glaring at the Lycan. "Did they get it back from her?"

Kellan gave an easy shrug, his thumbs hooked in his front pockets. "Not yet. But Seth assures us that they'll be bringing it back within the next day or so."

Noah made a thick sound in the back of his throat, hating the damn waiting. He wanted this war over and done with, terrified that any minute now one of those Casus assholes was going to take over someone in his family. Someone he cared about.

"You know what I think?" Kellan asked. "I think there's something else going on that you're not telling us." The Lycan's gaze was dark with concern. "And I think it's got something to do with that blonde witch we ran into back in the Wasteland. The one who was working with Gregory. The one you said that you knew."

Noah worked his jaw as he turned his back on the Lycan and headed toward the room's window, his muscles coiled, his insides cramping. He'd told the others he had no intention of talking about what had happened on the night Kellan had faced off against Gregory DeKreznick...and that particular witch had used her power to freeze them all in place, before disappearing. But Kellan just wouldn't let it go.

And until someone from the Broussard family answered those letters, he wasn't telling anyone a goddamn thing.

Bracing his hands on the top of the window frame, Noah stared out into the glittering darkness and pulled in a slow, deep breath. "I appreciate your concern, Kell. But I'd really rather just be alone right now."

The Lycan gave a worried sigh, but finally left him in peace...and Noah stayed at the window long after Kellan had left, lost in his thoughts, his rough breaths keeping perfect time with that ominous countdown in his head.

Tick...tick...tick...

CHAPTER EIGHTEEN

IGNORING THE PASSING scenery, Seth sat with his back to the train's window, his attention focused on the woman sleeping in the seat next to his. She'd wanted to simply go into one of her light trance states, but he'd argued that she needed a couple hours of good, solid sleep while they were traveling to Florence. Though she claimed she didn't need a nap, she'd finally relented after he'd explained that he'd caught a few hours earlier in the day.

And while trains usually made him feel restless and cramped, the seats too small for someone his height, Seth was feeling remarkably content as he sat there and watched her, soaking in her beauty the way a leaf soaked in rays of sunshine. It was a kind of sustenance, like manna that fed some inner hunger burning inside him.

He'd never realized what a difference it would make, sleeping with someone who knew *all* of him, instead of just the pieces that he chose to share. The sex had honestly been…mind-blowing, her body endlessly soft and sweet, drugging his senses with pleasure. He could have stayed inside her forever. Still wanted to, even though she was slowly killing him with her thirst for revenge. He was so damn terrified of losing her, he couldn't think straight, a burning urgency to hide her away and keep her protected boiling through his blood.

I should lock her in my room the instant we reach Harrow House. Should just keep her there until Westmore and the Casus are destroyed. Until it's safe for her again…

But Seth knew he'd only end up turning her against him if he followed through on the primal impulses. That he'd only turn whatever she felt for him to hate. He'd gotten lucky when she'd chosen to forgive him for going after the Markers without her, but to do something like that a second time would be pushing his luck.

The minutes stretched out, bleeding slowly into hours, the rhythm of the train's wheels the only sound but for the soft, husky murmurs she would make every now and then. Seth used the time to relive those heart-pounding moments when he'd had her naked and willing beneath him, the remembered pleasure scraping all the way down to his bones.

And yet…just because he couldn't get her naked now didn't mean he couldn't touch her. Powerless to hold back any longer, Seth leaned toward her, nuzzling his face against the side of her throat. He imagined laying her down in a field of soft, vibrant flowers, her pale skin shining like a pearl. Imagined all the wicked things he would do to her in that verdant field.

Breathing in a greedy lungful of her scent, he kissed his way up to her ear, whispering how badly he wanted her…how much he needed her, and she came awake with a small cry, chill bumps spreading over her skin as he nipped her delicate earlobe with his teeth.

"What the hell are you doing?" she moaned, shivering as he kissed his way back down the slender column of her throat, sucking at her soft skin, the pressure just shy of marking her.

"I don't want you to forget," he rasped, the husky words laden with hunger.

"Forget what?"

His reply was soft, his lips moving against her as he spoke. "How good we are together. How it feels when I touch you. When I'm inside you."

"Are you…are you trying to seduce me into changing my mind about continuing with the hunt?"

The words held a heavy note of suspicion, so Seth drew back until he could look her in the eye. "It'd be nice as hell if that were possible," he rumbled, "but no, I'm not trying to manipulate you." He brushed his knuckles across the softness of her cheek. "I just want to make sure you remember there are things worth living for."

"Like what?" she asked. Her voice was breathless, her slender hand trembling as she tucked a honeyed strand of hair behind her ear. "Pleasure? Sex?"

A wry grin twitched at the corner of Seth's mouth. "I was thinking of something a bit more specific. As in sex with *me*."

She laughed, her beautiful eyes sparkling as she gave him another one of those soft smiles, the second one hitting his system just as hard as the first—his chest tight, breath locked in his lungs—and Seth knew, in that instant, that he'd do whatever it took to keep this woman safe, no matter the consequences. Suddenly, everything had become so clear, it was as if he was finally seeing for the first time. Colors, shapes…*emotions.*

He *would* have a talk with her once they reached Harrow House, and try to make her see reason. Seth knew she planned on going into battle against the Casus with him and the others when they found Meridian, and he was going to do everything he could to talk her out of it. But if he failed, he couldn't keep worrying about how she'd react if he had to take action and have her restrained at the compound. Yeah, it was going to suck to have her angry at him, and he had no doubt that he'd be left groveling for years to come. But he'd do the time, if it meant keeping her safe. He *had* to…because he didn't have any other choice.

If that's what it came down to, he'd do it because *he loved her.*

Florence, Italy
2:30 a.m.

SETH HADN'T SAID much on the way to the villa, or as Raine had left him standing there with his shoulders propped against the door to their room when she went to take her shower. But as she came out of the bathroom, dressed in sweats and a tank top, he sent her a sharp look from his place against the door and finally said what was on his mind.

"It's over now," he rasped. "He was the last one, Raine."

Seth had cut his arm again as soon as they'd reached the city, giving her a hefty dose of blood, and then they'd immediately gone after Wentworth. Luckily, it hadn't taken long to find him. In less than a half hour, they'd managed to corner the Casus in a dark alley, the two of them working together with perfect timing and precision. And this time, Raine had allowed the soldier to be the one who used the Marker to fry the bastard.

It no longer felt strange or scary to have Seth helping her carry out her revenge against the Casus. What frightened her was what Calder had planned for the human once they reached Meridian.

"I said it's over, Raine." There was a sharp note of impatience in the words. "Your hunt is finished."

"In a way, yes." She sat down on the foot of the room's massive antique bed and forced herself to look at him as she said, "But Westmore is still alive."

His chest lifted, stretching the soft cotton of his T-shirt as he drew in a deep breath, his beautiful eyes dark with disappointment. "We got the Markers back from Westmore. And the Casus on your list are dead. That's what you wanted." His voice was getting harder…rougher. "I wasn't going to have this talk with you until we reached Harrow House, but it can't wait. I'm begging you, Raine. Just find a way to be happy and let it go."

"But Westmore's the one who gave the order for Rietta to be killed," she argued. "And Carlson isn't in hell yet.

When you shot him, his shade was sent back to Meridian. If I stop now, I fail, Seth."

He rubbed a hand over his mouth, his knuckles still scabbed from where he'd punched that wall in Paris three nights ago. Three nights that felt like a lifetime, but then, they'd packed a lot of emotion into the time they'd been together. Whatever else was said about their relationship, no one could ever call it boring.

"And what if I swear to you that I'll make sure Westmore and Carlson pay for what they did?" he demanded. "Will that make a difference?"

"Their crimes were against *my* family," she whispered. "You shouldn't be the one who keeps taking on the danger. You don't deserve that."

Bitterly, he said, "I'm a vampire killer, remember? I probably deserve that and more."

"You know I don't feel that way," she said, her emotions no doubt blasted all over her face, so easy for him to see. "You're a good man, Seth. One of the best I've ever known."

His eyes burned as he suddenly pushed away from the door and crossed the room to her, the color like bright chips of molten green. "So exactly when does it end, Raine? When you're dead?" A muscle pulsed in the side of his jaw as he towered over her. "Because you might be willing to accept that outcome, *but I'm not.*"

"But this isn't your choice," she pointed out unsteadily, her throat trembling with emotion as she craned her head back, holding his stare.

His nostrils flared, his voice strained. "You let me

in, Raine. Whether you wanted to or not, you did. That gives me—"

"It gives you nothing!" she burst out, cutting him off. She could sense the danger here—could sense that part of her that desperately wanted to surrender to his will and throw herself at his feet, saying to hell with revenge. But she couldn't let that happen. Would never be able to live with herself if she did. "Sex isn't love or a relationship or a commitment, McConnell. Sex is sex."

He lifted his brows. "So you're just screwing me?"

She flinched at the crude accusation. "You know that's not true."

"You can't have it both ways," he growled, scraping both hands back through his hair. "Either we're just screwing each other, or we're in a relationship, Raine. One that gives me the right to protect you."

"I'm sorry," she whispered, wetting her lips. "But I can't give you what you want, Seth."

For a moment, he only stared down at her, his gaze so narrow his thick lashes were tangled together at the corners of his eyes. Then he drew in a slow pull of air, and said, "Is this about feeding from my veins?" His voice was raw, his body vibing with hot, primal frustration. "Is that what it's going to take to make you accept me? Because if it's the only way to save you, then have at them, Raine. Drain me of every last goddamn drop," he snarled, holding his wrists out to her. "I don't care anymore! I just want you to stop trying to kill yourself before you push me to do something that's going to make you hate me!"

Since she knew the offer was only being made in anger, she quickly pushed past him and moved to the far side of the room, needing to put space between her and the mouthwatering scent of his blood. She'd sealed the cut he'd made when she'd fed earlier, but she could still smell the potent fluid rushing through his veins… and she wanted it. Badly.

Forcing her mind back to the argument, she faced him and said, "I know you don't understand, but I need to see this through."

"Yeah, I heard you the first time." He scrubbed his hands down his face, then braced them low on his hips as he lowered his head, his chest rising and falling with his rough breaths. "At any rate, there's no sense arguing about it now," he muttered. "We've got to get the Marker you took back to Kierland and the others. We can settle everything once we're at Harrow House."

He turned, and she couldn't hide her panic as she asked, "Where are you going?"

Cutting her a shadowed look over his shoulder, he said, "I'm just gonna grab my shower."

Raine watched the bathroom door shut behind him, and fought back the tears of frustration burning in her eyes. She could feel him slipping away from her, but didn't know how to hold on and still complete her mission. She knew damn well that he had no intention of allowing her to go into Meridian with him. He was probably planning to lock her up in a room at Harrow House once they'd returned the cross, and then leave her there… while he set off with the others.

And ends up walking right into Calder's trap!

His phone suddenly rang, making her jump, and she picked it up off the dresser, seeing that it was Kellan. Worried it might be something important, she answered the phone, explaining that Seth was in the shower.

"I was calling to let him know that we've finally got the last Marker," the Lycan said. "Can you give him the message?"

"Sure. But how did you get it so quickly?"

With a husky laugh, he said, "It ended up being buried here in England. In a place called Wookey Hole."

Thinking about the things she'd learned from the others, she said, "Isn't that where the Markers were originally found by one of the Buchanans' ancestors? The one who hid the Markers and created the maps?"

"Yeah, but the place has changed a lot since Alia Buchanan was alive." She could practically hear the Lycan cringing. "It's turned into a freaking tourist trap. You have no idea what I endured to get that last little bastard."

"Well, at least you were able to find it," she said, keeping one eye on the bathroom door. "And I imagine you're anxious to have the Marker I took as soon as possible."

"That'd be great, since we need to get all twelve together and see if we can form the map."

"Seth and I killed the last Casus on my list tonight. So I'm done with it."

"Ah, that's good."

"What about Westmore?" she asked. "Did Ashe tell

you we think the Markers they found in the Kraven's apartment are probably tagged?"

"Yeah, he told us. We all agree that Westmore will make some kind of move. We just don't know what he's got in mind."

"He's probably already watching Harrow House," she said. "Waiting for us all to show."

"That's the other thing I wanted to talk to Seth about. We're actually heading out of here. The odds are high that the gateway is somewhere on mainland Europe, so we might as well save time by getting over there. We're hoping you guys can meet us in Paris tomorrow at noon, at the Hilton near the Arc de Triomphe. I've already called Ashe to let him know, so he'll be there, as well."

"Not a problem."

"Great. And, Raine?" The background clatter of voices disappeared, as if the Lycan had just walked into another room. "Do you know anything about Ian's dreaming?" he asked, something in his tone telling her that this was going to be strange. Ian Buchanan was Saige's older brother, and like his sister, he had a special…gift.

"I know about the dreams," she said. "The ones he has of the future. What did he see?"

"He keeps having dreams about all of us standing at the gate that leads to Meridian," Kellan explained. "In most of them, we're all arguing about how to get the damn thing opened, and none of us can figure it out. But in the last one he had, Seth wasn't there with us. Is everything okay between you two?"

"I don't know." She forced the words past her trembling

lips, a cold sweat breaking out over her body as she resigned herself to the idea that had been brewing in the back of her mind. "He's… To be honest," she said, "I think he's tired of it all."

The Lycan's muffled curse made her wince, and she had to bite her tongue to keep from admitting it was a lie. Finally, Kellan exhaled a rough breath and said, "Will you do me a favor and tell him that we really need him there? I can't imagine doing this thing without him."

Raine said that she would, then quickly disconnected and erased the call from the phone's memory, before powering it off and putting it back where she'd found it. Just as she turned around, Seth came out of the bathroom, his magnificent bod naked but for the white towel wrapped around his waist. She couldn't control the violent wave of hunger that suddenly tore through her, knowing damn well this might be the last night they were together.

Driven by raw, pulsing need, she crossed the space between them and put her hands on his bare shoulders, shoving him against the closed bathroom door.

"What the hell?" he growled.

"I don't want to spend the rest of the night fighting," she whispered. "I just want to be close to you."

There was so much emotion in his eyes, Raine couldn't help but wish that she could read his thoughts. But despite the ease with which she'd finally gotten a read on Wentworth, Seth remained frustratingly closed to her, his mental guards thicker than ever.

He started to reach for her, but she shook her head, wanting to stay in control for just a little longer. "I'll let you do whatever you want to me, Seth. But first…first, I want to do something to you."

His lips parted as she gripped the edge of the towel and jerked it off him, her hungry gaze dropping to his breathtaking erection as she let the towel fall to the hardwood floor. Pulling her lower lip through her teeth, she listened to the rush of her pulse roaring through her ears as she reached for him with her hand. But the instant she wrapped her fingers around that hot, thick stalk, he caught her wrist, locking it in his grip.

"You shouldn't," he groaned, his eyes heavy-lidded and dark as she looked up at him, a warm flush burning along the crest of his cheekbones. She could see that it embarrassed him to be touched there—for his scars to be felt or seen. She hadn't expected the ruthless hunter to possess that kind of vulnerability, and it opened her up in ways she never would have expected.

Softly, she said, "Trust works both ways, Seth."

He stared down at her, his green eyes turning liquid and bright, searching for answers in her gaze. Then he released a ragged breath of air…and loosened his hold on her wrist.

CHAPTER NINETEEN

OH, CHRIST...

Seth's heart hammered with a painful, jarring beat as he watched Raine give him a shy smile, then slowly slip to her knees before him, her feminine little hand stroking his aching length from root to tip.

"I meant what I said about trust," she said huskily, grasping his wrist with her free hand...and pulling it to the long fall of her hair. His eyes went wide with shock, then narrowed with an intense rush of primal satisfaction as he buried his fingers in the thick, slightly damp waves, wrapping the honey-colored strands around his hand.

"Feels like silk," he muttered, his voice rough with lust as he curved his long fingers around the back of her head...then pulled her toward him, until that beautiful mouth was so close he could feel her soft breaths blowing against him. She breathed in through her nose and moaned, as if his scent excited her, and he had to lock his knees against the dizzying rush of pleasure that shot through him.

"I've never had this," he rasped, tightening his grip on the back of her head in case she misunderstood and started to pull away. "But I...I want it. *From you.* I want to know how it feels to have your mouth on me, Raine."

"Just tell me if I do anything you don't like," she whispered, the way her lips brushed the taut, sensitive crown making him shudder and gasp. Then she opened her mouth, her small pink tongue flicking against the slick head, tasting him, and his head fell back, thunking against the door, while something that sounded like a raw, animalistic growl tore from his throat, echoing through the room.

"More," he forced through his clenched teeth, unable to stop his hips from punching forward, pushing his shaft against her mouth. Then a graveled mix of sharp, hoarse curses burst from his lips as she took him in and started to suckle.

Needing to watch her, Seth lowered his head...and found the little crossbreed staring up at him, her gorgeous eyes hazy with pleasure as she swirled her tongue around the glistening head. Then she sucked him back in, taking him a little deeper, and he felt a sharp, searing release already bearing down on him.

Fighting for control, he covered her hand with his own, squeezing down *hard,* and moved his other hand to her face, the tips of her long hair still threaded through his fingers. With hot eyes, Seth watched as he rubbed his thumb against the corner of her mouth, the sight of his dark, scarred shaft sliding within the tight stretch of her lips the sexiest damn thing he'd ever seen. She moaned as he slipped his thumb beneath his cock, pressing it against that center crease in her bottom lip at the same time he pushed forward, giving her another inch—and as that erotic moan vibrated along his shaft, Seth knew he wasn't going to last a second more.

"Stop!" he barked, trying not to yank her hair as he pulled away, his back coming up hard against the door behind him.

She blinked up at him, her big eyes clouded with confusion. "Why? I thought you liked it."

"I loved it—but I don't wanna come until I'm inside you," he ground out, quickly reaching under her arms and pulling her to her feet. He curved a forearm under her sweet ass and lifted her against the front of his body, carrying her to the room's massive, wrought-iron bed. Setting her down on the edge of the bed's high mattress, Seth stood between her legs as he reached for the waistband on her sweats—but she flinched, sending a panicked look toward the two lamps on either end of the dresser, their bright glow filling the room with light. "What's wrong?" he asked, smoothing her hair back from her face with a shaky hand.

She wet her lips. "Can we please turn the lights off?"

"I'd rather keep them on."

She winced, mumbling, "I wish you wouldn't."

"Why? What is it, sweetheart?" It occurred to Seth that she'd always made sure their rooms were mostly in shadow whenever she'd gotten naked in front of him, never allowing him to see her as clearly as he would have liked.

When she didn't say anything, he murmured, "Trust works both ways, Raine."

She closed her eyes for a moment, then slowly opened them, a warm blush covering her skin as she said, "I don't want you to see my scars."

Seth frowned, wondering what the hell she was talking about. "But you don't have any scars."

"Actually, I do," she said, her gaze sliding from his. With an uneasy shrug, she added, "But they're faint enough that you can't see them when the lighting is low."

"Are they from when you were…attacked?" he asked, trying to recall if he'd seen any scars on her body when he'd carried her out of Westmore's compound. But it was hard to say, because she'd been so battered and bruised, covered with blood and soot from the explosions that had torn through the ancient fortress. Was it possible that he hadn't seen them?

Obviously, it was, because she nodded and said, "I got them during my captivity." Her voice was quiet, soft. "Normally, my healing abilities keep scars from forming. But they denied me blood for too long, which made it difficult for my body to deal with all the…injuries. Some of the wounds scarred as a result."

Wishing he could fucking kill Seton all over again, Seth smoothed a hand over her bare shoulder, his chest aching, his throat tight with emotion. "So you've been trying to hide them from me?"

"I'm not hiding." She gave a tired sigh. "I just…don't want you to see them. They're not pretty, Seth."

It made him furious that this beautiful, exquisite woman felt the need to hide from him, but he understood her fear, considering he'd spent his entire adult life having sex in the shadows, never trusting anyone with his secrets.

But he didn't want Raine to feel that way. Didn't want her to be embarrassed by her body, or to think he was a judgmental prick. "Raine, scars are only scars. They don't change who you are. And they sure as hell aren't going to change the way I look at you."

"That's easy for you to say," she whispered, locking her troubled gaze with his once more. "I mean, even with your scars, you're still gorgeous."

His lips twitched, and he shook his head. "Woman, I don't have anything on you. You're so far out of my league, I'm lucky you even gave me a second glance."

A breathless laugh spilled from her soft lips, and she didn't fight him when he reached for the bottom of her tank top and pulled it over her head, the scars just visible in the warm glow of light cast from the lamps. They were faint, silvery marks, covering her breasts and the slender curve of her stomach. Some of them were obviously bite marks, while others looked like she'd been slashed with claws. The skin was smooth, the scars pale enough that he hadn't detected them before. But he hated the pain that had caused them, his resolve to keep her from Meridian stronger than ever.

"See?" Her voice was rough. "I tried to warn you they were ugly."

"No," he whispered, pushing her against the bed so

that he could lean over her and place a tender kiss against one of those faint scars…and then another. "You're so beautiful, Raine." He nuzzled the soft swell of one breast while stroking his thumb over the other's tight nipple. "Every part of you. You don't ever have to hide from me."

She shivered, and he could feel the exact moment that she surrendered to him—that tight tension easing from her body as the warm spill of desire poured through her system, leaving her pliant and soft. With a provocative moan on her lips, she ran her smooth palms over his shoulders and chest as he covered one of those deliciously plump nipples with his mouth. Drawn tight by the urgency of his need, Seth hungrily suckled the sweet tip while he tore her sweatpants down her slender legs, then did the same with her panties.

Need her so badly. Every part of her. Now…

Bracing himself on a straight arm, he wedged himself tighter between her open thighs and struggled for control as he gripped his cock in his fist, fitting himself against her soft entrance. A drop of sweat stung his eye as he stared down at her, his body burning with heat, and then he pushed forward…and knew he wouldn't be able to take it slow. He was sinking into a plush, cushiony heaven, and there wasn't a chance in hell this was going to be anything but fast and raw.

"Put your heels on the edge of the bed and hold on," he told her, his voice gritty and thick as he gave her another inch. He put his thumb in his mouth, making it wet, then reached down and rubbed the callused pad

over her clit, her hips rolling as she took him deeper…
and deeper. When he was finally packed up inside her,
buried all the way to the hilt, he grasped the backs of
her knees and pushed them against the bed, spreading
her beneath him. "Tell me you're ready," he growled,
bracing his feet on the floor. "Because this is gonna be
rough."

"I'm ready." The breathless words vibrated with excitement, and he lifted his gaze to her face just in time
to see her wet her lips with a sexy flick of her tongue,
her beautiful eyes smoldering with hunger as she stared
up at him. She was so gorgeous she glowed, stealing his
breath, and they both gasped as he pulled back his hips,
then slammed back into her with a powerful, penetrating thrust that made him growl. Gasps quickly became
hoarse cries as he took her just like he'd said he would,
the rhythm hard and fast and grinding, blowing his mind.
She dug her nails into his shoulders as he kept her pinned
on the edge of the mattress, their bodies slapping together
with wet, erotic sounds, their skin so hot they should
have been steaming. They pushed and shoved in a violent
struggle to get closer…*deeper,* the sex more raw and
possessive than anything he could have imagined.

She thrashed beneath him, her hair tangled around
her flushed face, and Seth would have been terrified he
was hurting her, if she hadn't kept clawing to drag him
closer, the pleasure-thick sounds spilling from her lips
pushing him to a place that was dark and intense and
stunningly primal. And then she was screaming as she
crashed over the edge, coming so hard that she pulled

him right along with her, her orgasm lush and tight and devastatingly sweet as it milked him of everything he had, his body pumping into her for long, scalding moments that made him feel as if he was being turned inside out with ecstasy, as well as pain. Even though her fangs had released just as she reached her peak, he eagerly took each of her husky cries into his mouth, loving the way she tasted, unable to get enough of the way she kissed him back as their violent rhythm eased into a slow, gentle thrusting.

When Seth finally forced himself to pull out, knowing her tender body needed time to recoup, he crawled up onto the bed and pulled her against his chest. He wanted so badly to beg her to give up her fight again, but knew it was pointless. It'd taken him years to work his need for revenge out of his system. How could he expect her to give it up after only a few months? And for a man like him? One who refused to give her his vein? Who still broke out in a sweat whenever he imagined her sharp fangs piercing his skin? Though they'd each shown such a deep measure of trust that night, he simply didn't know if her bite was something he would ever be able to accept.

But it didn't stop him from dreaming of what could be.

"How does a relationship between a human and a vampire work?" he asked, sifting his fingers through her hair, loving the way those silken waves felt against his skin. Loving even more that she'd trusted him not to hurt her.

"What kind of relationship?" she asked, her fingertip tracing a scar that ran along his ribs.

"The kind that lasts, like marriage. I know it sounds crazy, but after all these years, there's still a helluva lot I don't understand about the Deschanel. Do they even believe in marriage ceremonies?"

He could feel the tension creeping into her muscles, a wariness in her tone that hadn't been there before when she said, "Why are you asking me this?"

"Because I'm curious." *And because I'm madly, desperately in love with you. Because I want to find some way to bind you to me that can never be undone.*

He could practically hear her brain working as she tried to figure out where this was leading, her voice hesitant as she finally gave him an answer. "Yes, there are marriages between human males and Deschanel females. It's also possible for a bond to be made that links the human's and the vampire's life forces together, enabling them to sense the other's emotions—but that's only if blood is shared between them," she explained, the words husky and soft. "If that bond is made, it also links their life spans, so that the Deschanel half of the couple isn't forced to live lifetimes without her male. But the female can't pass on any of her powers, the way a Deschanel male can when he mates with a human."

"I couldn't give a shit about powers," he rumbled, stroking his hand down her back. "I just want you."

She shivered in his arms, her breath hitching with a rush of nerves as she said, "But you haven't let me finish. You see, the Deschanel is only part of my bloodline. As one of the more powerful Alacea females, I'll most likely create a mental bond with the man I choose to pledge my life to."

"What kind of bond?" he asked, then immediately winced at the soft note of dread underlying his question.

She kept her cheek pressed to his chest as she answered. "One that would enable me to have complete access to most of his thoughts, memories and emotions." Her voice was starting to sound a little sharper. "He would have no shields against me, even with my powers as weak as they are."

"But doesn't caring about someone blur your connection with them?"

"It does, except in this case. A bonding merely solidifies the connection." She took a deep breath, then quietly continued. "And while it's not something I could stop from happening, I would learn to control it, giving him as much privacy as I could when it came to his thoughts, though I hear it's nearly impossible to control the emotional connection. But it's not completely one-sided, because he would be able to sense my emotions, as well."

Seth tried to imagine what it would be like, but couldn't. All he knew was that he didn't like the idea of being so open to her.

"I can feel the conflict within you, Seth. The thought of me being able to see into you so clearly makes you uncomfortable."

"There's a lot of shit in my past that I wouldn't want

you to be forced to live with," he said, pulling her up higher on the bed, so that they were lying face-to-face and he could look into her eyes. "But I still want you. After seeing the way I react to you, I don't think there's any way you can doubt that, Raine."

"It sounds crazy," she murmured, touching his stubbled cheek with her fingertips, "but I think I'm actually starting to believe you. But…" Sadness darkened her eyes, her lower lip trembling as she said, "But sometimes want simply isn't enough."

"I think you're wrong." He slid his hand over her hip, and satisfaction burned through his veins when she shivered from the simple caress. "The way we are together— that's a helluva lot more than most couples have."

And no matter what he had to do, he'd find a way to make it enough. He might not ever be able to give her his blood, but damn it, he'd keep her drenched in pleasure. Keep her so satisfied, she wouldn't care that she couldn't bite him…or that he'd kept her from her revenge.

"You know, when you look at me the way you are right now, as if you want to eat me alive, it… I don't know how to explain it." A soft smile touched her mouth, her eyes burning with a kind of bright, inner light. "But it makes me feel better than I've felt in a long time. So thank you for that. For this. For…everything."

"I have other ways to make you feel better," he rasped, running his mouth along the delicate edge of her jaw.

She tilted her head back to give him better access, and gave a soft laugh. "You're insatiable, McConnell."

"Just desperate." He groaned with enough feeling that

she actually giggled, the light sound filling him with a poignant shot of pleasure. If he could, he'd spend the rest of his life making her giggle and laugh and smile. Simply making her *happy*.

"You do know human males are supposed to have low stamina, don't you?" she teased as he rolled her beneath him, his weight braced on his elbows.

"Yeah, well, I've always been an overachiever," he drawled, and she was still laughing when he pushed back inside her, that sweet sound becoming an even sweeter moan.

As he started to move, Seth's throat burned with the need to tell her everything. That he was in love with her. Completely. Desperately. That he loved everything about her, every part of her, and wanted to spend the rest of his life with her. But he couldn't get the words out, too afraid of how she would react, terrified his confession would send her running.

So he gathered her beneath him and took her mouth, pouring everything he felt into the blistering kiss…and showed her with his body instead.

The following morning…

HE WOKE UP ROARING, but Raine had expected nothing less.

After all, there were only so many ways a guy could react when he opened his eyes and found himself cuffed to a bed. And considering she wasn't a dominatrix, he was probably going to assume that this *wasn't* fun and games, but the real deal.

"What the hell?" he growled, jerking at the handcuff she'd taken from his bag and hooked onto his strong wrist, the other end locked around one of the thick iron bars that ran vertically across the sturdy, antique head-board. Even though he was exceptionally strong, she didn't think he would be able to break free.

"I'm sorry, Seth." The words were hardly enough to placate him, but they needed to be said. The look of betrayal burning in his dark eyes cut straight through her like a knife, and she wished there was a way to make him understand. She had to at least try...

Quietly, she said, "I can't forget what Seton said about Calder." Her hands wrapped around the strap of the pack she'd thrown over her shoulder, the grip so tight her fingers tingled. "So I called my parents in the middle of the night and asked them to come here. They're waiting in the kitchen, and they're going to watch over you until I let them know that it's okay to let you go." She paused as she realized she might *not* be able to contact them if things went badly, then added, "Or in a few days, if, um, something happens and I can't get in touch with them."

He pushed himself up into a sitting position, his jaw locked so tight it bulged at the sides. "And just where do you think you're going without me?"

"Kellan called last night while you were in the shower. They've found the last Marker. I'm going to meet them in

Paris today, where we'll try to form the map. And then once that's done, we'll be going into Meridian."

"And you think you're going with them?" he demanded, the muscles in his chest and shoulders bunching with rage.

She nodded, and he strained against the cuff so violently that his skin started to tear beneath the metal, the scent of his blood filling the room.

"Please, don't do that!" She fought the urge to move closer to the bed, her eyes filling with tears. "You're hurting yourself!"

"You can't leave me here!" he roared, his deep voice bellowing with fury and fear. He twisted around, the sheet tangling around his hips as he used his free hand to wrench and pull on the wrought-iron headboard, but it wouldn't budge. Finally, he stopped the violent struggle and lowered his head, his breath rattling between his parted lips. "Damn it, Raine, you can't do this." He turned his head, locking that searing gaze with hers. "You can't do this to a man who's falling in love with you!"

She reeled, her heart stuttering as those rough words slammed into her. Shaking, she swallowed, then somehow managed to say, "If that's true, Seth, then it's even more important that I do this."

"How the hell does that make any sense?"

"If my life is ever going to be worth anything, then I have to know that I did everything I could to make sure that Rietta's killers pay for what happened to her."

"Then let me do it," he growled. "Stay here with your

parents and trust me to do this for you. I'll get you the revenge you need. I promise you. But I need you to be safe."

"I can't," she cried. "You heard what Seton said. If you go into Meridian with the others, they're going to kill you."

"You think I'm that easy to kill?" His expression tightened with a savage mix of anger and frustration. "Jesus, Raine. When are you going to realize that I can take care of myself?"

"I know you can. But they're going to target you because of *me*. And that's not fair, Seth. They were my mistakes, which means this has to be *my* fight."

"Like hell it does. When you love someone, you share the fights," he argued in a low voice, the look in his dark eyes tearing all the way to her soul. "I'd do anything for you, Raine. *Anything*. But if you walk out that door and leave me here, then we're done."

She flinched, her heart hammering as she took a step back, feeling as if he'd just dealt her a physical blow. "You can't blame me, Seth. You did the same to me yesterday. And I forgave you, because I knew you only acted out of fear for my safety. I'm just doing the same thing."

"It's not the same, damn it!"

"Why? Because you're the man and I'm the woman?"

"Yes. No. I don't fucking know," he seethed, his corded throat working as he swallowed. "But just because I know you're a strong woman doesn't mean I want to see you in the middle of a battlefield! I don't want to lose you!"

She didn't want to lose him, either. But she had to do this. She didn't want to spend the rest of her life like this. Didn't want to carry the crushing weight of guilt and failure with her every second of every day. It had taken Seth years to purge his demons. If they were ever going to have a chance, she would have to do the same.

"If you still want," she whispered, "then we can talk when this is over."

"You know, I knew it was going to come to this. That you'd run." His voice cracked at the end, but he shook his head and latched back on to his anger, his words coming hard and sharp. "I knew you were never going to have the guts to give me a chance."

"I hate that you feel that way, because it's not true. I just want to keep you alive, Seth. I can't let you throw your life away because of me. And I can't let you keep me from doing what I came here for."

He stared back at her, his cold gaze completely stripped of the warmth that she'd come to love. "You shut that door, and that's it," he muttered. "Don't bother crawling back."

The words were cruel, but she could see the hurt in the grim lines of his expression and knew he was striking out at her any way he could. Her tears flowed hard and fast and free, and for the first time in what felt like forever, she didn't try to stop them. It would have been impossible. They were coming from too deep inside her. A place that lay even deeper than her guilt.

"I'll try it, anyway, if I come through this in one piece."

"Jesus, Raine. Think about what you're doing. Are you really willing to break a sacred covenant? Do you know what that will mean? If the Grangers tell the Deschanel Court, the vampires will look down on you forever. Are you honestly willing to live with that for revenge?"

"No," she said from the doorway, choking on her tears, "but I'm willing to live with that for you."

Then she closed the door behind her.

CHAPTER TWENTY

Mount Agri, Turkey
Late the following afternoon…

NO MATTER WHAT Raine did, nothing felt right, as if she'd left Italy without a limb…or her heart.

No. Don't think like that, she silently scolded, following the others as they trekked their way deeper into the mountain. *You don't have time for it.*

And she honestly didn't. Traveling through an ancient tunnel that'd been carved into a mountain was harder than she'd thought it would be. But then, since the moment she'd walked away from Seth, nothing had been easy. She missed him so much she could barely function…and she wasn't the only one wishing he was there.

When Raine had met up with the Watchmen in Paris, the first thing Kellan Scott had asked her was, "Where the hell's McConnell?" She'd claimed they'd had an argument and he'd stormed off, leaving his bag and phone behind, shouting that he was done with her and the war. And while the others were clearly finding her version of events difficult to believe, at least no one had come right out and called her a liar. Instead, they'd grumbled and cursed, and then they'd gotten to work on the Markers, trying to create the map that would lead them all to Meridian.

Kierland had booked the group a massive suite at the hotel, and almost everyone from Harrow House had been there, with the exception of a few of the women and Aiden Shrader's adopted daughter. Even Aiden and Quinn had made it, hurrying back from Russia, where they'd been dealing with the latest Infettato attack. As long as the Death-Walkers were around, they were going to keep turning humans…keep creating chaos and spreading fear, and Raine knew it was a concern to everyone on the mission. After all, the moment they used the Dark Markers to kill the Casus shades, the monsters would be sent to hell…and the Death-Walkers would be released by the hundreds. Maybe even the thousands. Then it was *really* going to be a race against the clock to get the death journal deciphered, so that they could find a way to kill the psychotic creatures and save the world.

Wanting to help in any way that she could, Raine had tried using her powers to get a read on the Death-Walkers and their cursed Infettato, but she'd been unable to pick up anything from either species. That was another downside to having betrayed Seth. Ever since she'd left him cuffed to that damn bed, her powers had been growing weaker. With that one act, she'd managed to put herself back into a negative spiral of guilt and self-loathing, and she was now paying the price for her betrayal.

Though she'd wanted to simply go and hide away in

a corner, where she could have some quiet time to try and sort out the chaotic mess of her emotions, she had put on a brave face, knowing damn well that there was work to be done. She and the others had spent hours in that hotel suite, placing the twelve Dark Markers into different configurations, doing everything they could to create some kind of map—and then she'd finally seen it. Not landforms or coastlines. Not rivers or roads. Not coordinates or a diagram or even a map. But one simple word.

Ararat.

When Raine had pointed it out to the others, they'd frowned, not a single one of them making the connection. Rolling her eyes, she'd said, "Oh, come on. Are you telling me that I'm the only one here who ever went to Sunday school?"

"Sunday school?" Aiden had snorted, while someone else had muttered, "Is anyone else as confused as I am?"

Looking around the group, Raine had said, "Mount Ararat is the mountain where Noah landed the ark after the flood. It's actually a mountain in Turkey called Mount Agri."

"No shit? I know that name," Gideon had drawled, a wide smile spreading across his gorgeous face. The vampire had joined up with them a few hours after they'd gathered at the hotel, everyone agreeing that it was more important to have him there rather than waiting for Westmore to show back in Italy. And since Spark had finally been transferred to one of the Italian

Watchmen compounds, Liam had been able to come along, as well.

"Ashe and I have a niece who works in the town at the base of Mount Agri," the vamp had gone on to say. "She married a human who holds office in the local government. I've been to visit and we've gone skiing at one of the mountain's resorts."

So now here they were, in Turkey, freezing their asses off. Gideon had called his niece and asked her husband to have an avalanche warning declared, which had cleared the area of locals and tourists. But they were hardly alone. Watchmen from all over the world had shown up to help with the fight, and Raine had liked the ones she'd met, except for a guy named Remy from the Paris compound. The shifter had apparently met Seth when the soldier had stopped into his compound to pick up some weapons, and the guy had been vocal in his complaints about a former Collective officer being voted as the new security chief for their still-unnamed organization.

Remy had also enjoyed pointing out that Seth had failed to show for the fight. Kierland had warned the others from his unit to simply say that McConnell had been held up with some personal business that couldn't be ignored, but it hadn't done much to stop the talk that was spreading, which only added to Raine's feelings of guilt. Here McConnell was trying to start a new life for himself, and she'd managed to make him look as though he'd turned his back on everyone when they needed him most.

What made it even worse was that Raine knew, from

the hazy snippets she'd managed to pick up from the others' thoughts, that his friends were still holding on to the hope that the soldier would have a change of heart and contact them, which only compounded her guilt even more…further weakening her abilities. Then there was the issue of her family. Using her parents to keep watch over Seth had meant confessing to the lies she'd told them, which had been wrenching. But she'd needed their help. They'd been disappointed, but more worried than anything else. She only hoped they would honor her wishes and keep Seth from leaving that villa until it was safe for him to do so.

And yet, despite the fact that her powers were pathetically weak at the moment, Raine didn't need to be a mind reader to know what everyone was thinking. They were all wondering why Westmore hadn't attacked. Wondering what he was waiting for. Wondering what he knew that they didn't.

Even though the Watchmen hadn't been able to determine if those three Markers that had been in Westmore's possession had been tagged with tracking chips, they were still going on the assumption that they were bugged. So then why hadn't the Kraven made his move? Using the unique gift she had of "listening" to physical objects, Saige Buchanan had managed to find a hidden entrance about halfway up the mountain's side that led to a wide tunnel. They were already well into the tunnel, which they believed was leading them to the prison's gate, having made their way through a series of doors they'd unlocked by placing a single Marker into the cross-shaped niches carved into the center of each one. Raine had no doubt they were getting close to Meridian, the walls no longer even made of actual rock, but shimmering with some kind of strange crimson glow that rendered their flashlights unnecessary. But there'd still been no sign of Westmore.

Just as strange was the fact that there'd been no sign of Westmore's Kraven followers…or even the Collective Army. The weak readings Raine had managed to get on a few of the Kraven that belonged to Westmore's inner circle had shown them to be in South Africa, waiting on instructions from their leader. And what she'd been able to glean from the Collective soldiers assigned to Westmore was just as disappointing, since it appeared they were in America dealing with a rogue family of wolves. As far as she could tell, no one was preparing to attack them, and more than ever, she wished she could read Westmore and see what was going on in his devious mind.

"This place creeps me out," Aiden suddenly muttered, running one of his big palms along the glowing side of the tunnel. "Are we even inside the mountain anymore?"

"Don't think so," Noah Winston murmured, his deep voice rough with anticipation, his dark hair sticking up in crazy spikes from where he kept scraping his fingers through it. "We probably passed into some kind of alternate dimension when we went through that first doorway."

Over the next hour, they passed through another

seven doorways, which made twelve so far. One for each Marker in their possession.

And an hour after that, they finally found the gate.

Though Ian had seen the gate before in his dreams, describing it as a vast monstrosity that spanned more than fifty feet wide and rose thirty feet high, the group still gave a collective gasp when they saw it. The same demonic red glow that had bled from the walls of the tunnel emanated from the cavern that held the gate, reflecting off its gleaming surface, its composition the same dark metal as that of the crosses. And since Kierland's unit was leading the army of Watchmen, it was up to them to figure out a way to open it. They spread out, using their hands to investigate its warm surface, but could find nothing like the niches that had been carved into the doors they'd traveled through to get there. While Quinn used his wings to lift into the air, searching the top portion of the gate, Saige placed her palms against the engraved metal, once again listening with her power. After a moment, she took her hands from the gate and dropped her shoulders, her tone dejected as she said, "All it keeps saying is that the twelve Markers need to be placed at the same time."

"Placed where?" Kierland asked, frustration edging his thick words. Other than the strange symbols etched into its surface, matching those on the Markers, the gate was smooth.

When Saige said she didn't know, Ian muttered, "Well, here we are, just like in those goddamn dreams I keep having. At the gate, and not a damned clue how to get through."

"Wait!" Quinn called down, and they looked up to find him using his talons to scrape away what looked like layers of lime scale that had grown across the top of the gate. "I think I've found something!"

Within minutes, Quinn had uncovered twelve cross-shaped recesses, and Ian looked at his brother, Riley, asking, "Do you think you could move all twelve Markers into those slots at the same time?" Like his siblings, Riley also possessed a unique gift and could move objects with his mind.

Though it took Riley a few minutes to get the hang of handling that many objects at once, he finally managed to get them in place. A subdued cheer went through the group a moment later when a deep groan emanated from the gate. It shuddered as a fissure tore through its center, the ground vibrating beneath their feet. Kierland ordered everyone to draw their weapons, and then they put their shoulders against the heavy gate and pushed inward, forcing the sides to open. They kept pushing until both sides were flattened against the inner walls of what looked like an immense cave that grew wider as it spread deeper into the mountain…or wherever the hell they were. Riley retrieved the Markers from the two halves of the gate, then passed them around to the others, while keeping two for him and Saige.

There was nothing but the soft rush of a swirling, foggy wind as the group moved into the cavernous space, the moist air rank with the nauseating stench of rotting flesh. Despite the crimson light that glowed from the rocky walls, they could only see about fifty feet in any direction, the fog obscuring visibility, but the place still oozed with evil, as if the very air was drenched with it.

"Holy shit," Kellan whispered at Raine's side. "We're not in Kansas anymore, are we?"

"Definitely not," she replied, her hands tightening on the long, lethal knives that Noah had supplied her with. Though the men had tried to make her take one of the crosses for protection, she'd argued that it would be best if the supernatural weapons were carried by the trained warriors in their group, knowing they were better equipped to use them against the Casus. Since they didn't know exactly how the Markers were going to work within Meridian, she didn't want to be the one who screwed up and made a mistake. She just wanted the Casus to die.

And since Westmore was a Kraven, if he finally showed, all Raine would need to destroy him was one of the wooden stakes she had strapped across her back. Then she could return to Italy and release Seth…and beg him for his forgiveness.

But I'm only going to see him again if I make it out of here in one piece.

"Where the hell are they?" Noah growled as he pushed to the front of the group, standing between her and Kellan. His ice-blue eyes scanned the inner recesses of the cavern. "There's nothing here!"

"Quiet," Kierland whispered, staring into the distance. "I think there's someone coming toward us."

"Chloe," Kellan murmured, placing his hand on his fiancée's shoulder, "can you give us a little more light, honey?"

The half-witch had been learning to use her newly unleashed powers, and was obviously getting stronger, since a warm ray of light spread out from her lifted palms.

"It's Westmore," Raine said with a stunned gasp. "How did he get here?"

A slow smile curled the Kraven's mouth as he approached. "I came in through the back door," he drawled, and there was no mistaking the thick note of satisfaction in his tone. Something was coming…and Raine had no doubt it was going to be bad. As the Watchmen kept pouring into the cave behind them, she couldn't shake the feeling that they were walking into a trap.

"The back door? What the fuck does that mean?" Kierland snarled, sounding almost more animal than man. All around her, Raine could feel the shape-shifters giving in to their predatory natures as they prepared for battle, while the Grangers released their talons and fangs.

"Well, I meant it metaphorically," Westmore explained with a low laugh, his normally brown eyes burning with the bright, red glow that a Kraven could only achieve at night. "You see, while Meridian might be a bitch to escape from, it's not all that hard to get into, if you know what you're doing. Calder and his followers are powerful enough to do more than merely send shades across the divide. In the right circumstances, they can also pull a body from the outside world and trap them here inside the prison. Not often, mind you, because it's quite draining. But Calder was willing to do it for me. I didn't even need to know the prison's location. All I had to do was make my way to Marseilles, where I had a special altar waiting. Then it was a simple matter of having the Casus pull me across the divide that separates Meridian from the rest of the world, and now I'm here."

"But…why? Why trap yourself with the shades?"

"Because there were plans to be made. But really I just wanted to see the expression on your faces at this exact moment in time."

"But you've lost," Aiden growled, baring his deadly fangs.

The Kraven merely arched a brow. "Have I?"

"We opened the gate, you jackass. We're going to search this godforsaken realm and find the Casus. Then they're going to die."

"You may take out a few before you're all annihilated, but hardly many, because you don't know how to form the prime weapon. The one the Markers' creators planned to use to destroy the shades, before their untimely deaths prevented them from doing so. And you're wrong about me losing. Yes, I lost the Markers to you—but sometimes… Well, it finally occurred to me that sometimes you have to lose before you can win. That you have to sacrifice a few for the sake of the many," the Kraven said with another husky laugh. "You see, I wanted you to think that you had outsmarted me, so that you would come and open the gate. In essence, you've done the hard work for me, and now look at you. Right where we want you."

"We?" Raine whispered, a frisson of dread slipping down her spine as she caught a flutter of movement at the edge of her vision. She turned her head, then screamed, "Look at the walls!"

All around them, Casus shades were suddenly separating their spectral forms from the cave's ceiling and walls, where they'd been hiding, impossible to see. Though the monsters barely had any substance after so many years without sustenance, their fangs and claws glinted in the ominous lighting, looking more than capable of rending flesh. There were thousands of them closing in on the group, the shades trapped in their monstrous Casus forms, with leathery gray skin, ridged backs and wolf-shaped heads.

The Watchmen had thought they would be able to break into Meridian and work their way through the prison, taking many of the Casus by surprise. But it was a trap. They'd all been so sure Westmore would convince the Kraven and the Collective to fight for him, when, instead, he'd managed to set things up so that the Casus were the ones who would do all the work. And it was so simple. By warning the Casus of the Watchmen's plans, the monsters had been able to organize and prepare.

And until the Watchmen figured out how to use the Markers to make this "prime weapon" the Kraven had mentioned, it wasn't going to be a battle. It was going to be a friggin' bloodbath.

The realization sent a fresh wave of guilt clawing

at Raine's insides, since she knew the Watchmen were going to need all the help they could get, and here she'd cost them a talented soldier by keeping Seth from the fight.

She'd been so sure she was doing the right thing by keeping him in Florence. But if that was true, then why did it feel so wrong?

While Kierland shouted out orders and the group took up defensive positions, a massive Casus shade made its way to Westmore's side, and the Kraven gave the vile creature an eager smile. "I told you the plan would work, Calder."

"Calder?" Noah growled, surging forward, only to get hauled back by Kierland. Raine wasn't surprised by Noah's reaction, considering they'd heard rumors that Calder wanted to use the human's body as his host.

Westmore returned his attention to the group. "Allow me to introduce Anthony Calder, leader of the Casus… and my great-great-grandfather."

"You're…*related?*" Raine croaked, unable to believe what she was hearing.

"That's right." Westmore's smile spread like an oily stain. "You see, not all the Kraven births were a result of rape. My ancestors were lovers, and my line has continued to celebrate our Casus blood through the centuries, plotting for a way to bring about the flood."

"But what do you get out of it?" Kellan demanded, tucking Chloe behind him.

"What do I get out of it?" Westmore repeated, looking shocked by the question. "The Kraven are tired of being treated like weaklings. We want what's rightfully ours. Power. Respect. Once the Casus are free, our bloodlines will mix, and then the Kraven will no longer be considered an embarrassing secret. We're going to become part of a new race. One that will be the most powerful race on earth!"

"Enough talk," Calder snarled, saliva dripping from his gnarled fangs as he threw back his head with a harrowing howl—and in the next instant, the shades descended on the Watchmen in a great crushing wave. As the battle began, she could hear Kierland shouting for the Watchmen in the rear lines to make sure the gate remained closed behind them. Considering the lock was now broken, it was essential that the gate be protected until they'd managed to kill the Casus.

If we manage to kill the Casus, she thought, a cold fear slithering through her veins as she saw those shades that had been shot or stabbed already moving back to their feet. They'd been counting on conventional weapons taking the shades down long enough for those with Markers to finish the job, but it clearly wasn't going to work that way.

"How the hell do we form this prime weapon?" Kellan roared, only just managing to fry a Casus shade with the Marker in his glowing hand seconds before it took a bite out of Chloe.

Though they'd speculated during their journey there that the crosses might combine to form some kind of powerful weapon once they were inside Meridian, they didn't know how to make it happen…and they were running out of time. Ian and Riley had been mashing the crosses together the entire time Westmore had been talking, trying out every configuration they could think of, and nothing had happened. Now the Watchmen with Markers were using the ancient crosses to kill the Casus one by one with their Arms of Fire, but it was a losing battle…and they all knew it.

Cries of pain echoed through the cavernous prison as many of the Watchmen who had followed them into battle were cut down, the shades already gaining substance as they fed on the bodies. The scene was so chaotic, Raine knew she was never going to find Carlson, the Casus Seth had shot that first night in Paris. But that didn't mean she couldn't be useful. Doing her best to help the others, Raine slashed out at a nearby Casus that was already regenerating from the kills it had made, then twisted to avoid its snapping jaws. The monster gave her a slow smile, then parried with a swift rain of blows that caught her off guard and she lost her footing, falling down hard on her backside. As the Casus pulled back its arm, ready to deliver what would surely be a deathblow, Raine blanched with fear. But the strike never came. Instead, the creature's ice-blue eyes widened with shock as the raised limb was severed from its shoulder, its leathery body slumping to the ground.

Blinking with astonishment, Raine found herself staring up at the most beautiful face she'd ever seen. "McConnell," she whispered. "Ohmygod. What are you doing here?"

SETH STARED DOWN at the woman he loved, and struggled to control his rage. But, *Christ,* it wasn't easy when she was in the middle of a damn war zone, taking ungodly chances with her life. He could hear the others remarking on his arrival, but he ignored them, his attention riveted on the wide-eyed little vamp.

Offering her his hand, Seth pulled her to her feet as he said, "I caught up with the rear guard just before they slammed the gate shut. It's taken me this long to work my way to the front."

"But why did you come?" she demanded, glancing at the blood spattered across his torn T-shirt, then at the long blade he held in his hand, before lifting her bright gaze back to his face.

"Did you honestly think I wouldn't come after you? It's too dangerous for you to be here on your own."

"Are you mad?" she cried. "You're the one who's the bloody human!"

"That's right." His voice was hard with pride. "I'm the man who's meant to protect your ass."

"But you're meant to be in Florence!"

"Yeah, well, your mother had a change of heart about keeping me locked up." In fact, it had been one of her mother's glimpses of the future that had finally earned him his freedom, since the powerful psychic had seen that her daughter was going to die…and believed that Seth was the only thing that could keep her heartbreaking vision from coming true.

Thankfully, he'd been able to use the *Sangra* bond to track Raine, since he hadn't wanted to call any of the others and ask where they were headed, knowing she would read their minds and learn he was free. And considering what she'd done to keep him from joining this battle, he simply hadn't trusted her. Not about this. For all he knew, she might have taken off alone with the Markers, or any of the other hundred and one terrifying scenarios he'd tortured himself with while trying to reach her.

He couldn't let that happen, considering he'd finally figured it out. Finally gotten a handle on what he needed. Yeah, his past had been a bitch, but as he'd watched Raine walk out of that bedroom in Italy, leaving him behind, Seth had realized his past no longer mattered. What mattered was the little vampire who'd stolen his heart. The woman he couldn't live without—who he needed in *every* possible way.

Now he just needed to tell her. Yeah, he'd told her he was falling in love with her, but he needed to let her know how he felt about *everything*. The past and their future. Her fangs and her need for blood. But first he had to get her the hell out of there.

"Well, look what we have here," a voice suddenly purred off to his right, and Seth turned his head to find Ross Westmore standing beside a hulking Casus shade. The Kraven's red eyes were focused on him with a look that was pure anticipation, a blood-soaked knife clutched in his hand. "You're a little late," Westmore drawled, "but I'm so glad you could make it, McConnell."

CHAPTER TWENTY-ONE

"THAT'S CALDER STANDING beside the Kraven," Raine murmured, moving closer to Seth's side as they turned to face their enemies. She could hear Ian behind her, shouting that he'd found Gregory DeKreznick's shade, and knew the others were too busy fighting their own battles to offer them any help. She and Seth were going to have to deal with these bastards on their own, and she tapped into that inner well of hatred seething inside her, knowing she was going to need every ounce of its strength.

Taking a deep breath, Raine was ready to tell Seth that she would take Westmore while he dealt with Calder, when the soldier let out a furious roar and launched an attack without her.

"What are you doing?" she screamed, watching in shock as Seth drew a spray of blood from Calder's chest with his blades. The Casus leader's body was already regenerating, gaining substance from the kills he'd made, and while she hated that Watchmen had lost their lives to the monster, Raine was hopeful that Seth would now be able to injure the Casus badly enough to keep him down. At least until he could be killed with one of the Markers.

"I want you to run, Raine! Get the hell out of here!" Seth shouted at her, just as Westmore struck out at him with his knife. Seth lunged back to avoid the Kraven's blade, then slashed at Calder's arm as the Casus tried to swipe him with his deadly claws. Westmore immediately came at him again, and Seth spun, coming around with a powerful kick to the Kraven's temple that sent him slumping to the ground. With Westmore down, Seth turned his attention back to Calder, who was coming at him hard and fast. Raine couldn't help but wince each time the Casus got in a swipe of his claws, though Seth was quick enough to avoid any serious damage.

It was taking everything she had to keep from joining the fight, but when she saw Westmore move to his knees, she reached behind her and grabbed one of the wooden stakes she was carrying. The battle with Calder was heating up, and she knew that Seth hadn't noticed Westmore regaining consciousness. She could also see that the Kraven was planning to go for the soldier's back.

Gritting her teeth, Raine quickly covered the space between her and Westmore, tackling the Kraven just as he moved to his feet. They rolled over the gritty ground, grappling and clawing, before they both came up in a low crouch, preparing to strike. Then they both froze, gasping, their eyes wide with shock as they processed the situation they now found themselves in. Raine had her wooden stake poised directly over the Kraven's heart, while Westmore had the edge of his blade pressed tight against her throat.

It was a stalemate. She knew that if she tried to kill him, the odds were high she'd end up dying, as well. And Westmore was in the same dilemma.

Though she didn't dare take her gaze off the Kraven, Raine assumed Seth had managed to deal Calder a crippling blow, since the soldier's deep voice was suddenly coming from close beside her. "Damn it, Raine. He's not worth it. Let him go!"

"I'm sorry, Seth." She didn't want to die—but she desperately wanted to destroy Westmore. "I…I don't have any choice. I have to go through with it."

"That's bullshit," he growled. "We always have a choice!"

Before she could argue, Seth moved just behind Westmore's shoulder, giving her a clear view of his tortured expression, and pain twisted through her heart. She'd been so worried about putting him in danger, but *she* was the one hurting him. The one destroying him.

Oh, God, she thought, her resolve faltering. *What am I doing?*

"Don't let this bastard win," Seth pleaded, his words ragged and low. "Please, Raine. Do you really think this is what Rietta would have wanted for you? I know you loved her, but she loved you, too. She would have wanted you to go on living. For you to find a way to be happy and at peace."

She knew he was right. She was throwing away her one chance at happiness, and for what? Westmore's death wasn't going to bring her sister back. Nothing could do that. But that didn't mean she had to throw her own life away. Didn't mean she had to give up the miracle that she'd found. That's not what Rietta would have wanted, and as she stared into Westmore's crazed eyes, she realized that his death was no longer the thing she wanted most in this world. What she wanted most was the soldier. The man who'd stolen her heart.

She could see so clearly now—not with her eyes, but with her heart—and in that moment Raine truly understood just how stupid she'd been. It hadn't been her hatred making her stronger this past week. It'd been Seth. Hate and shame weren't the things that burned deepest—*love was*.

And she *loved* McConnell. Loved him enough to go on living. To forgive herself for what had happened and embrace this amazing second chance that she'd been given. To move ahead of the past…and *finally* reach for the future.

With a deep breath, Raine lifted the stake from Westmore's chest and jerked out of his reach. "He's yours," she whispered, looking at Seth, and with her surrender came a surge of power that nearly brought her to her knees. There were no more blocks. No more blind spots. Not even with Westmore. The Kraven's thoughts were now completely open to her, and as Seth took up the fight, catching the stake that she tossed to him, she could see everything that she needed to know about the Markers within Westmore's mind.

Just as Seth drove the stake through the Kraven's heart, she turned and shouted to the others, "I know how to form the prime weapon!"

One by one, the Watchmen with Markers broke away from the battle and began making their way toward her, when a bizarre burst of light appeared directly behind the place where Calder was still lying on the ground, a guttural snarl on his lips as the Casus struggled to get to his feet. Raine spotted a flash of long, pale blond hair whipping from the light as it transformed into a glowing chasm—that tangled hair reminding her of what the others had said about the mysterious witch who had been aiding Gregory DeKreznick. The blonde reached out of the light with one skeletal hand and grasped Calder by the ruff of his neck, her touch seeming to stun him into a trembling stillness as she started pulling him into the chasm.

"Don't let her take him!" Noah roared, racing past Raine as he dove for Calder. The Marker he'd been holding fell from his hand as he fought to get a grasp on the Casus's blood-slicked skin, struggling to pull the monster from the blonde's hold, but she was too strong.

"Sienna, no! Don't do this!" he shouted, scrambling up Calder's massive body. Just when he was close enough to reach for the female's thin arm, Calder snapped his jaws, a stark bellow tearing from Noah's throat as the Casus sank his gnarled fangs into the human's forearm. The blonde gave a powerful yank on the Casus's body that knocked Noah to the ground, and they all watched with wide eyes as Calder disappeared inside the chasm. As the edges began to close, several Casus shades rushed inside, following their leader.

Then there was another blinding flash of light, and the chasm was gone.

Noah pulled himself to his knees, clutching his wounded arm to his chest, and looked at Seth. "Take my Marker," he ground out, forcing the words through his clenched teeth, a wild look in his eyes that made Raine worry for his sanity.

As Seth picked up the Marker that Noah had dropped, Kellan pulled a hand down his face. "This has been the strangest damn day," the Lycan muttered.

"We can talk about it later," Raine said in a loud voice, drawing the attention of the twelve Marker holders while the rest of the Watchmen kept the remaining Casus shades at bay. "Right now, I need all of you to gather in a tight circle."

When they'd followed her instructions, she said, "Now raise the hand holding a Marker high into the air. And make sure all of your hands are touching." As soon as they did, a brilliant band of white light formed around their raised fists, binding them together, their arms glowing brighter as someone muttered that the crosses were burning even hotter than they'd been before.

"Now what?" Seth demanded, his rough words thick with pain.

She spoke in a rush. "Now throw the crosses on the ground as hard as you can."

"That's it?" Kellan asked, sounding less than convinced.

"Trust me. The blast's going to take care of anything in this place with Casus blood." Raine glanced at Noah, and quickly added, "Which means you should take cover, just to be safe."

He scowled, but made his way over to one of the rocky outcroppings at the base of the cavern's walls, then hunkered down behind it. When the others saw that he was sheltered, they shared a dark look, then slammed the glittering Markers against the ground. But not a damned thing happened. The battle continued to wage around them as the army of Watchmen fought to hold back the Casus, while the ancient crosses simply lay there on the cold, hard ground…doing nothing.

"Well, that was a bit anticlimactic," Aiden offered in a wry drawl.

"Just give it a minute," Raine snapped, knowing this was the way—that it would work. But when another thirty seconds went by and the Markers were still lying there, she started to tremble, terrified that something had gone wrong. Had she misunderstood what she'd seen in the Kraven's mind? Had his information been wrong? And then she finally felt it. At first there was just the slightest tremor moving through the ground, but then it began to rumble with a violent quake, the twelve Markers suddenly erupting into flames. Seth gripped her hand, tugging her back as the ground started to give way beneath the fiery crosses, a molten beam of light shooting up from the gaping hole. The beam soared toward the cavern's ceiling, then detonated in a powerful blast.

The explosion was so violent it knocked them all through the air, Raine's breath forced from her lungs as she slammed against a rocky patch of ground. She must have blacked out for a moment, because when she came to there was nothing but a choking cloud of smoke, the others groaning as they struggled back to their feet. Pushing her hair out of her eyes, she sat up, ready to scream for Seth, unable to see him in all the smoke, when he suddenly staggered down onto his knees at her side, his beautiful face smeared with ashes and soot and blood. But she'd never seen him look more gorgeous.

"Is everyone okay?" she asked. "Are the Casus dead?"

"Everyone's fine. And yeah, the shades are dead," he rasped, a crooked grin twitching at the corner of his mouth as he added, "Thanks to you."

"Are you pissed at me?" she whispered, her jaw trembling.

"I was when you left me. But then I remembered why I'd been planning to do the same thing to you, and I got over it." His strong throat worked as he swallowed, his voice even rougher as he proudly proclaimed, "You love me, Raine."

She could tell from his expression that he expected her to argue, but she was done fighting her feelings for this magnificent man. "You're right. I do love you. And I'm so sorry, Seth. For everything. Can you give me another chance to prove how much you mean to me?"

His eyes were doing that molten thing again—but with love, not anger. "I think I'd probably give you a thousand chances," he told her, framing her tear-drenched face in his hands, "because I want you so damn badly."

Raine gave him a watery smile. "Then this is your lucky day, McConnell. Because you've *so* got me."

Harrow House
The Lake District, England
The next evening...

IT WAS A BLOOD NIGHT, as the Deschanel liked to call them, the sun setting like a ball of fire on the horizon, painting the sky with primal shades of red, the moon already glowing with a scarlet hue. The kind of night meant for lovers—for hot, sweat-slick skin and shallow breaths—and Raine could hardly believe she was going to spend it with Seth. It seemed like a miracle that they had come through the nightmare in one piece...but she was more than ready to celebrate.

After the Casus had been destroyed, everyone had gathered around to offer their congratulations to the group who had held the Markers, and Seth had been given his share of shoulder slaps and handshakes. But there had still been work to be done. Once those who had lost their lives during the battle had been buried, the other Watchmen (she didn't know what else to call them, considering the new organization was still unnamed) had collected their wounded and left, heading back to their respective compounds. Then Raine had asked the group from Harrow House to gather around, and though she was nervous about how they would react, she'd come clean with her friends and confessed that she'd tried to keep Seth from the battle. Surprisingly, the others had been teasing rather than angry, and she'd taken their ribbing in stride, just thankful everything had worked out.

Then they'd gotten the hell out of there—the entrance to the tunnel had mysteriously disappeared behind them, as if it had never existed—and the group had started the long journey back to England. On the way, they had talked about what the future would hold. While they'd managed to destroy those shades trapped within Meridian, the Casus who had escaped during the past year and were living in host bodies would still need to be hunted down. Quinn had flown into the gaping hole and retrieved the markers, so they would be able to use them to kill the host-bound Casus. And then there were the Death-Walkers. With so many Casus shades having been sent to hell when the prime weapon had detonated, they knew the Death-Walkers would be escaping in frightening numbers, and soon the Watchmen and their allies would be fighting the second phase of the war.

When Raine had admitted she was worried, Seth had pulled her into his arms and whispered how much he loved her, reminding her that they would face whatever the future held together. Then he'd kissed her with so much passion, she hadn't been able to think straight for the rest of the day, desperate for the time when they could be alone.

And that time was finally here.

They were standing in Seth's bedroom, the door locked behind them, the rest of the house noisy with laughter and conversation, while Kierland was hidden away in his office, trying to learn if there had been any sign of the Death-Walkers.

But in here, it was just the two of them, a shivering wave of anticipation crackling in the air. There was so much to say, neither seemed to know where to start. And then Seth grabbed her hand and pulled her closer. His deep-grooved grin was unbearably beautiful, and Raine whispered his name, the soft syllable weighted with so much emotion, she didn't know how it managed to float in the air, instead of crashing to the floor. Two bedside lamps gave off a bright light that filled the room, but they didn't move to turn them down. They had nothing left to hide. Her arms went around his neck as his mouth covered hers, and he kissed her like he was starved for her taste. Like he never wanted to stop, his fingers shaping around her head, holding her to him.

Though she wanted to just keep going, losing herself in the moment, Raine finally forced herself to break the kiss and say the words she knew needed to be said. "Despite everything that's happened, there's still so much that hasn't changed," she whispered, her hands pressed against the pounding of his heart as she stared up into his dark, heavy-lidded eyes. "You know what being with me will mean, Seth. Even if I promised to never bite you, I'm not sure I could keep my word. I want you too badly."

"Stop worrying," he rasped, pulling her tighter against him. "I want everything you can give me, Raine. All of it."

"What are you saying?" she asked unsteadily.

"I'm saying that I love you. That I want to spend my

life with you. Every morning, every night. I want to marry you and grow old with you. I want it all, Raine. I want a life with you."

"A life?" she repeated, feeling as if she'd been smacked in the head. *Hard.*

With a nod, he said, "I know it won't always be easy, but as long as I'm with you, I don't give a shit about anything else." His smile flashed, wicked and slow. "Just think about it, Raine. You can teach me how to not be such a jackass."

She couldn't hold back a soft snort. "I'm a psychic, Seth. Not a miracle worker."

He was still laughing when she added, "And I like that flair you have for being a jackass. You always look so sexy when you're being bad."

"Face it," he said smugly, giving her a lopsided grin. "I'm *always* sexy." Then he cupped the side of her face in his hand, and she could tell from the subtle shifting in his expression that he was about to say something serious. "But all teasing aside, I meant what I said, Raine. I want a life with you. I want it all, including that bond you were telling me about."

She blinked with surprise. "You mean…"

"I want you to bite me." His dark eyes glittered with emotion…and desire. "I want us to share blood."

She shook her head, trying to think past her confusion. "But…did you listen to anything I said to you in Florence?"

"I listened, and you know what? I trust you, Raine. With everything. My past. My secrets. And I—"

"Wait. Just wait." She struggled to get her thoughts straight, but her head was spinning. "You need to think about this, Seth. Once it's done, it can't be undone. You'll be completely open to me. *Forever.*"

"I don't give a damn."

She pulled her lower lip through her teeth. "You'll never be able to lie to me."

"Not a problem," he said, looking too sexy to be real. "I have nothing to hide from you."

"But…are you sure that you want to spend the rest of your life with a vampire? With a woman who has fangs?"

"I'm sure that I want to spend the rest of my life with the woman I love. Being with you is all that matters to me, Raine. But if it makes you feel any better, then I can honestly say that my feelings about your bloodline have changed. I love the fact that you're a vampire, just like I love your beautiful little fangs, because if it wasn't for your Deschanel blood, I'd have lost you during this nightmare." His mouth curled with another slow, crooked smile. "I know it took me a while, but I guess there's nothing like the prospect of having his heart cut out to finally give a guy some real perspective."

"Wait a minute." Her voice was hoarse with shock. "Did you just say that you *love* my fangs?"

He gave a husky laugh as he pulled her closer…and answered her with his mouth, the devastating kiss so hungry and hot that Raine was surprised it didn't melt her down. Then he was carrying her to his bed, laying her across the soft, cool sheets…and coming down on top of

her. The clean clothing they had put on after their show-
ers was ripped as they struggled to get to warm, bare
skin, their breathing rough as they fought to get closer
together. Within seconds he had her spread beneath him,
his body sinking into hers with a deep, desperate thrust
that made her cry out. Then he gripped her ass and rolled
to his back, reversing their positions so that her thighs
were straddling his hips as she lay against his chest. His
fingers dipped lower, touching the soft flesh stretched
tight around his shaft, his big hands holding her steady
as he raised his knees and pumped up into her in a hard,
driving rhythm.

With a groan, he turned his head on the pillow, exposing the side of his throat. "Do it now," he growled, the
warm breaths she was panting against his neck seeming
to drive him wild. "Christ, Raine. I want to wear your
mark. Want my blood in your body," he choked out. *"Do.
It. Now."*

"But I don't want to hurt you," she whispered, her
mouth watering as she tasted his warm skin with her
tongue.

He pressed one hand to the back of her head, holding her against him. "You're hurting me by making me
wait."

Unable to hold back any longer, Raine made the bite…
and his reaction was unlike anything she could have ever
hoped for. Within seconds, they both came from the
explosive force of pleasure that seared through them,
his rough growls of satisfaction making her come even
harder. And as the moon made its slow climb through

the stars, he demanded she bite him again…and again, claiming he couldn't get enough of her "sweet" little fangs. In addition to the bite on his throat, she took sips from his chest and his biceps, and each time she pierced his flesh, he shuddered hard with pleasure, a graveled shout on his lips as he slammed himself into her with a visceral, breathtaking need.

And in those quiet hours of darkness, he finally lifted her wrist to her lips, his deep voice deliciously rough as he told her to make a bite. Then he pulled her bleeding wrist to his mouth and eagerly fed from the punctures she'd made, while pulling her face back to his throat so that she could take his blood at the same time. And, *God*, it was intense. The surge of emotion was blissful and surreal, the feedback loop of pleasure burning through their sweat-slicked bodies so powerful they nearly passed out when they found their release.

Raine eventually lost count of how many times they made love, his hunger insatiable. But then, she was just as greedy. At some point they scrounged for food down in the kitchen, then made their way back to his room, and he took her again in the shower. Then again in his bed, and as the first rays of dawn lit the sky through his bedroom window, Raine slipped into another lush, tight orgasm, her body floating weightlessly in that swirling maelstrom of sensation.

When she finally came back, she opened her eyes to find Seth's face close to hers. She started to give him a shy smile…then realized she was already smiling.

"I was right," he said, the soft words thick with satisfaction.

"Right about what?" she asked, looping her arms around his neck.

"I said I'd feel like the luckiest man alive when you came with a smile on your face. And I do."

Stroking her palms across his broad shoulders, she said, "I think I'm the lucky one."

He rolled them to their sides, and his eyes darkened with emotion. "I'd ask if you saw anything in my past tonight that bothered you, but I…I can *feel* that you're happy." His deep voice was rough with awe, and Raine knew it was going to take time for them to become comfortable with the powerful connection that now bound them together.

"I am happy," she whispered, pressing a soft kiss to his cheek…then his temple. "Because all I see in you is love, Seth. And it's so beautiful." She pulled back so that she could see his face, and asked, "Do you remember when you told me that I was afraid of letting something good happen to me?"

"Don't remind me," he murmured, pulling her closer to his chest. "I was trying like hell to get you to take a chance on me, but I know I sounded like a jerk."

Raine gave a soft laugh, then leaned forward and kissed that first bite mark that she'd made at the side of his throat, her voice thick with emotion as she said, "You sounded like you cared. And I just want you to know that being with you is so much better than good, Seth.

It's the best, most amazing thing that could ever happen to me."

He went instantly still, not even breathing, and then he gave a low growl, his hands tangled in her hair as he pushed her to her back again and claimed her mouth. With perfect trust in her heart, Raine surrendered to the dark aggression of his kisses, her hands pulling him closer, her body needing him with a hunger she knew would never be sated. There was so much love inside her, there simply wasn't room for anything else. Not the past or fears or worries.

Instead, Raine was filled with warmth and light…and a bright, beautiful hope for their future.

EPILOGUE

The following night...

AS A CLOCK TOWER struck midnight in the small village of Ransk, in the middle of the Polish countryside, the ground began to shake with a violent tremor. Villagers ran from their beds and poured into the streets, the cold wind carrying away their terrified cries as they stared up at the swirling mass of bodies filling the sky. A black fissure slashed across the moonlit heavens, a thick red smoke seeping from its gaping mouth as spectral figures continued to pour out, the winds rushing with a stark, harrowing roar.

There seemed to be hundreds of the creatures...and still they kept coming, until the sky suddenly went black. For a moment, there was nothing but a deathly silence—the winds calm, the earth still—while the villagers stood huddled together, staring up into that infinite darkness. A collective gasp sounded from the group when there was a sudden spark of color...and another...as the creatures opened their bright, yellow eyes, staring down from above.

Then the darkness descended...and the village was no more.

* * * * *

GLOSSARY OF TERMS

for the Primal Instinct Series

The Ancient Clans: Nonhuman races whose existence has been kept secret from the majority of humans for thousands of years, their abilities differing as widely as their physiology. Some only partially alter when in their primal forms, like the Merrick. Others fully transform, able to take the shape of an animal, similar to those who compose the Watchmen.

These are but a few of the various ancient clans that remain in existence today:

The Merrick: One of the most powerful of the ancient clans, the Merrick were forced to mate with humans after years of war against the Casus had decimated their numbers. Their bloodlines eventually became dormant, dwelling within their human descendants, until the return of the Casus and the time of their awakening. In order to feed the primal parts of their nature, the newly awakened Merrick must consume blood while having sex. Characteristics: When in Merrick form, the males have fangs, talons, flattened noses and massive, heavily muscled physiques. The females have fangs and talons.

The Awakenings: Each time a Casus shade returns to this world, it causes the primal blood within one of the Merrick descendants to rise within them, or awaken, so that they might battle against their ancient enemy.

The Buchanans: One of the strongest Merrick bloodlines, the Buchanans were not only the first of the Merrick to awaken, but they also each possess an unusual power or "gift." Ian has a strange sense of premonition that comes to him in dreams, Saige can "hear" things from physical objects when she touches them and Riley's telekinetic powers enable him to control physical objects with his mind.

The Casus: Meaning *violent death,* the Casus are an immortal race of preternatural monsters who were imprisoned by the Merrick and the Consortium more than a thousand years ago for their mindless killing sprees. Recently, however, they have begun escaping from their holding ground, returning to this world and taking over the bodies of "human hosts" who have dormant Casus blood running through their veins. The escaped Casus now prey upon the newly awakened Merrick, feeding on their flesh for power, as well as revenge. Characteristics: When in Casus form, they have muzzled faces, wolf-shaped heads, leathery gray skin, ridged backs and long, curved claws. The males have ice-blue eyes, while the females have eyes that are pale green.

Meridian: The metaphysical holding ground where the Casus were imprisoned for their crimes against the other clans…as well as humanity. Although it was created by the original Consortium, no one knows how to find it until the ancient archives reveal that the Dark Markers are not only the keys that will open the gate to Meridian, but that they will also form a map that leads to the prison's hidden location.

Shades: Because of their immortality, the Casus can't die in Meridian. They have simply wasted away to "shades" of the powerful creatures they once were, which is why they're forced to take human hosts when they return to this world.

The Deschanel: Also known as vampires, the Deschanel are one of the most powerful of the ancient clans, rivaling the strength of the Merrick and the shape-shifters. Although duality is a common feature among many of the clans, the trait is especially strong within the Deschanel, whose very natures are a dichotomy of opposites—of both darkness and light—which makes them complex friends…and dangerous enemies. Characteristics: Pale, pure gray eyes that glow after they've taken a blood feeding. Despite their power and strength, they move with a smooth, effortless grace that is uncommon among human males of their size. They also have incredibly long life-spans, until such time as they finally take a mate.

The Burning: The body of an unmated Deschanel male runs cold until he finds his mate. The phenomenon is referred to as being "in heat" or "burning," since his body begins warming from the moment he finds her.

The Förmyndares: As the Protectors of the Deschanel, it is the duty of these warriors to destroy any threats to the vampire clans.

Nesting Grounds: Ancient, sprawling castlelike communities where Deschanel family units, or nests, live for security; they are protected by powerful magic that keeps them hidden from the outside world. The grounds are located throughout Scandinavia and other parts of Europe.

A Sangra *Bond*: A bond that can be formed between a human male and a Deschanel female, enabling the male to track her over long distances.

The Alacea: A powerful, eclectic clan of psychics who have varying degrees of powers. Most can see into the past or the future, with a few having the ability to read another's thoughts in the present—but usually only one form of sight is given. Characteristics: Dark, sky-blue eyes.

Aldori Trance: A deep trance state that an Alacea with mature powers can enter, but there are often serious consequences.

Transsis: Light trance states that the Alacea use when they need to rest, but don't want to go into a deep sleep.

The Witches: Although there are many witch clans still in existence, their powers vary greatly from one clan to another. Characteristics: Physical traits vary according to the specific clan of witch.

The Boudreaux: A carefree clan of witches whose specialty is beauty spells.

The Mallory: A powerful clan of witches whose diverse powers were bound by a curse. Because of the centuries-old curse, they magnified the emotions of those in their presence to extreme levels—but the curse is now coming to an end.

The Reavess: A clan of witches who can communicate mentally with those in their families. They access their considerable power through the use of spells, and will bond their true loves to them through sex. They are also able to assume the traits possessed by their mates during "joining."

The Saville: A snobbish clan of witches who have little power.

The Regan: An aggressive clan responsible for hunting several rival clans to near extinction. Characteristics: Long noses, pointed ears and deeply cleft chins.

The Kenly: A mountain-dwelling clan nearly hunted to extinction by the Regan. Characteristics: Short statures and large, doelike eyes.

The Feardacha: One of several ancient clans that reside in Ireland. They are extremely superstitious, believing that the dead should never go unchecked. As a precaution, they tattoo pagan symbols on their hands and arms, believing the symbols will draw to them any evil souls that manage to escape from hell, so that they might kill them once again. Characteristics: Tattoos, mocha-colored skin and pale green eyes.

The Vassayre: One of the more reclusive clans, they seldom come out of the underground caves where they dwell. Characteristics: Dark markings around their sunken eyes.

The Deuchar: One of the most violent of the ancient clans, they are the mortal enemy of the Shaevan.

The Shaevan: One of several ancient clans that reside in France.

The Shape-shifters: A richly diverse, powerful collection of clans whose members can take either the complete or partial shape of a beast.

The Prime Predators: Consisting of the most dangerous, predatory animal species, they are the most aggressive breeds of shape-shifters, well-known for their legendary sex drives and their unquestionable devotion to their mates. In order to claim a mate, a Prime must bite the one who holds their heart, marking them with their fangs while taking their blood into their bodies. They are also known for their incomparable skill as warriors and their strong healing abilities. Examples: the tigers, jaguars and lycanthropes.

The Lycanthropes: Also known as werewolves, they are formidable warriors who can actually change humans to their species with the power of their bite if they are in wolf form. However, in order to mark their mates, they must make a bite with their fangs while still in human form.

The Raptors: One of the rarest breeds of shifters, the Raptors are known for being ruthless warriors and possessive, utterly devoted lovers. Although they do not completely shift form, they are able to release powerful wings from their backs that enable them to fly, as well as sharp talons from their fingertips for fighting.

The Charteris: Dragon shape-shifters who possess the ability to control fire, and whose bodies burn with a dangerous heat when making love to a woman who holds their heart. It is believed that no pure-blooded Charteris are still in existence.

The Archives: The records that belonged to the original Consortium which are believed to hold vital information about the ancient clans. Though the new Consortium spent years searching for them, the archives were eventually found by the Collective Army, then taken by the Watchmen.

The Death Journal: A journal found with the ancient archives that explains how to kill a variety of clan species, many of which are no longer even in existence. There is a passage in the journal written in an archaic language that the Watchmen can't decipher, but which they believe will explain how to kill the Death-Walkers who have escaped from hell.

The Collective Army: A militant organization of human mercenaries devoted to purging the world of all preternatural life. In an ironic twist, the Collective Army now finds itself partnered with the Kraven and the Casus, in exchange for information that they believe will enable them to exterminate the remaining nonhuman species.

The Consortium: A body of officials comprised of representatives from each of the remaining ancient clans, the Consortium is a sort of preternatural United Nations. Their purpose is to settle disputes and keep peace among the differing species, while working to hide the existence of the remaining clans from the human world. More than a thousand years ago, the original Consortium helped the Merrick imprison the Casus, after the Casus's relentless killing of humans threatened to expose the existence of the nonhuman races. The council fashioned the Dark Markers in order to destroy the immortal killers, only to be murdered by the newly created Collective Army before they could complete the task. Years later, the Consortium re-formed, but by then its original archives had been lost…all traces of the Dark Markers supposedly destroyed during the Collective's merciless raids, which nearly led to the destruction of the clans.

The Dark Markers: Twelve metal crosses of enormous power that were mysteriously created by the original Consortium, they are the only known weapons capable of killing a Casus, sending its soul directly to hell. They also work as a talisman for those who wear them, offering protection from the Casus. Although the Dark Markers were hidden in order to keep them safe, there is a set of encrypted maps that lead to their locations. The Watchmen and the Buchanans are using these maps to help them find the Markers before they fall into enemy hands.

"Arm of Fire": Weapon mode for a Dark Marker. When held against the palm, a Dark Marker holds the power to change one's arm into an "Arm of Fire." When the cross is placed against the back of a Casus's neck, the flame-

covered arm will sink into the monster's body, burning it from the inside out.

The Encrypted Maps: When Saige Buchanan discovered the first Dark Marker in Italy, she found a set of encrypted maps buried alongside the cross. The maps, which lead to the hidden locations of the Dark Markers, had been wrapped in oilcloth and preserved by some kind of spell.

The Death-Walkers: The demented souls of clansmen and -women who were sent to hell for their sadistic crimes, and who are now managing to return to our world. It is unknown how to kill them, but they can be burned by a combination of holy water and salt. Driven mad by their time in hell, they are a formidable force of evil, seeking to create chaos and war among the remaining clans simply because they want to watch the world bleed. Characteristics: Although they retain certain traits from their original species, each of the Death-Walkers has cadaverously white skin and small horns that protrude from their temples, as well as deadly fangs and claws.

"The Eve Effect": A phenomenon that affects various breeds of shape-shifters, causing them to be drawn to certain females who touch the primal hungers of both the man and the beast. If a male falls in love with one of these females and bites her, she will be bonded to him as his mate for the rest of their lives.

The Infettato: Humans who have been infected by the bite of a Death-Walker. Once turned, they become the "walking dead" and it is impossible for them to regain their humanity. They live only to consume flesh, tracking their prey by scent and blindly obeying the orders of those who made them. As they feed, they become stronger, and they can only be killed when their hearts are removed from their chests and burned. Characteristics: Mottled, yellowish skin, gaunt faces and sunken eyes. Black skin that looks as if it has been burned surrounds their eyes and mouths.

The Kraven: The descendants of female Deschanel vampires who were raped by Casus males prior to their imprisonment. Treated little better than slaves and considered an embarrassing symbol of weakness, the Kraven have been such a closely guarded secret within the Deschanel clan that the Watchmen have only recently become aware of their existence. Hoping to improve their circumstances and become more powerful, the Kraven are working to facilitate the return of the Casus. Characteristics: They are believed to have long life spans, and their fangs can be released only at night, causing their eyes to glow a deep, blood-red crimson. They can also easily pass for human, but can only be killed when a wooden stake is driven through their heart.

The Wasteland: A cold, desolate, dangerous region that was created by powerful magic, where exiled Deschanel "nests," or family units, are forced to live once the

Consortium has passed judgment against them. Protected by spells that make it invisible to humans, this vast region "shares" physical space with the Scandinavian forests surrounding it.

The Watchmen: An organization of shape-shifters whose job it is to watch over the remaining ancient clans, they are considered the "eyes and ears" of the Consortium. They monitor the various nonhuman species, as well as the bloodlines of those clans that have become dormant. Prior to the recent Merrick awakenings, the most powerful Merrick bloodlines had been under Watchmen supervision. There are Watchmen compounds situated around the world, with each unit consisting of four to six warriors. Characteristics: Physical traits vary according to the specific breed of shape-shifter.

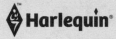

REQUEST YOUR FREE BOOKS!

2 FREE NOVELS
FROM THE SUSPENSE COLLECTION
PLUS 2 FREE GIFTS!

YES! Please send me 2 FREE novels from the Suspense Collection and my 2 FREE gifts (gifts are worth about $10). After receiving them, if I don't wish to receive any more books, I can return the shipping statement marked "cancel." If I don't cancel, I will receive 4 brand-new novels every month and be billed just $5.74 per book in the U.S. or $6.24 per book in Canada. That's a saving of at least 28% off the cover price. It's quite a bargain! Shipping and handling is just 50¢ per book in the U.S. and 75¢ per book in Canada.* I understand that accepting the 2 free books and gifts places me under no obligation to buy anything. I can always return a shipment and cancel at any time. Even if I never buy another book, the two free books and gifts are mine to keep forever.

191/391 MDN FDDH

Name	(PLEASE PRINT)

Address	Apt. #

City	State/Prov.	Zip/Postal Code

Signature (if under 18, a parent or guardian must sign)

Mail to the **Reader Service:**
IN U.S.A.: P.O. Box 1867, Buffalo, NY 14240-1867
IN CANADA: P.O. Box 609, Fort Erie, Ontario L2A 5X3

Not valid for current subscribers to the Suspense Collection
or the Romance/Suspense Collection.

Want to try two free books from another line?
Call 1-800-873-8635 or visit www.ReaderService.com.

* Terms and prices subject to change without notice. Prices do not include applicable taxes. Sales tax applicable in N.Y. Canadian residents will be charged applicable taxes. Offer not valid in Quebec. This offer is limited to one order per household. All orders subject to credit approval. Credit or debit balances in a customer's account(s) may be offset by any other outstanding balance owed by or to the customer. Please allow 4 to 6 weeks for delivery. Offer available while quantities last.

Your Privacy—The Reader Service is committed to protecting your privacy. Our Privacy Policy is available online at www.ReaderService.com or upon request from the Reader Service.

We make a portion of our mailing list available to reputable third parties that offer products we believe may interest you. If you prefer that we not exchange your name with third parties, or if you wish to clarify or modify your communication preferences, please visit us at www.ReaderService.com/consumerschoice or write to us at Reader Service Preference Service, P.O. Box 9062, Buffalo, NY 14269. Include your complete name and address.

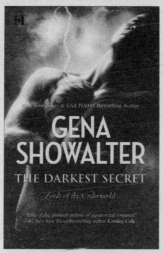

RHYANNON BYRD

HQN™

We *are* romance™

www.HQNBooks.com